A Harry Circus Mystery

ACROSS THE
SINGING BRIDGE

By E.D. Ward

Across the Singing Bridge
Copyright 2017 E.D. Ward

Published by Piscataqua Press
An imprint of RiverRun Bookstore, Inc.
142 Fleet Street | Portsmouth, NH | 03801
www.riverrunbookstore.com
www.piscataquapress.com
ISBN: 978-1-944393-56-4
Printed in the United States of America

For Lou and those who always said I would,

And those who never thought I could.

Thank you, Nichole, Jennie and Katherine.
Without your help and persistence,
the words of this book would never have seen
the inside of a printer.

PROLOGUE

I WOKE UP AROUND 8:30 A.M. drenched in sweat. My innermost mind remembered a neighbor telling me when I came here that I'd soon hate real warm weather, and I thought he was pulling my goddamned leg the way you string the new guy along. I've been in Isles Port, Maine for fifteen years, and it was true, goddamit; I had grown to hate the heat. Directly outside my window, summer was a-buzz. A large bee suddenly slammed itself into my window screen, forcing me to jerk my head in that direction. My eyes burned from deep within their sockets, while my friggin' tongue seemed swollen the size of my goddamned head. My first instinct was to lie back down and let it all pass, but it was just too hot. I had to get outdoors and breathe. I moved slowly through the dark, junk-laden hole I called home—wallowing in misery fifty percent of the time and complaining about it the other fifty. There just didn't seem to be any way out, but I probably wouldn't take one if I found it.

Hell would have to be a welcome diversion from this defecation I called a life. Nearing the door, I stubbed my big toe on a piece of steel I'd saved for only Christ knows why. Cursing as I approached the screened door, the light from outside was a welcome sight despite the heat. There were times I couldn't even remember what life was like on the other side of the "Singing Bridge." It seemed everyone that crossed it from the south had bigger and better cars and lots of fuckin' spending cash. They threw it around here and there, like tourists usually do, flashing C-notes under the noses of the locals, watching with much humor as they went into their little song and dance to earn their peanut share of it all. When it was all over and the cold finally settled back in and they were nestled in their warm, palatial palaces to the south, the rest of us slimmed-down, little swine stoked our wood fires, ate our potatoes, and waited for the sons-a'-whores to come back next year.

The heated scent of pine was heavy in the air, blown by a southerly breeze. I began to feel the need to relieve myself of what little remained of last night's supper. As I leaned against the front fender of my decrepit, faded-blue pickup about to let go, I heard the sound of an approaching vehicle. I didn't want to look up, but the intensity at which the tires hummed led me to believe it was in a direct path toward me. I was right; it was one of them sons-a'-whores come to force-feed me more alcohol. No way, Jose! The urge to throw up passed when I realized I was being summoned.

My eyes strained to focus, but the moisture formed from the heaves left my vision blurred. The big shit-eatin' grin behind the wheel belonged to my buddy, Bullet. Bullington Carter is his given name, and God protect the poor fool who dare call him that. Bullet lived some twenty-odd miles to the north of Isles Port, but he spent so much time here, there were people in town who thought he lived here. He was the very first person I laid eyes on while jumping from my fully loaded U-Haul at Phyley's Exxon in the center of town the day I moved here. We're about the same build, him and me; except for that beer belly of his that droops over the belt of his green work pants a little. He seems more rugged and wild-looking, I'd guess, probably from living out there in the woods from birth, eating all that wild game his entire life. In the fifteen years I've known him, I honestly don't think he's eaten beef—or even knows what it tastes like—and calls store-bought food "she-it." I guess you could call him one of the bad boys, but I'll tell you', he's got a heart of gold.

"Well, mista' man. If'n I di'n know no betta', I'd say you was gettin' ready ta puke when I pulled up." Bullet snickered as he spoke. I didn't say a word; I simply walked toward the door, and Bullet followed with his partial six-pack and the half-burned non-filtered Camel cigarette hanging from his oversized, chapped lips. We hadn't quite reached the table when I heard the sound of the first of what would become many beers that day pulled from its plastic ring. I couldn't help laughing, seeing the look on old Bullet's face as he passed me my first brew. The cold beer tasted so good in that sweltering heat, I actually lost the urge to throw up.

Bullet was the kind of guy who started drinking beer right after his first cup of coffee in the morning, and went right on drinking until his head slammed into the pillow late at night; then get right up early to do it again, never feeling any adverse effect whatsoever. It killed me the way he could handle his booze, but lately it began showing up in the lines on his face.

We did in the brew he'd brought with him, and then we started in on a fresh pack I pulled from the fridge. I really couldn't remember being this close to anyone before; able to share anything and everything and never fearing retribution of any kind. Bullet had a reputation that kept most law-abiding, upstanding citizens at least a decent arm's-length away. He was crude (I'd have to be the first to admit that), and a stiff shirt was definitely a turn-off, but if he liked you, he'd give you the shirt off his back and never ask you for it back. Yeah, that's old Bullet all right. I sat half-watching, half-listening to him talk, his puffy lower lip bouncing between syllables, while the rhythm of speech and swallows of beer were uninterrupted. He smoked one Camel after another, sometimes flicking the ash onto the floor and upon realizing what he did, apologizing and scuffing the ash with his work boot. Most of the time however, he did get the damned shit into the ashtray. He was one of them honest sons-a'-bitches whose honesty always got him into more trouble than he needed.

"Honesty is the best policy?" he'd always ask. "'Fuck you, bubba' is my policy, and if you don't like that, fuck you anyway!"

He rattled on for quite some time, but I was in no rush to go anywhere. His nervous leg pulsated as if it was a well-oiled piston in a fine-tuned motor, and while he spoke, his eyes focused directly on mine as if we were riveted to each other. I looked toward the clock for a moment, and realized I had swallowed three 16-ounce beers, and it wasn't quite 10:00 a.m. There was something about an early-morning beer buzz. I wasn't much for breakfast usually, but I suddenly felt rather empty and kind of weak. I walked toward the fridge while Bullet, never stopping his chatter for a breath, followed me with his eyes, watching every move I made. I slapped a couple of fresh deer steaks into the fry pan, and he stood immediately, walking toward the stove.

"I'm naut' real hungray," he said, "but I guess I could get somethin' down."

There's something about the smell of fresh deer meat frying in butter that just makes my stomach growl even more. Old Bullet cracked another beer while the smell of fresh meat filled the entire room. I'd thrown two more large steaks in for him, and from the looks he'd been giving me, I just knew that two eggs were in no way going to be close to enough. I cracked the whole dozen and started whipping them.

"Mix some cheese in thi'em," he said. I looked toward him with a kind of dry Down-East look, and told him the next time he came to visit he oughta bring a bunch of his own grub.

He burped a slight laugh and simply said, "Fuck you, Bubba." Then he guzzled the last of his beer. Breakfast was cooked, and I dished it out on two plates, watching as Bullet seemed to inhale his.

As we ate, I recalled Bullet telling me he'd had a rough time of it at the start. He was a mere twelve years old when he found his father up in the rafters of their old barn, hanging by his neck, dead. It seems he'd been there for quite a while; nobody really missed him, as he sometimes disappeared for weeks at a time. The goddamned maggots had started cleaning out his eye sockets. I suppose you never get over something like that, ever. Twelve years old, Christ. I wonder if anyone could get over something like that as long as they live. He only talked about it that one time, and told me never to say anything to no goddamned fool around here. I never did. I guess probably that started the true foundation of our friendship. That and the fact we both loved deer meat and couldn't get enough of it.

Surprisingly enough, considering the amount of time that Bullet had spent with me over the years; he'd had a wife, Millie, and two boys, Billy and Bobby. I'll never forget the first time I laid eyes on them two. Bullet and I had walked through the kitchen door of his place, and those two little fuckin' brats were lighting friggin' matches behind the cook stove. Billy was nine and Bobby was twelve then. Millie, sprawled across the couch, was just downing the rest of her Budweiser as if nothing were happening. That was par for the course where she was concerned. The minute Bullet laid eyes on them and the flame on the match, it was as if the goddamned flame had ignited him, sending him on a screaming attack at Millie after grabbing the two little rug rats by the scuff of their necks and dragging them toward their mother. She seemed puzzled, as if to say, "What the hell?" They screamed at each other for quite some time. I finally walked out of the house, sat on the porch and had a beer.

It was no more than a year after that incident that those two little fuckers burned that goddamned house down. It was the only house Bullet had ever lived in. Bullet sat and cried that whole day, never taking one single drink. I swear that was the only time I ever saw him go without a drink for one entire day. He's been making up for it ever since. He never touched the kids, and he didn't say a word to Millie about it. He simply stared at them for the longest time, and it was as if they knew better than to say anything. The very next day he started to clean the mess up from the fire, and I helped him to build them a new house–right on the very spot the old one was built. He said that he loved the view from here, and there wasn't any place he'd rather be than right on top of this ridge. Sure as hell, he built them a fine house, the very house he still lives in today.

Millie run off with a carnie who worked for "Opie's Shows" when they did the Bangor State Fair a few years back; she took the boys with her. It set Bullet back for quite some time, and I'm not really sure that he ever got over it. Oh yeah, he'd tell me that he was glad she'd left and took those two mangy brats with her, but those were his only sons. He has told me when we were alone that if he ever got his hands on that little fuck of a carnie we'd all see just how far that little fart's neck would stretch. There was something about the way he said it that left no doubt in my mind that he meant it.

There was a way of life out here that was so different from anywhere I'd been before. It was, without a doubt, the financially poorest population anywhere; but the people were not poor in spirit. In that respect, they were the richest in the world. Sure, you can go anywhere and find the same things you'd find here: incest, drug abuse, alcoholism, domestic violence, hate, cheaters, and murderers. The numbers weren't as great, that's all. People struggled for a paycheck here, same as anywhere else in this great country of ours, except no matter how hard they struggled for the buck here, they still came up with shit. Just like everywhere else, a small handful of folks had it all and passed out a few peanuts to the rest now and again.

As broke as they all were what seemed to be in ample supply was independence, sometimes to the point of arrogance. I've actually seen a man go without a meal so as not to accept a job from someone he didn't like, or had had a run-in with in the past—headstrong like none I'd ever seen. That's just the way it is here: you made do for yourself, or you went without. Sometimes, however, that was not the case. Some people believed that what was yours should be theirs, and helped themselves right to it, thinking nothing of it. A few learned to regret it, while others just didn't care. It was a strange place at times, but for me it had become home, and I couldn't think of anywhere I'd rather be than where I was.

Forest Bagley—now there was a character. He stood exactly six-foot-five, and was built like a brick shithouse. His arms were the size of my legs, and his head seemed too large for his goddamned neck. He had to weigh a good two-fifty. His entire life, all that man ever did was cut, load, and unload wood. Mostly firewood, which meant it, was hardwood, making it even heavier. He loved his work and he'd tell you that, as long as he could hold you captive in a conversation about firewood, the best kinds to burn and where the best could be found. All the time he'd be telling you his little story about wood, he'd be stuffing his face with ham and cheese sandwiches, potato chips, and cold Hire's Root Beer from a bottle, while leaning against the cooler at Filbert Cirone's store in Chesterfield. He was a regular at Filbert's.

Old Filbert made about the best ham and cheese sandwiches around; but after watching him make them one time, it was kind of gross to see how he could pet, then feed the mangy cat with the same hand he was layering the sandwiches with. I swore off ham 'n' cheese for quite a spell after that, and then I'd only eat them if I made them. That damned cat walked all over that counter. Sniffing at this and pawing at that, occasionally getting lightly backhanded by Filbert away from the open containers of food, and the cat would lie down on the cutting board while old Filbert would slap the mayo to the bread, half-listening to Forest's woodlot management course, half-talking to the friggin' cat. Filbert was around middle age, medium height and stocky built at this point. You always knew it was him with his red and black flannel shirt, green suspenders and blue jeans.

I remember the time, shortly after I'd moved to the area, when I stopped into the store to get a pack of beer or something, and the place seemed alive with an unusual hustle and bustle. Filbert seemed to be bouncing off the walls with joy, and it didn't take him long to draw me to the center of his happiness. Going down into the basement of the store, we found Forest chomping on a ham and cheese sandwich, gawking at the biggest bobcat (well, the only bobcat) that I'd ever seen hanging from the floor joists. Its bloody, dripping nose was almost to the floor, shot that very morning by Filbert himself.

There wasn't anything unusual about Filbert and his wife of thirty years, Heidi. They were as normal as normal was for these parts, and they were always involved with something or another of a civic nature. Filbert ran the store and was there religiously at 5:00 a.m. every morning; rain, sleet, snow, or shine, which wasn't a huge effort, considering they lived just behind the store. Most folks, being up early around here, always knew that Filbert would be open to get their newspaper and coffee or beer, whichever they needed to start their day.

One particular Wednesday in the fall sometime, that feels like a lifetime ago now, it rained hard, all day. That evening, as was customary on Wednesday night, the usual group of the town's women met at the Legion Hall for quilting. They used the kitchen, as it was the warmest area in the entire hall. The entrance to the kitchen was through the double swinging doors which were at the far end of the huge hall. Filbert had built the doors after the kitchen's remodeling, incorporating glass in each to avoid the inevitable collisions by the incoming and outgoing foot traffic to or from the kitchen. From its inception, the hall seemed to breathe a life of its own, centering on the variety of functions that made up the very life and blood of its existence.

Bingo on Saturday evenings drew a large crowd from surrounding towns, making it the hall's greatest financial supplier. It played host to an occasional wedding as well, and was always available for the renowned Friday Night Spaghetti Supper to raise money for a local family who might have lost their home to fire, or any number of worthy civic causes that arose from time to time.

The women huddled in their close-knit circles, gossiping and telling stories about their grandchildren, and seemed content. Heidi Cirone, looking up momentarily from her needle that particular Wednesday night, became puzzled at the sight of Filbert approaching the glassed swinging doors. Heidi had never seen the look he displayed, nor could it prepare her for the shock that was soon to become her reality. At the sight of him nearing the doors, her easily attainable smile surfaced, replaced suddenly by sharply protruding eyes. She stared in silent fear as Filbert slowly fell against a swinging door without saying a word, never taking his eyes from hers. His face pressed on the glass, disfiguring his features, and he slumped out of sight and fell to the floor with a huge thump. This was the first of his many heart attacks to come.

During the period between the late sixties and right through the seventies, there seemed to be an extremely large influx of young energetic families from a broad range of backgrounds and areas of the country rooting themselves in the area known as Down-East Maine. They came with new ideas, motivated with thoughts of accomplishment that seemed to overshadow the very life-blood of idealism already deeply entrenched in the lives of the local people; an emigration seen as an insurgence against the solitude and anonymity that the entire area had prided itself on for nearly two centuries. Nevertheless, they came and were tolerated by the locals.

It seemed to take forever for spring to come that year. The winter was as deep a freeze as had been seen for many years. Shallow-dug wells froze, leaving residents of small homesteads to transport water in fifty-gallon drums in the back of pickup trucks from springs scattered throughout the county. Winter was not only a time for Mother Nature to rest and rejuvenate herself, but it was a time for some to feel the effects of poverty deeper than most people know. True, in most respects, everyone made do with very little, and what was in the pantry was probably from the garden, or bartered for back in the fall. Few did not eat deer or moose meat, and for some, the regular diet of Partridge and Canada Geese was a wholesome winter necessity.

It was spring when Kenny Collins arrived in Chesterfield. A spring that many would soon wish they could forget. Kenny Collins was a drifter. He traveled light, you might say, as when he strolled into Cirone's store that first time. He carried a small backpack slung over one shoulder and a four-foot-long walking stick which, we would all learn very soon, he never went anywhere without. Many of the regulars were in the store when he ambled in, walking confidently, displaying an air of sarcasm. He looked at the group, gathered around their usual spot across from the counter at the Coke machine. A Coke machine back then was a flat-top cooler with sliding chrome doors on the top, making a very nice table to place sandwiches and soft drinks on while passing the time. Their eyes were upon the stranger from the moment he walked in, and he knew it.

It was as though his confidence welled up within him the more he became the focus of the attention. I was standing next to Bullet at the far end of the store, over by the meat counter, watching Filbert make a couple of his famous ham and cheese sandwiches. Bullet looked over at the stranger first, then poked me in the ribs as if to have me look up to see what the wind had blown in. I shrugged him off, trying to stay focused on what Filbert was telling me, and then he poked me again, and that's when I laid eyes on Kenny Collins for the first time.

His hair was straggly, long, and from the looks of it, he hadn't washed it for quite some time. He had it pulled back into a tail, but it wasn't long enough to hold in place, and there were loose hairs falling all over his face. He could have used a shave, but in these parts, most everyone could have used a shave. His long woolen coat blew back behind him as he walked, and from where I stood, there didn't seem to be any buttons to keep it closed. I tried to ignore the young man, who looked about twenty-five, though it was hard to guess his age from the tattered look. He simply meandered around the store, and when I looked back toward the counter, old Filbert had already started walking toward him.

"Howdy, howdy…what can I do for ya' today?" Filbert asked, in a tone that left no doubt that he was concerned with the young man's appearance. Kenny made no real attempt to respond other than a simple grunt that added a more defiant air to an already questionable look. Filbert glanced pointedly back at the two of us, and he didn't have to ask that we keep an eye on this one.

The very first word Kenny spoke was to me, as I stood at the far end of the store near the meat counter. Bullet had made his way toward the group at the cooler and meandered through the store watching every move Kenny made, trying to be inconspicuous, but looking more like a pounded thumb than a super-sleuth detective.

"What's new?" Kenny asked, and introduced himself to me at that point.

"Not a hell of a lot," I responded. I could tell from that simple "What's new?" that he was not your typical Down-Easter. What I did notice was that he looked me straight in the eye when he asked. Now that he'd made contact with someone, and that someone just happened to be me, the questions seemed to flow like beer and wine at a Down-East wedding or funeral. He was inquisitive as hell, wanting to know everything about the area: where he might find a small house to rent, who was hiring now, the best places to eat—which led me to believe he was looking to hang around for a time, and strangers didn't get a real cozy welcome 'round these parts.

The whole of Washington County was blueberry country, and many transients passed through this part looking for work, but most were looking for something they could put in their pocket rather than pay for, applying the simple mentality, "It wasn't what you did that was bad; it was if you got caught."

Kenny, as we were soon to find out, was not considering transience. He had left a well-to-do background in New York City (though no one would know that for quite some time), carrying with him in that small backpack a bankbook with a balance to die over. That, we would also find out later. From where I stood, I could overhear the group from beside the cooler and the occasional prejudicial slurs that always accompanied the arrival of any outsider. While the slurs, never hidden in whispers, didn't seem to bother Kenny, he continued walking through the store as though prepared to make an offer to purchase the place. Filbert went directly to the checkout counter, maintaining a stance that would have made any drill sergeant proud.

Oh, it wasn't as though we'd try to drive someone off just because he wasn't from around here, but folks were what you might call standoffish, hesitant to let someone from away into the inner circle. Kenny didn't hang around too long that day. He grabbed a couple of things from the shelf, paid for them and stuffed them in his backpack, then asked if Filbert could make him one of his famous ham and cheese sandwiches. Where he heard that term I'll never know, but it was all Filbert had to hear to change his mannerism toward the young man. He walked out the front door, munching on that sandwich and sucking on a cold Coke, as if the world owed him something. I had a feeling that it wouldn't be the last we'd see of Kenny Collins.

It was two months, though, before Kenny made another appearance at Cirone's store, and as usual, Bullet and I were at the meat counter. I'd completely forgotten about him until he walked in. At first neither one of us recognized him. He was clean-shaven. His hair'd been cut shorter; it looked as though he'd been down to Doc's barbershop in the harbor. Doc only knew how to give one haircut, and it seemed to fit every head that came under his shears.

Summer was coming on us quick now, and Kenny looked as though he'd been working in the woods from the clothes he wore. Upon seeing us, he walked directly toward us, and immediately began talking as if we'd been long-lost buddies.

"How we all doin'?" he asked. He had a smile that almost stretched his lips to each ear.

"Fair t' midlin', I guess," Bullet answered.

"I've been up workin' for Forest Bagley on Hardwood Ridge for the past couple a' months, and with summer comin' on and all, I sure would like to get out of them woods," Kenny said.

I knew from experience that working in the woods for a living was no place to be in the middle of summer. Hell, spring was bad enough, with the blackflies. With the heat of summer, you had the deerflies that were always able to find their way under your hat, burrowing deep into your hair and biting the hell out of you. Then there was the stifling heat. The wood chips flying from the chainsaw would stick all over you, and the more you sweated, the more they stuck. Bullet knew what that was all about—he was a veteran woodsman—but he came out of the woods when Millie and the two rug rats ran off with that carnie. He said that was the last time he was gonna cut wood for a living, didn't have to work that hard anymore.

Usually, I cared less what a flatlander said or did. Flatlanders were those who came here mostly from the southern New England states, usually apartment dwellers, and thus the term "flatlanders." Kenny was different. He acted with a sense of self, to me anyway; the way he spoke gave me a feeling that he didn't come here to make a statement; he came here to make his own way, make a few bucks, have a couple of beers and just get along.

On the other hand, Bullet didn't like him from the very start, and he told me so.

About the time Kenny was talking about getting out of the woods, along came Filbert asking if he could help the young man, never realizing it was the same character he'd had us watch only a couple of short months before. Well, he was a charmer, that Kenny. By the time Filbert made our sandwiches, realizing who he was, or not, he'd hired Kenny to work in the store, as he always needed an extra hand during the summer blueberry season. Kenny simply nodded in our direction as he left the store and now, he would be a regular.

It didn't take Kenny long to ingratiate himself with the local clientele of Cirone's store. He actually fit right in with his quick humor and ready smile, but there was something just below the surface that didn't add up. Oh, don't get me wrong, he was a good person, anyone could tell right off the bat; it was as if he always left a little something out of the equation that might add up to the whole Kenny Collins. He was the hardest worker we'd ever seen, and Filbert was glad to have him on board. I remember this one time, shortly after the transients arrived to start the blueberry season, when a young Indian walked into the store. It was very busy and everyone seemed to be preoccupied with one thing or another while the young chief wandered around, filling his pockets with little things like apples, small packs of crackers, and some slim-jims, and was making his way to the door when out of nowhere, Kenny stopped him and asked him to empty his pockets.

A scuffle broke out between the two, and before you could blink, Kenny had the chief upside down and inside out with his pockets emptied onto the counter. He held the young brave by the neck with that four-foot-long walking stick that he kept behind the counter, asking Filbert if he wanted to call the law. Filbert shook his head no, to the amazement of Kenny and the patrons who stood gawking at the situation. In a low voice, Filbert asked the young man if he was hungry, and when he nodded his head indicating yes, Filbert tugged him slightly by the arm and brought him to the back of the store and made him a couple of ham and cheese sandwiches. He let him keep the things he'd tried to steal, and sent the young man on his way after adding a cold drink to the collection. After he'd left, Kenny—perplexed with what Filbert had done—asked why he let the guy go. In a low, almost inaudible voice Filbert responded, "I was hungry once. It doesn't feel good." Kenny never said a word, and simply looked at Filbert with a newfound respect.

There was no doubt that Kenny attracted a certain type of crowd wherever he went, and the store seemed to be a gathering place for that kind. His customers, drifters mostly, came at all times of the day, bringing a small amount of business with them like cigarettes, rolling papers, beer. Cases of beer, which made Filbert happy as a hog in muck—but the locals, knowing very well what Kenny was doing, complained even more that the new boy was taking Filbert for a ride, and they made no attempt at keeping it a secret from him.

People made remarks like, "Now why do you suppose someone would need to buy rollin' paypaz' when they just bought themselves a pack o' cigarettes?" Filbert would simply shake his head, telling whoever would listen that Kenny was just a likeable young man who was helping to bring in some badly needed business, and he wasn't going to aggravate him by telling him not to bring people to the store. Although, as time passed, the strangers got a tad stranger and business from the locals fell off.

As usual, summer was flying by. The blueberries were the best they'd been in years, and everyone had money to spend—and spend they did. There was an unusually large amount of transients than there had been in previous years, and they were a tougher crowd. The local lawmen regularly broke up fights in and out of town, stopping every couple of miles to pull over a strange vehicle. We'd see at least one person sprawled over the hood for a search of some kind. Overall, it made for quite an offbeat summer.

But the end of the season is when it got really strange. Kenny's dealings with people from away got more involved, and the questions directed at Filbert were now coming from the local constable and the resident state trooper. It was as if Filbert was in some kinda fog and didn't make any attempt to question Kenny about his apparent soon-to-be troubles.

As the burning heat of summer left, so did the throngs of transients blown by the autumn winds to the apple and potato harvest up north. The green-leafed fields of summer were turning brilliant red, and the hellish sounds of harvest time slept in quiet solitude. It was the time locals loved the most—when the summer people left—but it was the time to get ready for the leaf-peepers of fall with their binoculars and cameras with telescopic lenses. It wasn't the people everyone wanted, it was their money. That's what makes it all go 'round.

The fall winds were blowing, and when the wind was right, you could get a good whiff of the pulp mills from Old Town down here across the blueberry barrens. With the coming of fall, it was rank. I never was able to get used to the stink of it; good thing Isles Port and Chesterfield were this far from it. Old Bullet called it "tree juice a floatin' in tha' air."

"Good for tha' 'conamy," he'd say. That wasn't the only stink floating on the wind those days. There was a stink of marijuana too—something else to get the locals' goats up. They knew right off if somebody was smoking the stuff. You could always count on someone coining the phrase, "Your eyes look like road maps, but for the likes o' me I can't figure out to where." I don't think it matters where you're from, when things start changing from the norm, people start gettin' nervous, and that's just what started happening here in Isles Port and Chesterfield. People started getting nervous and started pointing fingers at the ones they thought were responsible for the changes, and Kenny Collins was the recipient of more than a few finger-pointings. The more they pointed however, the more he liked it.

Kenny became involved in many activities in the area, especially if they involved making money. With the end of summer, all trade dropped off, and Filbert had to cut Kenny's hours considerably, but it was fine with him. The more time spent away from the store, the more time he had to pursue his evil ways. He had an entrepreneurial air about him that drew money, and draw money he did. He bought wood from his former boss Forest Bagley, and had Forest cut and deliver it, charging twice the amount to the customer, and they were happy to pay it. He sold Christmas trees and wreaths around the holidays to people from out of state, and when fishing season came along, he already had a fine stock of bait of every kind ready for the anglers. He was a fine young hunter, quick to learn.

Filbert brought him along everywhere he went, showing him his secret places to hunt and fish, and Kenny took advantage of every tidbit of info he got. Like anything good, someone had to take and wring the hell out of it, and Kenny was quite the wringer. He found out that a couple of disabled vets lived out in the woods by the river, and it just so happened that both of them had a serious liking for alcohol and drugs. The booze wasn't any problem with the State Liquor Store just down the road, but around these times Down East, it wasn't very easy to keep one's self stocked in all kinds of drugs. Kenny had some lucrative connections from out of state, and one phone call from him could get enough for all the vets in the entire area. Kenny took full advantage of those possibilities and prospered. It seemed rather strange how Kenny was so well liked and hated at the same time, by the very people he supplied. He knew it, and he always seemed to get even, one way or another. This ticked them off worse.

Mary Bagley—now there was a looker. She was born in Aroostook County, but her family moved here when her daddy's mother died and left him the farm, literally. The place was a twenty-five acre spread down along the Paguagus River just north of Isles Port, and there were five of them. Her mama was from Aroostook County and her daddy was an Isles Port'r. The kids' ages ranged from three years to nineteen, nineteen being the age Mary was when Kenny first laid eyes on her. She was the sweetest thing. She would come into the store with a list from her mama; with her little brother and sister at home, mama didn't get out much. It was strange, how being from way up in the county they seemed to speak more like southerners than Mainers.

It wasn't easy to live in these parts, not to mention having three kids to feed. Oh, there was some farm stock to care for. Three milking cows, that helped a lot. They had some chickens, turkeys, one big old workhorse that twitched the firewood out of the woods for them, and a couple of pigs every year to help feed them all. I guess you might say they were self-sufficient. With a couple of hundred bucks worth of food stamps each month they did alright, but 'round here if you got stamps, you were one of them, and the locals, either out of jealousy or greed for want, always turned their noses up to those who needed help for self-betterment. That never stopped Kenny, however, from flirting with young Mary every time she came to the store, and she never attempted to hide her feelings for him. It was an instant attraction, you might say, and everybody knew except her mama and daddy, but like everything else in life, all good things must end, and so would their little secret.

Autumn flew by and winter was on the doorstep. Kenny'd been extremely busy with his enterprises, and he'd let his relationship slide somewhat where Mary was concerned, and she told him so one afternoon in the back room of the store.

"I guess with the comin' of winta', I probably ought to find a thicka' blanket to cuddle with, as the ice around hea's startin' to build around the gutt'az," she said.

"Now Mary, you know how busy I've been these past few weeks, and all the money I'm making is going to be for us one day."

"Do you take me for some spill-ova' from Bangah' Mental Health?" she added.

"Now…come on, Mary, you know better than that. I've been real busy all fall and the money is coming in now. I'll be able to take part of the winter off so we can spend some time together out to Filbert's camp. You know how much you like the seclusion out there."

She remained quiet for a period, while Kenny laid it on with another layer to convince her that he meant what he said, and after a couple of minutes of the Kenny work-over, she bought it…hook, line, and sinker. That's the way it was with old Kenny-boy; he wouldn't rest until you bought the package, and for some strange reason, Kenny was always part of the package.

Mary was such a fine young woman, not only of physical beauty, but also of attitude. She stood about five-foot-five, about a hundred and two pounds and she had the shiniest dark brown hair, looking like silk flowing over her shoulders, and entrancing brown eyes. She appeared thin and gaunt, but mostly it was the baggy clothes she wore. Her voice was soft, and her little laugh could tickle a man's desires, and it tickled the hell out of Kenny.

Most everyone thought that Mary had been as pure as the driven snow when she first met Kenny. She wasn't. She had a decent way of hiding her faults from them that meant the most, and for whatever reason, she always passed herself off as the sweet little virgin, but she wasn't that either. She loved the sex and drugs lavished upon her by her bohemian boyfriend, and she wasn't the least bit intimidated by the company he kept. You might say it was her way to escape from the humdrum life of a poor farmer's daughter with younger siblings she was responsible for most of the time. You see, what most people didn't know was that having them kids wasn't the only thing her mama and daddy were good at; both of them were serious drunks.

Winter slashed in with a vengeance on Thanksgiving Day that year. The only thing moving, and it wasn't even 'til later in the day, were the plow trucks. It was kinda nice to see the snow. It put solitude back into the entire area—the type that only the locals could appreciate. Everyone simply stayed home with family and enjoyed the feast with their own. Yeah, there were those like myself who would have probably been alone anyway, stayed home watching it snow and drinking, but for someone like Mary Bagley, she would be with the only person she believed understood her: Kenny.

Mid-coast Maine and up north was in a power-out situation, and for the most part, it wasn't that common. It didn't much matter if the power was out; most folks heated with wood, so staying warm wasn't the problem. And, cooking the old tom turkey wouldn't be a problem either; most folks still had a wood-cook stove in the kitchen. I missed family and the little things that only family can get you through. Most folks had good memories when it came to family, at least most people I knew. It's strange though, when you think you know someone, down the road you find out that it wasn't as pretty-as-you-please for them. Terrible things go on behind closed doors, things that take the innocence away from the children and sometimes the adults who get in the way. That shit went on around here, just like anywhere else. Most of it went unnoticed, but in the case of a particular situation that involved Kenny Collins and little Mary, it would change things forever.

It was that very snowy holiday when all this shit with Kenny and Mary started. They decided to elope. Yeah, they took off for Augusta, thinking it was far enough to get away with it, never thinking about when they had to come back and face the music with her old man, Virgil Bagley. True, no matter how drunk a person might get, or stay, the one thing you can't overlook is the thought of a loved one going missing. Virgil was no different. He would have had the National Guard out if he could have. The local lawman's hands were tied to the area, and the resident State Trooper, Harry Circus went through the motions, but when you think about it, what the hell could he do except do his job and follow up on the information he got from the parents and the folks around town. No one had a clue what those two were up to. It was the best-kept secret in the whole Down East—actually, the only-kept secret in the whole Down East.

Well, they spent a couple of days in and around the Sugarloaf area for their honeymoon, never letting on where they were. Mary called home to break the good news to a couple of frickin' deliriously worried parents. But she was free now, she thought. Free to do the things she and Kenny had talked about since they'd met, like no more taking care of a couple of small kids. Sure, she'd help her mama all she could, but it was her mama's problem now. Her mama's and daddy's problem, and that's the way it would have to be from here on out. Kenny and Mary, or Mary and Kenny, any way she said it came out sounding right to her ears and Kenny's too. The future was looking bright. They had more money than her parents had ever seen at one time, and they had the rest of their lives to prove they could make it. They had big plans to set the world on fire, and right at that moment, they were both carrying a huge box of matches.

The winter's cold wasn't all that could freeze the tip of a kid's tongue to metal. When they got home, you might have thought the roof had blown off the place the way the verbal fireworks were going off in it. The only thing they didn't do was come to blows. Well, I think I told you before, old Kenny had a way of sliding out from in front of a pointing finger, and that's exactly what he did when the old man started in on them. He pulled up a chair and sat at the far end of the table, letting them blow the heat all over little Mary, and she didn't have any problem fending them off. Nothing her parents could say was going to change their minds and no way was there going to be an annulment. In his mind, Kenny had no problem thinking he could support a wife.

He had a small place down by the river he rented from Filbert, and it was just big enough for a love nest. Through the gossip-mill and from Mary's own mouth, they were very careful where birth control was concerned, and for the most part, neither one of them was ready to be a parent. There was only time for partying, and love-making, a little something to eat, make a little more love, and find another party, and around that time in these parts, if you wanted to find a party, you didn't have to look hard.

That's exactly what had the local old folks up in arms. Everywhere they went, the smell of pot was just floating in the air, and it was starting to piss a few people off. I guess that's when the shit started to hit the fan, and the stink spread to the far reaches of the county. But for some reason, old Kenny never stopped doing what he always did, and no one seemed to be able to catch him, while Mary became a major player in her husband's game.

The river flowed heavy just behind Filbert's store—even as cold as it was that winter—there remained several decent rifts in the ice, allowing water to flow over the top and creating a white water flowage that could be heard for long distances up and downstream. From inside the store, it sounded like endless thunder, even though the water level had dropped considerably in winter.

Kenny worked whenever Filbert called him, usually the night before he was to receive a truckload of something, stock shelves, or take a run to Bangor or Ellsworth to pick something up. One thing was for certain, when Kenny worked, Mary was soon to arrive at the store, and simply hung around, just because. Of course, she had a way to keep Filbert enjoying the company, and he always fed them while they were there. Filbert could be sure that the people that did business with Kenny, in or out of the store, would usually show up, and it seemed that the person they wanted to see wasn't Kenny, but Mary. It was at these times that Filbert began to believe the worst of the rumors that flew around town about the two people he truly believed in.

He and Heidi had started out pretty much the same way, not involved in the obvious shenanigans these two were into, but renting the same small place by the river before they eventually bought it and tried to make a go of it the only way they knew how, just the two of them. He tried to keep out of it until he saw Mary slip a small plastic bag to one of the regulars who always bought beer and cigarettes, but this time only came in for the little baggy. It was as if Filbert had sent the message telepathically, because as he approached, Mary obviously knew what was about to happen, and, grabbing her coat, she left.

She never returned that day except to pick Kenny up late that afternoon. By then old Filbert had cooled down and probably forgot.

As slow as it might have seemed, winter moved along like any other season that year. The holidays flew by, and before you knew it, Saint Paddy's Day had arrived. Some folks make a big thing out of all those so-called holidays; I suppose they're just looking for something else to have a party over. Not that there's anything wrong with that; it just seems like they never grew up as far as most folks around here felt. Monday was Monday and the rest of the days ended up flowing into the next. Bullet would be the first to tell you that.

"One day's no different than the next," he'd say. "Ya get up, have a little drink, and keep right on havin' em' all goddamned day."

Well, I guess I won't argue with that. Most of them parties ended up taking place at Bullet's house, since it was so far removed from the beaten path, so-to-speak, and with the party- people came all that shit and gurry (an old Maine term for fish guts and in this case described the undesirables) from town. It wasn't until Kenny invited himself to one of them parties that it all started involving me and my good friend Bullet. If you remember, when Kenny came to town, Bullet didn't like him, and since then we were being thought of and judged as one of them and it seemed to tighten the knot a bit tighter around old Bullet's neck. The last thing he wanted was to choke on someone else's phlegm (as he might have put it). And that is when it started to involve us.

And by the way, my name's Adver Bagley, no relation to them Bagleys upriver. I appreciate your taking the time to read my story. I've put it down just the way I heard it, and I hope you enjoy it.

'Judge not, that ye be not judged'

(Matthew 7:11)

T HE MORNING LIGHT WAS DIMMED by a sea smoke that seemed to have no end in sight, dampening clothes with only a few moments outside. A small group of men gathered out front of Filbert Cirone's store, clustered in a tight circle around the single gas pump to the side of the plate-glass picture window. One could tell from the tightness of the little circle that the subject was of a gossiping nature, as one by one the visors of each cap were seen swiveling from side to side, making sure they remained alone with their yakking.

"I'm thinkin' the little shit knows exactly what's goin' on," one of the men remarked.

"Well," another one added. "If he doesn't, he's a bigger fool than he makes himself out to be."

"Ayah," a third one said as his head swiveled from left to right, then back to a central focus on the group.

All the heads turned now, at the same time, and in the same direction toward the front door of the store. Filbert, on his daily routine of checking the pump gallon readings, frowned as he exited, knowing very well the group was up to no good, if only with their idle banter.

"What the hell aar' you all up to if it ain't no good, I'd like to know," Filbert said with a half-smile, indicating he was only foolin' around with them.

"You know, Filbert, supposin' you know most of what goes on 'round hea', I'd think you'd be the best judge about Kenny Collins thea'?" the tallest of the group asked.

"I'm no judge for anybody, and I think you boys already know that. I like to keep mine to me and leave theirs to them," Filbert said.

The entire group appeared to become tense at the tone Filbert took, and the short pudgy one, who'd been leaning against the pump's nozzle, began tapping a rhythm on top of the pump with his nervous little fingers.

Just across the bridge from where the men stood was River Street. Its name was synonymous for its location, running for several miles along the Paguagus River; the road being the only thing between the massive, colonial and Victorian homes and the swift-moving current. The huge homes, built by the lumber barrens and mill owners of a bygone era when the rich were most definitely separated and segregated from the working class poor, were a kind of monument to their accomplishments. However, many from that era, who enjoyed the luxurious lifestyle of their day, were ruthless and greedy beyond the realm of those who inhabited them now. At these times and in this century, the division between the classes was far less magnified. Nonetheless, there remained (and always will be) a division of the classes.

In the other direction, away from the towering mansions, River Road became gravel and narrowed to the width of one vehicle, with tree branch overhangs that swatted a vehicle while passing and kept the road leading to the dead end at the river and Kenny and Mary's place less used. Small towns like Isles Port and Chesterfield seem to cultivate rumor whenever the subject of the rumor-mill was a young and pragmatic newcomer, especially one willing to go the extra mile to stir the pot of town talk. Kenny Collins was more than willing. Most everyone however, did not want to label Mary as a willing contributor to Kenny's anarchy.

The group suddenly became still and straight-faced as Mary's mid-sized Chevy accelerated up the incline from River Road on its approach to Filbert's store. It was an easily recognized little car, as the exhaust leaked from the header at the engine, making the rumble more distinct and acute than if it were leaking from a location more toward the rear of the car. As if no one standing around the pump had been talking about them, Kenny and Mary were greeted with huge smiles and waves, as the car pulled to a stop in front of them.

"What's goin' on with all you piss-pots today?" Kenny asked.

A slight mumbling came from the group, but not one came out and said anything audible. Mary stayed behind the wheel, smiling as usual. Kenny went to the trunk and pulled the duffle bag out quickly, and hurried toward the driver's door. He and Mary exchanged a few short words, then he stuck his head in, and they kissed goodbye.

The group circled around the gas pump, cooing at the sight of the two kissing, but came to an abrupt silence as Kenny swaggered toward them, mocking them and wobbling his head in contempt. As he entered the store, the group disbanded.

Once inside the store, Kenny looked from side to side in an attempt to see Filbert, but he was nowhere to be seen, so Kenny walked straight toward the door at the back of the store, the one that led to the basement. Opening it, he threw the duffle bag up against the stone point foundation and onto a wooden deck at the top of the basement stairs, and then slammed the door. When he turned, he was met with Filbert's cold stare.

"Well, mista' man. I took the pump readings for ya," Filbert said.

"Yeah…sorry. Mary needed the car and took her sweet time gettin' ready. What do you have going today?" Kenny asked.

"I'll need ya' to go on over to Ellsworth. I was called this morning and they told me my supplies were in. And while you're thea', you may as well get the plate stickers. Registration's due in a few days," Filbert said.

Filbert wanted to just reach out and grab Kenny by the scruff of the neck and shake some sense into him—come right out and ask him if he was selling drugs and all the other stuff everyone was talking about behind his and Mary's backs. He couldn't, because he didn't believe it, and he let it go. Like so many other times, when he came so close to asking that his lips almost formed the words, his mind raced back to that first day when an arrogant young Kenny walked into his store, browsing through the aisles as though he owned the place, and he remained silent. How good a friend and hunting companion Kenny had become for Filbert and right now, someone completely invaluable to him. He knew the day would come when he would ask; unfortunately, today would not be that day.

The bell over the transom tinkled, and Filbert strode toward the front counter as Kenny clamored in the stock room preparing for his return with supplies for the store.

Most days when Kenny worked, Mary would visit her mom. There was always something to help out with. Nothing ever changed there. For the most part, it was what attracted her to Kenny. A wild side of a life she had only dreamed about before being confined to a home with difficult parents. There was never any quiet time in a house with kids and two alcoholic parents.

It seemed that when she visited, her relationship with her mother, Lucretia, was developing into a kind of woman-to-woman connection. Lucretia was well aware of the man her daughter was living with. She might not have been a frequent visitor to town, but she had a phone and a small circle of friends that kept her up to speed with the rumors about Mary and Kenny.

Virgil, her father, however, was not as receptive of the relationship. He kept his daughter's best interests at the forefront of his thinking, but cautiously, he kept Kenny at a safe distance, as far as a relationship went. Behind the scenes, he kept an open ear for the small talk around town, and for the most part, kept it to himself. On days when Mary spent mornings with her mom, Virgil kept himself busy, as most men in the Down East area do when avoiding a particularly uncomfortable situation. Mostly, he would greet his daughter with a half-hug and a grunt, then leave the two women sipping tea at the dining room table, and wouldn't return until well after Mary had left, quizzing his wife about every little detail of what they'd talked about.

While Mary visited, Bobby, who was too young to leave for school and the one who missed her the most, competed for her undivided attention, and usually found a way to get it. The house always smelled of rancid meat and dank diapers. Even though Bobby was too old for diapers now, his mother had never bothered to toilet-train him.

There was never a time limit on how long Mary would stay. She never seemed in a hurry to leave. While her brother and mother would fall just short of begging Mary to fix one of her favorite lunches, and it was clear to anyone who may have witnessed it, Mary loved every minute she stayed with them. When she finally left, it appeared that she had packed away any evidence of rancid meat and dank diapers with the cleaning effort she made.

Mary never regretted leaving home; maybe the way she left, but never the fact that she did. It's like everything else in life: the grass is greener on the other side of the gate. It's all part of life, and everybody gets a taste of it. There were times lately that she feared, if only a little, the way Kenny swung his life about on some thin string; dangling it like a hellish nightmare in front of her; and she, at times, was very unsure of herself.

She found herself having that very thought while stirring the tomato soup and watching the grilled cheese sandwiches in the frying pan as her mother rounded Bobby up.

Lunch was always special if Mary fixed it.

The last thing Kenny threw into the cab of Filbert's pickup truck was the duffle bag he'd thrown on the landing at the entrance to the basement. He had his own pick-ups and deliveries to make on his way to and in Ellsworth. He never viewed his relationship with Filbert as using Filbert as a means to an end—the end being the huge amounts of money he made from his private dealing, while using his work and personal relationship with Filbert as a front. He truly enjoyed being with Filbert, and always cherished everything he'd been taught about the great outdoors. Without him, it would have taken a long time to fully understand the secrets of snatching a brookie out of a crystal clear pool in some far-off brook deep in the woods, or comprehend the feeding habits of whitetail deer at the changes of the seasons. Because of Filbert, there was always fresh deer meat on the table.

From the first day that Kenny had arrived, he always envisioned himself and a fine woman living in one of those grand houses on River Road. After all, those houses weren't built with pure honesty and the sweat from the architect's brow. It was always other peoples' sweat and blood that went into success of that magnitude, and Kenny considered himself an entrepreneurial thinker with dreams of grandeur, never including into the equation the possibility of failure, danger, and risk in the type and design of enterprise he'd now embarked upon, or the area in which he chose to undertake it.

As Kenny pulled out from behind the store on his way to Ellsworth to run his and Filbert's errands, what he couldn't know was that Virgil Bagley was watching him leave from a tiny window just above the landing at the entrance to Filbert's basement.

2

A N UNEXPECTED SNOW FELL on the entire Down East area, forcing the normal daily routines to a standstill. Filbert opened the store during a heavy pelting mix. A day like this was common for Maine in spring. They were however, frowned upon, slowing the eagerly awaited transition from the long winter months, where most time was spent dreaming of this time of the year. The stored potatoes and canned vegetables were nearing depletion. The foil-wrapped pig meat and chickens frozen last fall were in short supply. And if you knew anything about Mother Nature, the last thing you wanted to do was drop a deer now, as it was hard to tell the bucks from the does; the bucks had shed their antlers by this time, and the does were probably carrying their young.

The lights flickered, forcing Filbert to look up toward them.

"Well, if you dim bastards go out, I'm outta' hea'," he said. Once he opened, however, he never left. At about the very moment the words left his mouth, headlights of an approaching vehicle, dulled by the flying snow, appeared in the distance, causing Filbert to turn his head in their direction. With much concern, he watched as the vehicle, indistinct as of yet, began pulling donuts on the slick snow-mix in the center of the roadway, just to the left from the center of the storefront.

"What kinda pecka'headedness…?" was all that Filbert could

get out when he noticed it was Mary's car, and the shit-eatin' grin behind the wheel belonged to Kenny.

Round and round, the vehicle spun wildly, seemingly out of control, kicking slush over the top of the car, to the exhilarating pleasure of the young attractive passenger. They skidded sideways toward the single gas pump out front, coming to what appeared to be a planned stop in a position ready for a fill-up.

The outside store lights burned brightly, and for the first instant since Filbert had noticed the car, he now saw Mary, laughing as though someone was tickling her from somewhere under the seat, latched onto her man, who also seemed to be overflowing with glee.

The blowing wind began to force the snow mix into drifts on the roof eaves and on top of the single gas pump. From his perch by the front door, Filbert thought that the side of Kenny's face, around and below the eye, seemed swollen and bruised, but he dismissed it as shadows that formed against the dull, early morning light and the driving wet snow. It was, however, as if Filbert had suddenly become invisible, and the two people in the car carried on an unheard conversation as if they were the only two people alive in the entire world.

Finally ignoring the two lovebirds, Filbert looked down the aisle that ran the length of the store from where he stood at the checkout counter. He could see the small gathering of chickadees, titmice, and blue jays gorging themselves at the feeder hanging just outside the tiny window next to his sandwich counter. The cat was lying on the counter with its eyes as large as quarters, watching the frolicking birds, and flapped its tail abruptly with aggression as if a pouncing were imminent. Even as late in the season as this storm was, being in the store on a day such as this gave Filbert a feeling of warmth. It provided a type of solitude that only a snowy day could offer. It fed the daydreamer's mind; a feeling that would soon fade with the coming of spring and the onslaught of the summer fury.

It took quite awhile for Mary and Kenny to leave the love nest, and when they finally did enter the store, they had apparently met up with Bullet Carter out front. For some unknown reason, Kenny and Bullet had begun quarreling, and brought it with them into the store. Filbert had strolled to the sandwich counter, stroking the cat as the whirlwind of two entered some eighteen feet away, spurring the cat to run off at the sound. It was from Filbert's view, at this distance, that the brunt of the anger belonged to Kenny. The taunting came from Bullet, and the subject matter was the shiner and swelling to the side of Kenny's face, confirming the sight that Filbert had originally dismissed as shadows. Mary followed the two at a distance, looking pale and frightened.

Filbert had never seen Kenny angry. He'd always remained calm, as when the young Indian had his run-in with him that summer past. Now, he was almost out of control, and Bullet was enjoying the contest. Mary tugged on Kenny's arm in an attempt to calm her man and slowly, he began letting her move him toward the sandwich counter as Bullet continued to taunt Kenny on his way to the beer cooler.

From Kenny's first walk through the store—the day Filbert had motioned toward Bullet to keep an eye on the young man as an ordinary transient—Bullet always appeared to be glowering whenever Kenny was underfoot, as Bullet would describe it.

"He's like a rodent, always scurryin' about, looking for a chance to swipe the last piece o' cheese."

Filbert didn't like any kind of squabble ignited by any two or any group that could eventually lead to serious trouble in the store. Sure, this was for the most part the local beer-and-cigarette run, but local families shopped here, just not as many as he would like. His was a small store, so his prices had to be higher than the IGA in Isles Port to make up for the slow turnover of the shelves, but you never knew when someone with a kid would walk in, so Filbert always kept his guard up for any sign of trouble. Right now, as much as he admired both men, he moved quickly to where they stood, getting right in the middle and in their faces.

"I'm naut' quite shoa' what this hea' squabble is all about, but if'n it comes ta' blows, you'd best be takin' it out a' doas,'" Filbert said as he squared off with the two.

Bullet stepped around Filbert and placed his six-pack of Bud on the counter, never saying a word. He'd known Filbert since they were boys; since Bullet was a couple of years younger, he respected Filbert. He would never have pushed Filbert into any confrontation in order to assert his bad attitude about the young drifter, as Bullet called him, infuriating Kenny into the type of outburst that had just taken place. Little Mary stood frozen by the sandwich counter, eyes wide with fear, holding the cat, which was large enough that she appeared to be wearing a fur muffler covering her entire front from her shoulders to her midsection. The cat's tail swayed as it hung down well past her waist.

"I'll take a pack o' Camel, non-filter, with this bea'," Bullet ordered. And because it was Kenny who'd slid in behind the counter, Bullet just couldn't help getting in one more dig.

"And if 'n' ya don't mind, wha' kinda' rollin' paypaz' you suppose 'ud be best?" Then he laughed an evil laugh. Filbert shook his head and turned now, going toward the back of the store, but Mary had already moved from her place and had taken the cat with her, knowing, as did Filbert at this point, the battle was over.

With their voices now lowered, the two men at the counter became civil with one another (for the most part), and concluded their business, then the clanging of the door chime faded, as did Bullet's voice with the overtones of ridicule as he left. With the store quiet once again, Filbert was no longer in a daydreamer's mood, and he wanted an explanation from one or both of the two people in his store right now.

It was apparent, by the way Kenny lingered at the checkout, that the last thing he wanted to do was talk about it, and Mary had suddenly pulled some kind of vanishing act with the cat. Filbert had an ear for the store and the sound of a closing door would have alerted him, had Mary used the back door to leave. There were only two; the front and back doors, and the back one squeaked like hell, so as far as Filbert was concerned, she was in the store somewhere. He headed for the only place she could be, the basement.

When he found her, she was sitting on a wooden pallet piled with fifty-pound sacks of potatoes. Given her tiny build, she would have had to jump up in order to seat herself where she was, and the cat, still cradled in her arms, purred happily. The basement was somewhat shallow, and a person of Filbert's stature needed to crouch in order to enter the basement proper, but he was able to stand erect once in. The walls were stone-point construction, giving the entire sub-layout a dark, dank appearance, yet it was quietly removed from the outside noises.

"What the hell was that all about?" he asked.

Mary, unwilling to look up at him, began to mumble in an inaudible tone, almost as if she were having trouble clearing her throat. It appeared to him that she might have been crying, yet he could see no tears, nor did she display any outward signs. Again, he asked, "What the hell was that all about?"

Slowly, she began to look up at him, and spoke clearly, but not before looking around to make sure they were alone. At the first sight of her looking around, Filbert did, too, simply out of curiosity or a suspicion that someone was watching from an unknown location. Whatever it was, he felt very strange in his own basement. Mary began relaying to him the events that had led up to Kenny's facial injuries.

"He got into a fight with someone in Ellsworth," She said, but would not go into detail about the events that led up to it or name anyone. Suddenly, none of what she said sounded right, and Filbert felt that Kenny was doing more than just running everyday type of errands.

"What were they fightin' about? Did he get into an accident with my truck?"

"No…no there wasn't an accident. He…" She hesitated for a moment. "Well, he had a few errands to run for himself, and he got back late." None of what she said made any sense to Filbert.

It had been several days before that Filbert had sent Kenny

to Ellsworth with his pickup. He'd never realized until now that Kenny hadn't returned until very late that night. It wasn't an unusual event; a trip to Ellsworth could take all day, and he always expected that anyone he might send for supplies would run a slew of errands for themselves. He could have cared less when the pickup came back, as long as it was emptied and its contents were stored in their proper places, and with Kenny that was never a problem. He had the run of the whole store, and as far as Filbert was concerned, nothing about that arrangement had changed.

Mary's left foot, barely touching the lowest sack of potatoes, tapped out a nervous rhythm, forcing the cat's bulbous head to bounce on her knee, and ushering the cat into a blissful sleep. Although subdued and obviously fearful that Kenny might come down the stairs at any moment, Mary told of her experiences with a different Kenny, who only three short years before had swept her from her family existence for the adventurous, socially radical lifestyle she longed for, helping her escape from the parental prison she had come to believe was her life. She told Filbert that Kenny was becoming more aggressive, occasionally grabbing her forcefully by the arm to keep her obedient to his impetuous whims. Filbert was realizing that the visage of the person he trusted was beginning to take on the role of an ogre. He felt sick to his stomach, and wanted to go upstairs and wring Kenny's scrawny neck, but at what cost to Mary?

Filbert looked at her with sympathetic eyes, remembering the little girl he'd first met when Virgil moved them all back down here from Aroostook County when his mother died and they took over the old homestead. Mary sat before him now a woman, but in many ways that little girl was still there, giving her the appearance of vulnerability. And she may have been vulnerable, but there were times when she used it and knew very well how to, in order to get things done her own way, making him wonder if this was all some little show to distract him from the actual Kenny-and-Mary antics.

Filbert was a good man, but he was not a fool. The rumors

spreading around about the two had confused even him, the last person who wanted to believe that the rumors were more than simply that. Lies made up by those, who for their own laziness, loathed the fact that someone else made a grab for success, whatever it might be.

Mary looked up suddenly, her eyes wide with a sense of urgency.

"Please, Filbert; you can't say anything of what I've told you to him. It'll only make him madder now that he had that run-in with Bullet."

He wanted to take this one step further, and ask why Bullet was so willing to create such bullshit so early in the day, but at the sight of his eagerness, Mary allowed the cat to slide from her lap and walked quickly toward the stairs.

She no sooner got halfway up when Filbert heard Kenny's approaching footsteps and realized that Mary had heard them long before he had. He listened to see what would happen. When Mary reached the bottom of the stairs, her face was the reflection of fear, drained of all color, and her head jerked wildly when Kenny bellowed out, "What's goin' on?"

3

MARY SPENT LONG DAYS ALONE at their little place down by the river. She had put some of her own touches to it. She kept it clean and added rustic collages in just the right places that would have indicated that a woman was the one to decorate, because a man, especially a Down East man, could not bother with, or even find the time to add such a touch to his abode. And cut flowers would never happen. Kenny thought that type of decorating was sissified. The only scent he wanted was the disguising smell from the odoriferous incense sticks which masked the pungent pot smoke that always seemed to permeate the entire building. So, Mary reserved herself to the little things that made a house a home.

There was a grapevine wreath that she had made on the front door. A very impressive ornamental grass wreath hung in the corner just above their tiny rectangular wooden table, which slid handily under the windowsill with their chairs facing each other so they both had an unobstructed view of a white water rip, which ran just below the window and about five feet out. The ceilings were beamed and low, making it easy to heat through the winter.

The woodstove was the focal point of the open concept living room, dining room, and kitchen, and was centered between all the rooms. Their bedroom was just off to the right as you walked into the living room. Kenny liked it because he said that he had an open view of anyone who might come in the middle of the night.

The very first time Mary heard him use that phrase "the middle of the night," she thought he was kidding; but as the months flew by, the middle of the night became as active as the middle of any day.

Kenny seemed to exist on Budweiser, pot, and some little black pills he'd begun using during the last winter. His moods would reach a flashpoint when the supply ran low or out, and when it did run out, it was as if the power switch flipped to the off position. The high-strung, high-powered Kenny collapsed in the corner or on the couch or in bed; and in bed was where he usually ended up until that expected little-black-pill-telephone-call came in. Then he dragged himself up and out of bed and became that whirling tornado he always was, but with a bigger chip on his shoulder and an attitude more hateful than ever.

He seemed to feel the need to lavish their relationship with all the things his so-called business rewarded him with, and the things he thought they deserved out of life. They sat for hours some days, when neither of them had plans to leave, Mary drinking gallons of coffee, and Kenny taking only his beloved Bud and rolling joints. For him, pot-smoking was a must with all that beer.

"You always have to take the edge off with one of these little beauties," he'd say. It got to the point both for Kenny and Mary, with Kenny taking two little beauties every couple of hours, that by noon they were ready to take on the world without batting an eyelid.

It was on those long, slow-starting days that the hordes of Kenny's so-called friends seemed to invade their little hide-away on the river.

The cabin was completely isolated from view, making it the perfect place for an arcane get-together, and lately, there had been many. The posted "Private" sign at the beginning of the road had been there since Filbert and Heidi first rented the cabin, mainly for the occasional out-of-town "sport"—a fisherman or hunter—looking for that special spot to snag his trophy salmon or that perfect ten-point buck. All the locals knew who lived there, and for the most part, there were no residents, outside of any of the small group handpicked by Kenny himself or Mary, who ventured down the narrow gravel road. Other people came from as far away as Bangor. Some could have inspired the original phrase, "Look what the cat dragged in." Over time, fear had begun to creep into Mary's consciousness, a dread that made her mother's intuition look like a drunken fortuneteller's story. Sometimes, it was a single individual who would drop by. Other times it might have been a couple. Those were the easy ones to take. A little small talk, pass a doobie around, and Kenny would take them out to the barn where he kept the stash, and in a few short minutes they were gone; most of the time, without even as much as a goodbye to Mary. The ones that Mary feared were those who focused on her—the ones with rotted front teeth and scruffy faces, who undressed her with their eyes. She was afraid one of them might venture back on a day she was alone when no one was within earshot of the house.

Mary was well aware of the goings-on and the politics of small town life. She'd been born into it. Kenny, on the other hand, only thought he knew. The phrase, "When your neighbor sneezes, you catch the cold," was putting it mildly in most respects. True, there can be nothing as quiet and free-spirited as life in a small, far-removed rural community, but the word "privacy," well, that was in the eye of the beholder. In a small town, your business was everyone's business. Mary might not have been born here, but her father had been, so she was thought of as a local. No matter how Kenny endeared himself, or thought he did to the locals, he would always be from away.

One person, considered by himself and everyone else to be a local, was Maine State Trooper, Harry Circus. He married after graduating from Paguagus High School; settled in the small town of Berryville, just north of Isles Port. Annie, his endearing wife and member of the Women's Auxiliary, which had been founded by her great-grandmother, was chairperson of the Annual Berryville Baptist Church Bake Sale, devoted to the church choir, and regular attendee of the evening knitting group at the Legion Hall.

When Harry was growing up, he'd been the focal point of high expectation in school and the community. After all, his dad was the resident state trooper—much pressure for a young man—but he was inspired by his father's accomplishments. As a second-generation state trooper, he had much to live up to, but it was who he was. He'd grown up with that type of discipline. He was expected to perform, whether on the basketball court or at the Criminal Justice Academy. He did exactly what he was supposed to do.

As the only resident trooper, his rule was supreme within the guidelines of his authority.

Kenny was rapidly becoming an attraction to the suspicious eye of the trooper because of the information being fed to him by the town constable. The constable was tight with the political agendas of most of the past and present selectpersons. The contrast between the constable and the trooper in appearance was an entire world. Circus stood lean, muscular, and his appearance jived totally with the standards set forth by the Maine State Police for all their personnel in regard to appearance and cleanliness. Ralph Bailey, the constable, however, looked ready to go hunting or fishing, with his green flannel pants held up with suspenders and the ever-present flannel shirt with the constable badge pinned to the flap on the left pocket. A constable only carried a sidearm when needed, and usually directed by the trooper, during an arrest, assist, or a questioning of a likely violent suspect.

The rumors were now rampant about the goings-on at the little cabin down by the river. Anything done or asked where Kenny and Mary were concerned happened on the sly, so as not to alert them to the behind-the-scenes digging for information about them. And so, the covert activities surrounding the two became less of a secret with each question asked by the two lawmen. Now, as the pressure cooker heated to a possible steamy blowout, Kenny and Mary cleaned house and went on a little vacation.

4

THE PAGUAGUS RIVER FLOWED through some of the most pristine wilderness areas in Maine, winding its way to the sea at Isles Port. It was the magnet that drew money from away and into the malnourished economy of the Down East area. The tourists came for the canoe trips that allowed them the solitude they craved, to escape from the monetary prisons they'd been sentenced to for life. A life most people here resented them for, yet would never trade for the mere wealth that kept them in that type of prison. The sports came for the salmon fishing, which had been depleted greatly over the years, but even a local who lived to land a massive salmon to cook with freshly picked peas from the garden for the Fourth of July dinner felt pride in this accomplishment, fit for a king.

The hunting was good, but not as plentiful as it was in years past. The only viable natural resource that was left was the lumber/pulp industry and the Maine Wild Blueberries.

Just north of Isles Port were the towns of Berryville and Chesterfield, Maine. The towns lived, breathed, and reeked of the little blue fruit during August, the height of the sometimes-delirious blueberry season. At every turn of the road where a fully loaded truck on its way to the processing factory changed direction, a slight shift in the weight of the load allowed a sloshing of the tiny blue balls to tap out their dry rhythm on the pavement below, to be pulverized beneath the wheels of any following vehicle, to bake and stain the blacktop purple under a sizzling August sun. An onslaught of transients came for the purpose of removing every blueberry from the natural low bush plants that spread for miles on the glacially flat and deserted landscape of the blueberry barrens. They brought with them backpacks with their belongings and very little cash (some without any) to support their needs for anywhere from three days to three weeks if the crop was good. They also brought their habits with them. Kenny fit the mold and was ready to accommodate. If you needed it, there wasn't much he didn't already have or couldn't get and word of his limitless supply and his daily drives through the harvest area made him very popular and an instantly recognized supplier. His motto: "Have car, will travel."

He never followed the same route or time-frame on any given day; he supplied on a whim. He might show up at a campsite at sunrise one morning and sunset at the same site a few days later, but, like clockwork, Kenny would show, and his duffle bag was full. He became familiar with individuals who only days earlier were complete strangers. Without effort, he gained their trust and knew before leaving an area how soon he would need to return and what they wanted. On most trips, when Mary wasn't visiting her mother, she was with him. She always thought of their little rides on the blueberry barrens as part of the adventure she had originally left home for. The danger of that type of life while she was with her man never entered her thoughts, and with their deliveries made, it was their turn for the pleasure. They loved taking long drives after the deliveries were made. They had no one to answer to other than themselves, and neither one of them knew what a time clock was; however, the amount of sampling they were now taking from their own supply was reaching dangerous proportions. Suddenly, they both seemed to be losing touch with rational thinking but, *"what the hell,"* they used to say, in unison at times, accentuating their obvious one-track minds.

Mary always felt that she was only along for the ride. The

bags full of cash and drugs were fine with her, but when the black handgrip of the pistol concealed by Kenny's black leather jacket made itself visible, she began to feel she might be in over her head.

The dulling effects that the alcohol and drugs had on their senses ushered them toward a sense of untouchable accountability. They took on a callous demeanor. For Kenny, this was simply one step up from an already well-displayed pompous self-portrait; but for the quiet, down-home, country girl Mary, the change was drastic. Her mother, who refused to listen to other people talk about those changes, was now seeing for herself each time Mary visited. She had become a short-tempered, unruly young woman who just didn't seem to have enough time or care to embrace her younger siblings with the tenderness and affection she once had only a few short months earlier. She hurried through her visits now, unable to simply relax for their extended tea times before fixing the children's lunch, and her restless energy overflowed with unnatural fidgeting. Kenny, on the other hand, never faltered in his high-speed pursuit of those he supplied and/or befriended, until supplies ran low. Until the supply was depleted, it was only business, and anyone was a potential client.

His high energy was at times contagious for people who encountered him on a daily basis, thickening the shroud of skepticism that had blanketed him since the first day he walked through Filbert's store like a buyer inspecting the property. The one person who had almost single-handedly woven that shroud from the very onset was Bullet Carter. He wanted only to see the day that Kenny Collins was well on his way. He wouldn't rest until he did, and it didn't matter to him how Kenny left.

An early morning sun radiated brilliantly through the plate glass window of Cirone's store. Virgil Bagley stood, leaning against the soda cooler, knowing very well that today was one of Kenny's days to work. He wasn't much for getting involved in his daughter's personal affairs, but he'd been watching from the sidelines since the first spark of their relationship as his beautiful young daughter had moved away from his parental authority, and it sickened him to know that a man like Kenny had so much control over her and kept her so distant from her family. He was not a meddling parent. For the most part, Virgil Bagley was somewhat distant from his children, at times throwing himself into his work around the farm, and even though it was often a financially futile effort, it helped to keep food on the table and milk for the kids in the fridge.

He was a man of simple taste. Blue jeans with suspenders and a belt with a multi-colored flannel shirt was the norm, although the hunting knife he always carried in his belt was a bit unusual. He never went anywhere without it. With heavy heeled woodsman's boots, Virgil Bagley was ready to attend any function, including the occasional funeral. Everyone who knew him had heard his motto at least once: *"It don't matta' what a man has on; it's the depth of his soul that counts."* He shared many of Bullet Carter's opinions, only Virgil had been quiet until now, but he was ready to give Kenny a huge piece of his mind.

It became obvious to Filbert after failing several attempts at conversation with Virgil that he was preoccupied with his own thoughts. With the rumble of Mary's approaching vehicle, Virgil was unable to hide his reason for being in the store. He made no attempt to move from his relaxed posture against the soda cooler, but his head did turn quickly in the car's direction, and he stared at the occupants. Mary saw her father through the window, and Filbert watched her frown.

For the first time since he'd arrived at the store, Virgil spoke. "Well, if it ain't 'dances with assholes' arriving at work, with a chauffeur at that." Filbert thought it wise to remain silent. Kenny made no attempt to acknowledge Virgil's presence, but from the look on Mary's face, he knew he was there. The two sat out in the car by the single gas pump as they always did when Mary brought Kenny to the store. It was as if it would be their last goodbye, and nothing and no one could distract them from it, not even Virgil's presence.

Virgil's angry stare was steadfast, but his patience was like a hunter in a tree-stand, knowing his buck-deer was just over the rise and soon would belong to him. Filbert busied himself with incidental chores, keeping an alert eye between the front door and the soda cooler, where Virgil stood motionless, and Filbert was pleased that no other customers arrived for their early morning fixins', whatever they might be.

It was difficult for a man like Virgil Bagley to expose his deep concern for one of his children, especially his oldest—the one who'd witnessed his earlier years as a drunken rabble-rouser with no intention in life except to be just that.

Mary remained behind the wheel, as usual, and the moment Kenny exited the car, Virgil exited the store and met him just outside the door.

Although they didn't come to blows, their facial expressions and body language spoke volumes to Mary, silently, through the barrier of the auto glass. She watched, paralyzed, as the two men warded off attempts by Filbert to calm them, and after several terror-struck moments, saw Kenny storm in through the store entrance, almost running, and leaving through the rear door.

Sixteen hours later, Mary still hadn't heard from Kenny. Alone in her bed, she was in the grip of a migraine nightmare, reliving the sight of her father and her husband locked in a vicious quarrel in the middle of Filbert's store entrance early that morning. She felt like her brain was seeping out slow, dissolving drips from a crack in her temples.

Suddenly, she heard the front door open and close behind Kenny's footsteps. He shuffled along like he was very tired. Although the migraine continued to intensify, she fought off the urge to remain in bed, making her way slowly toward him. Blinking now under the strain of the dimmed light in the living room, her surging need to vomit from the pain of the migraine was not enough for her not to be concerned for her man. He was smiling toward her as he sat beside the window at the dining room table. The dim light from a candle reflected on his face, while casting an evil shadow through his thick dark hair onto

57

the wall directly behind him. He was very drunk, and he wanted attention, but she could not give it to him, because the migraine swelled to a throbbing dizziness, forcing her to run for the sink and give in to the uncontrollable need to vomit. Kenny, thinking she had also spent the day and evening at her own party, became extremely angry and walked from the house, slamming the door behind him, yet, through her agony, Mary heard nothing and was again alone.

To be alone with pain,

There can be no greater hurt.

5

TWO MONTHS HAD PASSED since the evening of Mary's migraine and Kenny's all-night wandering escapade. During this time, between the height of blueberry season and the rapidly approaching winter, the cash flow the two of them had become accustomed to was disappearing. There was always beer however. Filbert ran tabs for most people from town, and in some cases, surrounding towns, for those who didn't have a year-round, steady income. And in Washington County, that was most of the population. Most folks in these parts knew from the get-go that a tab at Filbert's was a cash-cow loan that never needed paying back. They knew Filbert would never chase them for it, and he was always the prey to a sob story. He just couldn't stand the thought of someone going hungry, and that's why he never made any money. He broke even, and sometimes came out in the red. That was probably why he never took in the gossip about Kenny and Mary. They were like everyone else to him. If they needed help, he'd be there for them.

If they fell short, each one would offer to work it off with hours at the store, or by running errands for Filbert or Heidi. Mary would at times baby-sit for Lulu, the youngest of the Cirone kids as a means to pay off their tab, and that gesture alone kept Filbert on their side no matter how hard someone tried to dissuade him about his feelings for the young couple. It was as if Filbert had a slight leak from the brains department when it came to just accepting the truth about Kenny and Mary. They hadn't started out trying, but they were quickly pinning their own badges on their chests proclaiming themselves white trash and it didn't seem to faze them to within a heartbeat of their past pride.

Two people who were not dissuaded in their opinion of the two were Trooper Circus and Constable Ralph Bailey. The trooper generally kept an arms-length between himself and the general populous, socializing only with a small group of handpicked friends and family for personal relationships. The Constable, on the other hand, was infinitely social in all circles, like the spider to the fly, one might say, but he picked up little tidbits of information that had led to the solving of cases over the past several years, and as much as they were opposites, the trooper paid serious attention whenever the constable made his opinion or observations known.

Despite the fact that Kenny's illicit goings-on had by this time taken a financial plunge, he remained under the watchful eye of both lawmen, but the trooper kept himself out of the limelight. They would meet at the Quick-Stop every morning for coffee, as did many locals starting their day. They casually discussed the people who made frequent contact with Kenny, but only here, in their own backyard. They never followed him or Mary whenever they left town in any direction. What went on outside of here was none of their concern, though the trooper informed local law enforcement agencies in some of the larger towns such as Bangor and Ellsworth of the possible drug trafficking in their communities. If they saw Kenny doing business in their towns, he suggested they keep a watchful eye out for their "little man," a term they both used regularly, but only to themselves. Using the description "little man" would not allow an eavesdropper to know who they were speaking of, and therefore they could maintain a level of covertness with every conversation about Kenny or Mary, or both.

The two men sat with their steaming coffee cups in front of them; Ralph dunking what looked to the trooper to be a very dry, very stale plain donut. He had two, and offered one to Harry; when he refused, Ralph dropped it next to his cup, with a sound like a small piece of wood.

"So, you say that Filbert thought they might come to blows?" Harry said.

"Ya, he said they paid him no mind when he tried to get between 'em, and it was shortly after that when Kenny stormed off and went out the back of the store," Ralph said.

"Did he go after him, or did he just stay there with Virgil?" Harry asked.

"Well, he said things went pretty fast after that, 'cause by the time he turned back toward Virgil, he was standin' out by Mary who was sittin' in her car," Ralph said. The two men sat quietly for what seemed like the longest moment, the trooper looking down into his cup, while the constable watched as a hunk of donut broke off and fell into his.

The early morning traffic began to get heavy, as logging trucks and local handymen headed off to their jobs. The gas pumps were always busy from open to close. The Quick-Stop sold their gas for five cents cheaper than Filbert did. There were two pumps out front here, one regular and one premium. Filbert had one pump, and sold only premium, and for the amount of gas he sold he couldn't afford to sell his for less. The trooper looked up from the table out toward the gas island, and couldn't believe his eyes. Standing right in front of the window was the very person who was the topic of their conversation. Without looking away, Harry began tapping his finger on the table in front of him in an attempt to gain the constable's attention, and he did.

"What's that, a new drum riff ya' workin' on?" Ralph asked. Then he saw Harry's eyes moving from his toward the outside, and Ralph began turning his head in that direction when he was told not to look.

Ralph could project one of the dumbest looks when provoked, and right now was one of those moments that seemed right to let one hang out.

"The way your eyes were a-shakin' thea', I could have sworn you wanted me ta' look at somethin' out thea', but excuse me for checkin'," he said. Harry couldn't help the tiny puff of laughter that burst out of him, and excused himself for his apparent coarseness toward the constable.

"Sorry Ralph, it's our 'little man' right out front. I just didn't want you to be too obvious about our desire to check him out, if you know what I mean."

"Ah…ayah, Harry, got ya'. What's he doin' thea'?"

Harry lowered his voice. "Well, believe it or not, the little shit's buyin' gas. I guess I know where his loyalty pumps." A line was forming at the coffee dispensers, and the two lawmen knew the time to be right to end their conversation about Kenny. What they were not aware of at that moment was that Kenny was watching them as his own way of intimidating after he'd been told of their observing him. To add insult to injury, while the trooper and the constable prepared to leave, Kenny pushed hard on the horn, forcing both men to jolt their heads in that direction. There before them was a broad-smiling Kenny Collins in the front of his car at military attention saluting the two men, who now looked like teddy bears propped up against a pillow unable to move without assistance. Kenny walked casually to the driver's side, got in and began to drive away, waving to the two lawmen as he pulled out.

6

A CHILLING NORTHWEST WIND GALLOPED through the area like the headless horseman's heavily sweating steed, breathing hard and spraying sputum down the necks of the young ghosts and goblins making their way to the lighted doorways of their Halloween benefactors. The already hardened, rapidly drying leaves crunched underfoot, while the scent of autumn filled the night air. A group of mischievous pranksters roamed the thickets, lying in wait for the younger, unsuspecting, door-to-door tricksters, heightening the mood. In some circles, however, the candy handed out did not contain any sugar, at least not the kind of sugar a child should be exposed to. Small groups of adults met to celebrate their version of Halloween, and in one of those gatherings, Kenny Collins was not only a prankster, but also the ministrant of treats.

The small house by the river was dimly lit with candles throughout, while the walkway leading to the front door gathered tall, flickering shadows from the keenly placed garden torches illuminating the house in a Halloween glow.

As with any gathering, several people mingled about, stopping at little circles of close-knit friends drinking and passing around the ever-present joint, talking of things that seemed to matter only to them and their small group. Their costumes, far more theatrical than those worn by the children roaming the streets and side roads of Chesterfield and Isles Port, spoke volumes of their desire to escape from the doldrums of daily existence and the reality of life in a small Maine town, far removed from the active, hurried lifestyle of places like Ellsworth or Bangor. However, most who lived here would never change places with anyone from either one of those towns.

Kenny mingled, walking throughout the gathering with his little mirrored tray and expensive-looking little glass straw for the premeasured white lines of cocaine, and was met with wide-eyed reception from everyone. Earlier in the day, Mary had voiced her opinion over the expense of such a large amount of the drug, but, after Kenny dismissed her as a straight-ass, he explained to her that image was the equation needed to keep the level of dealing and the money they both had become dependent on at a level it needed to be for the upcoming winter months and their deflating economy. Friendships were not what he intended to cultivate. He knew that by spring, many of the people in this little house would be deeply indebted to him, and he would never hesitate to use it against them to maintain the level of his and Mary's lifestyle.

The last little group to receive tidings from the evenings prankster were in a darkened area that appeared set aside for only them. This small group of three, though not as heavily disguised as most who gathered, was not recognizable to the others, and it was obvious they were not from around here. There were two nice-looking women, probably in their late twenties, and a longhaired guy who looked like a runaway from an old pirate movie, in his early thirties.

All three wore Lone Ranger masks, while their designer jeans and jewelry reeked of money. They hadn't specifically chosen their little darkened corner; rather, the locals kept the strangers at a decent arms-length. From the looks on the trio's faces, it was fine with them. The mood and decibel level heightened during the party, which was typical of any gathering where alcohol and drugs become the catalyst for ambience.

Kenny was smothering the pirate fellow with exaggeration, and at times, when Kenny looked around at his remaining guests, the longhaired guy looked toward his two female companions with a "do you believe this shit" look, then he would turn quickly toward Kenny, agreeing with everything he had to say. Nevertheless, Kenny was not interested in making friends. Everyone was a potential business associate, and he always said that there was someone out there in the world just waiting to make him rich.

Suddenly, Mary, who'd been busy in the kitchen keeping their guests supplied with drinks and snacks, made her appearance dressed as Elvira, the 1980's iconic "Mistress of the Dark," and immediately caught the roaming eye of the longhaired pirate fellow. She was hot.

Though the icon Elvira had always displayed a well-endowed bosom, as petit as Mary was, the extent of her partially exposed breasts would have forced any normal male to stare, or at least seriously glance, with much delight and curiosity. She sauntered in elegantly, and was without a doubt enjoying every moment and compliment from her male and female guests. Had the pirate worn an eye patch, it would not have covered his eye now, for suddenly, it mattered little what Kenny had to offer. Mary became the focal point of his attention.

As she approached, both men stopped talking and began to fondle her with their eyes. Neither one was aware, at that moment, that the other one was gawking in her direction, but the first to notice was one of the young women who had come with the pirate. When it became clear to her just where his eyes focused, she kicked the pirate hard in the ankle, causing him to jump with a yelp so loud that most everyone in that section of the house became quiet, looking toward them with concern. The dude became so pissed from the kick, that without flinching or saying one word, he reached out and took the woman by the neck with one hand, pulling her toward him. The chair she sat on toppled beneath her, and she and the chair landed in a heap at the pirate's feet. In the scuffle, a candle was upset, and Mary, who was within a few steps of it, stomped the flame out with her foot while calling out for Kenny who was getting up from his chair, grabbing at the hand that seized the woman's throat. Several people from the closest circle of friends drew in tight to get a better look, but most of the guests remained at a distance, unwilling to get involved.

"What tha' fuck do you think you're doin', asshole?" the pirate screamed at Kenny.

Kenny's eyes were as large as silver dollars, and his face expressed total determination.

When it came to a physical scrap, Kenny was like a streak of lightning. However, unlike the incident in Filbert's store when Kenny subdued the young Indian caught stealing, the pirate was a formidable match for Kenny in every respect. They entwined themselves in a series of headlocks and releases, flinging themselves about in that little corner of the room, resembling a couple of reptiles in mud vying for possession of a bug-infested puddle. Blood began to flow from the pirate's nose, and the woman who'd been the focus of the scuffle began screaming at Kenny. Kenny was distracted, thinking that the woman was upon him, and the pirate pulled a knife from his boot and began waving it under Kenny's nose with the obvious intention of cutting it off.

"I'm gonna rectumize you, ya' little fuck. Nobody puts a hand on me and gets away with it," the pirate wheezed.

Then he looked toward the woman who'd kicked him, and threatened her with the knife with periodic stabbing motions. It was bizarre how quickly the two men who'd been so deep in conversation to the level they'd reached only moments earlier could be such adversaries now. With the knife reflecting light from the room off of its six-inch blade, a majority of the male guests began to show their disapproval with the pirate's approach to fighting. They moved closer and began to roust him with their chanting.

"Root, root, root, root!"

The chanting and the inevitable insurgence against him from the encroaching group of drunken men gave the pirate much to dread, and he became visibly shaken, retreating toward the front door, which was the only unobstructed egress from the little corner of the room. Though all of this took place in less than five minutes, Mary stood fast to the spot and her foot, the one she'd used to smother the flame on the upset candle, seemed frozen in time. The only visible movement was her anxious breathing.

Mary's thoughts raced from the present to the not-so-distant past, and her intuition allowed her to envision the very thoughts that had given her doubt from the very start that Kenny would one day end up on the wrong end of a gun, or in this case, the chrome-plated blade of some longhaired freak's knife. She knew very well that her father had had his share of trouble while being held in the grip of alcoholism for all those years when she was growing up, but for the life of her, right now she couldn't remember any stories where any mention was made of someone pulling a knife or a gun in a fight. That was the big thing about her father's generation; you weren't a man unless you could settle it with your fists. The mix of the drugs and booze always played a role in making Kenny crazier, out of control, than if he only did one or the other by itself.

A huge dude from the group of rooters moved slowly through the crowd, inching his way forward. As the only thing moving in the entire house at that moment, he was caught in the knife-man's peripheral vision, and he jerked himself and his blade in that direction; bringing the dude to a one-step stop. That was all that Kenny needed: a lapse in concentration. And with one swoop no more than three-feet away, the sickening sound of the bone in the knife-wielders wrist snapped with one quick twist from Kenny's strong hands. The knife fell free to the floor and the quickly retrieving grasp of the huge dude's hand. The two women the pirate had come with, who until now had remained quiet and well out of the way, ran to his side, bawling like a couple of children, probably more out of fear for themselves than the wellbeing of their escort, who lay in a heap in the center of the room. With the knife firmly in his grip, the huge dude was making every attempt to flaunt it in plain view of the man who'd held it ready to stick someone with only moments earlier, and he stuck it, half-blade deep, into a wedge of cheddar cheese in the center of the table. Mary ran to her husband's side and clung as though she would never let him go.

So many people were standing between the knife and its previous owner that it would have been impossible for him to retrieve it without having more damage done to his already painfully fractured wrist. With the help of his frightened fair maidens, the pirate got himself to his feet and began walking toward the only door that was not blocked, but not without some explicit threatening directed at the man who just broke his wrist.

"Don't turn your back, you little cock, 'cause when you do, I'm gonna be right there with a brand-new blade to give you a real close shave". He continued shouting out threats while being escorted to the door by the still-whimpering women in masks. As the door slammed behind the trio, life and movement re-established in the guests, and some began to move closer to Kenny, wanting to know what had just happened. Kenny however, was unwilling to discuss it, and made it very clear to those interested that he would not. Mindful of it or not, Kenny was rapidly making as many enemies as he was friends. With Kenny, however, a friend, or an enemy was a renewable resource, and in his own words, spoken many times to Mary, he wasn't out to make friends, he was out to make money. And if anything got in his way, it would be left on the side of the road, dead.

From that point on, the evening moved quickly, and so did the guests. They left in small groups, offering their thanks to Mary for a great party, and condolences to Kenny after hearing the threats directed at him from a man who looked like a pirate, and whom most of them had never seen before this evening.

A few die-hard stragglers hung in for a last drag off of a still-burning joint, while guzzling the remaining drops of beer left in their bottles, but shortly after midnight, Mary and Kenny were finally alone.

They sat quietly for the longest time across from each other at their window perch, listening to a long, hypnotic instrumental by Pink Floyd, bringing a quiet end to a noisy evening. The radiant beams from the spotlights at the outside corner of the house filled the entire room from the bow window, and a few candles still flickered throughout the house. Mary sat with her eyes closed, simply enjoying the mood and the music.

"I think we need a dog!" Kenny said loudly, ending the tranquil moment.

"A dog?" Mary responded, wincing in confusion.

"Yeah, a dog." Kenny looked toward the table where the knife was still jabbed into the now-discolored cheese. "I don't trust that little bastard, and if for some reason he decides to come back here to get his knife—I don't think he will, but if he does and I'm not here, I think he oughta be met with a huge mouth fulla' teeth."

"Do you think he will?" Mary asked, feeling uneasy about the whole event.

"Like I said, Mary, I don't think he will, but who the fuck knows with a shit-for-brains like that?" he responded curtly.

Mary didn't respond; she simply looked out onto the spotlight-lit water-rapids just outside the window, and wondered what life would be like without all of this hell that was always in her face.

What she didn't know was that the descent into hell was only just beginning.

7

MONDAY MORNING CAME FAST. It was almost as if the weekend had lasted for a lifetime, yet it was now Monday. Lucretia stood on the wet asphalt of Eastern Maine Medical Center's parking lot, sucking deep from the Marlboro Light 100 cigarette, thinking how she figured she would arrive at this point in her life one day, *"throat cancer, lung cancer, pancreatic cancer, asshole cancer, cancer, cancer, fuckin' cancer!"*

She looked around and realized how much she hated Bangor. She'd have much rather been in her dining room with a drink and a fresh butt burning between her lips. On the heels of that very thought, she saw Mary walking from the far end of the lot where she'd parked the car.

With a sarcastic ring to her voice, she asked her mother, "Are you enjoying all that foul smoke you're pulling into your destroyed lungs?"

As soon as the words left her mouth, she was overwhelmed with guilt. Lucretia acted as if she never heard a word that Mary said, but her eyes gave her away, while she continued to draw deeply from the cigarette. "What time is it?" she asked. Mary looked inside the lobby through the immense glass front of EMMC. The huge clock over the reception area indicated 10:15 a.m., and she told her mother.

"You made good time with that old shit-box car of yours. If I'd had anything to gamble, I'd a' put my money on us not makin' it on time, or even makin' it period," she said.

Mary remained calm, breathing in deeply, trying to take in as much of the early morning air before beginning the possibly long indoor stay in this disease-infested complex behind her, but was only able to take in a whiff of the second-hand smoke from her mother's cigarette.

Mary and her mother had known for quite some time that things were not right with Lucretia's breathing, but she had never considered quitting the smokes, or the booze—as much as she may have cut back on the latter of the two evils—and it was obviously too late in many respects. It took Mary a solid month of phone calls, even a couple of letters to doctors and health organizations to find someone who would see her, knowing up front that she had no insurance or the means to pay for the inevitable accumulation of bills that would follow the tests scheduled to start in just a few minutes.

"We have to get you upstairs now, Mom," Mary said, in as soft a voice as she could. She watched as her mother silently tapped out the red-hot tip of what remained of the Marlboro against the handrail, sliding the remainder into the half-smoked pack and putting it into her purse.

She took a deep breath, saying, "Yeah', I'm ready."

As they entered the swinging doors to the huge lobby, their thoughts at almost the same millisecond were identical.

They both prayed to their Holy Mother of God, and the prayer was that the findings in this hospital today would bring about a cure, and thus an end to what had become a free-fall into the depth of fear that only being a potential cancer victim could create in the mind and soul of the one who would be afflicted.

As they walked, almost arm in arm, but never touching, Mary could feel a sense of emptiness, dreading the unknown. It could conceivably take weeks for all of the tests to return, confirming their fears, or setting them all free of the monster. Yet, all of this was simply another spike in Mary's heart, punctuating the life she had lost control of and felt there was no way to regain the feeling she'd once had for her dreams and a life of freedom.

8

W ORD SPREAD AS RAPIDLY AS A CONTROLLED BURN on the blueberry fields in autumn about the fight and wrist-breaking party at Mary and Kenny's place on Halloween night. Even more rapidly, it reached the ears of the local lawmen. What fueled their interest was that no one knew the victim of the broken wrist. All anyone had to offer was that he looked like a pirate and the two women with him were a couple of hotties.

Harry and Ralph sat across from each other at their usual table at the Quick-Stop. As steam rose from their cups, the coffee still too hot for gulping, they agreed that they were mutually concerned about the threats directed at Kenny Collins from the fellow who looked like a pirate. It could and probably would lead to no good, when after the broken wrist healed, the little twerp came back for revenge. It wasn't that the two men necessarily shared concern for Kenny's well-being; after all, he'd broken the wrist, and had to know there could be some sort of reprisal coming his way. Their concern was for any overflow of violence involving an unsuspecting, innocent citizen.

Though all rumors filtered into the gossip funnel, the one that got the most attention from the two men was that Kenny and that guy had been in an intense conversation moments before the fight started. The trooper posed questions and built scenarios as to what had transpired between the two men, yet without actually talking to either man, they were getting no farther along as to the why than they'd been at the beginning of their conversation.

As much as the trooper wanted to stay out of the limelight, he told Ralph, "Kenny Collins seems to think he's becoming immune to the laws that govern the rest of us, but without a complaint from the guy with the broken wrist, the only thing I can do is talk to Kenny, hoping he might volunteer something," he said.

"Fat freakin' chance o' that," Ralph said between bites of his stale donut and slurps from his hot coffee.

Harry could never understand why Ralph always picked up the stale donuts, when all he had to do was ask for a fresh-baked one and he would've had one.

"You know I'm going to have to be the one who talks to him about this. I'm not sure just how far out of control he is at this point, and I don't think he'll give me as much crap as he might give you, Ralph."

Ralph nodded his head in agreement without looking up from his coffee and donut.

"I'll stop in at Filbert's store first thing in the morning to see if he's working, and if not, well, I'll stop by their place." Harry sipped his own coffee. "Maybe they will both be there," he added.

While Mary sat anxiously awaiting her mother in an upstairs waiting room and the two officers concluded their daily talks about Kenny, he aggressively worked a remote trout brook off the Stud-Mill Road, a huge gravel logging highway running between Woodland, around Pocomoonshine Lake all the way to the pulp yards at Costigan —a location far removed from the trampling of everyday life and people. His hip basket was near-filled with plump little brookies, yet a few more would only help to fill the fry-pan. While the chances of being seen by a warden out here were pretty slim, even if one did make an appearance, Kenny would have seen him long before any contact were made. Hunting and fishing laws were for those who bought licenses, he believed, not for those who relied on the natural resources for sustenance and survival, and around here you did what you had to do. Out here, Kenny had time to think. The little things that made up an everyday cramp (as he liked to describe the monotony of day-to-day life) he could run away from here, in the deep, green moss-covered forest alongside a slow-moving trout brook with shimmering pools that thrived with life. The quiet solitude was, at times, almost overpowering, yet other times empowering. It was good being alone with one's thoughts in nature.

Enjoying the solitude of nature was at the other end of the spectrum from Kenny Collins' public personality, or what he wanted to project from his self-made world of chaos—a world that was rapidly coming into the light. He projected to all who would notice that he couldn't give a shit for another's well-being, but as he watched his feather fly create a circular ripple on the smooth surface of a pool, his thoughts seemed pulled by an invisible force to Mary and her restlessness at being unable to help the situation that enveloped her as she sat quietly in a poorly colored waiting room awaiting the completion of a second round of tests on her mother. Suddenly, Kenny felt very clearly that all she could do was think about him and how much she wished he were there with her.

With this almost telepathic feeling, Kenny's need to be alone gave way to his need to be with Mary. In his mind, it was as if he was re-visiting their beginnings, and for the life of him now, unexplainable. However, despite Kenny's ability to allow his mind to drift between good and evil, he nevertheless maintained at the forefront of his thoughts the information afforded him on Halloween by the very fellow whose wrist he had broken. That information, to this day, he shared with no one.

The subject matter of that conversation, taking illicit pictures and using blackmail against the subjects, in most circles, would likely be considered perversion, but it tickled Kenny's imagination to the point where it made him feel almost sad to think that because of what he'd done to the guy, he would never be able to tap into his obvious wealth of money-making ability, on an entrepreneurial level—no matter how perverse it might be—that impressed Kenny beyond his own belief and his original religious up-bringing.

He was convinced, because of his open relationship with Mary that she would be completely accepting of it. Now that his thoughts fell from his original concern for her and Lucretia in Bangor and thrust him into a yearning for her return, that he might share, for the first time with her, his new plans that would usher them to wealth beyond their dreams.

With excitement pulsing in the back of his twisted little mind, he pulled his line, stowed his gear, and began strolling back downstream with a newfound energy that set him even freer than he'd become in the last several hours of solitude. As far as being able to talk to the little pirate fellow again, that would most probably end up being like their first encounter—simply perchance. The reality of meeting him again for revenge was very likely, and Kenny turned that thought over as he walked.

The soft, mossy trail following the winding brook made for a quiet advance toward the gravel road where he'd parked Filbert's truck, somewhat hidden beneath a thick pine grove and down a slight embankment. A light breeze began to howl through the pine needles of the giant trees, creating a natural symphony blending with a shallow waterfall, as the brook made its way beneath a narrow, wooden bridge at the end of the path alongside the road.

Kenny had almost reached the hidden pickup truck when he heard the sound of a rapidly approaching vehicle. His first instinct was to heave the trout basket into the thicket at the edge of the road, but the vehicle was upon him long before he had time to slip the basket from his belt. At almost high noon, the sun, well out of the eastern sky, was blinding Kenny. Allowing himself to fall prey to such a mistake suddenly made him feel foolish, like being naked in public, with a basket full of out-of-season trout. What he didn't know was that Bullet Carter and I, Bullet's close friend Adver Bagley, were in the vehicle.

The old rusty truck pulled up right next to him, and Bullet hung his beefy arm out of the window, his sickeningly familiar voice reverberating from behind the sun-glared windshield. "Well, if it ain't the biggest little poacher Down East. Wha'-chi-do, steal the truck, too?"

As close as Bullet and I were, I can honestly say that the only time I'd seen him display such animosity toward someone was when he'd threatened that little fuck of a carnie who stole away with his wife and only two boys. Kenny stood to the spot, displaying a defiant stare at the voice, as the sun continued to blind him from actually seeing the face that went with the voice.

"Yeah, and I suppose you're down here for a casual romp down through the pansies?" Kenny shot the response back to antagonize the situation further.

"Wha'-chi-got in the basket, looks as though you' been out pickin' daisies," Bullet fired back. And at that point he began to laugh nastily, forcing Kenny to flip him off and start walking toward Filbert's semi-hidden pickup truck.

"I oughta punch you in the fuckin' mouth, you little weasel," Bullet shouted out.

At that point, I could see that this was getting more serious than need be, and I reached out to grab Bullet's sleeve as he attempted to jump from the driver's seat after Kenny. He tugged at my grasp, giving me a dirty look, but I maintained my stare, apparently instilling in him the difficulties this shit could amount to, and he settled back into the seat, but not without throwing in a few more slurs of insults toward Kenny. It seemed strange to me that Bullet, who had only come out here for the sole purpose of poaching a deer before hunting season (which went into full swing in another week)—and had one deer in the freezer—was a good indication that the kettle was calling the frying pan black. But it obviously never entered his mind as he continued ranting insults in Kenny's direction, until we heard the sound of Filbert's pickup sliding sideways under the heavy acceleration of Kenny's foot on the gas. I found some humor in all of this, as everyone throughout the entire area knew how well Kenny Collins could handle himself in a scrap, but it was clear he did not intend to apply his techniques of self-defense against the likes of Bullet Carter.

"It doesn't matter where I go these days, someone is shovelin' shit into the fuckin' fan and I always seem to be standin' in front o' the blades." Kenny was yelling to himself and pounding on the steering wheel as the pickup fished-tailed onto the gravel road.

We sat and watched from Bullet's truck, expecting to see a rollover, as the area we were in was rutted and rock-exposed, and blowouts were commonplace. The truck then roared out of sight, and soon the sound of its tires on the gravel faded and the woods were quiet again.

Bullet and I sat for quite some time, and I had to know what it was about Kenny that set him off whenever they came in close proximity to one another. At first, he didn't want to talk about it, which was usual with old Bullet, but with patience and some coaxing, he began to open up about his feelings.

"You gotta remember the first day that little slug walked into Filbert's store?" Bullet asked.

"Ya', sure I do."

"Well, call it a feelin' or whatever ya' want, but from the very start I had no use for 'im. He's a sleazy little frig' and usually up to no good. He reminds me o' that little fuck of a carnie, ya' know?" He stopped talking and simply looked out onto the woods that surrounded us. I didn't really understand what it was that he was trying to tell me. It wasn't like Bullet to pin a badge on someone without a good reason. He just didn't give a shit about stuff like that. We sat there without saying a word for a long time, and then he took a deep breath and began talking again. "Ya' see, Mary and me are... well... we're cousins twice removed. When I heard he was seein' her shortly afta' he got hea', I knew he was feedin' her thi'em' drugs and getting a little from her, and it kinda got the old blood a pumpin'." Bullet hesitated for a moment before going on. "Well, ya' see, ya' might say we was kissin' cousins."

I thought I stopped breathing for a moment. "Are you telling me that Mary, your cousin, was also your...?"

"Ya' might say that, though we only did it a couple o' times, but when they... started bein' an item, well, I guess, in a way, I lost it."

All kinds of things ran through my head. The one that bothered me the most was that as close as we were, Bullet and I, this was the first time I'd heard about this. Now I wondered if this had in some way forced his wife, Millie, to get involved with that carnie at the Bangor State Fair for revenge, and then she found herself in over her head. Shit, I didn't know what to think at this point. Bullet kept looking at me for some sort of response, but as sure as a fella takes a healthy crap in the mornin', I was definitely stumped for something to say about this one. From the look on Bullet's face, he was happy as a pig in shit that I couldn't. I popped a cold beer and took a huge guzzle, and without looking in his direction, I heard Bullet do the same.

We'd come out here in hopes of knocking a deer or two down before the shootin' started on opening day, for the sports from away, anyhow. The sight of Kenny Collins and his fishing gear is what got Bullet going, and now I had a better understanding of why. We sat quietly drinking the beer we'd opened for as long as it took and then Bullet started talking again.

"I knocked 'er up ya' know," he said.

He said it with such callous indifference, my head jerked as though I'd heard what he said, but really wasn't sure that I had. I looked over at him, and he was looking into his can of beer as though something were about to climb out. I was speechless.

"Ya'...she lost it a couple a' months into it. No one ever knew, so we just went our separate ways. You're the first one I've ever told and I'm kinda' thinkin' that it oughta stay that way, if'n ya' know what I mean?"

"Ya'...sure, no problem," I said.

9

Filbert opened the store right on schedule. On this day, however, he wasn't his usual, upbeat self. What had haunted him since last Friday evening was the thought of possibly ending his relationship with Kenny. He'd heard all of the rumors spreading around like a bad cold of Kenny's Halloween escapade, but the stories surfacing now of the drug party that took place in what used to be his and Heidi's place and was still owned by them turned his stomach. He felt betrayed beyond belief, and for the first time, for as long as he could remember, he wanted to get even for being made the fool.

He knew how people took advantage of him when it came to repaying what was owed on a store account; that was just the way people were around here—not all of them, only the ones most hard-pressed and disadvantaged. No, this was a slap in the face to his total confidence in the two people whom he'd placed so much faith—they had let him down so hard. He knew the hardship it would cause them if he let Kenny go from his little job at the store, and Kenny was such a help to him all of the time and a companion the likes of which Filbert had forgotten existed since he'd been a young man himself.

That was minuscule in comparison to his thought of evicting them from the property. Sure, the image of the place being empty and subject to break-ins crossed his mind, and he felt an overpowering sense of guilt for it, but how long could he continue to encourage such bad behavior while allowing his property to be used as a den of sin? The more his mind pondered on the possibilities of both situations, the more he could feel depression begin to overwhelm him.

After turning the lights and gas pumps on, instead of placing himself at his usual favorite perch at the checkout counter, which gave him an unobstructed view of the road into and through town, he stood stroking the cat at the sandwich counter, paying no attention to the frolicking birds at his cherished feeder.

The front door chimed open, barely noticed by Filbert until he heard the approaching footsteps. It was Bullet Carter. "Sun-ova-bitch, mista' man, if'n you don't look reedii' for tha' fuckin' undatayka," he said.

"I feel as though I'm ready for the undatayka," Filbert replied, stressing the last word with a slight chuckle in his voice.

"Havin' one o' thi'em' days, aar' ya'?"

"You could say that," Filbert answered.

Bullet mumbled something inaudible to Filbert's ears as he ambled toward the beer cooler. Bullet was a good one for walking away in the middle of a sentence, allowing the end to trail off into the stratosphere somewhere, leaving the listener wondering, and by the time he returned with the ending, if you asked him what it was that he'd said, he'd look at you like you had a booger hanging from your nose.

Filbert thought that Bullet had a slight problem with his short-term memory, but you didn't want to tell old Bullet something like that. Filbert could hear him faintly, from the opposite end of the store, rummaging around the shelves, for what, only he could know. He always found something that Filbert had stocked for so long he'd forgotten he had it, and Bullet would begin a friendly wrangle, eventually getting the item for a lesser price than was stickered.

The door chimed once again; this time it was a regular morning stop-in for beer and a newspaper. Bullet began a chit-chat with the person while Filbert, feeling the effects of his depression, began to smother his persona. He moved from the sandwich counter toward the front of the store. He could not however, join in the conversation that the two men carried on. It was the usual stuff—"Got enough wood stacked? Get ya' deer yet? How's the wife and kids?'—all the day-to-day chatter that a bout of depression detached a person from. Filbert was bored stiff. However, he would never say a word that would indicate to them that there was anything wrong, and so he simply smiled, nodding his head whenever one or the other looked in his direction for approval, or a comment.

With beer and newspaper in hand, the man left the store, leaving Filbert and Bullet alone, and the very thought of holding a long and drawn-out conversation with Bullet this morning was the last thing Filbert wanted to do. Normally, it would have charged his need to know; whatever it might be that Bullet, or anyone for that matter, wanted to share with him. He liked and respected Bullet, and had known him all of his life, but he knew how much Bullet hated Kenny, and the last thing he needed this morning was a long talk about the source of his oncoming downheartedness.

"So…what in tha' fuck is eatin' you this mornin', mista' man'?" Bullet asked.

Without revealing his innermost feelings and letting on about his thoughts over the Kenny and Mary thing, he simply responded with, "Not gettin' as much sleep as I need these days," he said.

It seemed to be enough for Bullet, because he lifted his head with a quick jerk, and used his eyebrows to indicate that he understood, but Filbert doubted that he would simply go quietly. Without the time allowed for a second breath, Bullet brought up the subject of having seen Kenny out by the bog, fishing illegally and using Filbert's truck to do it.

Filbert actually did not know what he was referring to, because Kenny's use of his pickup truck was a standing invitation, with permission granted long ago by Filbert as long as the tank was where it was when he took it, and the keys were left in the ignition so he was never stuck without his own truck. However, with Kenny, the tank was always where it was when he took it, and Filbert had never given it a second thought that the gas came from his own pumps.

A slight ray of sun reflected off the top of Chesterfield Ridge, illuminating the entire store-front through the plate glass windows and shining on the top of Bullet's six-pack, nearly blinding Filbert and forcing an almost dry-heave from his depression as he moved quickly to avoid the glare. Thinking back to a moment earlier and half-listening to Bullet ramble on about catching Kenny fishing out of season, he couldn't help but wonder if Bullet had been out there to do the same thing, or even to try for an early deer before the shootin' started Monday for all hunters, including out-o'-staters.

It just didn't matter to him at this point. His thoughts were eating him up from the inside about the thing he was sure he had to do, and no small talk from Bullet or anyone else was going to make that responsibility any easier.

"When did you see Kenny with my pickup truck out to the bog?" Filbert asked.

"Ah…oh ya', Monday morning, real early. The little slime-bucket was makin' his way from the path to the truck when me and Adver seen 'im. He stopped dead in his tracks, let me tell you, mista' man, thinkin' we're the warden, ya' know," Bullet said and then he started laughing. "That little fuck ain't no good, and you have ta' know goddamned well that he ain't. If you don't know what's goin' on with him and Mary…"

Filbert put up a hand and walked away from the checkout counter.

He made his way toward the rear of the store, his heavy-heeled walking alerting the cat, which jumped from the sandwich counter and disappeared in one of the aisles. He didn't hear any trailing footsteps, but by the time he reached the counter and turned, Bullet was standing on the other side of the counter.

"Jebus Christmas, I thought you'd left!" Filbert said.

"I don't think it's faya' that ya' keep runnin' from the truth where those two aar' concerned. That boy seems to be able to make an ass out o' anyone he wants to, but I'll be a sun-ova-bitch, mista' man, if'n I let him make an ass out-a' me," Bullet said, his lower lip bouncing as he drew from the non-filtered Camel cigarette hanging from it.

"Why do you hate those two so much?" Filbert asked, and his voice rose in an unfamiliar tone.

"I don't hate those two, I just don't have any use for him especially, the shit-pot little freak from away. All was good with little Mary until that shit-bag made his appearance when he did." Bullet shook his head. "I never liked that little shit-hole," he added.

It was an extremely slow morning at the store. For some reason, even the regulars failed to pop in, and so the two men talked for a long time, each man learning about things that they'd never known. As they rambled on, Filbert's depression dissipated, and he began feeling himself once again.

Though they had always been fond of one another, today seemed to bond each man's soul to a level of understanding neither one of them had ever shared before.

Less than a mile from where the two men spoke heartily in the quiet store, Kenny was unable to shake the shadow of apprehension that hindered his ability to speak to Mary about his new money-making approach to living in Washington County, Maine. He was convinced that she would be able to look at it as simply another way to subsidize their income; however, it was a step out of the norm, and he wondered just how far out of her comfort zone she might be willing to go. He chugged what remained of his bottle of Bud, then took a huge hit from the joint before passing it to Mary as she sat across from him at their window table.

As she reached for it, a tiny tip of the ash fell into her hot cup of coffee, igniting a barrage of profanity that Kenny himself was unsure he'd heard from her in the past. What Kenny could not know was that the bag of nerves in front of him right now had something she needed to share with him, and her anxiety had reached a level of equal proportions with his. Neither one knew how to begin, fearing the other's response.

Ironically, they began speaking at the very same moment, apparently motivated from the effects of the pot, and then each told the other, "Go ahead, you first."

It was obvious to Kenny that whatever it was that Mary wanted to tell him had her on the edge of her seat, and as much as he believed he would excite her with his plan, he thought it best to let her spill hers first and get it out of the way.

"Go ahead, Mary, I'll roll us another one and you tell me what has you so pumped up," Kenny said. Mary's face beamed with excitement, and she began.

"Well, Monday when I took mama to Bangor for her tests, I ran into an old friend I went to school with up in Aroostook County. Funny as it might seem, she has a job in a small nursing home in Ellsworth, and she told me they're looking for some help."

Kenny was confused, but he wanted to hear more, and remained quiet while Mary rambled on enthusiastically about the work schedule, and how the benefits were unbelievable—sick time, vacation time. She went on and on, and without sharing the freshly rolled joint, Kenny drew from it while he listened, and he never said a word.

His mind at this point was working overtime, and it wasn't at some nursing home in Ellsworth. What Mary shared with him stuck a huge pin into his over-inflated balloon, and he could feel the heat of his anger rising through his jugular with a pounding of suspicion in his head. As she continued speaking of the positive value of a position of this sort, all Kenny could think of was why she hadn't mentioned it before now, since it was Friday and the end of the week.

Jealousy, to this point in their relationship, had never raised its ugly head from either of them, but suddenly, perhaps from the long-term effects of the alcohol, or drugs, or both, Kenny felt that he was losing control of his little world. A world before this very moment in which his biggest fan, his most sincere supporter, his most loyal counterpart, his wife and best friend was now turning her back on him, like everyone else in the world had done to this point in his life, and it didn't feel good.

Upon finishing her little tour of the nursing home, Mary instantly realized from the look on Kenny's face that happiness was not the rule for the day.

"What's wrong…? I thought you'd be happy to know that I had a chance to help us out a little financially, now that the cold weather is coming and things are a bit slow for you," she said.

Kenny went into an explosive, verbal assault on her, saying things that made no sense to her about the two of them and the way things used to be for them, and how he supported her through thick and thin, and now she wanted to leave him here in the dead of winter.

"Why don't you just stick that pirate's knife in the old ticker and put an end to it, eh, Mary?" he roared.

She couldn't believe her ears. Since they'd met, he had never, ever talked to her in such a violent tone, and it frightened her as deeply as the fear she'd had as a child when her father would go into wild drunken rampages of accusatory innuendo against her mother about things they all knew were untrue.

"What do you mean; stick a knife in your heart, and what does any of this have to do with me getting a job in Ellsworth? A job I don't even have yet, but a job that could help us get ahead this winter?"

He turned from her and looked out of the window behind him, and saw it was just starting to spit light snowflakes from a deep, gray sky.

Instantly, a huge lump formed in her throat, but she would be damned if he was going to make her cry the way her father had made a fool of her mother all those years ago. While he looked out of the window and pouted, she got up from her chair, went directly to the door where their jackets hung, swatted hers from the hook, and opened the door and slammed it behind her as she left. By the time she got to the car, started the engine and began driving away, his fury was all the more intense, invigorating his desire to become more drunk and stoned. The snow, though only a flurry, began in earnest as Mary pulled from the driveway, giving her a feeling of emptiness deep within her soul. The only man she had ever loved, the person she had run away with for her freedom, had just made her feel like a prisoner.

Mary's old car lumbered its way over the gravel road away from the house. She was so overwrought that she wasn't paying attention to the rutted areas, and several times the car slid dangerously close to the embankment high above the churning waters of the river. She suddenly felt the loss of a sense of direction, feeling more alone than she had ever felt before. Her thoughts went to her mother, and she wanted to be with her; however, it would force her to sacrifice face with her parents for having defied them in the first place. She knew exactly what her father would say, knowing very well how he hated Kenny, and the way he had warned her about how her marriage would turn out.

No, going home to her mother was not an option. She'd drive around for awhile, she thought, and then go back and see just what in the hell was eating Kenny.

10

Thinking that he didn't want to charge into anything where Kenny Collins and his young wife were concerned, Harry Circus finally made his way over to their place down by the river. His car, heavily laden with electronic equipment up front and highway-safety and first aid equipment in the trunk, bottomed out several times on the way down their rutted gravel road. Harry winced with each hit to the undercarriage, thinking of how easy it would be to send a small dozer down with one pass and level it all off. The fact that he was one of only two troopers responsible for covering a huge area (and having to leave with a moment's notice) he was happy to have a driveway less than thirty-feet long, allowing for a quick departure during the day, or the middle of the night in any weather. Traveling down this particular road allowed him to daydream of a time gone by, when, as a youngster; he walked this very road to enjoy his favorite pastime, fishing. It was still his most cherished hobby, if he could only find the time. Through the thickness of the surrounding trees, he caught several glimpses of the house and the river, glistening under a partially hidden autumn sun. The scattered white from yesterdays light snow had drifted at the bottoms of trees.

As he rounded the final turn that would head directly into the front door-yard, the absence of Mary's car gave him a pang of disappointment, and he thought that maybe he had waited too long and missed his best chance to catch them at home. Nevertheless, he was here, and he would at least knock on the door. Upon entering the open expanse of the turn-around driveway, the trooper became very happy at the sight of the man-of-the-hour himself, sitting on the front steps, obviously enjoying what little sunshine filtered through the overcast sky.

The trooper stopped his vehicle a short distance from the front of the house. The last thing he wanted to do was to intimidate Kenny into a defensive attitude from the onset, though he doubted that he would. As he was about to exit the car, his radio sounded a brief report from a dispatcher in Machias, the town in which his Troop Headquarters were located, about something happening in that area, but it wouldn't interfere with what the trooper had in mind for the next twenty-minutes or so.

He got out of the car and as he did, Kenny flipped something into the bushes off to the side of the steps. The rancid scent of pot became apparent, but faded quickly in the slight breeze. The two men stared into each other's eyes as the trooper came near; neither one opted to speak first. The trooper eventually opened the conversation.

"Kenny, what's goin' on?" the trooper asked, standing tall like a tree in a clearing.

"Oh, same old shit, but I got a big shovel now," Kenny said.

The trooper knew how quickly the young man could become agitated, and that was not his intention, or his reason for being here. He was, however, the local trooper, and he wouldn't stand for any so-called shit that might be shoveled in his direction, no matter how big the shovel. They made small talk for several minutes, the trooper inquiring about how Kenny had found the brook trout fishing this summer. He knew, but didn't understand, the extent of Kenny's poaching of game of every kind and the level at which he took game out of season. Although, if Kenny was in any way confused as to why the trooper was here in the first place, he gave no indication through either facial expressions or body language that would have aroused the trooper's suspicions, nor did he respond to the trooper's question about the brook trout fishing. As it was, the trooper prided himself on his ability to detect the slightest nuance in a facial expression that might lead him in another direction in a questioning situation.

At that moment, Mary's car approached slowly down the driveway.

The timing couldn't have been more right as far as Harry Circus was concerned. Having both of them here now, was for him, the perfect situation, even before getting into the meat and potatoes of his visit. Kenny stood up straight from his casually slumped sitting position on the third step and leaned against the front door at the sound of Mary's car.

For the first time since his arrival, the trooper detected an unmistakable change in Kenny's facial expression which led his naturally suspicious mind to punch-in for overtime. It became obvious to the trooper that the two were angry at each other the moment Mary stepped from her car, which she parked under a large pine tree about ten yards from where the two men stood watching her. Upon seeing the look the two displayed, Mary made no attempt to hide her concern for the trooper's presence, and ironically, used the exact phrase the trooper used on his arrival.

"What's goin' on?" Mary asked.

Both men chuckled slightly, and moved apart after realizing how close they'd been standing to each other. When Kenny moved down the several steps to greet her, Harry nonchalantly moved toward the steps where he'd seen Kenny flip something into the bushes on his earlier approach to the house. As he strained to see into the bushes (his curiosity always getting the best of him) he could see nothing through the lush foliage and flowering plants. Mary and Kenny touched hands briefly and then moved apart, suggesting to the trooper that they might have been quarreling, and they were remaining somewhat stand-off-ish toward one another.

"So, what's goin' on?" Mary asked once again.

To the trooper, this was an open invitation to move forward to the business at hand.

"Well, I can't seem to get out from under the rumor-mill about the going's-on here on Halloween night," Harry said.

The two looked at each other, displaying no guilt, yet it was obvious to Harry that some concern sparked from his question, as it was visible in their facial expressions. He continued, after deciding that he would search a little by making up a bit of information about the pirate's hometown.

"From what I've been told, some guy from Bangor pulled a knife on you, Kenny, and you proceeded to snap his wrist. I'm kind of wondering what the chances are of him coming back looking for revenge, at whatever cost?" The trooper focused his stare at the two, expecting some kind of response, yet they simply looked at each other and said nothing. This time it was Kenny who came back with a question, bordering on sarcasm.

"Who the fuck said he was from Bangor? I never told anyone he was from Bangor," Kenny said.

"If you could keep the vulgarity down to a minimum, we do have a lady present," Harry said.

"Yeah, Harry, I'll be real careful with the fuck-talk," Kenny responded defiantly.

Harry wasn't exactly a soft-shelled egg when it came to wise guys like Kenny Collins, but he did have his limitations to being insulted outright. Trying to be diplomatic, he let that one go without a response, thinking it better to leave the conversation on friendly terms.

"So, what about the guy that everyone said looked like a pirate? Should I keep an open eye for trouble? This is our turf, yours and mine." He looked toward Mary when he said this, knowing very well that Kenny was from away, while Harry and Mary's father had been born and bred here. There was no denying where the trooper's loyalty lay, but as a state trooper, he had to control his emotions and the predispositions ingrained in him since childhood. Any biased attitudes could be stacked against him if push came to shove.

The swift current of the Paguagus roared above the slight breeze blowing through the tall pines, and the trooper longed to be somewhere else, without confrontation. They went back and forth for about ten minutes, and the three-way conversation went nowhere. When the trooper pressed either Kenny or Mary, they came to each other's defense, shattering any hope the trooper might have had for finding out more about the pirate fellow, or any of their guests. Making small talk about anything was like pulling teeth without Novocain, and with these two, it wasn't going to happen. *"These two are a pair,"* the trooper thought.

Harry became extremely agitated at his inability to control the direction of this simple questioning of what should have been a couple of country bumpkins; yet as he found out in quick order, they were far more reticent than he could have possibly imagined. Finally, before losing all control of his emotions and letting fly with any unsubstantial threats, he looked around the property, with an occasional glance toward the river, and wished once again that he could just go fishing.

"Well, folks, it seems pretty obvious to me that you hardly knew anyone who stopped by your place on Halloween night, including the little twerp whose wrist got broken." He looked directly into Mary's eyes. "You're convinced he won't come back, and it looks as though the last thing on your minds these days is some pirate with a big knife looking for revenge, right, Mary? You both know how to reach me if need be, and Ralph Bailey is also a phone call away," he said.

Then, just to make it perfectly clear exactly who this man in the blue Stetson hat was, he couldn't see the harm in pitching one little curveball before leaving.

"Oh, by the way, you may have a neighbor who might be smoking a little weed, because when I pulled in here, I thought I caught a whiff of the foul smellin' stuff." He said this with a weird-looking smirk on his face. Then he continued, "Oh, Mary…You really need to get that exhaust-pipe fixed."

Without saying another word or offering a wave, the trooper

got into his car and drove around the U-shaped drive, slowly making his way toward the blacktop.

Mary and Kenny, standing much closer now than they had been when Mary pulled in, watched as the trooper's blue car drove out of sight.

As pleased as they both were to see the car vanish beyond the thick trees and bushes on their road, it did very little to ease the friction between them, given their little spat last evening. This was truly the very first time they had fought. Before last night, Mary had generally given in, or as she mentioned to Filbert that morning in the store's basement, an occasional tug on her arm forced submission in most cases. Like every couple, after a period for adjustment to each other little things began to mean a lot, and so it was with our two little lovebirds in their nest by the river. Some things Kenny said to Mary hurt her, and when she had left the previous evening, she'd had no idea where she might go, but as she drove, it had come to her.

The friend who told her about the job in Ellsworth had also told her where she lived, and said that if there was anything she could do to help, in any way, all Mary had to do was ask. Last night, as a second thought after their fight, Mary had gone right to her friend. After spending the night and getting all of the details about the job, they'd left together this morning and not believing it herself, Mary had managed to get an interview. They'd hired her on the spot.

The thrill of getting a new position can make it feel like Christmas in July, or whatever time of the year it is when someone who needs the money gets the job. It was no different for Mary; the only thing different for her was that she had to go home and tell her husband, which she was about to do when she came upon the trooper in the middle of their driveway, and suddenly, her mind had gone blank. All she could think about was that huge bag of dope Kenny had scored only last night, and seeing the trooper, she wondered if he was there for that reason. At that moment, Mary's dreams of telling Kenny the good news came to a sudden end.

However, now that the trooper had gone and taken those fears with him, only one remained. She had to tell Kenny that she'd taken the job in Ellsworth. This job was something she had to do for herself, something that would help them to stay financially afloat during the most difficult season of the year Down East, winter.

11

THE REST OF THE DAY AND EVENING WENT without incident, yet both Mary and Kenny kept their distance, while still remaining civil toward one another. Each of them now had a secret kept from the other, and neither one knew the best way to bring it to light. Mary's mind raced in many directions at once while she put together a simple evening meal of macaroni and cheese from a box—not the kind her mother used to make from scratch, using three different types of cheeses, diced onions, garlic, and fresh herbs from her garden. Mary fried up a bunch of hot dogs, and since she hadn't remembered to buy buns, sliced them up and threw them into the finished mac and cheese. With several homemade biscuits smothered in butter, a cold beer for Kenny and a cup of tea for herself; that was supper.

After an unusually warm, partially sunny day, the evening brought the crispness of autumn air in, and Mary could hear the crackling of kindling wood as Kenny stoked a small fire in the woodstove, giving her a warm sense of security that a comfortable house can give, even at the expense of a false sense of entitlement. She heard the clunk of a large log, placed heavily atop the fire, then the stove door closed with another clunk and she heard the sound of Kenny's footsteps coming toward the scent of supper that filled the tiny house.

They looked at one another, sitting in their usual seats at the table. It's strange, she thought, *"when you live with someone for a period of time, you both pick up little habits that seem to fit into the day-to-day existence of co-habitation, something that you never think about while you are adapting to those little idiosyncrasies."* They ate in silence for the most part, with only an occasional comment from one or the other about some tidbit of gossip from town or up-river. Both had heard them all; it was simply their way of breaking the ice after their spat, in the hope that they would make up later.

When they had originally moved in, Kenny made it a point to ask Filbert if they could install a spotlight at the corner of the house facing the river, because Mary wanted one. They told him it was for better security, but actually, she liked the way that a spotlight revealed the surrounding woods and the water on a dark night. Filbert agreed, and paid to have one installed. Tonight, it illuminated another early-season snow flurry, and with a fire in the stove and love games in the air, it could be the perfect evening.

"Night is where it's at," Kenny would say, quoting a phrase of Charles Manson's in a book he'd read about him and his little family of murderers, when Charlie, after dark, would feed his little band of followers their daily ration of drugs. He couldn't even remember the actual name of the book, whether it was *The Family* or *Helter Skelter*; it didn't matter—he just liked using it after their supper. Drugs were a large part of their existence now, but tonight, for some reason, his quote didn't come out. He wasn't jumping up to get the stash from where they kept it in one of the drawers of the old sewing machine Mary's grandmother had left her, and Mary never indicated she wanted anything.

They simply remained where they were at the unclear table in silence. The CD player pumped out bluesy instrumentals by Albert King and some early Fleetwood Mac, but now, their little game of chit-chat took on a more sexually suggestive tone, and it appeared that playtime was imminent. Even when preparing to make love, Kenny's thoughts wandered to every crevasse of his mind's capability. He never was able to concentrate on any one subject for a decisive outcome, and at times, Mary truly believed that he might be afflicted with ADHD. When he sat down to relax, one leg, or foot, pumped continuously, to the point of annoyance for the observer, yet Mary was the only one to say something like, "You left your motor running, or is that a well-oiled piston?"

Kenny never responded; he would simply relax his foot or leg, whichever it might be at that time, and within a few minutes, without realizing it, the leg or foot began pumping once again. For as long as they'd been together, Mary had simply dismissed it, or often truly didn't notice it any longer—one of those little idiosyncrasies of co-habitation.

Kenny got up without speaking a word or indicating his intentions, and went into the bedroom to light several scented candles. He walked up behind Mary as she remained seated at the table. He lifted her hair with both hands and placed his lips against the nape of her neck. Shivers ran up her spine, goose bumps began to form instantly on her arms and legs, and she closed her eyes to allow the sensation to move freely throughout her entire body.

He moved his lips slowly, softly kissing the side of her neck, and felt the heat on the surface of her soft skin. He ran his fingers through her hair and allowed it to fall slowly over her shoulders, and she breathed deeply as one of his hands massaged her where the hair had not yet fallen. She turned toward him, his lips met her partially opened mouth, and they began to kiss deeply as their breath caressed each other's cheeks. All anger was forgiven and forgotten as the sensation of love entwined itself into their beings. He took her gently by the shoulders, turning her slightly and directing her to a standing position in front of him, and he pressed himself tightly against her, allowing the heat of their bodies to warm them sexually.

Yet, even now while they shared this private moment of togetherness, Kenny's mind drifted to his stress and the lack of money he earned at the store (despite what he earned on the side from cash drug deals), which alone amounted to about two hundred dollars a month, which for Washington County, wasn't all that shabby. He thought of his Christmas wreath business and another couple of hundred bucks a week from that and the firewood sales. All this was going through his thoughts while the woman he supposedly loved was breathing deeply with desire in his arms at this very moment. In addition, all that he could feel was the stress of his so-called life and Mary wanting to take that fuckin' job in Ellsworth. Not knowing at this time that she had already taken it this very day, and around the same time he intended to let her in on their new venture into the world of money, or so he thought, is when she intended to share with him her little secret.

What neither one knew was Filbert's intention where their lives were concerned. That would be the ultimate, unsuspected surprise that would temporarily wipe out their dreams for a so-called good future, and it was coming sooner than they knew.

Kenny's eyes widened as Mary removed her sweater, revealing her bare breasts standing out firm and perky from her slender body. Kenny stared with much delight, as a feeling of inadequacy came over him for having let himself go physically over the past couple of years. His beer paunch was his greatest embarrassment, and the only time he took his shirt off now was to shower or have sex, and he had several times left his t-shirt on for the latter. When she came toward him, naked, reaching out for him to take her, his mind went blank, the turmoil he had gone through only moments earlier falling away. He took her into his arms, feeling her smooth, soft skin from her shoulders to the silky softness of her firm bottom, causing a tingle to flow into his groin that would not allow him to think of anything but her. They lay together with their arms and legs entwined, their lips pressed tightly in a deep kiss. The crackling embers from the stove popped, while outside the early-season flurry grew into a blinding snow-squall, typical for this area near the coast this time of the year; yet they were unaware of it and they were warm and safe, just the two of them.

The evening hours vanished. The music had long since stopped on its own. Kenny and Mary lay together in an exhausted heap in the center of their bed. Being together, naked as they were, despite what could have produced a natural sense of vulnerability, always encapsulated them in a cocoon of security. Lying quietly now, the time seemed right for either of them to open the can of worms each had kept closed about their little secrets. Since Mary's had more of an innocent nature, and was confident that what she'd done was for their good, she began by saying, "I love you, Kenny."

He displayed his usual look of arrogant confidence and said nothing in response, and so she continued. "I have a little surprise for you."

"You're not pregnant, I hope?" he asked.

"No, I'm not pregnant," she retorted.

He looked deep into her eyes, yet could read nothing of what it might be she'd conjured up as a surprise for him.

"Well Mary, go ahead, tell me. You've been hinting around for a couple of days now, and when you get done with your little thingy, I've got a beaut' for you, too," he said.

Suddenly, she felt a pang of indecision as she looked into his questioning eyes, but it had to be now—after all, she would be starting her first day on Monday, and if she knew him, and she did, he would need from now until then to digest what she was about to tell him.

"Well…" she began.

Instantly he interrupted with, "Deep subject for a shallow mind." He laughed cynically, while frustration grew on her face, and then she continued.

"Last night…when I told you…about the possible job in Ellsworth…then we…got into that little, you know…and then I left…" His stare was penetrating, and his sigh of boredom somewhat restricting, yet she continued.

"I stayed with Callie, you remember the girl from up in the County I told you about. Well, this morning before I came home to find you and 'trooper boy' out front, I went with her to the nursing home where she works for an interview." Then with a burst of enthusiasm, jumping on the bedsprings, she blurted out,

"I got the job!"

Kenny propped himself up on one elbow like some mythical, naked Greek God being hand-fed grapes. His facial expression never faltered from the poker-faced stare that had enveloped it from the onset of Mary's news, and all that he could say was, "What fuckin' job?"

She wanted to say something cruel, just because, but nothing came out, and for the life of her, she just couldn't figure out where the nice guy she had met only a couple of years ago had gone. Had he acted then as he did now, she would still be home with her parents, and for the second time in as many days, she thought about being with her parents: *"Shit! I can't believe I want to go home to them after all the things we said to each other, and now my husband is acting like some shit-head toward me, when all that I want is to help us out,"* she thought.

"Wow…aren't you the little… now-woman. She doesn't have to talk things over with her husband; no, no…just do what she wants to do," Kenny said. Then he got out of bed, put his pants on, and stormed out into the dark, little house, slamming things as he went, like a child throwing a tantrum. Mary lay in the center of the bed, her eyes closed, wondering if the relationship was worth the trouble she went through. She sat up, looking into the mirror on the top of her dresser, and seeing her reflection, she began speaking to herself in a low voice.

"What have I done to let all of this happen?" She was placing the guilt for all that seemed to go wrong with the relationship on her shoulders, as she always had. "It feels like yesterday we were inseparable and now…" She shook her head and continued to stare at her reflection with self-contempt.

12

WITH THE FIRST INDICATION OF DAYLIGHT, formed by a pinstriped, crimson line at the horizon, the early risers found themselves with a fresh dusting of snow, and since it was hunting season, the snow was a welcomed invigoration, making it so much easier to track deer for anyone whose intention it was to place venison on their table this winter.

Filbert opened the store about an hour earlier than usual, anticipating frenzied stops for last-minute supplies by the "heater hunters"—anyone who hunted, specifically from the front or back seat of a vehicle. Many old-timers did, especially those having problems with their legs either from poor circulation or arthritis, or those who were just plain overweight and lazy. Although it was against the law to drink and drive, or drink and use a firearm, if you were going to spend four or five hours driving around the woods on deserted gravel roads, you wouldn't be considered normal if you didn't have a couple of six-packs of cold beer in a cooler, some sandwiches and chips, and a hand full of Slim-Jims. In most cases, a decent-sized bottle of coffee brandy or peppermint schnapps was the rule to take the chill off in the event the passenger wanted the window open for a quick draw, if and when a deer crossed the road in front of them.

Now that Filbert's hunting time was generally restricted to

Thanksgiving Day, and since he'd shot more deer in his day than his memory could recollect, it didn't matter to him if he ever shot another deer. He thought, *"I would much rather get caught up in the chatter of those who did while stopping in at the store for their supplies and sharing their little stories about the hunt."* For Filbert, however, the thought of getting lost in discussions about hunting was the farthest thing from his mind that morning. He had, with the help from his newfound comrade-in-arms, Bullet Carter, come to a decision where little Mary and Kenny were concerned.

It was Saturday morning. The early-morning cumulus clouds were thinning, giving way to a bright morning sun, yet the lingering chill from the radiational cooling of the newly fallen snow remained in the air. Believing that the couple would be at home, Filbert asked Heidi to come in and hold down the fort as soon as she had the kids settled in for Saturday morning cartoons on the TV. As many times as he'd gone over his little rehearsed spiel in his mind, it didn't change the feeling of dread, because he'd never evicted anyone in his life; yet he was going to because of the way they'd disappointed him after all that he'd done to help them. Their drug dealings and whatever else they were involved in made the chore all the more necessary to clear his own conscience from what he thought was right and wrong. He would, he thought, give them ample time to find another place, keeping in mind the time of year, but along with being reasonable, he would maintain his stance on his disappointment with their behavior.

It was plainly visible to Heidi when she walked into the store from the rear entrance that Filbert's heart was heavy with anguish from the burden of his responsibility, and she understood because she also kept a place for the two of them in her heart, like one of her own children, although she did support her husband in his decision. "Good morning" was not the first thing out of her mouth when she came close.

"You cannot encourage that type of behavior, especially while they use our property to do it, and being this close to our children." She told Filbert this after seeing him struggling with what he was about to do.

"It's like having a part in a chapter of a poorly written book," is how Filbert described it to her as she stood alongside of him near the checkout counter.

At that moment, with as much pomp and circumstance as he could muster, Bullet Carter walked in through the front door, swinging it open then partially closed several times, ringing the transom chime incessantly. The big shit-eatin' grin and the non-filtered Camel cigarette hanging from his lips were in place as usual, and the clopping sound of his large, insulated boots echoed through the aisle as he made his way toward the beer cooler, mumbling something as he went.

"Well, mista' man, thea' won't be nothin' flyin' around out thea' this mornin' with Black-fly tendencies, I'll tell ya' that much. It's as cold as a witch's titty this mornin'," he said.

Filbert couldn't help but smile at that one from where he stood at the counter. Heidi simply held her stare with a less-than-favorable expression, turned, and walked up an aisle.

Heidi busied herself at tidying up the shelves that received most of the foot traffic—usually the last two nearest the wall leading to the beer cooler—which connected at the rear of the store with the sandwich counter.

Those last two aisles, by Filbert's design, held items like potato chips, cheese-curls, Slim-Jims, mini-sausages, and all of the snack foods that went well with beer and soda, which had a separate cooler to the side of the beer. Heidi was well aware of the recently resurrected relationship between her husband and Bullet, although the relationship by itself was not the problem for her; it was the lifestyle that Mr. Bullington Carter led that made her leery of him. Her feelings were not of mistrust as much as a level of concern.

As Filbert had suspected, the idea to open early was proven a necessity with the steady flow of customers through the front and rear doors. Because of the lack of parking space out front, some made their way in through the rear door, which was of no concern for either of them, as shoplifting was something that occurred more at the big stores in Bangor and Ellsworth. It was rare when someone walked in that they didn't know; mostly everyone who stopped here was a local, unlike the influx of transients that frequently traded at the Quick-Stop because of its location at the lower corner and the intersection of Route 1 North and South.

Bullet made himself at home, seating himself on the flattop soda cooler directly across from the checkout counter. He knew everyone who walked in, and generally struck up a conversation with all of them. Usually, on days like this, later on in the day Filbert would place a bottle of rye whisky behind the sandwich counter for the regulars, and most of the time, he took part, but that wasn't going to happen today. There was a seriousness about him that left no doubt in anyone's mind that something was consuming Filbert with an underlying interest, which he was not willing to share. Bullet tried several times without success, while Filbert remained pleasantly evasive.

"Ya' goin' huntin' today, big boy?" Bullet asked.

"No, I'm kinda' stuck hea' in the stoar' today. With all this goin' on, this bein' a huntin' Saturday and all, no, I'll be here all day, ayah," Filbert said.

Bullet placed a fresh cigarette between his lips while nodding his head in agreement...

"Ya' goin' to talk to thi'em' little shits today?" he asked.

As Heidi approached the counter from the back of the store, she couldn't help hearing the question, and saw the uncomfortable look on Filbert's face.

"Don't you have somewhere you have to be...Bullet?" she asked.

Both men recognized the tone in her voice, looking toward her and then quickly toward each other.

"Well..." he began, and was quickly interrupted by Heidi.

"Maybe you don't, but Filbert does. Chop-chop, let's go boys, yaw' burnin' daylight," she said.

Bullet figured they'd been fightin', and that would be the

reason for Filbert's inattentive attitude, and he wanted no part of a quarrelsome couple. His past was full of it, and he had no desire to be in the path of the results of ruffled feathers. With Heidi's comment, Bullet snatched up his six-pack of pounders, tucked his fresh pack of Camels into his shirt pocket, and without a word and a simple salute toward Filbert, he was out the door, with a few clumps of snow falling onto the vibrating door chime from the shingles overhead.

Within a few minutes of Bullet's departure, Filbert was driving down the narrow gravel road leading toward the river and Kenny and Mary's place. His heart was barely beating in his chest and his breathing was shallow, and the weight of a depression the likes of which he had not experienced in years, began to smother him.

The rusted rear fenders of the pickup truck rattled loudly over the rough, uneven gravel, and he knew the two young people whom he had admired and relied upon so intently up until a few short weeks ago were sure to know of his arrival long before the vehicle made its first appearance in the clearing. *"They can have no way of knowing what dreadful consequence my visit will have on them and how, very shortly, their lives will change for the very worst,"* he thought.

Despite the early season's dusting of fresh powder snow blanketing everything, Kenny sat on the stairs by the front door, the third step from the bottom. When he heard Filbert's truck, Kenny snuffed out the joint on the step he sat on, and put it into his jacket pocket. It had been at least four or five days since Kenny had worked at the store, and the first thought to cross his mind on seeing the old pickup was that Filbert needed something done today.

As the vehicle came to within a few yards of the house, Filbert, partially blinded from the reflected glare of the sun on the top section of glass on the storm door, shielded his eyes, as Mary came out onto the top step to see who it was that had pulled into the driveway.

Her ready smile immediately formed on her face, and Filbert's stomach began to produce bile that now burned his windpipe.

Her smile alone made him want to vomit and he truly did not know how he could go through with this eviction. However, facing Heidi after not following through would be of greater consequence, as she'd made it perfectly clear where she stood on these two and their goings-on. His first responsibility was to his family and his moral predispositions. It was true, he'd once admired these two as being most like he and Heidi when they first started out, but he thought, *"It's not the same anymore."*

Filbert sat in his vehicle preparing himself to face these two unsuspecting young people who, in his words, were "out of control."

Filbert slid himself from the driver's seat, and as soon as his feet hit the ground, his stomach began to excrete hot bile into his throat that burned him to an extent that no antacid could cool.

"Hi, Filbert." Mary exclaimed in her childlike tone of voice. He reciprocated with something inaudible, and instantly, Kenny exhibited a facial expression that seemed to question Filbert's tone, and the intensity of his stare forced Filbert into a more uncomfortable stance.

"What brings you out here this early?" Kenny asked.

The tone of Kenny's voice made Filbert feel unwelcome, but he was sure the feeling originated from his own resentment and insecurity from deep within his subconscious about what was to take place, and not from Kenny's perception of why he was here to begin with. He forced a smile as he stood facing them, and his mind formed visions of happier times when he and Kenny, still new to the area, had fished and hunted at Filbert's secret locations. When he had taken Kenny under his wing and taught him the essentials for survival, he reveled at how quickly the boy from the city picked up the knack for fly-fishing and hunting and life in Washington County. He soon fit in and became unrecognizable as someone from away.

"I'm fine, thank you, Mary. And how are you two doin' this mornin?"

They nodded their heads in the affirmative, though Mary was the only one to respond.

"Good, Filbert, good," she said.

The uncomfortable moment gave Filbert every indication that what he was about to do would flop at his feet like cow-dung spread on a plowed field in the spring. He took a deep breath and began.

"I suppose you two have heard all the rumors goin' round about your little party out hea'?" He said that and then cleared his throat. "It kinda' gave Heidi a bit-ova' cramp, if ya' know whadi' mean?" Then he laughed a nervous laugh.

"Don't get me wrong, kids"… And when the word "kids" came out, Kenny and Mary exchanged disgusted looks, making Filbert's mind go blank for a moment; then he regained his composure at the thought of Heidi, ripping him a new one if he went home and told her he couldn't tell them what he'd come to say.

"Ya' see," he started hoarsely; "we're both a little nervous about the talk of drugs and fightin'. Don't get me wrong K…" He stopped short at the sight of their facial expressions. "I mean, when I was younger I used to like tipping a few myself, and rabble-rousin' was the norm for a Saturday night, but…you know…things are different now. We got the three kids and all, and Heidi's a bit tense—what if they should stop by and see something they shouldn't?" He stopped to take a deep breath, and at that point, Kenny opted to throw out his two cents, starting out with a question.

"So, Filbert, what exactly are you tryin' to say? You don't want us givin' your kids drugs, is that it?" He said this with such a vengeful tone that it immediately allowed Filbert to overcome his inhibition to move forward, placing him in a defensive posture. His anger at Kenny's snide remark gave Filbert the confidence he needed to get to the point without any further hesitation.

"I wasn't thinking that exactly, but now that ya' mention it, yah', we don't want the kids around that shit, and you must think I'm some kinda fool if ya' thought I couldn't smell that crap in the air when I pulled in," he said, surprising himself with what he'd just said.

Mary's eyes were as large as fifty-cent coins, and there was a fear in her expression that settled deep into Filbert's soul, making him feel empty once again. She was the last person he wanted to hurt; he didn't want to hurt either one of them, but Kenny's remark had pissed him off and Mary was Kenny's wife, so she very well knew what the score was and was no longer the innocent little girl that had moved down from the County.

Filbert wasn't the type to stay angry for long, and he wasn't actually angry at this moment; however, he needed to stay on course with the reason he was here in the first place. He couldn't look Mary straight in the face when he began speaking. He couldn't gamble on what her expression would do to his newfound courage, and so he looked to the ground as if some divine inspiration would eventually lead him out from this scourge of unhappiness.

"Look, the way things have gone, we…me and Heidi, have to come to a decision. You're going to have to find another place to live." He said it so abruptly and it came out without hesitation, it surprised even him, not to mention Kenny and Mary, if the looks now displayed by the two people he most admired not so long ago were any indication.

"Where in the fuck do you think we're gonna go this time of the year?" Kenny asked coldly.

"I'm not sayin' ya' have ta' leave now, but ya' have to leave in a fair amount o' time. That's all there is to it," Filbert said.

Mary was about to interject when Kenny threw up a rigid arm, his open hand facing her, and she stopped speaking abruptly.

"Seems to me there's more to it than that, old boy. Trooper stopped by to chitchat about nothin' in particular. Old Bullet wants to get into it with me the other day, now you, the last person I'd figure to fuck us, is fuckin' us."

Filbert began to say something, but Kenny got up, went into the house, slamming the door behind him, leaving Filbert and Mary facing each other in silence. Mary stood silently watching Filbert leave, the clanking sound of the rear fenders on the pickup truck echoing long after it disappeared behind the thick stands of fir and pine trees midway to the blacktop. Although less than five minutes had passed from the time Kenny had climbed the steps and gone in the house, when Mary went to join him, he'd downed one full sixteen-ounce bottle of beer and started on the second.

"Yo, just in time, Mary. I figure we've got nothin' left to lose from this asshole day, so we might as well get loaded and stay that way," he said.

She couldn't agree more; yet something in the back of her mind—call it intuition like her mother used to—told her the surprises for the day weren't over yet.

At that same moment, at the other end of town, the trooper and constable were seated at their usual table at the Quick-Stop, discussing the very subject that everyone seemed to be interested with lately, Kenny and Mary. They'd been meeting lately every other day to talk about the situation. The trooper relayed to the constable his meeting at their place and how both of them, after Mary's arrival, had become defensive, and how keenly they averted his questions about the fellow who looked like a pirate. At this point, the information seemed sketchy at best.

"Unless there is a specific complaint about these two, or him especially," the trooper emphasized, "there won't be a whole lot we can do except to keep an eye on the entire mess and see what happens."

The constable dunked his donut and nodded his head in agreement.

13

DEPRESSION WILL SOMETIMES MAKE A PERSON do and say things they would not normally do and say. For some, alcohol and drugs can be the catalyst, while for others, heredity or even a decrease of daylight hours in early winter can be enough to shove a normal person over the edge into the deep, dark zones of depression. Sometimes, depending on the strength of an individual's metabolism, the usual setbacks in life—like limited resources, family bad news, and everyday trials and tribulations—can trigger the onset.

Unfortunately, all of the above at some level played a role in the insurmountable depression that overshadowed both Kenny and Mary. The only good news the couple could have shared, the start of Mary's new job, was now snuffed out with Filbert's eviction notice and his and Heidi's need to dissolve the relationship—the one thing both couples had depended on. What Mary couldn't know then was that about the same time of the eviction, a telephone call was made to the Bagley's residence, giving Mary's mother a telephone number for Eastern Maine Medical Center in Bangor. Generally, when test results of this kind performed on Lucretia were received, whether it was good news or bad, the doctor would want to speak to that individual in person, and this would be the case for Lucretia.

An appointment needed to be made, and since it was Friday, the upcoming weekend would prove to be less than relaxing for everyone concerned.

When Filbert returned to the store, Heidi heard the rumble of the old pickup as it made its way to the space behind the building. She shared her husband's anxiety about the eviction and how it would affect the two young people she'd grown to know so well and trust. Her deep-set fears about alcohol and drug abuse reached far beyond the arrival of Kenny Collins and his bohemian behavior. Her brother, who was younger by five years, was an alcoholic drug user who had been found face-down in an ice-fishing hole, his face frozen into the refrozen puddle in the lake. No, she could never take the chance that one of her children would come across the temptation from either Mary or Kenny, as both were loved and admired by the three impressionable children.

She considered her need to protect her children seriously, no matter how ludicrous real-life was at times. She thought the chances were good that at least one of her children might become afflicted with a substance curse. *"By the time the kids grow up,"* she thought, *"society will have one foot in the grave by then anyhow."* She promised herself, however, that she would do all that was in her power while the power was hers to protect her children the best way she saw fit.

As he entered the rear door, Filbert's shoulders drooped like a man who'd spent the day chopping and stacking firewood, or someone who'd spent the last several hours fightin' northbound traffic on I-95 from Kittery to Portland in August. She didn't have to say anything or ask a word. She only needed to look into his sad eyes to know that the task he'd set out to do was done, and she would give him all the space he needed.

Less than a mile down the road, Kenny and Mary sat at their favorite places at the table; yet today the rapid water of the Paguagus River seemed invisible to them. They remained silent for a long period, and neither knew exactly what time it was. Even though he didn't speak, Mary saw how drunk Kenny was getting. She wasn't a drinker. She had a little wine occasionally, but she never said no to anything rolled into a cigarette paper, or stuffed into an old corncob pipe. Suddenly, the silence was broken with the sound of Mary's soft voice.

"What are ya' thinkin'?" she asked.

"Not what I'd like to be thinkin'," he answered.

"Ayah," she answered with a slight inhalation of breath, and then the silence continued.

But the silence lasted only briefly before Kenny began speaking.

"Mary, for the life of me, I just can't figure out what in hell crawled up Filbert's ass for him to come over here, without him callin' first, or somethin'. Did he or Heidi ever hint around that they were pissed at us for somethin'?" he asked.

"No. It was as much of a surprise to me as it was to you when he said it."

"What in the hell are we gonna do now? The last thing that would have hit me, would a' been that we'd be lookin' for another place this time of year. This fuckin' rent was so cheap, and now that you're startin' that job in Ellsworth, it looked as though we'd be gettin' up a bit with the money-bags for a change," he said. This was the first time he'd spoken of the new job since she'd told him about it.

"Well, thank Christ I did get it. We'll need the extra money… and by the way, he did say we didn't have to leave right off, so, I say we take aar' sweet-assed time lookin'," she said.

"Yeah…lookin' for a place in the goddamned snow. Oh-yeah, just what I wanted to do. I should of shot that scrawny little fuck while he was still standin' there, out front," he said.

Mary knew he was venting, so there was no need to add anything to that type of comment. He would calm down as time passed, she could only hope. She would have to be the one to stay cool. *"We'll find a place, and it'll be better than this one,"* she thought. *"The job will work out. I'll make the extra money we'll*

119

need to pay for the other place, and we'll move on like people always do." She looked at the river from her window seat, and was already missing it.

The beer cap flew through the air, flicked from Bullet's middle finger and thumb and in a split second, it tinked against the empty Dinty Moore Beef Stew can on Bullet's kitchen counter. He never ate the stuff; he saved it for the stray cats that came his way at the house on a regular basis. It was several hours after the eviction and Bullet had returned earlier to the store for more beer before inviting me over to his place.

"Adver," he said, "it was the best thing Filbert could do was to get rid o' thi'em' two free-loaders out o' that camp. All those two want ta' do is drug-up, drink-up, and fuck-up." Bullet was ranting. He did that, he said, whenever something stuck in his craw. After he told me of his past, and how Mary was involved, I finally understood his feelings about Kenny. I kept telling him that I understood with a consistent nod of my head, but it wasn't enough to get him to just drink his beer and plain old shut-up.

I could see no good would come from their eviction, especially this time of the year, when all anyone wanted to do, besides hunt, was to be indoors snug and warm, not out lookin' for a new place to hang their hats. I didn't tell Bullet or Filbert what I was thinkin', nor did I side with them during our long, regular visits at the store afterwards. All I did, when the subject came up, and it did, regularly, was to nod my head and shrug my shoulders, remaining neutral on the subject. Apparently it worked, because neither one ever pressed me for more than that. The resentment that festered in Bullet for Kenny was now implanting itself into Filbert's subconscious, as far as I could see, forcing him deeper into the depression that was taking over his personality.

—

Bad news travels at the speed of light, and sometimes latches on to certain people faster than others. Several hours after the eviction, Mary received a phone call from her mother, who said she needed to contact a certain doctor from Bangor.

"The tests are in, Mary, and for Christ's-sake, why don't they just tell me what…" and Lucretia started coughing. It sounded as if she could cough up one of her lungs at any moment.

"Mama…are you ok?" Mary asked, while her heart beat several times faster than normal.

It was a regular procedure to see a doctor to find out the results of cancer tests. It just wasn't hunky-dory for Lucretia.

She never let anyone but Mary drive her anywhere, so that meant Mary needed to check her schedule for off-time, and now that she would be starting the new job, and though Mary would do anything for her mother, the added stress of the extra trip to Bangor would only add to the confusion that was Kenny and Mary's life.

Lucretia gave Mary the number for EMMC and the minute they hung up, Mary called the hospital and made an appointment for her mother. Thinking ahead with her thoughts, all she could do was to inform the nursing home of the need to have some time off and the reason. As far as Mary was concerned, they would have to accept it, because the way she felt today, nothing really mattered anymore.

It is universally accepted that weekends shoot by like rockets from hell, and Mary found herself on Monday morning alone in her car on the road to Ellsworth and her new job. The nursing home maintained a laid-back environment for attire, and the office atmosphere was to remain comfortable and casual. With money she'd borrowed from her mother, Mary had bought a sporty, long-sleeved sugarplum-colored cashmere sweater, which she wore over a crewneck white T-shirt and navy blue corduroys with berry-pink, slip-on skimmers. It wasn't a stones'-throw away, but at the speed limit, it was about a half-hour drive down the Black Bear Road.

By itself, the road was not difficult to negotiate—an environmentally scenic route not much traveled by anyone from away, winding its way through some of the most thickly forested, natural areas of eastern Maine, with a multitude of scattered ponds and lakes, their expanses relieving the feeling of isolation that the thick forest instilled in an individual's psyche. There were many dark sections, making it unfavorable to women traveling alone, yet for Mary, it was simply another jaunt through the woods to Ellsworth. Even with her casual acceptance of the road as a means of getting from point A to point B, she could never shake the feeling of complete loneliness that encapsulated her each time she reached the summit of Cathance Hill.

The road wound its way to the top from the Hancock, Washington County lines by Chock Lake, and went all the way down through an unorganized township, Frankfort, then onto Ellsworth. The summit, some nine hundred and forty feet above sea level, offered no visual outcroppings on which to view what lay below, which was the site of a long-ago, forgotten homestead. When Mary had been driven over the top of this hill as a child, a menacing feeling had always enveloped her.

As she neared this location now, the thought crossed her mind about how well the road would be maintained during the soon-to-arrive winter, where the top always received a decent snow shower or significant dusting most evenings and early mornings, turning a simple commute into a slip-sliding nightmare. As she drove, she became doubtful that taking her new job had been the right thing to do.

"I should be home taking care of the house and my husband." She was whispering, almost inaudibly, and could barely hear herself over the drone of the old engine's exhaust leak and the road noise from the partially bald tires. Without a doubt, she was getting cold feet, exacerbated by the fact that Kenny had not gone out of his way to support her on this one, and that made her resent her decision even more. Several times during the drive, she had half a notion to turn around and go home, and she would have, had it not been for her friend Callie, who had gone out of her way to get her the interview. There was no way she'd do that to her friend. She took a deep breath each time the weakness came over her, and continued driving.

As much as her determination ruled in favor of the direction she was going in, she looked forward to the end of the day when she could return home. She couldn't count the times she'd traveled this road for whatever reason, but it never seemed as long to get there as it did this morning. Her thoughts wandered in several directions simultaneously, and she suddenly wished she were high. At least that way, she could minimize the guilt that overwhelmed her.

As bad as it had felt a few short minutes ago, when the road sign indicating three miles to Ellsworth came into view, a pang of indecision rumbled in the pit of her stomach. She knew she should have eaten before she left. She felt the unsettling need to vomit, and pulled the car over, hard onto the shoulder, leaping quickly into the frosty, morning air.

Kenny found himself in the midst of a role reversal, no longer being the sole breadwinner and supporter; and with Mary working in Ellsworth; his resentment now brought him to the brink of an explosive anger. His anger was not reserved for Mary alone—for taking the job despite his verbal disapproval of it—it was an anger that welled up within him for Filbert and those he thought conspired against them, like Bullet Carter and Harry Circus. And he knew his own father-in-law was somehow involved in this insurgence, waging war against his and Mary's way of life.

Kenny was the farthest thing from an intellectual type, though he truly wanted everyone to think that he was. It was his personality which led people to believe he was a copious thinker. It was all in the façade of Kenny Collins. With the added amounts of alcohol and drugs, his elevated sense of paranoia allowed him to believe that anything was possible, by anyone, when stacking the deck against him. He was always the victim. In his mind, it was always about Kenny.

There was a serious level of mistrust in his mind brewing for a certain few. The three people who were directly involved with him from the onset of his arrival in Chesterfield, were now the most menacing in his mind. The first was undeniably Bullet Carter. He was one of the first people Kenny had spoken to that very first day anyone laid eyes on him while he sauntered through Filbert's store knowingly, with an air of sarcasm, which became embedded in Bullet as the dislike that festered to this day; and only added to the decaying bag of garbage that Bullet referred to as Kenny Collins.

The second person was, without a doubt, Mary's father, Virgil Bagley. The best thing that could describe Virgil was that he was a good family man. Virgil believed that Kenny had stolen his little girl from his family, but in actuality, Mary had run away from home to free herself from the confining (and her self-described) hateful existence. In Virgil's mind, Kenny had taken her, when in reality, Virgil's little girl had been simply a means to accommodate his and his family's daily domestic needs, giving him and Lucretia more time to enjoy their sometimes daylong Happy Hours. Along with that, unknown to anyone living or dead, Mary and her father shared a secret that bound them for all eternity—a secret neither of them was willing to share or bring to light. That was the only thing Kenny did not know, or suspect.

The third person, and the one who Kenny found to be most difficult to view as a back-stabber, was Filbert Cirone. He was the only person, of all those he interacted with, that he'd trusted. True, he and Mary had taken advantage of a good situation whenever they could, but he would have done anything Filbert asked before this. Now he felt this was a different ball of wax. The game had new rules, and Kenny appointed himself the umpire. However, the last thing he envisioned was waging all-out war against Filbert. No, in Kenny's mind it was the other two sons-a'-whores that had somehow talked Filbert into kicking them out, and it was those two who would see the war brought to their front-door-yards, if it was the last thing Kenny did.

14

THERE IS SOMETHING ALMOST SOLEMN about the transition from one season to another, especially autumn to winter. A calm stillness envelops the earth, forecasting (as only Mother Nature can do) the need to prepare oneself for the onset of change. The old-timer's predictions, used sometimes and by many, remained a viable tool in preparing for those changes. For instance, when a hornet's nest was seen constructed high above the ground, a deluge of snow upon the land was expected. For some, it was a welcome change. Yet sometimes there can be no greater feeling of depression than to awaken to an overcast, dismal morning, knowing very well that the security of your warm, little house and your ability to remain in it is dictated by the imposition of the hourglass of time. The anguish that now filled Kenny's existence, in light of his need to find new shelter and cope with the oncoming changes in his life, was insurmountable.

For the first time since Mary told him she would work in Ellsworth, Kenny remained silently grateful for her position, though he never told her that. Along with the eviction came the end of Filbert's need for Kenny at the store. He'd never come right out and told Kenny he was fired, but because they'd been thrown out, his pride would never allow him to step foot in the store ever again. The camaraderie ended the day they became homeless, if only in their minds.

Kenny's supply of drugs was running on empty, and the bankbook he'd carried in his backpack when he first arrived in town had a zero balance. Its source had dried out. However, his breakfast this morning consisted of the entire pot of coffee and a frugally rolled joint. Getting high was probably the last thing he needed now, but since he was a creature of habit with an addictive personality, nothing could be more needed than Kenny's own way of life. He made mental notes of what his approach to the day would be, the first being the need to secure a new place. He spoke to himself mentally, never speaking aloud—he believed that anyone who actually spoke to themselves in an audible tone had to be afflicted with some sort of mental problem. He remembered his mother saying in jest, "Those who talk to themselves have money in the bank." His response to a comment of that nature was the same: "'Yeah, right, but it sounds to me like there might be a loose screw to the vault door." He had his own agenda where the rest of the world was concerned, and even now, at this crucial stage of adjustment, Kenny was most unwilling to make any changes in his belief in self-reliance.

With Mary working about thirty miles away, Kenny could no longer count on the use of her car for any local or long-distance transportation. There was no way he'd get up and be out that early to drive her, and at this point, they could no more afford the extra gas than they could extra groceries each week. They both knew that eventually it would all level off financially as Mary's steady paychecks began to add up, but until then, they would hold everything together with fine twine, an ability they both had which most people from away could not comprehend.

The last thing Kenny would consider as an option was to go back in the woods for Forest Bagley, but he was sure that Forest would be a wealth of information and in some way a great source for someone who needed cash. So, first things first, contacting Forest took over the first slot on Kenny's to-do-list.

He was convinced that through the grapevine, gossip would have Forest's ears filled with the goings-on where he and Mary were concerned (Forest being a daily two-ham-and-cheese 'r at the store), and the fact he was Virgil's cousin left no doubt he already had an opinion on the matter. Kenny had to put that behind him in order to persuade Forest they both could create a win-win situation in the wood business. Kenny had it in his mind that he would be working for himself. Money was easy in the drug-trade business, when people had money. What he needed now was cash and a roof over their heads, and Forest Bagley was, as far as Kenny was concerned, the best likelihood.

He set out on foot just after 8:00 a.m., walking slowly at first, enjoying the solitude of the long driveway out to the blacktop, wishing it were summer once again with the transients hungry for his supplies. It was cold, with an unusual lack of snow for the middle of hunting season. Kenny, with one deer tagged and one taken under a tarp', was stocked with meat, which took some of the stress out of their money problems in terms of the need for food. A fresh supply of home-canned veggies from Mary's mom filled their shelves and freezer for now.

He wore a fluorescent orange hunting cap—the norm for a Washington County male in-and sometimes out-of-season—and shin-high insulated rubber boots with black Levi jeans tucked in. Under the navy blue pea coat, somewhat out of the norm for hunting season, underneath, he wore a red and black checkered woodsman shirt.

He carried a pint of coffee brandy in his left coat pocket, for lunch if need be, and several joints in his shirt pocket, with the flap buttoned down. He always tucked a doubled-bladed, eight-inch jackknife in one pocket, and in the right coat pocket, which was somewhat deeper; Kenny always carried his new .32 caliber semi-automatic pistol. If his timing was right, he would have no problem finding a ride to almost the very location of Forest's logging operation off Stud-Mill Road in one of the unorganized Townships to the north of Chesterfield. Most of the logging trucks going back to that location would pass through town on their return from Bucksport, a southern coastal town with a pulp mill.

Shortly after reaching the blacktop, he stepped up his pace in an attempt to keep warm. With the sun still at an autumn low in the sky, the warm rays felt good on his face, and he appreciated the stillness of the early morning air. As he made his way up the slight incline toward Filbert's store, a pang of resentment tingled in his stomach, and he wondered what he would do if he came face to face with either Filbert or Heidi in that area.

As the thought came and went, he heard the sound of an approaching vehicle from the bottom of the hill, and not wanting to appear needy for transportation, he waited until the vehicle came abreast of him before looking in its direction. He recognized the driver immediately. Kenny believed the woman to be close to his own age, though her young features and stylish attire were deceiving. She was almost five years his elder and he had, long ago, found her most attractive, yet kept his distance for obvious reasons.

She was known locally as the hot little divorcée from down by the river, and she knew of him also. Her place was a large circa-eighteen-hundred farmhouse with an attached L-shaped kitchen and small barn. It was located at the southernmost boundary line of Chesterfield by itself in a clearing. The property was envied by most sportsmen, Kenny included, for its location, bordered on two sides by the lower West Branch of the Paguagus River, about a mile above the dam, allowing for deep and slow-moving water. The property consisted of mostly open fields, which yielded a bountiful crop of clover when maintained, and because of its proximity to the river, became a resting point for Canadian geese on their migratory route south each year, making it a handsome place for anyone looking to fill their freezer with goose for the long winter. Crossing the river at this point put one in prime deer-hunting country, and its remoteness from the ears of the town made it the ideal bad-boys' hideaway.

The divorcée kept her friendships to a small group of hand-picked alter-ego types who never seemed to fit in with the Down East lifestyle. Their flamboyant dress helped to keep them a safe distance from the crowd, and at events like the annual Fourth of

July parade and gatherings of that kind, they corralled themselves in their own little corner of the world and maintained that safe distance from the onlookers.

His attraction to her was spawned from their similar characters and their ability to amass a deeper sense of allurement in the eyes of those they were both able to attract. She was partially hidden behind the fogged-over, driver's-side window as the vehicle came to a full stop in the middle of the roadway, and she immediately rolled the window down, allowing him an unobstructed view from the top of her head to the area just above her breasts.

"It seems as though we're lacking in the transportation department this morning," she said.

"I'm walkin' for my health." Kenny answered curtly, not wanting to appear needy to her.

And without a millisecond passing between comments, she added, "Well, from here you look pretty healthy." Then she simply smiled in his direction, waiting for another curt response, but didn't get one.

"Thanks, you look pretty healthy yourself, at least from here," he said.

They stared, smiling toward each other for several seconds. "I hear your wife got a job in Ellsworth. Does she like it?" the woman asked.

The last thing Kenny wanted now was to be reticent, because he wanted to continue the conversation with this woman, who seemed to be making herself available to him right now and was tugging firmly on his fantasy string. If his senses were on, he felt the attraction was mutual.

"Well, well, how quickly news wings its way through the endless miles of forests. Yeah, she likes it fine. I think it'll be good for her to get out and about, you know. Keep her from getting moldy, you might say," he said, and kept his stare focused on her.

He kind of half-grinned, and wanted to go on with something, but waited for some sort of response, and when she made none, he began again, remembering his plan for this day—and that included finding a place to live. Networking was a fine tool that Kenny made good use of in every walk of his life.

Even this woman, who now had him pinging back and forth inside, was no less a consideration for that mind-set than was the pirate fellow the night of the party. He knew very well that finding a place to live was the most important thing to him right now. It was the difference between remaining under the watchful eye of Filbert Cirone and the cursed eviction, and regaining control of his existence as he meant it to be. Without a doubt, money was essential to make it all come together, but that's what Mary was taking care of these days, and he was quickly seeing how that could work to his benefit by allowing him the freedom he needed to be himself.

An uncomfortable silence lingered until Kenny said, "Well, to be honest with you, I was takin' a gamble on a loggin' truck passin' through for a lift to where Forest Bagley's workin'. You know Forest?" he asked.

"Ya, I know Forest. He sells me wood," she said and looked at him inquisitively. "Are you lookin for work?"

And the moment the question left her lips, she regretted asking it. She knew of Kenny Collins through rumors of his furtive activity, and wondered why their paths had never crossed until now. She too was a lover of illicit endeavor, and had some of the same addictions as he did.

She began quickly, "I didn't mean…" and was immediately interrupted by Kenny.

"No big deal, no big deal," he said.

Miles away in Ellsworth, while her husband made what appeared to be a lead-in to promiscuous small talk with a divorcée, Mary felt the first ever pang of uncertainty in her subconscious mind about her relationship with her husband since their very first meeting and subsequent relationship and marriage.

Mary had never doubted the strength of their love, though she knew very well the extent of her husband's ego and self-centeredness, but the uncanny feeling that overpowered her at this moment made her want to call him at home, for no other reason except her need to do so and to satisfy the intuition burning a hole to the center of her soul. Had she been at her assigned place, her desk, she could have masked the obvious scowl that created deep furrows in her forehead, down vertically to the bridge of her nose, but since she was in the employee break room, it was impossible to avoid the scrutiny of her fellow workers.

"Mary, are you all right?" one of the office girls asked.

"I'm fine, I just have a headache that won't quit, that's all," she responded. Without saying another word, she bolted from the room, leaving her half-filled coffee mug and a plain donut minus one bite behind, and going directly to her desk, where she sought the privacy of her desk phone. She sat, hunched over with one hand resting on her forehead, the other holding the receiver tight to the side of her face, listening to the endless ring-tone through the earpiece. Without the luxury of an answering machine, the fever grew within her with every unanswered ring.

It is funny how, while the phone is ringing, your mind registers what the sound of a familiar person's voice will be when they finally answer. It can also sometimes allow you to picture that person's face and every expression it displays while they are speaking. In some cases, even though you've never seen the person before, your mind perceives a face and attaches it to the voice. For this particular call, however, Mary attached a face to the endless sound of the ringing, and hoped her intuitive restlessness was unfounded.

Up to this point, Kenny had never given her reason to doubt his loyalty and devotion, but she knew that when a man was put in a position such as Kenny was in right now, the need to protect that virile aspect of masculinity could be consequentially damaging to any relationship.

Meanwhile, Kenny and the divorcée were talking about his need to find a new place to live.

"Oh, you're kidding. I'm planning on closing my place up indefinitely, or at least for the upcoming winter. I have a…" she stopped speaking as if she were about to say something that needed to remain a secret, and then she began laughing, almost with the intensity of a happily misbehaving schoolgirl. While he stared, listening to the laughter, he turned his head toward the sound of an empty, twenty-two wheel logging truck barreling down the opposite hill toward them. He motioned to her to angle the car nearer the shoulder, but it was as if she had no clue of what he'd indicated by his gesturing until his voice rose, almost ordering her to move the car out of the way of the approaching logger. As much as his fantasy tingled in his groin, he couldn't avoid thinking that he would have had the ride he'd intended to take, and with the easily recognizable vehicle, no more than a couple of hundred yards from where he stood, he realized he wouldn't have had to wait long for the lift. The sound of the vehicle being downshifted and the rattle of the Jake-brake echoed through the cold stillness of the early morning air, and gave Kenny a nostalgic urge for the woods and the time he'd spent there, not so long ago.

Kenny recognized the driver immediately as the tractor portion pulled alongside them. The baseball cap and the wrap-around sunglasses were on the head of none other than the young Forest Bagley II, a very willing candidate for taking over the family woods operation one day. He waved to Kenny, making an arm motion indicating an invitation to come along, as if Kenny had placed a telepathic request, but Kenny waved him off somewhat reluctantly with a smile, and then returned his full attention to the giggly divorcée as the big diesel chugged away up the incline.

The woman inserted a cassette into the dashboard player unit while Kenny was momentarily distracted by the trucker, and a bluesy guitar riff by Dire Straits drifted softly from the open window.

The car's interior emitted warmth through the partially open window, making it most inviting as the early morning air began to penetrate Kenny's outerwear, though he would never let on that he was cold. His eyes swelled to almost twice their normal size when the woman lifted between her forefinger and thumb the largest marijuana joint he'd ever seen. It was the size of his middle finger in girth and length, and the look on her face said, *"Come and get it."*

Without an actual invitation, Kenny strolled around the rear of the car and got into the passenger front seat. She handed him the unlit joint and a Bic lighter, and the moment he took it from her, she placed the transmission into drive and sped away. It was just as well that they left when they did, for as far as Kenny was concerned, it was just a matter of time before some snoop passed by with the hope of writing a book on what they'd seen: Kenny and the hot little divorcée from down by the river, together.

Being somewhat of an entrepreneur herself, where her needs were concerned, she wasted no time, and as Kenny filled his lungs with the heavenly smoke, she came right out and asked if he would be interested in seeing her place with an eye toward renting it. He was convinced at this moment that she knew more of the eviction than she offered, yet he thought better than to question, or attack her for it, as he wanted to hear more.

"I'm sure we can come to some sort of agreeable terms where the rent is concerned, and I might even be willing to sell, if the price is right," she said.

Not wanting to seem overly excited, Kenny passed the joint over to her, and blew what smoke remained in his lungs over the top of the steering wheel, filling that corner of the dashboard with thick, blue smoke.

"Ayatollah, who gives a fiddlin' fuck about what it's gonna cost. Let's just go take a look at it," she said. Kenny chuckled.

He found much humor in the way she spoke, and he loved the way her face moved when she did speak. He didn't want to be obvious and stare at her, but it was difficult to keep his eyes off her. It was a short ride to her place from where they'd first met, just below Filbert's store, and they pulled into the driveway before finishing their smoke.

"Dump that into the ashtray, I'll fish it out later," she said.

With that said, they got out of the car at the same instant, yet their doors slammed one after the other. Kenny had always loved the location of this old farmhouse. The place he and Mary were in now was far more private and removed from the hustle and bustle, but this place was big, and he could always make good use of the small attached barn.

He remembered the first time he'd seen it from the opposite side of the river while hunting with Filbert. The old man told him to stay away from that one, meaning the very woman he stood next to at this moment. She had parked close to the barn, the driveway curved in at an angle, and it was obviously her usual parking spot because the gravel was eroded. When he first got out of the car, he caught a glimmer of light reflecting on the river water through the trees, and he liked it immediately.

They entered through a low-framed door between the barn and the L-shaped kitchen addition to the house. The contrast between the light from outdoors and the near-absence of light in the barn, with its few, small windows, left Kenny squinting to see, but as his eyes adjusted, he immediately began dreaming of a life of grandeur. Many thoughts passed through his subliminal psyche at the same moment, so much so that he was oblivious to the things she pointed out to him while they made their way toward the kitchen entrance, which was diagonally across from the door they just entered.

Stepping into the kitchen, they went one -step up, and the first thing to catch his eye was the large cast-iron cook stove just inside the door and to the right. He could smell the remnants of nearly burnt bread, and knew that the top of the stove was used for making toast. The lingering heat from an earlier fire gave the small kitchen a warm, inviting ambience.

From the moment they entered the house, however, the conversation became wantonly suggestive, giving a rise to the inside temperature without the assistance of wood in the stove. They weren't able to hide their mutual feelings of attraction any longer. They stopped for a moment at the base of the staircase, silently looking into one another's eyes.

"You've got my hormones standing on their little heads, and it feels as though they're lathering up to give me a bubble bath." She said this as her eyes suggestively went from the top of his head, slowly down, stopping abruptly in the area of his groin. Her lips were seductively parted, revealing the tip of her tongue through an evil little smile, making him tingle all over. He moved toward her with determination, and luckily, her denim shirt had snaps and not buttons. He gave a rough tug at the neckline, and the sound of the snaps popping forced his eyes to open large with excitement, revealing her bare breasts and her erect nipples, which were the same color as her lips.

15

NEEDLESS TO SAY, with already too much detail—some made up, some provocatively true—word of the farmhouse escapade between Kenny and his little divorcée playmate ran rampant through the grapevine. Whether someone saw them together at some point, or the little lady found it difficult to maintain the proper level of discretion needed to withstand the scrutiny of such an act in such a small town remained a mystery, if it mattered at all at that point. Bullet and I became aware of it shortly after Kenny and Mary moved out of Filbert's place, during the first week of December. They made no fanfare of it, actually packing and leaving in the middle of the night, avoiding 'The Nose', as Kenny began to call the local gossipers.

They left without as much as a word to Filbert, but knowing Kenny as we all did, it wasn't a surprise. They left the place as neat as the head of a pin, just the way they'd found it. Mary was a good housekeeper, before and after she went to work full time. There weren't many a man who didn't envy Kenny for that. It must be nice, comin' home to a squeaky-clean house. That's more than I'll ever know.

Because of the rumors about the fling, there was no secret about where they moved to; however, not a soul made any attempt to venture any closer than simply passin' by for at least the first week to see the new residents, and it didn't take long for the little divorcée to leave town either. She left with the clothes on her back and a trunk load of personal stuff, leavin' most of the old place completely furnished, which for Mary, anyway, was a dream come true. Having a house with all of the rooms filled, even though most of the things belonged to someone else, for the time being, it all felt like home. Most folks 'round here thought there might be somethin' more to it, because of how fast the divorcée left, but just as well, most everyone said. She wasn't from here anyway, which made it all the easier to watch her go.

After a time, through the rumor mill, it became general knowledge that there'd been a problem with her trust fund, and she'd gone home to a ritzy section of Connecticut, where she stayed with her family. All Kenny and Mary had to do to maintain the lease on the old place was to get a check to her by the first of every month, which they did, thanks to Mary.

It seemed strange that weeks went by and the rumors about Kenny never reached Mary's ears, until Virgil, knowing very well that his shit-bag son-in-law—as he was now called by Virgil— was on the road one frigid, Sunday morning, so Virgil decided to drop in for an uninvited cup of tea with his daughter. Mary was somewhat stunned by the visit, knowing her father kept a decent arms'-length distance from them most of the time. She had good reason to be uncomfortable with her father, yet she was always aware and her senses kept alert whenever he was around her. They made small talk for some time, and as much as Virgil wanted to blurt it all out, he found it difficult to form the words to the first sentence that would break his daughter's heart. They both knew that Lucretia didn't have long to live, but none of the three wanted to talk about it. They smothered themselves in denial, and nothing and no one would change that. Virgil knew this would be just another knife in Mary's heart, but he would not stand by any longer and watch her made the fool, by a fool.

He watched his daughter cross the room toward him from the kitchen with two, steaming cups with dangling tea-bag strings and tabs. Virgil preferred freshly brewed tea, but he had barged in without a call. A tea-bag is what he got.

"I hope this is hot enough for ya'?" Mary asked as she set the cups at opposite sides of the table.

"Oh, I'm sure it'll be," he said.

"I must say, I'm quite surprised to see ya', ya' know...by yourself, poppin' in like this," Mary said while taking her seat across from him.

"I hope it's not a problem. I didn't tell your mama I was comin'..."

Mary interrupted immediately. "Is it mama, is something wrong?"

"No, no, Mary it's not that, your mama's fine this morning; same as she's been for a week now. She's good one day, not that good the next, ya' know," he said.

Mary sat quietly, waiting for what had actually brought him here in the first place, but he kept hedging on whatever the subject might be, and that was as plain as the nose on his face. Finally, after a long silence, while both suffered in discomfort with the whole situation, Mary blurted out, "Fa' Christ's sake, daddy, why don't ya' just come right out and tell me whatever the Christ it is?"

He sat there looking completely distraught, with the same look, Mary noticed, that had covered his face when they received the news about Lucretia and the cancer.

"Well...Mary, it's your husband. Couple o' things you outa' know 'bout him."

Being out on a Sunday in the early morning cold didn't faze Kenny in the least. The money Mary made at the nursing home had reestablished their personal economy, and the extra money first went to the rent, then if there ended up being a surplus for the month, and there was most of the time, they spent it on themselves and the non-essentials for life's easier times. One of those easier-times--expenditures, but equally necessary, was the beat-up but mechanically sound 1957 Chevy pickup Kenny had found in a run-down old barn north of Isles Port. It belonged to an old woman living alone whose husband had died some years earlier, and she just didn't seem to be able to part with it until Kenny charmed the hell out of her and she practically gave it to him.

It wasn't much of a looker at first, but after hookin' a set of jumper cables to it, when he turned the key, it started up and ran like a fine, old watch, and the heater worked. He was in that truck right now, and on the front passenger floor, covering the empty Bud cans, was his duffle-bag, the same one he'd been carrying his life's belongings in when he first arrived in Chesterfield, and still used to transport his secret cargos. Today was no different. Had he known, however, that his father-in-law was now seated in his kitchen, in his favorite chair, at his table about to change his life, probably forever, he would never had been so cheerfully high, knowing that the contents of the duffle-bag would begin a new phase of subsidizing their income. With his newfound free time, thanks to Mary's stability and devotion for her work, he'd been able to reconnect with the dark side of society, the people he'd come to need, and the lifestyle he wanted to dominate.

He never had, however, told Mary about his new idea for making money, an idea kindled by the pirate fellow's words the night of the party. His newest relationship with his landlady friend had reignited the need to explore this fantasy. The basis for the success of the plan lay in his ability to manipulate and deceive, like the evil land barons who had built the empires of Chesterfield's yesteryear. The only thing Kenny had overlooked was the depth of his social roots—the one thing that the land barons of long ago had had were social and family roots as deep as time itself. Kenny was from away, and if time ticked for him, as it did for those like him, the only thing that would work was a bus ticket outta here.

The plan, which had been briefly explained to him that night, was simple if you were of a corrupted mind-set. Kenny had always been quick to learn new procedures.

First, you needed a willing female participant; second, a decent video camera; and last, but not least, a drunk, stoned, and also willing male sucker. Once the guy was drunk and stoned, persuading him to take part in any type of sexual encounter with the woman would be easy, and if for some reason, during a bout of indiscretion, a few pictures were taken to blackmail the male participant, that would provide another way to subsidize one's income. One would have to be completely stupid or desperate to attempt such a venture, but when the equation of money, sex, drugs, and greed enter an egotistic mind, who could calculate the results?

As Kenny made his way toward Chesterfield, it began to snow heavily, and with the spirit of the holidays tucked away in his subconscious mind and duffle bag, he began singing Christmas songs while the old pickup truck fishtailed in the heavy, wet, rapidly deepening snow.

16

"I WANT YOU TO TELL ME THE TRUTH!" she screamed. "Were you screwing that bitch?"

Mary stood across the room from Kenny, and after that question, neither one seemed to be able to find another thing to say for the longest moment. The room filled with a menacing quiet. There was a look of total anger on her face, but it was softened with the overtone of a serious hurt. Invisible to him was the trembling, originating from deep within her, and she stood firm in her place, waiting for a response. Kenny faced her with a stupid look on his face.

"Are you out of your mind?" he asked, and the sweet tone of his question belied his usual character.

Her father's words to her only this morning rang coldly in her thoughts, and her mind's eye saw her little traitor and that tramp together, probably in this very house, and as her stomach turned she wanted to run for the toilet, but she stood her ground.

A sudden feeling of dread came over Kenny, as he studied the stare focused on him, and he sat heavily on the over-stuffed couch that had belonged to and was left by the little lady who owned the house.

He suddenly remembered the words of an old man, many years ago, who lived in a less-than-favorable section of his hometown, where he used to buy drugs as a teen-ager, telling him, "If you're going to be a good liar boy, you'd better have a good memory."

Those words rang louder than ever in his mind now, though once they sounded like the ravings of an old fool.

His mind ran in circles. *"What was more important here—the simple act of having sex with a little rich pig, or the fact that I, through my manipulation of the divorcée, got us into this place and away from Filbert's dictatorship?"* he asked himself.

Right now, however, he felt a slight pang of fear in his stomach, an uncertainty for matters left unfinished. What pissed him off the most was not knowing who had told Mary about the little thing he thought was quietly between himself and someone who was no longer in the picture. However, negatives of photos sometimes have a strange way of becoming developed as time passes.

"Well, are you just going to sit there fluffed-up on that fuckin' couch, or are you going to answer me? Did you sleep with that little bitch?" she asked him again.

"Mary…" he started, and she immediately cut him off.

"No! Don't…Mary' shit me with a bunch of your cold crap! Did you sleep with her, or not?" she demanded.

"No!" he said firmly.

They began staring once again, and then Kenny looked over her shoulder through the window in the corner of the room, watching a snow squall developing out of the north. It chilled him to know that he and his wife might be facing the beginning of a winter in their relationship.

Mary was faced with two possibilities now. First, she knew her father might have fabricated the story, which for him was a method that he'd used many times to create havoc with people he took issue with, and she knew very well the extent to which he took issue with Kenny. It was, however, beyond her to believe that he would go so far as to accuse him of adultery. Second, her father's story wasn't the farthest thing from possible where Kenny was concerned. She knew his ability to charm the ladies and how far he'd taken it on the barrens, with those little drug-queens, who so desperately needed their fix, and the compromises they were willing to make to get it. Kenny had always been there to make sure they complied so he would be paid. Then, too, there were those long nights, she thought, when she couldn't go with him for their long rides, and when he returned, early in the morning, looking worn out, he'd never offered a reason for being out all night, and she'd never asked.

Right now, silence was the best keeper of time, but how long he'd be able to maintain this silent machismo while pitted against Mary's anger remained to be seen.

Kenny sat by himself on the sofa, quietly thinking about the stuff Mary asked.

"And who in the hell knew and told her about this in the first place?" he wondered.

There was no worse time in Virgil Bagley's life that he could remember than watching as his wife, withering away before his eyes, continued smoking and drinking like a woman possessed. He knew there was nothin' he could say or do that would change anything. Now, Mary and her little dirt-bag husband were traveling toward their own hell, and since he'd been the one to tell Mary about the fling, he would now have to hold himself responsible for opening the doors to their inferno.

"I'm one ta' talk," he thought, looking down at his hands, shaking for need of a drink and displaying permanent amber stains between his index and middle fingers from smoking.

This time of the year was no help, being shut in for a solid three months fighting off the boredom of winter, struggling with cabin fever.

Some people found it easier to fall prey to alcohol or drugs of some kind in order to deal with the wicked demons of winter's isolation. The cat was out of the bag, or in it, depending in whose boots you were standing in. Mary was as meek as a lamb, but when provoked, she could turn into a wildcat. That sudden up-and-down temperament is what had attracted Kenny in the first place, and it kept him coming home every night. Kenny was no pushover; he was quick to explode and even quicker with his fists when he needed to be.

Until now, however, he had never hurt her, and for all practical purposes, she hadn't given him any cause to, but things were different now. Mary's job gave her a sense of self-sufficiency. It was her money that paid the rent to that lavish bitch from away, and her money paid for the pickup truck Kenny used as the dope-mobile. Earning a regular salary allows for an entitlement of opinion in most status-quo situations and Mary was getting very used to being a breadwinner.

The evening continued with an eerie quiet, broken only with an occasional slamming of a cabinet door, or a pot or pan tossed aggressively under the kitchen counter, creating a deeper sense of frustration and isolation between the two, as for now, the noise was Mary's only release from the pain that drilled its way to the center of her being.

Kenny felt the urge to leave several times, yet he was convinced that doing so would only jeopardize his ability to convince her of his fidelity. *"Play with matches, get burned. Live by the gun, die by the gun,"* he thought.

Suddenly, his life—their life—was becoming a huge blur, and it pissed him off to think that someone other than he had caused it, again. It was always someone else's fault.

Outside, the wind howled with the intensity of a winter's gale, and it hit Kenny, for no apparent reason other than the fact his thoughts were bouncing around in his head, that they had not yet cut and brought home a Christmas tree to decorate, nor had Mary taken out any decorations. She always had the place lit and feeling like the holidays long before this, the end of the third week in December. True, they had moved the first week, but Mary had everything in its place now, and that cold feeling came over him again as he slumped on the couch and wished it would all go away as the words of an old poem flashed into his memory.

The music's playing in my ear.

I don't want to hear it anymore.

Life was easy once upon a time,

Days are short now and nights are long.

The winter wind blows my soul about.

The fire we once shared is out.

I'll calm myself with a little drink,

While the flame on the candle near the window flickers.

17

The spirit of the holiday season was blanketed in a near-total silence. Five days had passed since their fight. Today was Christmas. When one of them did speak, it was usually Kenny, who began with what he thought was a humorous anecdote to an around-town happening, but his comments were shrugged off by Mary's low-volume utterance that she'd heard it yesterday. This alone began to spark anger from deep inside Kenny, and his substance-induced paranoia kept generating pictures of people feeding Mary with more innuendo, increasing the decaying state of their relationship.

Mary's immediate family was the only family Kenny had, or was willing to speak of, and that bond didn't mean much to him. They both showed up at the old homestead late on Christmas morning, to Virgil's obvious dismay. At the sight of Kenny walking in behind Mary, who was carrying the bulk of the presents, he gave only a jerk of his head in Kenny's direction and then walked into what they called the sewing room, where Lucretia had a portable sewing machine, and stood in front of the TV, where some pre-game sports show was just starting. Kenny was not an avid sports fan, but he was a huge follower of the fight game.

He prided himself on having seen almost every fight that young Cassius Clay, later Muhammad Ali, fought, right up until he moved Down East and Pay-Per View became the norm.

Lucretia was always thrilled to see them both, and she had, because of her deteriorating physical condition, lost track of the going's-on spurred by the rumor-factory from town. Despite her frailty, it was obvious to her that all was not well in the relationship department where Mary and Kenny were concerned. She sat where she always sat, in the same chair at the dining room table, which gave her an unrestricted view of the fields and the river in the distance. It gave her the opportunity to simply daydream if she had the mind to, and she said it took her away from the things she didn't want to think about, like her failing health; yet the ashtray, overflowing with crushed butts, and the half-filled glass of bourbon on the rocks, were like fixtures beside her.

The kids frolicked around the Christmas tree, which was sparse of limb and any deep color of green. It stood less than five feet tall, supported by two pieces of board nailed cross-wise to the base of the trunk. When they awoke, they got to open all of the presents marked from Santa. It was always Santa who brought gifts; yet Tabitha, the older of the two, displayed a squinting eye at the signature appearing on the presents, especially those brought in by Kenny and Mary, which were also marked from Santa.

Mary had pre-cooked a large, stuffed turkey overnight, which needed only a warm oven to finish, and after she shoved it in the oven, the aroma filled the entire house, adding much-needed holiday warmth. Kenny tried several times to break the ice by offering Virgil a cold beer, but Virgil met him with a vacant stare of dismissal. Kenny returned to the warmth of the large kitchen with attached dining room to share the company of his very receptive mother-in-law.

He sat himself in the chair next to her, and he could almost feel her disease emitting itself from her gaunt body while her disheveled hair and unironed housecoat hung lifelessly.

Lucretia, unlike her husband, loved Kenny. She loved him like a son, and dismissed the ranting of those who had no use for him; but lately she found it difficult to overlook the negative sentiments charged by her own husband against him. She had always thought of Kenny as a rebel—which for Down East Maine, he was—and knew how easily he could stir the cauldron of ignorance. She also knew of his deep-set unwillingness to accept change. Her intuition read him like a book, and despite her love for him, she knew what men like him were capable of; after all, she'd been married to one for nearly thirty years now.

Sure, Virgil was more laid-back now-a-days, and his rabble-rousing escapades were over. Now the highlight in his life seemed to be finishing a six-pack of beer in one sitting, then getting up without falling over the chair. He would, however, always be Virgil Bagley. That she was sure would never change.

"Well, dear mother-in-law, how are you doin' on this fine Christmas Day?" Kenny asked, displaying the dumbest grin Lucretia had ever seen, and she was unable to stop herself from bursting out in laughter, which felt somewhat uncomfortable in her mid-section, but felt good at the same time. She reached out for him, while his stupid stare remained focused on her. It had been so long since she'd laughed so heartily, the children came running from the living room and their tree to see what was causing their mother such happiness.

"Kenny, you're so funny! If it gets any better than this, I'm gonna staat' thinkin' that there is somethin' wrong," she said, laughing happily. The children clustered around their mother enjoying the moment and the spirit of the day. Though Virgil made no appearance from the sewing room at the sound of merriment in the dining room, he was simply being himself, and everyone was used to it.

While the children danced and played around the table and the area surrounding the stove, giving Lucretia an almost-new lease on her ill-fated life, Kenny, distracted by movement near the stove, looked away from the kids. Mary was leaning over the open oven door, basting the turkey. He examined her, with his eye for sexual detail, and her profile revealed the firm slender body that had always turned him on—a body she'd denied him access to for almost a month now, since their argument and her questioning him about the little fling. He had never known the level of frustration and desperation he felt now, after not having sex with her for so long. As he'd heard it said from another's words, the thought crossing his mind at that moment was, *"My hormones are standing on their little heads, and it feels as though they're getting ready to give me a bubble bath."*

Mary hadn't failed him, nor had he failed her.

They were simply products of their own world and generation, where sex and drugs were the focal point. As beautiful and sexy as Mary was and no one could compare in his eyes, he just needed more of everything. Those were his warped sense of values.

She felt his eyes on her, and looked in his direction. Their eyes met, and from the look on his face, she knew exactly what he was thinking. She may have shunned him his conjugal rights this past month, but her doubts of him were insurmountable in as much as justified. Outside of what her father had told her, she had nothing else to go on, and no one was willing to give her anything. She also desperately needed to be with him, and she knew deep down that her abstinence could not last forever. She was as addicted to her needs and vices as he, and apparently, always would be.

Without speaking a word to him, her facial expression appeared to send him a telepathic message that made his groin tingle, and suddenly his need for a turkey dinner was the last thing on his mind. Mary announced that the meal was ready, and that if anyone wanted to eat, the dining room table would have to be cleared and set for Christmas dinner. The children came running at Mary's call, and Lucretia, for the first time since they'd arrived, got up from her chair and went toward the sewing room and spoke quietly to Virgil; after several minutes of silence, they came out of the room and joined everyone.

There was a visible coolness between Virgil and Kenny, but they remained civil toward one another.

"Pass the butter, please," Virgil said to Kenny.

"Here you are," Kenny said politely.

It was a huge charade, but Mary was grateful for the kids' sake.

Outside of the large window across from Lucretia's favorite seat for daydreaming, a cold wind blew the powdery snow across the field into drifts along the uneven landscape. Though not everyone in the house agreed on every aspect of their existence, they all agreed that they were happy to be together, in the little house by the river, on this frigid, windy Christmas Day. In her weakened physical condition, Lucretia settled herself at her place at the table, watching delightedly as Mary brought in the fixins' for a huge dinner. Mary gleefully explained, as she placed the turkey in the center of the table, "It's a twenty-five pounda."

Kenny, before leaving home, had prepared some thinly sliced venison from a very lean loin, fried in butter. At the sight of them, Virgil's eyes widened, and a smile became visible.

The bread stuffing had cubed apples, venison sausage, bacon and mushrooms, the tantalizing aroma filling the entire house and stimulating everyone's appetite. The rest of the dinner was more traditional. Mary had baked several pies for dessert, which were set on a small table at windowsill level, tempting the diners with future indulgence.

The meal, the opening of presents, and the remainder of the day went without incident. As with any holiday or typical day off, the time flew by like a rocket to hell, and the time came for Mary and Kenny to say their goodbyes. The kids were hyped up from the sugar in the pies topped with ice cream and the Christmas candies that Kenny had scattered throughout the house, knowing very well the kids would find it.

All day, it had seemed deliberate that each time Kenny and Mary passed they brushed themselves against each other, playing that little tingle-in-the-groin game, which they had lost during the past month of disassociation. However, despite the teasing that had gone on at the old farmhouse, the ride home was in near-total silence. The drone from the pickup's hotrod exhaust appeared to dampen the awakened sexual mood. Neither one wanted to be first to break the ice of a feverishly long dry spell for the both of them.

"Your mother looked the best that she's looked in a long time," Kenny began. "I couldn't believe how much turkey she ate and…oh yeah, it was the best I've had in a long time, too. Thanks," he said.

Compliments from Kenny were a rare occurrence, but for some reason Mary felt he was being sincere. She knew him as not many did; though he kept his cold side for the world at large, she knew his softer, tenderhearted side.

He had decided to fry venison in butter because it was one of Virgil's favorite dishes, and he'd taken the time to slice the meat into thin medallions as a good-faith offering with Christmas dinner. *"If he only knew it was Virgil who told me of his fling with the little tramp, landlady,"* Mary thought.

She was completely unsure now that the encounter had even happened. She'd been unable to uncover any more, in spite of all the digging she'd done since the day she'd confronted him to his face and he'd flatly denied it. That was the norm, if you were from around here. Talking of someone's misfortunes or indiscretions were saved for those tight, little groups of gossip-mongers who acted as though they'd never heard any of it when they came face to face with the subject of their little dish of dirt.

As much as Mary wanted Kenny right now—and she knew the feeling was mutual—she couldn't fight off the need to still be alone. The sanctuary, for her, was their place. She had come to love it there, and it fit her style so well. She loved the country kitchen with its open concept, and the upstairs bedrooms with their privacy. Just the thought of the bedroom fanned her need to be with him, yet she simply did not know how to re-open this door of uncertainty that had closed between her and the only man she'd ever loved.

She felt in her heart that he was jealous of her job in Ellsworth. *"Oh, it would have been different had he been spending that much time away from home; giving no credit to my ability to bring home the bacon,"* she thought. These visions were streaking through her consciousness like lightning over the blueberry barrens during an August thunderstorm when she suddenly realized Kenny was speaking, and the sound of his voice ushered her back into the moment.

"Earth to Mary. Have you landed yet?" he asked.

"Sorry, my mind was on a couple of things at the same time. I'm sure you've been thea' a few times yourself," she said.

"Yeah," he said and left it at that.

"Ya' know Kenny… my father was thrilled with the deer meat. I could tell by the way he relaxed as the day went on." She looked out the truck window into the encroaching dark night. "My mother doesn't look all that well, does she?" Kenny was silent.

The last mile or so to the house went by quickly; neither one spoke after Mary's comment about her mother. As Kenny swung the pickup wide to enter the driveway, the headlight beams fell upon an unfamiliar vehicle parked at the unlit end of the driveway, and Mary's heart sunk heavily at the sight.

"Who's that, Kenny?" she asked anxiously.

"Not sure yet, can't say I've seen that one before." He said this with an almost relaxed tone, giving Mary a feeling of uncertainty. He kept the truck running, with the lights focused on the car, indicating to Mary that he was concerned, and several seconds went by before the driver got out, waving as if he knew them.

"Oh for Christ's sake! I didn't know that asshole had a car like that!" Kenny said.

"You know him?" Mary asked.

"Yeah…yeah I forgot that I told him to stop by tonight. He's cool," he told Mary.

As the driver approached them, Mary noticed his gait was long and purposeful. He was wearing a western-style denim shirt and faded blue jeans, and what caught Mary's eye and seemed most out of place for this cold, winter night, were his orange-brown cowboy boots, which made his legs look even longer. She couldn't believe he was outside without a coat and that he'd left the engine running, as the plume of vapor rose from the exhaust and encapsulated the entire rear portion of his car.

"Well, shit-for-brains, what's goin' on?" Kenny asked, grinning from ear to ear. Mary noticed that "Shit-for-brains" displayed a smile equally broad, but he had his middle finger raised in Kenny's direction. They met about halfway between the parked vehicles, hugging one another as though they'd not seen each other for quite some time. Mary stood by after getting out and following Kenny, expecting an introduction, and when none came and the two boys became boisterously loud, she made a beeline toward the warmth of the house.

As she entered, never giving a thought to the two outside, she suddenly became overwhelmed by the absence of the Christmas spirit that they had so lovingly experienced all day at her parents'. When she'd been living at home with her parents, she'd trimmed the house with the warm glow it always had for the holidays. She generally began decorating the day after Thanksgiving, and left the decorations up until January 2nd each year, filling the beginning of winter with lights to warm the soul, as she would say. Besides, Virgil and Lucretia's youngest child, Bobby, had been born on January 1st, which allowed the holiday celebrations to last just a little bit longer. Tonight however, it simply felt very cold in Mary's warm house.

She could hear Kenny and his friend speaking in the attached barn, where Kenny always entertained the people who came to see only him. Just as well, as far as Mary was concerned. Most of the visitors that did come were not the type she wanted to meet anyway. Her job in Ellsworth and the goings-on that had forced her suspicions about Kenny had changed her feelings for the things she did now. Had this been a year ago, she would have been right out there with them, needing to take part in whatever it was that interested Kenny. Now, his needs and interests were the farthest things from her desires.

True, she couldn't escape the hollow feeling of not being the wife she once had been, and those little things she'd done for him had made her happy. She put water on to make tea, and sat in the rocking chair next to the stove while she waited for the water to boil, listening to the nondescript happenings in the barn just beyond the closed kitchen door.

18

WITH THE HOLIDAYS BEHIND THEM and the envelope of unresolved issues left unopened, Mary and Kenny took one step at a time where their relationship was concerned. They spent a quiet New Year's Eve at home and for the first time in over a month, they made love. Neither realized until then how much they needed this close togetherness; yet for Mary, there was something missing, and a deep sense of emptiness came over her.

She went alone to celebrate her little brother's birthday on January 1st—not that Kenny was a regular children's birthday celebrant, but Mary never offered an invitation. After the little birthday get-together at the farmhouse, Mary came home to an empty house, and she was happy now that she hadn't decorated. The last thing she would have wanted to do today was to take it all down by herself and stow it until next year. She enjoyed her alone time, and never once gave a second thought to where Kenny was, or might be. And for the first time in her short, married life, the feeling of guilt never interceded with her thoughts.

She truly loved her job at the nursing home; even more, she loved the steady paychecks and the financial freedom it gave her. She loved Kenny. However, she could feel the tugging of change that was enlightening her persona, and those around her noticed.

In most cases, change is good, but Mary knew that too swift

of a change would threaten Kenny's way of life, a way of life he expected his wife to be a major part of. She couldn't stop herself from thinking of New Year's Eve and their being together. It was so right. It was the way it was supposed to be.

"Why then, did that little bitch from away have to come between us?" she thought, as the whistle of the kettle played a favorite tune boiling the water for her tea. Even though she could never prove that the encounter between Kenny and the woman had occurred, her intuition was far too strong to ignore. She had learned early to trust her feelings when it came to matters of love and war, and she considered this situation to be both.

During the time between Thanksgiving and the first of the year, Kenny had resumed ties with most of his so-called clientele. He much preferred to deliver his goods, making him all the less conspicuous to anyone who wanted to know more about the elusive Kenny Collins. He had become more self-promoting in every respect, and he even went as far as buying himself a cellular telephone, which for these parts of Maine was considered a step up on the ladder of social status, since not many from around here could afford one. The cell phone placed him, in the eyes of many, on the next higher rung. True, the onslaught of drop-ins at the house kept Mary feeling insecure, never knowing who these people were, and in most cases, never seeing them again. Whether or not they came while she was at work, it made her uncomfortable either way. However, she did thank her lucky stars that none came while she was at home alone.

"Look at that little toilet CEO," Bullet said, while staring out of the storefront window at Filbert's. Kenny, at the wheel of his pickup, sped past, in an obvious direction toward home. "The little bastard was probably out poachin' somethin'. Imagine... on New Year's Day, and out breakin' the goddamned law." Bullet laughed at his own comment. "I'd say that things were a bit quiet where those two aar' concerned, lately." Bullet looked around to see where Filbert had gone. He'd been standing at the counter when Bullet first saw Kenny, but when he turned with his second observation, Filbert was gone.

Just then, the trooper's car pulled up to the single gas pump. He got out and walked directly toward the door. There was something about a Maine Trooper: you didn't see them all that much, but they were always around.

"Well," Bullet said to the trooper as he walked in.

The trooper responded with a dry laugh. "Deep subject for shallow minds."

"Just seen that little dirt-bag fly past hea' and well ova' the posted speed limit, I might add," Bullet said.

The trooper looked at him with a smirk of questioning concern. "What's that, a flyin' dirt-bag?" he asked. He looked past Bullet as Filbert made his way from the storeroom to his usual perch behind the counter.

"Happy New Year, Harry. What brings you out on a holiday?" Filbert asked.

"Ayah', you're the only place open right now. Got any coffee goin'?"

Filbert pointed to the usual pot behind and to the right of the counter, knowing very well that the trooper knew he'd find a fresh pot brewing at Filbert's no matter what time or day it was.

The trooper sipped slowly from the hot paper cup, then looked toward Bullet and asked, "What was that about a dirt-bag flyin'?"

"Well, I thought everybody knew that Kenny Collins was a flyin' dirt-bag," Bullet responded without a moment's hesitation.

"Oh…Kenny Collins. I must say, he's been out of the local picture lately. I'm not sure where he's hangin' out, but I'm not hearin' the usual chatter about him and Mary."

"Lucretia is pretty sick these days, and I know Mary's been spendin' a lot o' time ova' thea' after work." Filbert added that, with a look of sadness on his face.

"Yeah." Harry grunted and shook his head in the negative.

Since he couldn't catch the men up in gossip, Bullet began

mumbling something, inaudible to either man, and left the group, wandering toward the rear of the store. Filbert thought he was probably heading for the beer cooler. The trooper followed Bullet with his eyes, and when he was convinced that Bullet was out of earshot, he turned toward Filbert, raising his eyebrows and head simultaneously, indicating he had something to share with the storekeeper.

Filbert got the message, and began making small talk with Harry, believing Bullet would soon make an exit with a fresh pack of butts and beer. There was no problem between Bullet and the local law, but there was also no love lost between them either. Bullet was an outlaw, and small talk, just short of cut-up, was all he could usually muster for the police, no matter what insignia they displayed on their chests.

Filbert had left the Christmas lights inside the large plate-glass window lit, and the trooper stared at them while sipping his coffee, becoming somewhat entranced with the dull glow against the frosted edges of the glass. Both men remained unmoving in their places beside the counter, and heard the returning footsteps from the rear of the store. Bullet's mumbling continued.

Filbert was right. Bullet carried a six-pack of Bud pounders, and pointed toward the cigarette case as he approached.

"I'll have a couple o' thi'em' Camels to go with these hea' beea's," he said.

Harry Circus couldn't help making just one tiny dig. "I hope you're not goin' to open any o' those beea's while ya' drivin'," he said.

"No sir, mista' troopa'. I don't drink 'n' drive, and you, of all people, should already know that I'm a law-obidin' citizen." And Bullet laughed so brazenly, Harry's ears began to ring slightly; then he left like the whirlwind that he was, and the lights, which had hung so peacefully only a moment earlier, shook in sync with the sound of the transom chime at the slamming of the door.

Both men watched in silence as Bullet's pickup truck slowly climbed the hill, taking him in a northerly direction out of

Chesterfield. As the vehicle vanished over the summit of the road, Harry Circus looked toward Filbert.

"I know darned well the extent that Mr. Carter thea' dislikes Kenny Collins, and there's no way I wanted to add more kindlin' to that fire, if you know what I mean," he said.

Filbert simply nodded his head in agreement. However, what the trooper could not know was that Filbert and Bullet had become somewhat aligned in their thinking where Collins was concerned. Had Harry known this, he never would have shared his information with Filbert.

"You realize, I'm also trying to get something on Collins myself—he's a rare bird—and this was given to me from what I feel is a very reasonable and reliable source. As you and I know, you've been involved with Kenny here at the store for quite some time, and I wondered if you ever heard him talk about making movies?" Filbert felt a pang of ambiguity at the trooper's tone; it was as if he was trying to connect Filbert with some sort of Kenny-type of perversion. "Hey, now…you wait one minute there, Harry, I…" The trooper interrupted.

"No, no, I didn't mean that you had something to do with that…" Harry said.

"Movies, what kind of…movies?" Filbert asked.

Harry stared intently at Filbert as if pondering the proper response. "Smut movies, Filbert. The kind of movies that would make a God-fearin' man sick."

The two men looked directly into each other's eyes without speaking for the longest moment. A thousand thoughts ran through Filbert's mind simultaneously, and he remembered how adamant Heidi was in wanting the two of them as far away from her kids as could be and as soon as possible. He wasn't the God-fearin' man the trooper referred to; though he did believe; he simply didn't worship as often as he might. It wasn't that he hadn't heard the worse about most folks—and some of the stories were pretty bad—but he was getting sick to his stomach over the thought of Kenny producing smutty movies. This was more than just wrong if it were true. Now, in his soul, he knew Bullet's ranting was not all made up, and he knew there truly was a good reason why he hated the man.

"I'll be honest with ya', Harry, this is news to me. I know they were smokin' a little o' that wacky-tobacky, but movies of any kind—this is news to me, Harry. Ya' don't suppose that little Mary..." He stopped suddenly.

Filbert stood silently, wondering where the trooper had gotten the information. He prided himself on always being at the forefront of first-hand news, but this was breaking news to him. Harry rambled on for several minutes, taking small sips from his coffee, looking directly at Filbert occasionally, as if looking for a change in his facial expression that might indicate some knowledge of what he was sharing; but to Harry's dismay, Filbert's face never changed from what appeared to be a sincerely, surprised expression.

Not wanting to appear overly interested with the news, Filbert kept his questions to the bare bones, and for the first time in a long time, did all of the listening. The point of no return came when the trooper mentioned a woman who vaguely resembled Bullet's ex-wife Millie, and he was unable to contain himself any longer.

"Tell me, Harry, where did you say this woman was from?" he asked.

"I didn't. You see, no one I've talked to has been able to say where the movies are being made, or who exactly are in them, and the movies themselves haven't surfaced yet," he said.

"How long has this been going on?" Filbert asked.

"Not sure," Harry replied.

"Did you say that you saw this movie?"

A strange look came over the trooper's face, one that seemed to reveal he'd said too much already, and with every prying question from Filbert, Harry began to withdraw into a no-man's zone of communication, and it became, for Filbert, like pulling teeth with a pair of needle-nose pliers.

The two men were distracted from their thoughts by an obviously overloaded logging truck which rattled the entire building as it passed, resurrecting a scowl on the trooper's face, yet he made no comment. He finished his coffee, moving toward the rear of the counter and the resident trash can, where he made his deposit. It was Filbert's nature to want to continue asking questions of the trooper, but stupid he was not. He would do his own questioning of his own group of very reliable sources, and the one person he couldn't wait to get in touch with was Bullet Carter.

Kenny zoomed up the road toward home, and in his mind, as warped as it had become, he was not thinking of this as New Year's Day, nor did he consider the windfall of cash he carried in his duffle bag from the lucrative deliveries he'd just concluded. No, he was wondering what Mary was up to in Ellsworth. *"She's probably with some little twerp, playing some touchy-games, in a back-office closet,"* he thought. His jealousy of her being away as much as her position needed her to be was reaching a dangerous level. His self-implanted untruths about his wife consumed him, induced by his over-indulgence of substance.

Suddenly, a pronounced questioning stare came over his face as he came to within several hundred feet of his driveway and saw Mary's car where it always was when she was home. He simply did not have a clue as to what day it really was, nor had he spoken with her before leaving early this morning. His thoughts at times, though he never shared them with anyone, especially Mary, were frightening had he shared them with a counselor.

He walked through the kitchen door, and for the first time in over a month, Mary felt that old flutter of love come upon her when she saw him. The feeling surprised her, but she associated it with guilt for what had taken place between them last night. However, Kenny did not feel the same fluttering. The questioning began as soon as he'd hung his leather jacket on the hook by the cook stove.

"What are you doin' home in the middle of the afternoon?" he asked sarcastically.

Her heart fluttered once again, but this time, there was a severe absence of love.

"It's New Year's Day," she answered softly.

She watched with questioning observation as Kenny, without saying a word in response, instead of taking his usual trip to the fridge for a cold beer, took a chilled glass from the freezer section and filled it with ice. He went to the cupboard beside the fridge and pulled a half-gallon of what looked to be vodka or gin and filled the glass. He turned and gestured with the bottle, offering some to Mary, but she shook her head in the negative.

"When did ya' start drinkin' that stuff?" she asked.

"As soon as I felt like it," he answered.

It would have been very easy at that moment for Mary to fire off the starting gun for another huge argument, and cram the rest of the day down the toilet, but she knew how he was when he first got home from wherever he'd been. Whether he'd been working in the woods or on the drug-trips, he always needed his time to unwind, so she let it slide, as any good wife would do, and she waited a few minutes for the booze to touch bottom. It eventually did, and Kenny began ranting about seeing Bullet's pickup parked at Filbert's store.

Mary was fearful of the negative sentiment building against her husband. Even if she told him about it, he would likely have shrugged it off as being bullshit stirred by the morons of the town who had nothin' better to do with their time.

She noticed that the more he drank and rambled on, the more red his face became—something she'd never noticed when he drank beer.

It had been a solid month now since Mary had used any type of drug, with or without Kenny. It was a milestone as far as she was concerned, but there was a part of her that cradled the addiction, and watching him indulge, her month-long abstinence came to an abrupt end.

The inquisitive little girl had returned, even if she convinced herself to be more conservative and aware of how fast it can all creep up on you and you become a victim, but drugs and alcohol had the power to sheen everything over with a rosy glow until the fire raged out of control. It was early in the day when they reunited themselves in substance, and as the afternoon ticked away, it was as if nothing had come between them, physically, or emotionally. He threw more wood on the fire. She closed the curtains, and neither one ventured out again that day.

From his nearly twenty-year experience as a Maine State Trooper, it was obvious to Harry that Kenny Collins was rapidly forging the chains of his own destiny, although no one who knew of Kenny's subversive behavior could provide an eyewitness account of a buy or sell.

"The law must sustain a level of monumental patience to apprehend an offender." Those words, drilled into the mind of a young Harry Circus by his father, a well-known and renowned Maine State Trooper, gave him the patience to see Kenny Collins brought to justice. Harry always said that he never allowed his personal agenda to intermingle with his authority, despite the difficulty he faced in the small community to decipher rumor from fact, and he tried to keep that sense of integrity about his work. He would have to go with his gut on this one.

Nevertheless, there were two men at this moment that had rapidly entwined themselves with their own belief that the law and its patience did not apply to them.

Bullington Carter, the more radical of the two, would have stirred the cauldron of lies more easily than his counterpart Filbert Cirone, who maintained a sense of level-headedness. Both men now loathed all that Kenny was, but each man's agenda was based on different past experience. Bullet's view was far more of a personal nature, trumped by his natural dislike for Kenny. Filbert's, on the other hand, was a true disappointment in a person he'd so loyally trusted and helped. His fears, like those of his beloved wife Heidi, were real. Their need to do the right thing where their children were concerned was sincere. And, there was another person, watching from the sidelines, who was building a head of steam and a fervent dislike—to the point of hatred—for good, old, Kenny Collins.

Virgil Bagley was a man of few words, and he would honor his wife's wishes as a token of his love, due to the enormous suffering her illness caused her. He would not antagonize either of them in a public forum, but he would not change his feelings for the man that had taken his little girl from his home. He would never allow himself to forgive Kenny, or, for that matter in a lesser way, Mary, for abandoning her family in their time of profound need. He was just another name added to the list of those who would be far better off without the likes of Kenny Collins in their lives.

19

WINTER HELD ITS SELFISH GRIP on Maine for the duration that year. The pantries of even those frugal enough to conserve were becoming meager of provisions, yet for the most part it was a winter void of unfortunate loss of life. Usually, winter and the isolation encountered by those who couldn't flee and follow the migration south can sometimes bring a frigid death, for man and beast alike. Survival of the fittest is not reserved for the wild creatures of the forest. Man sometimes falls prey to the confinement that only winter can impose. Starvation however, was not necessary. When it came right to it, someone would help. That's when they usually came to Filbert.

The weather wasn't too bad generally through the first half of January; then it was as if the entire world had frozen over, Mother Nature allowing a mere smidgen of life to survive. In the correct arena, when necessary, food stamps could and would be used to get the non-essentials for survival.

Cigarettes, beer, wine, and sometimes even products to assist with birth control could be obtained with stamps, and for the most part, no one really gave a shit as long as the merchant received his or her cash redemption. Who could fault such a tried and true way of life? Oh sure, if you got caught, you'd probably get spanked real well, but when it came to the actual lynching, they needed to simply look at the needy one, and things were dismissed with a moderate plan for re-payment. After all, it would cost more to send 'em upriver, than it would to keep 'em on food stamps.

Filbert however, was one of the good ones. He listened to all of the sad-sack stories, and in most cases, the individual or couple doin' the cryin' came away with at least a decent-sized box of groceries, and if there were kids, there'd be a nice bag of mixed candies stuffed in there somewhere. He used to jot things down on a store receipt, giving them the carbon copy and telling them if they could pay it by the next blueberry season (when most debt could easily be paid) it would be good, but seven out of ten never paid him back, and he never went after anyone for it. Most of the time, it seemed as though he threw the slips away as the winter got worse, and he'd fill another box for the same people, going over the same spiel again and again, never getting a dime. There was one merchant though who took only cash for his goods. Kenny Collins. It was true; with a small group he'd exchanged drugs for wood, or for the labor to work on his old pickup truck, a vehicle that required a regular mechanic to maintain its finicky disposition. Other than that, it was cash on the barrelhead.

He had begun during the holiday season that year, keeping the company of a younger crowd. He was seen regularly behind the Quick-Stop in the early evening hours, sitting in his pickup, usually surrounded at both doors by high-school-aged people. Occasionally he was seen driving around town, or between towns, with local teenagers in the vehicle, and there was always an unfamiliar car or truck in his driveway, keeping the mystique of his association with strangers alive. But he was never seen giving or taking anything from anyone. It was one thing to take money from adults to contribute to their depravity; it was another to take money from young adults for the purpose of corrupting their impressionable minds.

No one would argue the fact that those young adults were far more mature than they would have many older people believe. Some people believed in the old adage, "Live and let live;" and then there were those who believed because it was illegal it should be enough to instill the fear of God in anyone trying to ruin the sanctuary that was the human body and soul.

After the conversation between the trooper and Filbert on New Year's Day, Filbert revised his relationship with Bullet, and their conversations led him to further mistrust Kenny. The limits of their inquiring seemed endless, and their energy was boundless.

All they ever ended up with in their search were dead-ends, same as the trooper, but at times, persistence pays off. The last person Bullet wanted to share information with was the state trooper, or his counterpart constable, Ralph Bailey. Bullet held grudges. Many years before Harry became a trooper, Ralph was the constable under the jurisdiction of Harry's father, who was then the resident trooper. Bullet had been handcuffed by Ralph Bailey after an incident involving an Indian transient from Canada, who came Down East to rake blueberries. The Indian had found himself in a knockdown, drag-out fistfight with Bullet over some still-unresolved issue, and the incident had ended with both men being arrested. Bullet never forgave Ralph Bailey for… "taking the side of some drunk, fucked-up Injun' against me, a local resident," as Bullet had put it.

Ralph had tried many times to alleviate the bad feelings between them, but Bullet would have none of it. To this day, he still stared with a frown whenever the two of them came within close proximity to one another. As strange as it might seem, every time they did see each other, no matter what the situation, Bullet actually visualized the entire episode as it unfolded, right up to the handcuffing all those years ago.

Filbert and Bullet began to develop a panoramic picture of the unadulterated Kenny Collins—a picture they most wanted to share with Mary's father Virgil, knowing very well that as an ally he would become energetically aggressive in digging a more suitable grave when it came to the truth about his less-than-favorite son-in-law. In all of their digging to date, nothing had been uncovered about any movies, leaving them puzzled as to where the trooper had gotten his information.

In addition, the subject matter that piqued Filbert's curiosity about the woman who resembled Bullet's ex-wife Millie had never come to fruition.

Only one time did Mary see a youngster riding along with Kenny, along the Black Bear Road, when she was coming home from work one day in the late afternoon. She wasn't one for recognizing someone's vehicle on the road, but Kenny's truck stood out in a parking lot, you might say. She waved as the truck approached from the opposite direction, heading toward Ellsworth, but it was as if she and her highly recognizable car were invisible. The pickup blew by at a high rate of speed, and Kenny was obviously engrossed in conversation with the young man, whom she did not know. Kenny's head faced away, and he never saw her pass.

"Wow! Whatever he's smokin', I hope he brings some of it home with him tonight," she whispered to herself.

Word was spreading rapidly that Kenny had resumed his dealings, and once Mary had gotten wind of the movie thing, she tried to dismiss it as the extent to which folks go when they allow their jealousy to cloud their thinking, but there was doubt in her mind, since she'd never been able to prove or discount his fling with the little divorcée who owned the house they lived in.

She had sent along a letter with one of her monthly rent checks, coming right out and telling the woman she would like to meet her in person the next time she was Down East, to discuss the rumors about her and Mary's husband. The woman's reply came about a week later, handwritten on an index card with the rent receipt, that it wouldn't be necessary, as she had no idea what Mary was talking about, infuriating Mary further, and giving her no more information than she had already.

The dulling effects of the drugs did not allow Mary to dwell any more deeply on Kenny's superficial behavior, but she couldn't deny his mood-swings and the anger with which he lashed out at her for no apparent reason, at any time, without warning. Most of the time, it was his unfounded accusations of her infidelity with some mystery man that neither of them knew, generally while she was at work and out of his immediate control. There were times now that life together was unbearable, and she was becoming fearful of him. To this day, he had not hit her, but lately she feared that a beating might be imminent. His anger was monstrous, and like Kenny, completely out of control.

The only time they seemed to melt into an oblivious state was usually after their evening meal and the ritual that had now became their life: getting high.

It was during one of those "getting high times" when the phone rang. They had an old rotary phone, which was the norm Down East, where you couldn't limit the number of rings before an answering machine and message could tell the caller to call back at a more convenient time. Normally, the phone would have rung several times; the calling party would have become bored and hung up and tried later, thinking there was no one at home. The ringing however, became incessantly distracting from their relaxation time. Mary could see the aggressive change in Kenny's demeanor, and fearing an outburst that would probably last the rest of the evening; she leaped from her place on the couch, running toward the phone, which was on a small shelf between the dining and living rooms.

Nothing could have prepared her for the subdued, depressed-sounding voice on the other end. It was Virgil. His voice broke with the first syllable.

"Mary. You have to come home right now. I can't wake your mother up," he said.

With the sudden click of the receiver on his end, he was gone. Mary dropped the receiver to the floor, the sound arousing Kenny's curiosity with a howl of disapproval.

"What in hell?" he asked, in a loud voice.

She was crying hysterically by the time he blurted out the question, and was running toward the door before he could get up from the couch.

"There's something wrong with mama. I have to get home,"

she cried as she jerked the door open.

"Wait, I'll go with you," he hollered.

It was such a surprise that Kenny ran out behind her in his stocking feet, and was halfway through the barn before realizing it, so he turned back toward the kitchen for his boots, struggling over the hard-packed snow on the driveway. Mary had run out without a coat, and Kenny brought it with him and met her in the pickup, which he'd parked just outside the barn door. The keys were always in their vehicles, and by the time Kenny jumped into the driver's seat, Mary had the motor running. Kenny mashed the gas pedal down, forcing the truck into a frantic fishtailing on the snow-packed driveway and out onto the heavily sanded blacktop of the roadway. He could feel the heat of Mary's anxiety next to him, and he dared not speak a word to break her anxious silence.

A snow shower developed as they drove, leaving a fresh blanket of white on everything. Kenny's pickup was heavily weighted with cinder blocks in the bed, and the truck rolled on over-sized, studded snow tires, giving the vehicle an aggressive traction and allowing the driver the sensation of riding on their own set of tracks. At this early hour of the evening, most folks were still enjoying their supper and watching the evening news, leaving the roads vacant of traffic.

The dim lights shining from the houses they passed gave Mary a warming sensation, but did little to ease her concern for her mother and what she would find when they arrived shortly at her parent's home. It's amazing how a person's mind can take them back in time, without any obstacles to prevent the good or the bad from coming to the surface of the memory. At this moment, Mary's mind was doing just that. Suddenly, a feeling of loneliness encapsulated her, like a winter's coldness. She found herself, through her mind's eye, in that dark, dingy bedroom in their run-down little house in Aroostook County. She remembered shivering, not from the cold, but from a fear that a child could not put into words, betrayed by those who should have protected her fragile childhood: an innocent soul sent to a hell on earth, never being able to reason why, and forced to live in denial of the truth to protect the core of her young psyche.

Mary closed her eyes and trembled, envisioning the sexual abuse and ensuing pain inflicted upon her by her own father, so drunk from alcohol, his face distorted, almost unrecognizable, while her mother, another supposed defender of innocence, had long since passed out from her own overindulgence.

The sound of her father's voice on the telephone, dry and cold—just the way Virgil was–and the way he'd told her about not being able to wake Lucretia, had triggered her memory to carry her back to that first frightening night. Now she would have to face him after going back there by herself, if only in her mind.

She wanted to tell Kenny everything, but it couldn't happen now. All she could picture was Kenny going off on Virgil, while Mary went to her mother's bedside, not knowing what she would find. Her mind was so messed up at this point. She opened her eyes and watched the silhouettes of trees passing quickly in the dimming early evening light. Kenny noticed that she was again in the moment, and could not hold his silence any longer.

"Hey! Are you all right, or what?" he asked.

"No, I'm not. I can't help worrying about what we're going to find when we get there. My father's such a crusty-ass. I wonder just how long he waited to call me." She withdrew again.

Kenny was obviously puzzled at her comment about her father. He never heard her say anything derogatory about him before, but being Kenny, it tickled him to hear her say something like that about Virgil, as there was no love lost between the two men. They were less than a mile from the house when Mary's hands began to tremble again, so much so that Kenny noticed from the corner of one eye, and he looked in her direction with concern.

Mary was off once again to places only her mind could know, and they were there. Kenny slowed the vehicle before entering the partially hidden driveway. It was ice-rutted from lack of plowing, and Mary opened her eyes, as her worry grew. Kenny pulled to within several feet of the side entrance, and when they got out of the truck, the heavy, rancid smell of creosote from the chimney overwhelmed them. Already feeling light-headed from her mental excursion to the past, Mary felt her stomach heave from the smell of burning green wood.

Kenny looked up toward the top of the chimney. "What in hell?" he said. "He must have the damper on that stove closed up tight and just leavin' it a-smolderin'. Christ, what a stink."

They both walked toward the door, and Mary's thoughts went to her mother, with no further thoughts of her nightmarish past. When they entered through the door that opened into the kitchen, the house was cold and dark, with a faint light coming from the tiny room where the TV was.

The first thing Mary noticed was that the kids didn't come running toward her, as they normally would have at this time of the early evening. This should have been right around their suppertime. Kenny went directly to the stove, while Mary moved toward the TV room, hoping her father was there. The volume was set so low it was nearly inaudible, and the two kids were huddled together on the small couch wrapped in a quilt. Virgil sat in his usual perch, the overstuffed brown chair, in a t-shirt, steadying a can of beer on the armrest.

"Well, this looks cozy if it wasn't so damned cold in here," she said.

The two kids looked up, smiled at her, and as kids of any age will do when hypnotized by their favorite show, returned their stare toward the set, while Virgil simply grunted, never taking his eyes from the tube. Mary stared at him for the longest moment, feeling repulsed at seeing him sitting in this cold house in only a t-shirt.

"Where's mama?" she asked coldly.

Never moving his eyes from their position, he simply gestured by lifting the can slightly.

"She's in her room." Mary's heart pounded heavily in her chest, and she turned quickly, leaving the room and meeting Kenny just outside of the door.

"What's up?" he asked.

"Come with me, Kenny, Mama's in her room."

Seeing the concern on her face, he remained silent, following her down the long, narrow hallway leading to the staircase and the upstairs. It seemed colder at this end of the house, and she asked Kenny if he'd flashed the stove.

"I loaded it and it…is… cookin', babe. It'll be warm in here soon."

With much reservation, she climbed the steep stairs with Kenny directly behind her, remembering the days when she'd lived in the house, and her room at the far end of the upstairs hall. There were doors on each side of the hallway, typical of old New England farmhouses. Theoretically, the long, narrow hallways and small rooms made it easier to heat during winter, but in actuality, it did nothing to allow for any flow of warm air that might have risen from the first floor and the rooms with the wood stoves.

Lucretia and Virgil's room was the last room on the right, and the room directly above the open-concept kitchen and dining rooms downstairs. This room offered the same view of the fields and the river that Lucretia loved. When they arrived at the corner room, Mary stopped at the threshold, peered into the semi-darkened room, and saw that her mother was covered to her chin with heavy blankets. It was a relief to her, knowing how cold the rest of the house was, that her mother was at least warm in her bed. She entered the room as quietly as possible; Kenny remained at the doorway, not wanting to make Lucretia uncomfortable, if they awakened her, to see Kenny in her room. Mary walked to the foot of the bed, focusing her vision for the lack of light, but nothing could have prepared her for the sight of the discolored, drawn skin of her mother's lifeless face, her head facing the window and the view she always said she needed most.

20

THERE WAS NO PUBLIC VIEWING or church service for Lucretia. She had specifically not wanted them, and though few words passed between Mary and her father, they were able to agree on those two things.

The funeral was three days after Mary and Kenny had found her. Mary spoke little of it to the children, who appeared stunned for most of the three days; yet being kids, they amused themselves with triviality, allowing their immature minds to move forward. There was a gathering of family and friends at the Bagley plot in a small, ancient cemetery at the southern edge of Chesterfield less than a hundred yards from the Isles Port town line, in the deepest of forest that remained uncut, especially at the far corner where Lucretia was laid to rest. It was a quiet, solemn place to remain for eternity.

Mary did not cry at the cemetery, but not because her heart wasn't broken from her loss. She was going to miss her mother and their little visits together at the farmhouse, and she was happy that her mother's suffering was over, but the thought of the two young ones left home with Virgil gave rise to a sick fluttering in the pit of her stomach. A thousand thoughts flashed through her consciousness while she half-listened to the preacher, comprehending little of what he said. Her eyes moved from the plain, pine wood casket with a single rose on the top to the gently swaying treetops.

The weather, unseasonably mild for this time of the year, would normally have delayed the internment until spring due to the frozen ground, but Virgil's cousin, Forest Bagley, had a backhoe, and had offered his service so the funeral could take place without everyone having to suffer through the sorrow of Lucretia's death again in warmer weather. Everyone was happy for that gift from heaven, not only for them, but also for Lucretia.

The heaviest of Mary's sorrow came over her as the preacher was about to conclude his eulogy. Her eyes fell upon the two kids, each holding one of their father's hands, yet they both looked at Mary. At that moment, it became impossible to hold back her tears any longer, and for the first time in quite a spell, Kenny held her close to him and gave her comfort. They all stood silently, watching the casket lowered into its final resting place.

Several peered into the grave, and tossed more flowers, yet the only sound was the wind through the trees.

Then the small group of mourners began to leave, some holding hands, some walking aimlessly through the old cemetery looking and sometimes pointing to the almost illegible words on the cold, dark stones. Suddenly, a heavy massing of dark clouds began to smother the light of the fading sun, while a chill fell over the area as winter again re-settled itself.

It wasn't until Kenny and Mary turned to join Virgil and the kids that they came face to face with Heidi and Filbert, standing close together at the rear of the gathered mourners. It was obvious to Mary that Heidi had cried heavily during the ceremony, as both her eyes were very red. Upon seeing them, Kenny let loose of Mary's arm, turning abruptly away from the two, and leaving Mary to approach alone and thank them for coming, which she did.

They were so cordial toward her; it was as if no hard feelings had passed between them, and Heidi held Mary with a tenderness that only a woman could bestow upon another at a time of such loss. Filbert looked on quietly as the two women chatted softly, and when the time seemed right to leave, they kissed each other on the cheek, and Mary walked away. She was less than five- feet away from them when she felt a huge lump form in her throat, and the tears she had been saving flowed freely. This time she was alone with her heartfelt sorrow until the tug on her coat sleeve forced her to turn her head in that direction. It was the older of the two kids, Tabitha, looking up at her.

Mary wiped her cheeks abruptly, trying to hide her tears from the child, yet the tears were far too heavy to hide, and she crouched down and took the young girl into her arms, as if she would never let her go. Tabitha was ten years old now, and already beautiful. Her natural curly blonde hair flowed over her shoulders, covering her upper body, while her tall, lanky frame resembled that of a child model. Bobby Bagley, their younger brother, was still holding on to his father's hand, several feet from the grave. It was Tabitha, however, that Mary most concerned herself about, more so than Bobby, simply because she felt Tabitha could be in danger, living at home with Virgil. The nightmare of her own childhood—so vividly revisited only a couple of days ago— replayed itself now, as she held her sister, so much younger than herself, and without a mother.

Her mind raced as her eyes darted from Virgil, to the grave and back, and she knew then that somehow these two children would have to be with her.

Mary took the three-day bereavement leave with pay, a benefit generously offered by her employer and a time she needed to adjust herself to life without her mother. She was grateful that she'd spent a good deal of time with her mother during the last several months, even though she'd been filled with desperation about her mother's physical deterioration.

Despite Mary's low spirits, having her home during the past several days, was like being on vacation for Kenny. For him anyway, once the funeral was over, it was time to take care of business, and he did just that. He left Mary to herself for most of the day, and because she was at home and not in Ellsworth, he found no need to badger her with questions or unfounded innuendo. Right now, however, what Kenny might be thinking never entered her mind. The situation with Tabitha and Bobby absorbed her entire attention as she thought about how she could find a way to have them live with her. Two obstacles stood in her way: Virgil and Kenny.

As it was, the final day of her leave came on the Friday after the funeral, giving her two extra weekend days to collect her thoughts and spend some time with the kids, who were spending the last of Mary's time off with her and Kenny at their place. It made Mary feel whole once again to have them with her. She saw so much of her mother in Tabitha, and ironically, so little of her father in Bobby.

Mary used her place as home base during the three days following the funeral, cooking meals for the five of them, and on occasion, when family members from the County on her mother's side or from Isles Port on her father's came by, she made sure there was enough for all. She was surprised at how well Kenny maintained his cool disposition throughout, but his patience with her father was being shaven to a thin layer.

She realized that her need to have the kids with her would involve some type of legal issues that would undoubtedly create quite a stir with both men, and though she could not know at this time how much or how little trouble it would be, she knew it was for the children's best interests. She could not visualize any kind of a life for them at that old farmhouse with their father, who could never remember to come in for dinner most of the time, never mind provide a safe and secure environment in which to grow up.

She wondered how her job might affect all of this with both kids in school all day. She would work it out. She would wait for the right time and place, and go to work on both of the men-folk, and she would make them see it her way. This was something that would go her way. This was for the kids.

During the days following the funeral, life resumed, though not at the normal pace everyone was accustomed to. But for Kenny, the memory of Mary's name-calling comment about her father and his "crusty ass" still produced a chuckle, and the time was rapidly approaching when questioning her to spill her thoughts of why she said it would be at hand. He was well aware that as the weekend faded to a memory, so would having Mary at home like the old days of their relationship to cook and clean like any good wife, instead of tramping off to a job in Ellsworth.

Despite the gravy train her income produced for them, he still resented it because it took her away from him. Sunday evening, Mary had the two kids tucked away in their temporary bedrooms. She had borrowed a couple of cots from a friend, making the short stay with them as comfortable as possible. The house was quiet; Mary had refrained from using any substance for about a week at this point. Kenny walked in through the kitchen after burning a joint, so as not to allow the kids to smell the rancid aroma, at Mary's request.

She recognized his broad smile and squinting eyes as a successful completion of his self-assigned task. There were several scented candles burning in the living room, the light was dim, as they liked it, especially after smoking, and for them it was a great way to relax.

Kenny sat on the couch next to her, and they simultaneously exhaled a sigh of relief after the arduous week.

"How you holdin' up, baby?" Kenny asked.

"I'm ok. I'm just glad that it's over," she said.

"I know what you mean, babe. It still feels a bit queer that your mom ain't at home like she's supposed to be. She wasn't my mom, but I'm gonna' miss the hell out of her."

Mary expelled a deep breath, and rested her head on the back of the couch, closing her eyes to enjoy what was left of the rapidly moving evening.

"I wish you didn't have to go to work tomorrow. I love it when you're home." He said this at just above a whisper, but Mary read each syllable for what he actually meant it to be. He just wanted her here, at home.

She offered no comment and remained still; hoping he would simply sit back and enjoy his buzz, but knowing Kenny, that probably wasn't going to happen. It didn't take long. Kenny was thinking of a humorous way to bring up the "crusty-ass" comment, but didn't want to press her about it. He knew there had to be more to it than just a stupid comment. Mary had a correct way of saying things, and flat-out cutting someone up with a backbiting slang phrase was not her style. He, on the other hand liked the term and in the future, it would be a well-established cut-up in his vocabulary.

He thought about it for a moment, and then he broke the still of the evening with an emphatic burst of laughter.

Without opening her eyes, Mary asked, "What?"

"Mary, I've got to know—why did you call your father a 'crusty-ass' the other night?"

He asked her this with a hint of honest inquiry, yet he could not mask the sarcasm that glimmered from the question.

The last thing Mary needed now was to take that cold, debilitating journey into nostalgia she prayed had somehow dissolved itself and faded in the recesses of her mind. However, here it was again, right in her face and splattered there, in living color by her husband.

"Why are you bringing that up, and when did I say that?" she asked, trying to hedge the subject, and honestly, at this moment, she could not remember the exact context in which she had used the term, or when.

He giggled, with an immature, almost childlike sound—he acted quite silly at times when he was high—and Mary, though she made no comment about it, was annoyed by his foolishness and hoped he would let it go, but he persisted.

"Well, the night we were on our way to your mom's and Virgil's after he called you. Your mind had obviously lifted off to places unknown to me anyway, and you called him that just before we got there. Something about him not calling, or waiting too long to call, I'm not sure myself now, Mary, but you did call him a 'crusty-ass,'" he said as he began his insane laughter again. She opened her eyes, looking at the ceiling and the bouncing shadows created by the flickering candles, and wished she had a place of her own to go to, a little hideaway just for her where no one could find her. She turned her conscious mind at that moment to the question of why and when she'd called her father that name. She was being ushered back into her memory—to that cold, frightening night as a child in the County, and she became angry, because she knew that nightmare was re-awakened from a long, deep sleep. What worried her the most was that eventually, Kenny's persistence from his obvious need to deposit the new word in his slang-folder (for the purpose of enlightening the less brilliant of his associates) would never disappear until Mary told him why. Doing so would open that proverbial "can of worms," and would most likely be bigger than both of them.

"So, ya' say he just turned like a scared rabbit and left Mary standin' alone when he saw the both of ya'?" Bullet asked. The two men stood across from each other at the counter the next morning.

"Ayah," Filbert said. "Like he never knew who we were. Guess he holds a grudge, but for the life o' me, I never had the notion he was that type o' baby when he worked for me."

"I told ya' a long time befoa' this, he ain't nothin' but a little shit-pot," Bullet added.

"Ayah." That was all that Filbert had to add, and both men stood shaking their heads in the negative, simply for a lack of something else to say. At that point, Heidi, who was in an aisle rotating canned goods, moved slightly toward the center and interjected her thoughts.

"I feel so sorry for little Mary. You know very well that she is going to get the brunt of the responsibility where those two kids are concerned. It won't be Virgil, or that magpie, Kenny, who are going to take a' good care o' them," she said.

Both men grunted slightly at the same moment, but she didn't hear them. Thinking them both deaf, or simply ignoring her, Heidi shrugged her shoulders and went back up the same aisle, resuming her chore. She spoke aloud, several times, but neither man attempted to answer, though some of the things she said forced them to look in each other's direction and raise their eyebrows, a gesture indicating their agreement to what she said. Still, they didn't reply. When they realized she did not intend to end her little barrage about Kenny and Mary, Bullet made his usual saunter toward the beer cooler, and Filbert realized that Bullet was about to set himself free, leaving Filbert to deal with Heidi, alone.

The death of any person generally brings out the best and worst in those who remain, whether related to the deceased or not. The fact that Bullet was a distant relative on Virgil's side, though he never made it to the funeral, he took full advantage of anything he could dig up against Kenny, and would offer it to anyone who would listen. Lucretia's death had nothing to do with Kenny, but just the fact that he was married to her daughter was more than enough for Bullet to feed the gossip-fire of a solid, winter shut-in time. By now, most everyone around town knew everything that went around about Kenny and Mary, but since Mary had become a working girl, most of the crap had fallen on Kenny's shoulders, and for the most part, the rumors weren't just rumors.

21

MARY'S HEART FILLED WITH ANGUISH after getting the kids off to school on Monday morning and then going on her way back to Ellsworth and work. She knew that today, the kids would have to go home to Virgil after school, and the thought of him forgetting their schedule gave her anxiety attacks during the drive and while she was at work. She spoke to several individuals there who had knowledge about obtaining guardianship over family members, and with a good lawyer, it didn't seem that difficult to do. Convincing the two adult males of concern in this matter would be the bulk of the problem.

First things first, as anyone might agree, and number one on the list would have to be Kenny. He was not a lover of children. Many times she'd heard him say in reference to kids with friends of theirs, "Glad they're not mine," and laughing coldly at the parents for having them. But she would never be able to live with herself if she didn't at least try. The thought of anything happening to them because of Virgil was more than she could bear. She had to prepare herself for battle. Though she hoped it wouldn't turn into a fight, she had to be ready for whatever came her way. Kenny, on the other hand, didn't appear to have a care in the world, except when he thought of Mary working in Ellsworth.

It was still a touchy subject for him, because he thought of himself as a macho-man. And there was one other thing he couldn't loosen from his craw: Mary's obvious avoidance of speaking about the "crusty-ass" comment. Kenny was convinced there was more to it than just a release from a moment of frustration on Mary's part. Tonight, he thought, would be a good time to explore the possibilities, as long as it didn't interfere with the important things he had on his agenda.

There was a huge shipment of grass on its way to him, via fish truck from Boston. He would meet the driver, a very close friend and associate, alongside of the Chesterfield airstrip, which had long been abandoned except for small, private planes. If everything went according to plan, Kenny would turn a very nice profit by the end of the week. To camouflage the cargo, he'd told the driver to pick up several sacks of stinky strip-fish for him, usually dried cod fillets, mixing the bagged weed in amongst the fish.

The cargo from Boston would fit in between the four-foot long bundles of firewood he'd loaded in his pickup before leaving to meet the truck. He would deliver it, along with the weed. The strip-fish was an easy sell along Main Street in Isles Port to any old codger who was on his way home with a fresh bottle or six-pack, to enjoy as a snack. Kenny hated the smell of the fish, and hated the taste even more, yet it did so much to hide the skunkie aroma of the fresh pot.

Kenny's cell phone rang. He got so many calls that it was as if his cell phone was surgically attached to his ear, leaving little time to finish a chore before being interrupted. He loved the attention and never missed a call. "Money talks and shit walks," he loved to say to whoever was close when his phone rang, and he never minded breaking away from someone, no matter what the situation, to answer his phone.

With this particular call, he knew that the entire shipment, due to arrive shortly, was already spoken for, and he would have to place his order for next week's fish run from Boston.

The driver had made several offers for Kenny to make the trip to "Bean-Town";' but he never wanted to know who supplied the stuff or where it came from. No contact, no connection. The truck driver was good enough for him, and he paid him well to do the run while keeping his mouth shut. It was almost time for a call from the driver, barring any unforeseen problems on the road. When the truck was twenty to twenty-five miles out, the driver would call Kenny, simply for a time check, never discussing anything over the phone, and Kenny would leave for the airstrip, hang out and wait.

Right now, he thought, it was about time to make a little location check on Mary.

His suspicions about her were unfounded, yet no one, not even Mary, could convince him that she was true-blue and faithful. He called her several times each day, always at her desk phone, and if for some reason she didn't answer, he would immediately call the main desk, not waiting for a transfer there, and ask some stupid thing like, "Did Mary report for work today? I've tried calling her desk phone and she's not answering."

After a couple of repeats of this, the receptionist got wise to him and told Mary. She simply shook her head, and for her, it was totally believable. When the phone rang this time, Mary looked up at the clock on the wall at the far corner of the small office. Thinking it was Kenny calling at his usual time, she wanted to answer with, "Hi, Kenny," just for spite, but she was more of a professional than that. She let it ring to the point just before the call would automatically kick over to the reception desk, and then she picked it up, answering as she would normally for any other incoming call to her phone.

"Well, I was getting ready to call the main desk, Mary. I figured you must be in the coffee lounge at this time of the mornin," Kenny's voice said over the phone.

She could visualize the smirk on his face from the tone of his voice, and wanted to say something sarcastic, but to what end of accomplishment could that reach? Being nice, she thought, would feel like salting the wounds, yet it did nothing to make her feel better about her feelings, for so many things that frustrated the hell out of her. She knew that striking up a conversation with him about her job responsibilities would turn the table of frustration, and he wouldn't stay on the phone very long—and she was right. About two sentences into a phony client report that she said was consuming her when the phone rang, and sharing absolutely no personal information about anyone, his silence alone confirmed to her that he might have already heard enough and was ready to move on with his own chores of the day, but not before giving the knife just one little twist.

"Well, Mary, it sounds like you're pretty busy, so I won't keep you. I'll just move my 'crusty ass' and see you when you get home from the grind. B-bye," he said, and was gone.

Not wanting to display any outward sign of anger, she placed the receiver down gently, but could not refrain from releasing a long sigh of exasperation.

She became overwhelmed, knowing that he would not give up until she revealed to him the feeling that had overtaken her that night when she called her father that derogatory phrase. Oh, how she wished she'd controlled herself, if only for a few more minutes until the feeling left her. Telling him, she feared, would ruin them.

Kenny would never be able to swallow the truth about her father and his ultimate, parental abomination. She seemed frozen to the spot for several minutes, unable to pick up where she'd left off, until she was jolted from her thoughts by the sound of a co-worker's voice inviting her to come along for coffee.

Kenny's timing was right on. As he pulled onto the airstrip's access road, he saw the fish truck approaching in the distance. The airstrip had been built during one of the World Wars. Most young people from around here didn't know which one, or even cared. However, the runway was paved at military length and width, allowing military aircraft of any size a quick in and out if needed. It was located on the flat and mostly deserted blueberry barrens at the northernmost end of Chesterfield, about ten miles north of Isles Port.

This was a great location, day or night, for any clandestine rendezvous. Kenny pulled the pickup to the farthest end, where a gravel road began and the terrain dropped off slightly, which made a vehicle seem to disappear, swallowed up by the vastness of the surrounding wilderness. The distance between objects on the barrens was at times deceiving to the naked eye, and it took nearly ten minutes for the fish truck to arrive at Kenny's location.

"What took you so long, Bubba?" Kenny asked with a drone-like exaggerated Down-East accent, knowing very well that he was mimicking the driver. The driver slid from the cab, saying very little to Kenny. It was a long trip from Boston to Isles Port, and it was apparent he wanted this trip to be finished. As he opened the rear door to the box section, the rancid aroma of stale fish overwhelmed Kenny, yet the driver seemed unfazed, and he climbed into the truck, making his way toward the front through the stacked fish-totes.

The totes were stacked within themselves, from the floor to almost the ceiling, which kept them secure for traveling, with a thin alleyway down the middle. The driver looked like he was dancing a shimmy, because of the still, wet floor as he made his way through. He kept some of the dry fish Kenny ordered close to the door, keeping any fish-cop (as everyone called Department of Marine Resources Officers) who had a nose for and the authority to stop a vehicle that looked like a fish truck anywhere in Maine, from the front and Kenny's prize cargo.

Kenny became so excited about what was coming to him shortly that his foot began tapping out a rhythm on the gravel, suggesting agitation at the driver's slow-motion movements in retrieving the goods. "C'mon, Bubba, I don't want to be out here when some simpleton decides to take a Sunday drive down the runway," he said.

The driver, obviously tired and disconnected from his surroundings replied, "It's Monday."

Kenny's eyebrows rose, and he simply offered the driver a slight shake of the head and a grin, yet said nothing this time. He breathed in deeply and exhaled slowly, looking around in every direction for any sign of movement on the distant horizon.

The very second that Kenny took hold of the brown-paper-wrapped package, he handed the driver his usual plain white envelope. Without saying another word, he walked to his pickup, placed the wrapped package deep in between and under the wood, then he placed the smelly fish on top, got in, and drove away, without the faintest disturbance of the gravel beneath his wheels. He did not leave the way he entered by way of the access road.

He remained on the narrow gravel road at the end of the airstrip. His intention was to follow it as it wound its way toward Chesterfield over the barrens and wooded areas that skirted the river flowing downstream. Taking this route home, his truck and the fish truck would never cross paths, and the likelihood of even passing another vehicle at this time of the year on these roads was fairly nil, as better than fifty-percent of the way would be iced over and difficult to pass. It was worth the gamble and the time to Kenny.

Kenny's income from drug sales, which was now his predominant income, and things like seasonal firewood and Christmas wreaths were surpassing Mary's from the nursing home. Along with the capital gain, psychologically his head had grown several sizes larger, making Kenny Collins about the farthest description from a nice guy as one could get. It had gotten to the point where he actually enjoyed watching people squirm if they came to him for a handout of any kind. After all, firewood and a good supply of drugs was like money in the bank around here, any time of the year, and Kenny was loaded for bear with both however; Kenny's relationship with Forest Bagley, his former employer and supplier of firewood was strained now because of the information passed to Forest by his cousin Virgil from everyone's friend, Bullet Carter. Most people, it seemed, kept Mary right out of the equation, whenever it came to character assassination. Kenny had become the person everyone loved to hate, and he made it easy for them, whether he realized it or not.

Mostly, he just didn't care what people thought. He had forged his destination in life long before he'd known this place existed, and nothing and no one would stand in the way to the level of success he desired, whatever the cost.

The travel was extremely rough over the road Kenny had chosen, but after several hours alone in the backcountry, and stops to sample his new supply from Boston, he looked forward to the couch at home and Mary's return from Ellsworth. It was late afternoon when he finally reached the couch and his head began to tilt toward a nap. Not a single thought crossed his mind before sleep came.

Mary had finally forgotten about his phone call to her earlier that day, and prepared herself for the long, enjoyable drive home. It had become second nature to her now. She actually looked forward to the time alone. It gave her time to think the little things over without the constant interruptions Kenny was notorious for. Right now, she was consumed by thinking about the kids and how she would get them away from her father. She couldn't be vicious toward her father, despite their past; yet it was true that she didn't trust him around the kids, and she believed that she was the best thing for them now, without Lucretia. Although their mother had done very little to make their young lives better, at least during the past six months due to her failing health, in Mary's mind, it was a damned sight more than Virgil could do in six years alone. Besides, the way she looked at it, she was setting him free.

The stunning effects of that evening phone call to her remained vivid in her consciousness, and as a consequence, she now felt differently about many aspects of her own life. Suddenly, her feelings about the way Kenny treated her as less than an equal resonated in her subconscious mind, and as she placed that on a level playing field with her father, she began to feel the same toward him as she did toward her father—a feeling that had slept for many years until just recently. She was in the process of questioning everything about herself and her life, so her time alone was more valuable than ever. She began to formulate a plan to get the kids.

The travel time between home and work was in the neighborhood of about thirty minutes one way, allowing her an hour per day to think her own thoughts. Today was Monday, and it thrilled her to think that she had devised a plan so quickly to get the kids. *"Evil versus evil,"* she thought. With her old man, she would use threats to expose his past. For Kenny, it was sex, drugs, and rock 'n' roll.

When she pulled into the driveway, she saw the thin plume of smoke rising lazily from the chimney. Kenny's truck was parked in the usual place, yet the house was dark. Not even the barn lights were on, which they usually were if he'd been tinkering or smoking out there. A slight fluttering in her stomach due to the thoughts she'd had during her ride home made itself known as she parked the car. Looking toward the house, she sat for a moment longer after turning the engine off; simply enjoying the peace and quiet, knowing it might be all the quiet she would get for the whole evening. She had figured out the approach she would use on each man, and like everything else in this crazy world, timing was everything. She would play her hand when the cards fell in her favor, and each man was different, yet she truly believed their reaction would be very similar.

The night sky was black and clear as far as the eye could see. Quadrillions of stars made themselves visible, and the cold night air pushed her along hurriedly toward the warmth of the little house. As she entered through the barn, a pang of uncertainty filled her senses along with the soured air of a dirty chimney. Since she was uncomfortable with herself about the plan, her desire to get high and maybe have a small drink, which was unusual for her now, grew strong as she entered the kitchen.

In the dim light, she saw Kenny's outline stretched out on the couch, and as she approached, had it not been for his deafening snore, she would have thought he was dead. His open mouth gave the appearance of a corpse that had fought desperately for its last molecule of air before expiring. She thought it best to let him sleep—for selfish reasons—because she would enjoy an extended quiet time for herself, but as she turned toward the kitchen, her dreams were dashed with the sound of Kenny's deep breath and a slight moan.

"What's goin' on?" he muttered.

"Hi, I didn't want to wake you. It sounded as though you might need the extra sleep," she said.

"Yah," was all that he replied.

She went directly to him, sitting beside him on the couch. Though he'd been lying there uncovered, when she hugged him, his body emitted a warmth that soothed her, and she wanted him to hold her as he did when they had truly been lovers, not like an old, married couple, as they sometimes acted now. They remained quiet for a long while, holding each other warmly. Kenny spoke first.

"Wanta get high?"

"I'm not sure. Is the stuff any good?" she asked.

With that question, Kenny was up and running off at the mouth, ending Mary's quiet time. She honestly didn't want to get high, but it was all part of her plan now. She had to make him see it her way, and she was prepared to do whatever it took to make it so. *"Oh, what the hell,"* she thought. *"I could use a stiff drink and a good buzz to calm myself down."* She watched Kenny, the little tornado, going through the house getting the stash and mixing the drinks to unwind.

Suddenly, the thought of the kids' first day back at school interrupted her need to relax, and she called out to Kenny.

"I'm going to call Virgil. I want to see how the kids made out at school."

Kenny barely heard any of what she said, yet he nodded his head and continued preparing happy hour. She dialed the number, and the phone immediately began to ring—once, twice, and then during the third ring, the receiver came to life with the sound of Tabitha's voice, alert and upbeat as usual.

"Hello!" she said.

"Hello, yourself, how was your day at school?" Mary asked.

Tabitha began immediately with a rapid verbal accounting of almost every minute of the entire day, possibly leaving out any time she may have used the girls' room, yet toward the end of a winded description of what seemed to be an actual toilet scene, Mary stopped her.

After a short pause to catch her breath, Tabitha began, once again as a child possessed for the need of attention. Mary was reminded of her closest friend as a pre-teen, and their plain old girl-talk. It was an essential part of growing up, and Mary feared it would be missing in Tabi's life now, without Lucretia.

Mary sat back, listening to her sister, and became more relaxed and happier than she would have been after ingesting any substance. A sheer brightness beamed from her face, leaving Kenny puzzled as he entered the room carrying a bottle of Bud, an ice-filled glass of rum-and-coke, and two joints hanging from his lips.

He placed the drinks, one in front of Mary, the other beside it on the coffee table, and sat heavily on the couch, listening to the conversation whenever Mary interjected.

For Kenny, however, patience was not a virtue. His leg began to pulse, and since his foot was resting against the table-leg, it sounded like the beat of a drum in Mary's other ear. After several minutes of the pounding, she looked at him in agitation, and he slowed the piston, as Mary called it. Reaching for the ashtray, he fired up one of the fatties and waited for Mary to finish.

The conversation continued right through their intended happy hour. Kenny was visibly antsy, and guzzled what remained of his first beer, pointing to it while showing Mary, then left to get another. While he was gone, Tabi's voice became strained, as if being prompted somehow on her end, to what extent Mary couldn't tell. But the child was breathing deeper with every syllable, and it wasn't because she was talking up the same storm as when she'd started the conversation.

Tabi sounded distracted. "Well, Mary, I've got to get this homework done. The teacher's been savin' stuff for me while we were with mama...you know." For the first time in a very long while, she told Mary that she loved her, and then she was gone, and Virgil came on the line. Mary attempted to say something in response, but the lump in her throat and the surprise at hearing the sound of her father's voice resounding in the earpiece prevented her from talking.

The last thing she would have wanted now was a conversation with Virgil, but there he was, at least in voice only. *"Thank God,"* she thought. He rambled on for several minutes, and Mary began worrying that he might be drinking more because his words were slurred. Kenny kept making questioning gestures with his hands and arms, keeping Mary on edge, and occasionally she returned a response by flipping her free hand, then he went back to drinking his beer. Mary's mind was traveling at the speed of light as her father continued speaking of things that at times made no sense to her, keeping her plan to get the children concealed in the back of her mind. Her patience began to run thin. Kenny finally left for the barn, giving up on happy hour for tonight, and through her frustration she now prepared to cut her father off and end this, at least for tonight, when Virgil fell silent on his own, and all that Mary could hear was the sound of his labored breathing. She wondered silently, *"What shut him down?"*

"Are you all right, or what?" she asked. He didn't speak immediately, and she was about to repeat herself when he began speaking, at a slow speed like an old record player.

"Yah'...Mary, I'm alright...I think. I'm not sure about anything anymore. Without your mama bein' hea'— ya' know how she kept things together, and you, Mary, you helped her to keep things together. I don't even want to think about what it would o' been like without ya' bein' hea' as much, to take care of her." He paused, breathing heavily once again.

"Don't worry about that..." She realized she was about to call him "dad," but then she stopped short. "Nothing could keep me from her when she needed me the most, you know that."

"Yah'...I know that—I just don't know about me anymore," he said. Then he was silent.

She would not have been able to explain the feeling that came over her now. Her silent thoughts raced, questions streaked through her subconscious mind. Most of them she could never ask, and Mary could not perceive what would come next, because her father was so indecisive. She'd spent the last five days mentally consumed with her younger siblings and their obvious need for structure, something Virgil Bagley had lacked from the moment his suspenders snapped against his shoulders every morning until his alcohol-saturated head hit the pillow each night. She wanted to burst out with the questions that filled her with concern; some of which she feared the answers to, but she knew the questions needed to be asked eventually in the process of her pursuit for guardianship of the kids. She was prepared to do anything she had to, at any expense—financially or emotionally.

She was distracted briefly as Kenny re-entered the house with the slamming of the kitchen door. He was scowling at having been put off from their happy hour by the phone call. Still on the phone, Mary dismissed him, surprising herself with the dismissal. All of her attention was focused on the troubled voice on the other end of the silent telephone line, at the other end of town. The silence had become uncomfortable, and suddenly, both Virgil and Mary spoke simultaneously.

"Look," Virgil started. "I…" He stopped as Mary started.

"I think…" she stopped, then said, "No, you first."

He began again in the same slow tone, seemingly confused as to the direction he intended to go. With Virgil, that was the norm, but Mary wanted to hear everything her father had to say about anything, storing it to memory in the event she needed to use it later where the kids were concerned. Expecting him to rattle on about nothing and with nothing decisive to say, Mary could hardly contain her emotions at what her father began to say.

"Mary, I'm naut' gonna be able to caya' for these kids. Your sister's becomin' a young woman faster than I can tell, and Bobby, well, he's a real handful. I ain't the kind o' person who can handle that kind o' stuff by myself."

Mary's heart pounded heavily in her chest, as if any moment she expected it to break out of its cavity and fall to the floor, still pounding. She wanted to let out with a howl, but remained quiet. This was the biggest break of her life, next to running away with Kenny. If this was going where she thought, she'd never have to bring up her plans with Virgil, who obviously wanted the same thing she did. When he began again after a lengthy pause, his voice became clear and decisive, leaving Mary somewhat confused, yet she remained still.

"Mary, I need ya' to take these two kids and make a home for 'em. I can't even boil water without burnin' it, and little Tabi ain't gonna' spend time carin' for me. She's too smaat' in school to be wastin' her time on someone like me."

She couldn't have agreed more with anything Virgil ever had to say than the words that had left his mouth just then. She could no longer contain herself and she blurted out, "YES!" Kenny jerked his head in her direction. They made small talk for several more minutes and then decided that it was time to call it a day. Mary said goodbye and placed the receiver softly into its cradle. Her eyes were wide open and a smile stretched across her lips.

"What was that all about?" He asked. "From the look on your face, ya' might think it was Christmas all over again."

"You're not going to believe this, but my father wants us to take the kids and have them live with us."

Kenny remained looking in her direction, yet he sat silent. Although, if vomiting had a specific look, it was the look that Kenny displayed at the very moment.

22

DURING THE DAYS FOLLOWING the fateful phone conversation between Mary and Virgil, Kenny remained, surprisingly, to himself and without critical comment. Mary, however, prepared herself for the moment he decided to change his approach to the new situation at hand. She busied herself at work, and during her breaks and lunch-times she spoke with and made contacts that would allow her to move forward legally in the attainment of her guardianship over the children.

After her enthusiastic "YES!" response to her father, she'd told him about the legal process which they both would have to follow. Virgil obviously thought she knew of these procedures from her experience at the nursing home, and she allowed him to go with that, never having to add her intentions preceding the call or her earlier research on the subject. Her feelings for Virgil had never faded since that dark night they found Lucretia, when her mind had carried her back in time and brought up frightening memories.

She never brought the subject up with Kenny, knowing his desire to find out what the insulting comment about her father was all about, and now, since it had been a couple of weeks since that night, Mary felt that the heat for his need to know had cooled enough for her to breathe easier. With Kenny, however, if you let your guard down, he'd burn you, and she knew it better than anyone.

As much as Mary kept the goings-on about the kids in and around town under wraps, something like this needed speaking of only once to have it take flight, almost on its own, and Virgil made no effort at discretion about the matter. Overall, Mary couldn't be happier knowing that her younger brother and sister would soon be living with her and Kenny, away from the nightmare that could become their life with Virgil.

She began to believe that Kenny might be remaining silent because he was quietly deliberating the issues, pro and con, and just didn't want to discuss it until he was ready, when suddenly the realization struck her that he hadn't called her at work for almost the entire past week. She looked quickly toward the wall-clock, and his usual time to check up on her had passed, yet he hadn't called. She exhaled a long sigh of relief, sparking the attention of several women seated at their desks, but they simply smiled in her direction, knowing of her recent loss and Kenny's daily calls. Though many at the nursing home had never had the pleasure of meeting Kenny Collins in person, most had become familiar with the sound of his voice.

Mary focused her attention to the work at hand, giving no further thought to Kenny, Virgil, or any one of the many things that had distracted her during the past several weeks, until the bellowing sound of Kenny's laughter echoed through the entire building, making Mary's heart leap into palpitations while hot bile rose in her throat, causing her to feel nauseous.

A thousand fears ran through her mind, but the most profound was that this was how Kenny chose to deal with his silent deliberation on the issue of the children.

He had never come to the nursing home since she'd begun working, though he'd been to Ellsworth many times during that period. All worked stopped now in Mary's shared office—several people recognized Kenny's voice and whispered to others, and then everyone wanted to meet and place a face to the mysterious voice on the end of their telephone lines.

Mary remained seated at her desk as one of the nursing home's attendants escorted Kenny to her office. Without making a huge production of it, Mary opened the top drawer of her desk and removed two antacid tabs from a roll, chewing and swallowing them quickly, extinguishing the burn from the hot bile, which seemed hotter now as Kenny entered the office with his high-energy personality and proceeded to suck most of the air from the tiny office.

"Mary, I never knew you were surrounded with such beauty while you were at work," he said, and glanced around the room, making eye contact with each woman employee. With this positive comment, it was impossible for each one not to return a blushing smile in his direction, and he loved every second of the attention. Mary, not knowing the true reason that he was here, began to feel even more nauseous.

Due to the laid-back environment, a demeanor the home prided itself on in order to maintain the level of tranquility for the residents, no one would question Mary if she decided to leave her work station and take her husband on a guided tour of the facility; something all employees did when visited by a family member or close friend. Both Kenny and Mary made small talk with the women in the office. Mary made every effort to leave quickly, but nothing moved rapidly when Kenny was in front of a new audience. His gift of gab overflowed. When she finally tugged his arm slightly, she felt an undeniable resistance, and fearing his temper, released her grasp immediately.

He continued schmoozing with the women uninterrupted for several more minutes before Mary asked, "Hey, would you like to see the rest of the home?"

He turned his head toward her slowly, as if about to chastise her for something she'd done to dissatisfy him, but never looking directly at her, and then turning to the other women, ingratiating himself with them for the chance meeting.

Mary attempted to take his hand when leaving the office, yet he gently pulled away from her, and she felt the heat of whatever had impassioned him to make this visit. They went through what was known as the Service Wing, and continued along a narrow corridor leading to the central area, which included several offices, one being the administrator's. He was at his desk, and looked up as they passed. Mary stopped to introduce Kenny and they exchanged informalities before moving on. The administrator was in his early fifties, not exactly overweight but bulging at the beltline. His hair receded broadly, and he always wore a white shirt and tie. That's probably what turned Kenny off. He hated what he called a "stiff shirt."

When they were out of earshot of the office, Kenny remarked coldly, "I've heard it said that the forehead is the sign of intelligence. If that's true, Mary, then that simple fuck is a genius."

Mary felt a flood of embarrassment come over her from his imbecilic behavior, but knowing how easy it would be for him to lose his temper, which lately was all of the time; she refrained from comment or any facial expression that would have him question her in any way.

She wanted to come right out and ask why he'd come to the nursing home. Had this been only a couple of years ago when they had first become an item, she never would have hesitated to ask him anything, but things were moving in a different direction now where they were concerned. The thought of the two kids came into her mind suddenly, and she was afraid that Kenny could become like Virgil. She questioned herself once again as to whether she would be making a huge mistake in taking the kids away from the man who was her childhood nightmare.

They strolled through the halls, staying away from the private areas. Kenny maintained his aloof sarcasm when making observations to Mary, but he put on his best "Eddie Haskell" face whenever meeting a resident or one of Mary's co-workers, and for that alone, Mary was extremely grateful. She was unable to remain still any longer as they came to a common area somewhat removed from the morning's activities, and motioned for him to go inside the empty room.

"So, what brings you to the big city this morning?" she asked.

"Nothin' special...can't a guy come to see his wife at work?" He mimicked the tone of her question. But Mary had had enough. She spoke clearly and expressionlessly, so as not to disrupt Kenny's mood.

"Kenny, since I started here, you've never walked through the front door, or the back door, of this place, and today, you walk in here like some fat-assed tour-bus driver on his way to a Cabbage Island Clambake with a busload of old ladies. I can't help wonder, for the lack of your morning call-in, that some other reason brought you in here."

Kenny proceeded to look around the room, which, because of its southern exposure, was set up as a sunroom, with white wicker furniture and color prints of the rocky coast of Maine on walls where the incoming light was crucial to the depth perception of the paintings. He walked slowly, swiping an inspectorial finger over the tabletops as if to indicate the need for dusting, and then he turned from the corner he was in and walked directly toward her. When he reached her, his stare was penetrating, and without saying a word, he grabbed her arm forcefully, just above the elbow, striking a pang of fear that leapt from her mid-section to her chest. When she tried to pull herself away, his grasp cinched her tighter, and he spoke in a low, threatening voice.

"Ya' know, Mary, lately you've been leaving me out of the important stuff where decisions need to be made. You took this job without telling me first, now this fuckin' kid thing." His eyeball-to-eyeball stare was unflinching, and he gave her arm a little jerk. He was about to start talking again when the sound of approaching footsteps caused him to look toward the hallway, and he released his hold on her at the very moment the administrator and several guests came into view through the doorway. All they saw were Kenny and Mary looking toward the group, smiling.

"Oh, I didn't realize anyone was in this section of the building right now," the administrator said, and looked toward his little group. "This is Mary Collins and her husband, Rickie." He blinked as he realized he'd gotten Kenny's name wrong. "Mary is a rapidly up-and-coming young administrator in her own right," he said, and the obvious appreciation and sincerity in his voice forced Kenny to want revenge by removing Mary from the sudden spotlight she was now in thanks to "Baldy," as he would have liked to call him now. He immediately corrected the man for calling him the wrong name.

"I'm so sorry, Kenny, I..." the administrator's voice trailed off as a question was fired at him from one of the elderly guests accompanying him on the tour of the facility.

Kenny's ego saw these simple occurrences as dismissals, and took them as insults added to injury. His anger flared and became apparent to Mary through the throbbing jugular in his neck.

Mary's arm ached where he'd held her, and she sidestepped slightly as the group prepared to continue their tour, readying herself to avoid another grab for her arm. The administrator broke with formality, waving toward the two in the sunroom, and they listened to the sound of fading footsteps in the distance. When Kenny turned, noticing the gap between them, he moved closer, and Mary moved away.

At this moment, Mary's intuition rumbled in her midsection, telling her to be very careful, and she began speaking to Kenny, who had moved across the room and was ignoring her.

"Kenny, why did you come down here today? You didn't just come down to say hi, and by the way you're acting, it seems to me you have something you really want to say. I need you to talk to me now, because I only have a few minutes before I have to get back to work. I can't let the boss see me out here again if he decides to come back this way with his little tour-group."

"Oh, the boss—you mean "baldy," don't you?" Kenny said sarcastically.

They were silent for several moments before Mary finally said, "Ok, I'm outta hea," and she began walking toward the door and the hallway. The move sparked his attention.

"Yo...yo! Mary! Get a grip! I'm just takin' a break here," he said.

"Well, why don't you take it while walking me back to my

office?" Mary responded with confidence. "I do have work to do, and I'm not plannin' on being here after quittin' time." Kenny felt a pang of anger rise to the top of the fury that permanently resided in his spirit now. He kicked the wicker coffee table in passing, his way of showing his displeasure, and when Mary turned at the sound, he was smiling at her as if to say, *"You'll never get the best o' me."* She shook her head, yet said nothing, and continued walking with him in tow.

It was obvious from her silence that she felt comfortable here at the nursing home, yet she knew that it didn't change his need to dominate her through the declining closeness of their relationship. He loved Mary as his wife, but he loved his "Kingdom of Kenny" more, and he would stand for nothing that might cause the kingdom walls to crumble.

Suddenly, the scent of what seemed to Kenny to be cafeteria or institutional cooking filled the hallways, causing a rumble of hunger in the pit of his stomach.

"Hey, what are the chances of us getting a little something for lunch?" he asked with a slight laugh. "The shit's startin' to smell pretty good around here." When Mary didn't answer, he got serious once again. "Ya didn't let me finish back there in that funny, sunny room. Baldy kinda interrupted, if ya' know what I mean, Mary."

She knew what he meant, and if she could help it, she would rather keep it for an at-home discussion because time was running out for her break, and this was not the place for an important discussion.

"Your old man got on the phone and told you he couldn't take care o' them kids. You get all hot and bothered, don't say a goddamned word to me about it except, "We're taking the kids, with Virgil's consent. They're gonna be livin' with us," he said.

She knew he was right to a point. It wasn't exactly how she'd planned to get the kids, but when Virgil had opened that door, she wasn't going to be the one to close it in front of her.

She spoke in earnest. "Kenny, I wanted to talk to you. I wanted

205

you to be a part of this…" Then she caught herself, not wanting to take it as far as telling him she'd been thinking about this since her mother died. "You were…well—so out of it that night, when Virgil took the phone from Tabi …When I started telling you about it, you just got up and walked out on me. What could I do? They're my brother and sister! Would you like to live with Virgil if you were a kid?"

They stood in the middle of the narrow hallway, not far from the kitchen. Neither one was willing to take another step farther after Mary's question to Kenny. They were standing close, looking into each other's eyes, and in an odd way, it felt like the old days. They always seemed to get lost in one another simply by looking into each other's eyes. It felt good to Mary, but it just wasn't the same.

"I suppose I'm the 'crusty-ass,' now that you're on speaking terms with your old man. Look, Mary, those kids are goin' to be right in the fuckin' way where my business is concerned, and it appears that you have no problem with that. As far as what interests me, you could care less about what I do now that you have this big job and a nice paycheck," he said loudly. Mary turned in every direction at the sound of his voice, making sure they were alone, and they were for the moment.

"Kenny, I have to get back to my desk. The first thing I want to do when I get home is to talk to you about this. I'll pick the kids up on my way home, get them squared away with supper and homework, and the rest of the night is ours. Whaddaya' say?"

She waited for a response to her statement that she would pick the kids up and get them squared away, but to her surprise, he didn't say a thing. He simply shrugged his shoulders and made his way toward the rear door, and was gone with a slight wave.

Mary's apprehension rumbled once again, leaving her puzzled as to why. She wouldn't find out until later that at that moment, Virgil lay passed out in the middle of his kitchen floor, completely drunk.

23

Despite Kenny's best efforts to remain out of the limelight of local gossip, just being who he was made it unavoidable. Rumors of Bullet's ex-wife Millie began to resurface when an extremely revealing photo of her with several unclad men had been found in a snow bank behind Filbert's store by a bunch of teens hanging around the previous Friday night. Had they simply flipped the photo back into the snow after their gawking session, it might have deteriorated and never been found. No one would know but them. One kid, however, thought he recognized her, and gave the photo to his father, who did know her and gave the photo to Bullet.

There's an old saying, I'm sure anyone over twenty-one has heard: "When the shit hits the fan, the last place you want to be standing is on the blowing side of the blades." That picture went round and round before it fell into Bullet's hands, and then last, but not least, into the hands of Maine State Trooper, Harry Circus.

"Judas Priest!" Harry said when Bullet handed it to him with a shit-eating grin on his face at the Quick-Stop on Monday morning while Harry and Constable Bailey prepared for their ritual coffee-and-stale-donut breakfast.

"Where did you get this snapshot from hell?"

"Well, without givin' ya' any names, it was handed to me by

the father o' one o' the kids that found it behind Filbert's last Friday night," Bullet said.

"I assume you don't mean little kids found this smut," Harry said.

"Yah…yah, teen-agers," Bullet answered.

"Let me see that!" Ralph demanded. His eyes bugged from their sockets. The last person Bullet wanted looking at his naked ex-wife was that piss-pot constable. Not that he had any feelings for her any longer, but it was just the principle of the matter. Harry flipped it, photo side down, on the table in front of him. The constable reached for it, but saw the recognizable scowl develop on the bridge of the trooper's nose at eyebrow level. After a moment, Ralph picked it up to examine the photo

"This brings me back to the movie smut I talked to Filbert about not too long ago. I can't help but think this is all connected somehow," Harry said, then wondered why Bullet would want to show him this picture, had he not discussed it with Filbert knowing very well the closeness of the two men. At the same moment, Bullet reached around them, pulled a chair from another table, and sat between the two lawmen at their table. He said nothing, yet he looked toward each man expecting some sort of comment.

"Holy shi…" The constable stopped short, remembering he was in the presence of a non-swearing man with a badge, and then continued. "I can't for the life o' me figure out who those men are with their heads cut off like that," he said.

"*Dopey little bastard,*" Bullet thought to himself.

The trooper was thrilled to hear Ralph's comment about not knowing anyone in the photo, as everyone was naked. It was true, for obvious reasons, because whoever had taken the photo did so at an angle eliminating all of the men's heads, yet there were no visible marks, scars, or tattoos on anyone that might lead to identification. Ralph continued to stare intently at the photo, causing the trooper and Bullet to look in his direction with concern.

"That shit-ass Collins is involved in this, I know it," Bullet said. The trooper breathed deeply, trying to overlook his foul language.

"I didn't realize he even knew Millie," Harry said.

"Neither did I, but if he isn't involved in this somehow, and I know he is, I'll take a bath in a bucket o' bat crap," Bullet spewed angrily.

Harry put his cup down and looked out of the window. For no apparent reason, he focused his stare on the wheels of an eighteen-wheel logging truck parked across the road from the Quick-Stop. He sorted through his thoughts about the photo while half-listening to Bullet ramble on about this, that, and other things, yet nothing Bullet said registered in Harry's consciousness.

"There isn't any law against pictures like this, as long as they're consenting adults," he thought. *"It's unfortunate that a group of teens found it, but it is what it is right now."*

Despite Bullet's well-known dislike for Kenny, there was nothing about this photo that could connect him to it. The constable continued staring at the photo, saying very little to appease Bullet's comments and questions, except for an occasional nod of his head, and Bullet became frustrated at being ignored by the two men.

Outside of the regular morning noise level of the store, it fell on deaf ears at the small table by the window. Bullet, though a regular at Filbert's, knew almost every second person walking through the door, and either he or they acknowledged each other with a low hoot or grunt and a slight wave. Bullet was rapidly losing interest, and was about to get up when suddenly Ralph spoke up.

"Wicked! I thought I saw somethin' in this picture when I first looked at it, but then I lost it for a minute. Take a look at this Harry. Tell me what ya' see in the background."

He had both men's undivided attention. Bullet slid forward on his chair, bringing the rear legs off of the floor. Harry cocked his head to one side slightly as Ralph passed the photo back to him.

"There, right there in the background." He pointed his finger from his place across the table. "Doesn't that look like the reflection of the person taking the friggin' picture?" Ralph asked.

Harry studied the photo intently, yet seemed to be having a problem seeing what it was that the constable saw. Bullet nearly broke his neck trying to get a closer look, but Harry had the photo in the palm of his hand, making it impossible for Bullet to see any of it due to the reflection from the window behind the trooper and the glossy finish on the print.

"Who is that, Harry?" Ralph asked.

"I'm not sure, there seems to be some kind of glare from the flash on…a piece of glass or something," Harry said.

Bullet's eyes were now bugging from their sockets.

Ralph continued to stare, displaying one of his famous dumb looks, which brought a rumble of laughter from Bullet, yet Harry appeared unfazed by the goings-on around him, and his stare became intense, as if he would try to enter the picture from where he sat and apprehend the photographer.

"Judas Priest, I'll tell ya', that is the reflection of the person taking the shot, but darn' if I can make out who, in the goodness of the Almighty it is. Good eye, Ralph," he said.

"Let me see, will ya'?" Bullet blurted out in frustration, yet the trooper appeared to have gone into the photo somehow. It was as if nothing and no one existed around him. His concentration fascinated the two men beside him.

It is worse than a crime; it is to blunder.

(Joseph Fouché)

24

No one ever found out about Virgil's drunken flop to the floor. It was lucky for all concerned that Mary moved as quickly as she had when getting the kids. The situation at hand, however, was Kenny's obvious disapproval. As far as Mary was concerned, those two kids were little angels. Not just because they were her siblings, but they were polite, considerate, and caring children, something she knew their mother had instilled in them. They appeared comfortable in the rooms Mary had chosen for them at the rear of the upstairs. They were set apart from Kenny and Mary's room downstairs, and though she never forced it on them with any kind of discipline, they were the kind of children to be seen, but seldom heard.

She believed that Kenny would grow to love them; however, it felt as though the two of them were moving farther apart in every way. Mary lived for the weekends now. Saturday mornings, she spent doting on the kids' needs to relax and be comfortable in their new lives. Whatever they wanted for breakfast, Mary made it. Cartoons on TV until noon, with snacks served, Mary on the couch right along with them.

Occasionally, Kenny went out and got high, and took much humor from the animations on the screen when he returned, but it was rare. Most weekends he was out early doing things he was not willing to share with Mary, and especially the kids.

His energetic drive to achieve new levels of success, and what he did, forced him to abuse his own supplies, which now consisted of more than just pot, and word of it spread far and wide. Things began to change for Kenny. It wasn't as though he was softening his views about the kids; he was still an angry young man, and he always used his anger to keep most people at what he thought to be a safe distance from the "real" Kenny. Sometimes, the things he did threw Mary surprise curves.

One day when Mary pulled into the driveway, arriving home after work and picking the kids up after school, Kenny, standing in full view for them to see as the car pulled in, was pointing toward the newly installed basketball backboard with hoop and net, laughing like a schoolboy and bouncing the brand-new Spaulding Official game ball out front of the barn door.

Despite the highs and lows of Kenny's temperament, Mary could not bring her emotions back to the days of happiness the two of them had shared early on in the relationship. The children were her solace now. She knew it was simply a matter of time before Kenny would unleash his personality monster and reveal himself to the kids, whatever the prompt might be. He no longer controlled his emotions as he once had, and it was that control that had turned her on to him in the first place. She now found herself in the same subordinate role she'd been forced to play out as a child and young woman before freeing herself, at least for a time, from the same type of prison.

The kids, as far as Mary knew, did not know the real Kenny as of yet. They loved him and worshiped the ground he walked on.

Never anticipating what life would be like with two grammar-school-aged children living at home, with their involvement in school activities during and after school hours, Mary was now thrust into the role of not only guardian, but also mother wanting the best for them.

This situation demanded an unequivocal surrender of the life she'd once desired for herself and her husband. She could never have dreamed, however, that the transition would be so easy, but she was not prepared to speak for Kenny.

What no one could have predicted was an association developing between Bobby and Lulu Cirone, the youngest of the Cirone children, who were the same age and in the same class. Mary and Heidi would soon come face to face, which for both of them would be a warm, but unexpected reunion.

Due to his late evenings out, Kenny remained in bed most mornings while Mary and the kids prepared to leave for their daily jaunt into the world. During the past week, Mary had offered a heads-up to alert Kenny that this evening, Bobby's class was displaying their Poster Projects, and both Mary and Tabitha looked forward to the completion of Bobby's project, as he had been feverish when asking for suggestions for the poster's development.

Although both had been careful not to be involved in any of the actual designs, leaving that to him, they simply wanted their evenings free to do their own thing after a solid month of "Poster Talk." Ironically, Bobby's poster theme was about the evils and end results of alcohol and drug abuse, and a note arrived from his teacher congratulating the family for Bobby's first prize, to be awarded by State Trooper Harry Circus that evening.

In his anticipation of the long day's events, culminating with the poster ceremony, Bobby, naturally over-active after a large glass of orange juice, began a nervous pacing through the entire downstairs, unknown to Mary or Tabitha, who were busy with their own routines. Not realizing it, and without malice, the noise level produced from his restlessness ushered Kenny into an angry awakening. The crashing of the forcefully opened bedroom door against the wall reverberated throughout the entire old structure, rattling the glassware in the cupboards, forcing Mary to run in the direction of what sounded like a cave-in in the kitchen, fearing the possibility of what had already happened.

When she arrived at the threshold between the kitchen and living rooms, her heart swelled with fear. Kenny, screaming at the top of his lungs and grasping young Bobby by the shirt collar and waistline, held him high above his head, shaking him, while reprimanding him for disturbing his desperately needed sleep. The boy looked to Mary with his eyes full of horror, and she screamed, forcing every eardrum in the room to ring with pain.

The level of anger in Kenny plummeted suddenly as he became aware of his actions, yet at the sound of Mary's screeching, it returned to a violent forte. He literally threw the boy through the air and stood watching with no apparent remorse as Bobby bounced on the over-stuffed couch, biting his lower lip and causing an instant flow of blood to stream down his chin and onto the clean, pressed blue shirt Mary had set out for him no more than fifteen minutes earlier. Mary paid no attention to the foot patter from behind her, knowing very well it was Tabi, and ran to console the boy, who now lay in a heap, visibly shaken and in disbelief of what Kenny had done to him.

Mary let out several swears in Kenny's direction, taking Bobby into her arms, and going directly toward the kitchen and running water. Tabitha, standing between the two rooms, looked to Kenny with a concerned, questioning stare as he stood in his Jockey-shorts only in the center of the room, head down, breathing heavily, knowing fully what he'd just done to a boy he'd come to admire.

The damage to the lip was far less than Mary anticipated at first sight of the wound. The cold water compress stopped the flow of blood, revealing a shallow laceration in the top layer of skin. Bobby, surprisingly calm after the encounter with Kenny's angry outburst, fidgeted as a boy his age would. Mary pressed the cold cloth against his mouth, despite his attempts to turn his head toward Kenny in preparation against another attack; however, the living room was quiet and empty, and Tabi came to their side, holding her brother's hand and confirming that Kenny had retreated to his room and closed the door behind him.

"Why did he do that to me? I didn't mean to bother him," Bobby said.

Mary looked into the boy's sad and questioning eyes, yet could find no words to console him; a lump formed in her throat, stifling any speech.

The day moved at variable speeds for everyone who lived in the farmhouse by the river. Mary was basically useless at work, keeping up a good front. No one noticed, or they simply didn't ask why. The two kids went through the day, up and down with their moods, and when asked about the fat lip, Bobby said what Mary had told him to say: that it was a piece of firewood falling from the pile that bounced and hit him in the face. The teacher kept her comments to herself, though she did not completely believe the story.

Kenny, on the other hand, went about the day with business as usual. He got high with coffee. Got high on his way to a delivery, and did the same for lunch; only once giving a thought to little Bobby and the damage done. Unfortunately, the thought didn't include the emotional damage. He did, however, feel a pang of uncertainty, but only for a moment, thinking of what might happen when the four of them returned home at the end of the day.

Kenny was now dealing his little bags of fun in broad daylight. At this time of the day, his younger clientele were in school. During the day it was the adults who came to him at his pre-arranged locations. Most of the time, however, he delivered his goods right to their front doors, usually staying to sample a little with them, then moving on to the next drop. This moving around, dropping-off plan kept most everyone from suspicion of the goings-on. True, there were still those who came to the house—only when the kids were in school—but they were very few now.

Despite his clandestine movement, there were eyes watching him. They watched from the windows of stores and houses, and everything they saw—and at times things they didn't see—were spread around like manure on freshly tilled earth. Those tilled gardens became more visible with the coming of spring.

With the new season at hand, Kenny could only foresee a bountiful summer, evolving into another blueberry August and the transients he loved so much, or rather the love of their money.

Finally, evening arrived and with it came time for the "Poster Contest Awards." Bobby, a typical rough-and-tumble boy, relished the praise and honorable recognition of his fellow students for his injury, soon forgetting the pain and fear that had followed the event earlier that day. Though enjoying hero status at school, he could not avoid looking over his shoulder at the slightest sound of a hastily closed door at home, wondering if Kenny was returning for a second round. Mary tried her best to keep him calm, reassuring him that all would be fine, but for a young boy with his past, the rule "once bitten, twice shy" applied.

Kenny didn't make an appearance at home that evening before they left for the school. The last thing Mary felt was sorry. She didn't want to see him, nor did she want to hear some lame excuse that had prompted him to do what he'd done to Bobby. Unfortunately, there would be plenty of time for that later. Right now, her focus was on Bobby's accomplishments and receiving the award, even if it was handed out by the trooper.

There was never any love lost between her and law enforcement people, but Harry holier-than-thou Circus, was an especially grand turn-off for Mary. He was, as far as she was concerned, a church-goin' hypocrite. In his opinion, there was a certain group of people who would be saved to the Lord; the rest he considered either out of control and be damned, or simply not worthy of being saved. That meant anyone who didn't go to church, his church, and that was Mary and her whole family.

Mary left the house with the two jittery kids. No one wanted to eat anything before leaving, and the fact that the school was less than a mile down the road eliminated any need to rush. Bobby looking over his shoulder at every unexpected sound added to the tension.

Being shy worried him, and the thought of having to stand up in front of an entire audience seated across the gym floor looking up at him didn't help much. Tabi was nervous, but not for the same reason. True, she remained skeptical of what might happen if and when Kenny showed up, but she had befriended a boy from school and they kept the relationship to themselves since before Lucretia died. Tonight, they would come together with everyone they both knew, and she worried what Mary would think if it all became apparent they were an item. She and her sister had the best relationship right now, and for a girl her age, it was everything in the world to her. She simply never could figure out how to tell Mary she had a boyfriend. Cooping things up was just the way it was at home with Virgil.

Mary wasn't completely thrilled about making this appearance tonight either. Since taking the job in Ellsworth, she'd been to the school only once since the kids moved in to inform the school of the changes, and she'd vanished as far as the eyes and ears of the town were concerned—and for her, right now, it was exactly what the doctor ordered.

A pang of fear rose in the pit of all three stomachs as Mary pulled the car into the school parking lot and realized, because of the huge turn-out, they would have to park in the road. Right out front, in the first place near the door, was the shiny clean, blue trooper car parked where it could be seen by all. Most people showed up real early so as to get a good choice of seats at an event like this, but Mary just hadn't given it much thought before leaving.

As they entered the building, the sound of the gathered anticipation seemed to resonate from the walls, and Bobby squeezed Mary's hand, pulling back slightly, and she stopped and bent over slightly, looking down at him.

"Hey big boy, if you don't want to do this, we can leave right now. No one is going to make you do what you don't want to do." She said this while looking into his eyes and a reassured look of confidence came over his face as he reached out and hugged her.

"Thanks, Mary. I'll be ok now," he said.

When she returned to a full standing position, feeling more at ease with Bobby willing to go through with it, she came face to face with Heidi, who was smiling broadly and standing right in front of her.

"Well stranga', where ya' been keepin' yawself, and whatcha been doin'?" Heidi asked, maintaining the broad smile.

"Well, I'm doin' soo good, I should be twins," Mary responded with a laugh.

"Oh, that's a good one, I have ta' rememba' that one," Heidi said, laughing out loud and reaching forward to hug Mary.

It felt a bit uncomfortable for Mary, not having seen Heidi since the funeral and eviction; yet strangely enough it made her feel good to be this close to another woman, something she'd believed went to the grave with Lucretia. Heidi was always the only other woman in Mary's life, and since the eviction, though she had considered going to see her and the kids, Kenny kept a tight rope on that type of forgiving. Heidi suddenly looked down toward Bobby.

"Well, young man, I hea' you've been a busy boy with that poster o' yaw's," she said, with one hand on Bobby's head, and before he could respond, Lulu came over to greet him. When she did, the boy's face lit up like a Christmas tree.

"C'mon, Mary, we've saved a place fa' you people next ta' us up front," Heidi said.

Mary pulled back slightly, and Heidi turned to reassure her that all was good with a simple nod and a smile, and Mary went willingly. In the back of her mind, she could see the resentment on Kenny's face, and he wasn't even in the school. When Heidi said "up front," she meant it. The first row of chairs was center-stage, and there was Filbert. It looked as though he'd just closed the store from what he wore, although that was what Filbert wore most of the time, and he was just as happy to see Mary as Heidi.

"Mary, it's so good to see ya," he said, and reached out and also gave her a hug.

The buzz of multiple conversations made it difficult to speak and be understood by the person seated next to her, and it sapped Mary of what energy remained of her fading constitution. The day had been long, and she had a ways to go before it ended. In her heart, she didn't want Kenny to show up here; yet, she couldn't shake the need to know where he'd been all day, since he hadn't called, and where he might be now.

Several teachers rounded the kids up, seating them with the rest of the students, while the recipients of awards were in a section nearer to the stage. Mary found Bobby in the middle of the small group. She tried several times to get his attention, finally waving to him, and he saw her. Not wanting to be known as a mama's boy, he nodded his head regally in her direction, and Mary got the message.

From where she sat, the swelling on his lower lip wasn't noticeable; yet knowing it was there made it visible to her. The crowd became restless, the children louder, and though she'd gone a long time without a migraine, Mary felt what could be the onset of one at the point between the end of her eyebrow and the bridge of her nose. She shrugged it off as a sign of being overheated.

As it is the case whenever a large crowd gathers tightly in a hall or similar confined area, body heat forces the temperature to rise in that space, and so it did in the seating area of the gym. Mary removed her coat on arriving, as did most everyone, yet she never gave a thought to the fact that she was wearing a short-sleeved blouse, exposing her uncovered arms to above the elbows. Her focus was the posters on stage. When she finally noticed, Heidi was staring intently at the large bruised area on her arm that remained surprisingly black and blue where Kenny had man-handled her at the nursing home.

Though Heidi hadn't commented on Bobby's fat lip or the bruise, Mary could not dismiss the look on Heidi's face, wondering if she may have associated the two injuries with Kenny's temper, but she couldn't overlook her own paranoid mind working overtime.

25

F<small>ILBERT, STANDING BEHIND THE COUNTER</small> for probably the millionth time, squinted against an early morning sun shining through the plate-glass window, and though he didn't wish to be disrespectful of his wife, wished he could block his ears against Heidi's third verbal onslaught about her observation of Mary's bruised arm and Bobby's fat lip.

"Filbert, when I saw that little angel's lower lip, well, I shrugged it off as normal for a rough-and-tumble boy, but when I saw Mary's arm and how bruised it was... If I knew he was beatin' on them..." She stood looking into Filbert's eyes with a determination he hadn't seen there in ages.

"We've got no proof that he's hittin' them. Besides, Mary's no fool. If he was, I'm sure she'd o' said somethin' to someone by now," he said.

"Don't be too sure o' yawself, old man. Love is blind, and don't you fauget it," she replied.

Several people came into the store simultaneously. Heidi dropped the subject like a hot potato, and went about her daily routine of straightening the shelves and tidying up.

She didn't like waiting on customers, and there were not many she liked to associate with. She wasn't snooty; she just didn't like most of the folks that came in. Most customers here wanted beer and cigarettes, never seeing the store as a viable place to shop for groceries. The price was too high for their blood, but when they found themselves in a pinch, Filbert's high-priced grub looked pretty good to them.

All that morning, Heidi couldn't get Mary and the kids out of her mind, and lost in her thoughts, she made every attempt to avoid anyone that came in that morning. Arriving at the rear of the store after one of her avoidance detours, she grimaced at the sight of the clumps of cat dander on the top of the sandwich counter, and began cleaning and disinfecting it thoroughly. She made a mental note to have a little talk about it with Filbert later.

Several minutes passed, while Filbert remained busy with the same two customers. Heidi, not being able to contain herself any longer, left the area of the sandwich counter and looked toward the front of the store, making sure Filbert was out of ear-shot of the phone beside the basement entry, and dialed Mary's number. She never turned to see if he could hear her. She never feared voicing her opinion to her husband, or anyone else for that matter. She just didn't want his opinion right now. She knew he would do his best to discourage her from becoming involved with anyone's domestic situation, especially Kenny and Mary's. She could hear Filbert ranting on about the lack of snow-cover this winter, keeping an eye in his direction when the phone began ringing.

She felt a butterfly-jitter in the pit of her stomach with the clicking sound of the receiver on the other end being lifted.

"Hello." Bobby answered the phone.

"Hello thea', you little daalin', how aar' you doin' this mornin'?" Heidi asked.

Seemingly confused at first, not immediately recognizing her voice, Bobby responded slowly.

"Oh… Hi, Mrs. Cirone. I'm good. Mary took my award as soon as we got home and put it high on the shelf next to the TV for everyone to see." His voice filled with excitement and enthusiasm, and Heidi suddenly became unsure whether or not it was right to call, thinking momentarily that she may have acted too quickly. But it was too late for that. As the boy finished saying "for everyone to see," Heidi heard the sound of Mary's voice becoming louder as she obviously came closer to the phone.

"Hello," Mary said with an inquisitive tone.

"Good mornin', dea'. I hope it's not too early to be callin'," Heidi said.

"Good morning, Heidi. No, no it's fine. The kids and I have been ready to go for a while now. We're just killin' time. Is everything ok?"

"Oh, it's all good, Mary. It was just soo nice ta' see the three of ya' last night, and I kind o' hoped we might get to see ya' all again, soon. Oh, by the way…how is that little angles lip? Did he fall or somethin'?"

Mary felt the inquisitiveness in Heidi's voice, but she knew that Heidi had no problem getting to the bottom of the little gossip boxes that were all over Chesterfield and Isles Port waiting to be filled, and that Heidi Cirone was not a vengeful woman, she just wanted to save the world.

The phrase, "hope to see ya' all again soon," did not register in Mary's mind as an invitation that included Kenny; but knowing the Cirone family, if Kenny showed up they would welcome him with the same enthusiasm as they'd met her with last night. Now, she couldn't help know that Heidi was wondering about the fat lip and the bruise on her arm.

"Well, that would be nice, Heidi. I'm sure the kids would love getting together outside of school and all. Let's work on that, and see how the schedules work out. I'll get back to you," she said, and immediately after the words left her lips, she regretted being so easy and available. And, Bobby had an unfortunate run-in with a huge piece of fire wood. Hit 'im right in the mouth." There was an uncomfortable pause on Heidi's end, when suddenly, she said somewhat distracted, "Good, good, Mary…" With those words, Heidi turned toward the front of the store to see where Filbert was, and came eyeball to eyeball with him. She had forgotten to keep him in sight during the conversation with Mary, and overhearing the distant talk, he'd come to see what it was all about. Heidi's stare became submissive, and she thought it best to end the conversation quickly.

"Ok, dea', I'm gonna' let ya' go. I'm sure yaw' busy to get goin' and we'll talk soon. Bye-bye now."

"What in hell was that all about?" Filbert asked and from the look on his face, he was not a happy camper.

Kenny never returned home on the evening of the Poster Awards. He never called at home, or at the nursing home the day of or the day after. Mary, seated at her desk, not only contemplated the possibility that something had happened to him, which worried her occasionally, but she was also faced with Heidi's sudden interest in resurrecting the relationship Mary thought long since dead. The phone call from her this morning had pretty much confirmed that she suspected something was wrong, and knowing Heidi, Mary thought she figured the bruised arm fit right in line with the fat lip. Needless to say, Mary's day was going along like a train without tracks. She couldn't get anything done. She felt she handled the incoming calls poorly, and simple everyday communication with her co-workers plain-old sucked as far as she was concerned.

The last place she wanted to be was here. She considered calling home just to make sure everything was okay, but interestingly enough, the way her life had gone in the past several months, deep down the thought of Kenny not being home was soothing to her. She was just tired of the nervous stomach each time she came to within several miles from home. She was fed-up with his calls to her at work.

"*How could two people, so much in love a few short years ago, drift so far apart in body and soul so quickly?*" she thought.

In the store, Filbert was so angry with Heidi for calling Mary; he completely ignored her for the entire first half of the day.

In return, she ignored him for spite, causing him further

irritation. At the sight of Bullet Carter parking just off to the side of the gas-pump, Filbert, knowing how Bullet irritated the hell out of Heidi, took much delight in his boisterous self-announcement of his arrival. Hearing her husband, Heidi took a deep breath, exhaled rapidly, and left through the rear door, slamming it as she went. Filbert chuckled, feeling victorious, despite the relative insignificance of his victory.

Disregarding the earliness of the day, Bullet Carter stormed in and ordered breakfast in a loud, sing-song voice.

"Two hot-doggies, mustard and relish, pleeease."

Filbert simply shook his head in disbelief.

Although Filbert was reluctant to side with Heidi and her suspicions about Bobby's fat lip and the marks on Mary's arm, he was bubbling over with the need to say something to Bullet, knowing how easily it would be to stir the old pot of hate which seemed to overflow where Bullet and Kenny were concerned. Filbert prided himself on being a man of great restraint, but he was rapidly becoming dissuaded of that trait, won over by those that believed Kenny to be an anti-Christ sent to change the world as a Down Easta' saw it.

Neither man had discovered any leads to Millie and her involvement with the men in the infamous photo, increasing their frustration at their inability to pin something solid on Kenny. Bullet told Filbert he'd tried his best, yet it was as if she didn't exist—not here in Washington County, or anywhere else for that matter.

Kenny was becoming careless in most things that he did now. What he was careful about was anything that involved his master plan, the one he never got to share with Mary. He broadened his arena, taking several trips to Boston in the fish truck with the driver. That was the reason he never showed up at the award night. On one such trip, returning from Bean Town, and thinking he was unrecognizable in the truck, he saw the little pirate fellow out front of the diesel pumps at Dysart's Truck Stop off I-95, just south of Bangor. The last thing he needed was a knock-down, drag-out battle in the middle of this parking lot full o' long-haul truckers who would love every second of it, especially with the size of load the supposedly empty truck he was in was hauling Down East. He sank low in the seat, focusing a watchful eye on the guy. This was the driver's regular fuel-and-eat stop. Kenny told him to use his regular route as if he were meeting him at the air-strip, so as not to throw any suspicion on the truck or the driver.

He couldn't help but wonder when seeing the pirate how many times he might have crossed the path of this very truck, in this jungle of trucks, never knowing where and to whom the vehicle and the contents were headed. He laughed to himself, watching him gas up at the pumps directly opposite him, and his warped sense of humor coaxed him to get out and just say hi. When the driver returned to the cab after filling the tanks, he suggested they go in to get some lunch.

"You go ahead, I'll be in to join you in a few," Kenny said, holding up his cell-phone. The driver pulled the truck to a parking slot on the side of the building, as Kenny swiveled his head with every direction change of the truck, keeping the guy in sight at all times with his eyes or through the mirror on his side. It was lucky for Kenny that he remained cautious, for when the pirate fellow finished filling his car, he also went into the building and didn't come right out. Though Kenny's stomach growled with hunger, another few hits from a joint and gulping a little black pill would soon allow the pangs to subside.

This was far better than a confrontation that could bring in a State Trooper, being this close to the interstate, or some local country bumpkin cop from nearby. He sat back, resting his head on his folded leather jacket, the pocket containing his .32 semi-automatic pistol, and relaxed while waiting for the results of his indulgence to take effect. Keeping an eye on the front of the building, he fell fast asleep.

26

T<small>HE ROADS WERE ONCE AGAIN CLEAR</small> of snow and ice, but the remnants of winter remained with the residual salt, sand, and gravel, and some less-pronounced frost-heaves, for lack of direct sun, were left unsmoothed in the shaded areas. People in the midst of commerce, along with those who'd wintered here, began to poke their heads toward the sunlight and hopefully a new season of prosperity.

With spring came many cleanup needs. Tree and limb blow-downs from winter's fury needed to be cut and hauled away. Roofs needed to be re-shingled. Automobiles needed inspection stickers, and with sand and gravel on the roads all winter, lots of people needed windshields and various auto parts. The old adage applied: *"Them that have get; and them that don't…."*

Bartering went so far, then cash was king, and you didn't need to live Down East to understand what that meant.

There were those who lived well through inheritance or hard work, and in most cases, both applied. Bullet Carter was set apart from the two. It was true, he'd been left the family homestead, which his two boys had burned down while playing with matches.

That's what most people believed ignited the fury and finally the separation between him and Millie. From the onset of his existence, the only thing Bullet ever did to make money was work in the woods early on during their marriage, and later drive the loaded blueberry trucks from the fields to the factory and back throughout the season, which for the most part began around the first of August. In Bullet's case, the season could run into the second week of September, depending on the size of the annual crop. Those late-harvested fields were given to the locals, and paid much more per bushel than the high-season rates paid to the transients, who by then were already up north picking apples, or diggin' up potatoes.

Rumor had followed Bullet all of his life about his financial situation and his socially detached lifestyle, but he had no creditors. He lived off the land, and took what he could, and that usually meant wild game taken out of season, but the way he saw it, the government took plenty from those less fortunate and he was only takin' what was rightfully his anyway. In most cases, he made no secret about it, which distanced him further from the self-righteous, God-fearin' folks who lived in the big houses along the river in Isles Port and Chesterfield. The law, as he understood it, was for folks like them along the river. They had more to protect than he did, and what he needed to protect, he could do with a shotgun and a bunch of 00 buckshot.

Most everyone had a certain level of respect for the law, but those like Bullet, living out away from town, seemed to feel the same about self-protection: laying their head on a pillow each night that covered a loaded .45 was their law.

Bullet wasn't a cold-hearted person; he simply lived by his own set of rules. All this talk of Millie being back, and that picture of her and men he didn't know, or maybe did know, is what burned him down deep. He no longer had feelings for her, and he'd come to accept life without his only two sons, but he couldn't stop wondering where they both were while their so-called mother was exposing herself in a picture with a bunch of naked men. Like a fool, he'd given that picture to Harry Circus and that little toy cop, Ralph Bailey. What he wanted now was to get that photo back, and if it was the last thing he did, he'd find the photographer who seemed hidden by the flash.

Filbert wanted to keep his and Heidi's interaction with Mary to a minimum. He just didn't want any trouble with Kenny, and right now, Kenny was the last person he wanted to reconnect with. Sharing that with Heidi would only cause her to dig deeper as to why, and he was not going to let her in on his and Bullet's small-scale investigation into Kenny's possible involvement with the glossy print or the still-elusive movies. He knew Heidi would get her way when it finally came to inviting Mary and the kids over, probably for a mid-Sunday afternoon dinner. Usually, if it was slow on Sunday, and it generally was, Filbert would close the store early, and that became family day for whatever Heidi planned for them. A walk along the river just below the dam was a favorite, or taking the kids swimming with the canoe upstream to the slow, moving water of the West Branch of the Pauguagus River when the weather was warm enough.

It was still early in the season for the river adventures, but with the coming of spring, Easter was just around the corner, and he shuddered at the thought of Heidi being the producer of an Easter-egg hunt around the store and the house out back.

Filbert was the placement director for the multitude of colored eggs, reducing his profit margin once again. There was no use arguing with her once she set her mind on something. Easter was still a few weeks away, and so he dismissed the thought as a premature worry that might not even come to light. He still had a difficult time shaking the thought while waiting on customers all morning long. He was anxious for this day to end.

The spring rains came in torrents nearly every third day, maintaining a continued winter chill, much to the dismay of all who cherished the uplifting of spirits from a new beginning. For one person however, a new beginning did not mean anticipating fair weather. Kenny was pushing hard to maximize his supply to those who craved his commodities. In his own estimations, this year would blow the lid off all past ventures, and he no longer considered firewood and seasonal Christmas wreath-making anything but a Down East Dork's way of wasting time for a peanut share of the wealth. This attitude he projected to any and all who would listen, creating a viral animosity toward him.

Those he supplied thought of him as being inspired. Those who watched from behind curtains thought of him as evil, and a cancer that needed to be cut out.

Kenny increased his consumption of vodka to a fifth every second day, and he consumed far more of his own supply, which included a huge assortment of prescription and illegal drugs of all sorts. For the chosen few who associated with him, he appeared to be floating on a cloud—a cloud that began to resemble fog as time went on. Though he was becoming more careless in every aspect of his life, no one saw it more than Mary and the two kids. His attitude toward them, or anyone for that matter, could change as quickly as the weather in New England. One minute he was lavishing them with ideas of getting ice cream and taking a ride to the city for shopping; the next minute he was savagely scolding young Bobby for some minor insignificant deed that could have easily been overlooked.

Everyone felt the need to walk on eggshells when he was around. It became more comfortable to be away from him than to be with him. There was one thing he remained conservative about, if someone like Kenny could be considered conservative: he was extremely careful who he approached about his little movie money-making venture. He hadn't made any money from it yet, but his portfolio of success was becoming quite large, and he wanted to add one more masterpiece to his collection.

One windy, rainy day he decided to make contact with the key figure in the plan, the only person on earth who knew of it—someone he knew to be extremely discreet with the subject matter. Kenny's intuition ruled his life's direction, and for whatever reason it prompted him, he thought it best before leaving to make a thorough cleaning of his pickup. He removed the resident fifth of vodka from under the driver's seat, and cleaned out the ashtray of residue from smoking material, and even decided not to carry any with him. Hesitating, he removed the pistol from his jacket pocket last.

"*There, clean as a freshly sliced cucumber ready to be served,*" he thought to himself while inspecting the truck.

Though he remained in his fog from an evening of heavy substance use, he gave no thought to his lack of awareness for his surroundings. Yet for some time now, the effects of the drugs and alcohol had been slowing his reaction time to a snail's pace, whether he realized it or not, and nothing Mary could say had any effect on him any longer. He left the house just before noon, usually a slow time around town and the surrounding by-ways. He felt exceptionally well this morning, buzzing along on caffeine alone.

He was several miles from home, on a deserted section of gravel road, when a glimmer of sunshine broke through the thick ceiling of clouds, and when it did, Kenny became distracted by it momentarily, gazing up at it and thinking of a song from years earlier with the phrase, *"But mama, that's where the fun is."* And at that very moment, he raced through a cross-road intersection and was broad-sided by another vehicle, sending the pickup spinning wildly out of control into a field, coming to a stop facing the opposite direction he'd been traveling.

It happened so suddenly, there was no time to think before it was over. Sitting behind the wheel, both hands resting at his side on the front seat, stunned and disoriented, Kenny looked around in an attempt to regain his bearings. The first thing he saw was steam rising from the front end of the other vehicle, which was about a hundred feet or so away. It appeared totaled. Strangely enough, thinking back to the actual crash, Kenny was surprised at how much it had sounded like something popping as opposed to a loud crashing sound with breaking glass. He'd never been in an accident before.

"Well, that's what you get, Kenny-boy. You should 'a got stoned before leavin' the fuckin' house. Now look at this shit!"

He looked again toward the other vehicle, and saw no sign

of movement, yet his first thought was not of the individual in the car, but the thought of being thankful for having cleaned out the truck before leaving. Several moments passed as Kenny sat quietly, noticing now that the car was a small foreign job, and he slowly slid himself from the seat and concerned himself with the damage to his truck. He gave no thought to the person in the car who might have been injured and still had not, at this time, begun to move about.

The truck had been hit on the passenger side; when reaching that side it became obvious to Kenny that the reason for the major spinning was that the damage was reserved to the extreme end of the rear fender—very little damage as compared to the other vehicle. He formed a smirking, nonchalant expression at the sight, and began a casual saunter toward the other car. Surprisingly, he lacked any outward sign of anger, which was unusual, since an incident of this magnitude should have pushed him over the edge.

"What were the fuckin' chances of meetin' another car here, at the same fuckin' time in the middle of some forgotten blueberry field, out in no-fuck place?" He thought as he neared the car. He wasn't really angry at that point, but just then, the sky opened up, releasing a torrential downpour that soaked Kenny to the bone, which released a barrage of profanity that appeared to have no end. His leather jacket kept his upper body dry, and he was thankful for that, because his cell-phone was in the pocket where he generally carried the pistol. He was several feet from the car when he reached for the phone, and at the same instant he noticed the young woman whose head tilted back against the headrest.

She was bleeding from the nose, and a huge swelling appeared over her left eye. At the sight of her, a pang of nervousness rumbled in his midsection, but only for a second, then Kenny's cold heart iced over once again.

"Shit, she's a little hottie. How come I've never met this little cutie?" he thought. Then he hollered out, "Hey…hey! Are you all right? Do I need to call 911?" She opened her eyes at that point and looked at him.

"I'm a bit dizzy," she said, then her head fell back against the headrest and she closed her eyes and appeared to be out cold again.

Without another word, Kenny reached for his cell phone, and surprisingly enough, the number to call the cops was programmed; he hit the buttons and the phone began ringing. He explained to whomever it was that answered where they were and what had happened, and while relaying the information, he subconsciously hoped it wouldn't be "holier-than-thou Harry" who responded. They were only a couple of miles as the crow flies from the tarred road, but the twists and turns over the gravel had them closer to five miles in. He knew that the information he passed along would bring an emergency vehicle as well.

"Just what I fuckin' needed. The cops and the medics. Great way to start the day." He said this at just above an audible level.

The young woman asked, "What?" Thinking he'd been talking to her.

It couldn't have been more than five minutes after he called and ten to twelve minutes after the crash when Kenny noticed the blue strobe-lights cutting through the thick ground fog which had developed quickly after the downpour. He strained his eyes, focusing on the rapidly approaching police car, and his heart skipped a beat, not from fear, but simply from the realization that it was Trooper Harry Circus.

He looked in on the woman and asked once again how she was, and told her that the cops were here and the ambulance would be soon, and that she would be okay now. She thanked him without opening her eyes, and he looked down, shook his head, and then kicked a small stone in an attempt to release some of his frustration. Right now, he wished he'd decided to stay home with a huge swallow of the clear liquid he'd become so fond of lately. The last place he wanted to be was here.

Harry barely had time to stop the cruiser before the EMT van appeared at the same distant location where Kenny had first noticed the trooper's car, and right behind them was Ralph Bailey, who also served as the local tow truck operator when not on constable duty.

Kenny felt like blowin' chow and crappin' at the same time.

"*Great, the place is crawlin' with morons,*" he thought.

The trooper simply looked toward Kenny with a shit-eatin' grin, then toward his pickup truck which remained in the field where it had come to rest after the crash.

"Are you all right?" Harry asked, looking at Kenny while walking toward the young woman.

"Yeah," Kenny responded.

The trooper reached the door of the smashed car, and talked in low tones to the woman. She seemed to be more alert than when Kenny had spoken to her.

Kenny looked toward the approaching tow-truck, and when he did, the sight of Ralph Bailey behind the wheel forced him to laugh out loud, saying, "I swear to God that guy's got his finger so far up his nose, I think he's scratchin' his friggin' brain." Harry looked in his direction, thinking Kenny was talking to him, but he only saw Kenny laughing even louder than before.

No one saw Ralph except for Kenny as of yet, and Harry dismissed Kenny's comment as another level of his sarcasm toward an authority figure. At this point, the EMTs had reached the car, and were making arrangements to transport, never hearing Kenny's remark.

Less than fifteen minutes after the emergency team arrived, the young woman appeared to be resting comfortably in the back of the ambulance and on her way to Machias and the hospital there for observation for the blow to the head. It was determined that she'd slammed her head into the steering wheel on impact. All that remained now were a few questions for Kenny-boy.

Of all the company Kenny preferred not keeping, these two men were at the top of the list. He and the two lawmen stood by the wrecked car and watched as the ambulance and its brilliant red strobe lights disappeared through the thickening fog. It had been several months since Harry was this close to Kenny. The last time he remembered was the day he stopped in the driveway at their place to talk, or rather he'd been hedged, by both Kenny and Mary about the pirate fellow.

Not wanting to be obvious, Harry moved a bit closer to Kenny in an attempt to detect any rancid aroma of pot, yet there was none, so he moved away. Harry and Ralph walked toward the tow-truck, conferring in undertones, and it appeared to Kenny that they were intentionally ignoring him, which irritated him further for having been here this long already.

He began pacing around the wreck, kicking gravel against the hubcaps in an obvious attempt at distracting the two, who now began to show signs of their own irritation toward Kenny's antics. Kenny, taking a deep breath and exhaling loudly, rubbed his hand over the leg of his jeans, still soaked from the earlier downpour. The two men broke from their parley, which was obviously about their "little man," right in front of them.

Ralph went to the controls on the hoist, preparing for the tow. Harry walked with an almost imperious stride toward Kenny, and the trooper's facial expression could not hide his anxious desire to question him.

"Ok, tell me all about it. What happened? How? When? Where? All of it," the trooper demanded, not bothering to hide his sarcasm. But Kenny was having none of it.

"Look, *teacher*. I'm not raising my hand to go pee-pee for you, or anyone else, so cut shovelin' the crap and we'll get this behind us. That ok with you?" he asked.

The trooper's jaw nearly came unhinged at the comment, and from the look on his face, he would have none of what Kenny was shoveling.

"I'm not going to stand here and be insulted by the likes of you. You're the one that got into the accident; I'm the one that's going to find out all about it. Is that clear?" he asked.

"Clear as clean water, chief," Kenny responded in a lower tone.

Without saying another word, Harry walked at a quick pace toward the pickup, which appeared to be high on one side, but lacking as much damage as the car that Ralph was now preparing for towing.

As they neared the truck, Harry realized that the rear wheels were down from a slight shoulder on the edge of the road, and when he noticed the angle of the tire skid-marks in the gravel, he realized it was probably the way the vehicle had come to rest after the crash.

"She came out of nowhere. I never had time to blink," Kenny said, then, thinking how badly he wanted this to be over, he began reconstructing the accident for the trooper.

Harry, as if paying no attention to what Kenny said, examined the truck, and much to his surprise saw very little damage. He gave credit for that to the age of the truck, knowing how well vehicles from that era had been constructed. However, in actuality, he listened attentively to every word, and for the life of him, there didn't seem to be a single point exaggerated, but being Harry Circus, he simply needed to think there was more. Trying not to be provocative, the trooper asked, "Do you come out here much?"

"Excuse me?" Kenny replied.

"I'm just asking. There isn't much out here, and both these roads, on either end, don't go anywhere except back to the black-top," he noted.

"Yeah. No...Whatever," Kenny said.

Both men looked toward the sound of Ralph's air-horn slicing through the still- thickening fog as he pulled away with the car chained to the tow-truck's boom. Harry flipped a half-wave in his direction, and Kenny, spit onto the shoulder, giving a rise to the trooper's growing disdain for the young man standing beside him. Everything appeared to be going as normally as possible for a trooper responding to a fender bender, and that's all it was except for the young woman's injuries and the fact it involved Kenny Collins.

"*Nothing out of the ordinary. I just want to have a look inside the truck,*" Harry thought. All was fine until he put his hand on the driver's side door handle.

"And what in the fuck do you think you're doin'? The little

girl's car hit me on the rear fender, not in the fuckin' driver's seat, or anywhere else in that fuckin' truck," Kenny said coldly.

"You watch yaw' mouth young man! Don't you tell me how to investigate an accident!" Harry responded with an authoritative bark.

"Well, you keep your sticky little fingers out of my truck."

"I was simply looking for the mileage on this old clunker," he said and Kenny took immediate offense.

"Look, you holier-than-thou piece-o'-crap cop. You're no better than the rest of us. I'd like to see you in ten years, see how you make out!" Kenny said loudly, as a tiny bit of spit flew from his mouth.

"You watch yaw' mouth, little-man. Don't you tell me how to do my job! You probably won't be around hea' in ten years; the way yaw' goin', you'll probably be sleepin' with the fishes," Harry barked back, and he was so furious, his lower lip trembled.

27

T HE ARGUMENT BETWEEN KENNY AND THE TROOPER only intensified the already strained demeanor that overshadowed them both concerning their feelings toward each other. Kenny remained pumped with anger, increasing his need for defiance against conformity of any kind, and lessening his respect for authority even more. The first thing he did upon returning home was to reach for the bottle of vodka and roll a joint. The second thing he did was to return the pistol to his inside jacket pocket, vowing never to remove it again.

From the time he'd left the house just before noon and the time he downed the last drop from his first drink, a little more than two hours had passed. He hadn't called Mary at work for quite some time, and his first thought was not to call her now, but as the effects of drinking and drugs began to take hold of his decision-making, he thought his experience with the trooper to be worthy of sharing. He was proud of the way he'd put the trooper in his place.

He poured himself another drink, while half remained of the smoke, and he took them along with the cell phone out to the side of the house where the reception for the phone was best. Upon reaching the outside, he noticed the sun breaking out through the rapidly thinning clouds.

The direct sun caused steam to rise from the damp cedar-shingles and the tall grass on that side of the house. The field between this side of the house and the river was hidden from the road, making it a conveniently private spot to enjoy the sun, out of sight from passersby. He continued to feel angry from the confrontation, and he hoped that the trooper felt the same. He laughed now, remembering the sight of the trooper's trembling lip after telling him to watch his mouth.

"You watch your mouth!" he said to himself, mimicking Harry. Many years before, he had told his mother that it was only nuts who talked to themselves, although his mind never allowed his memory to trigger a route to that time in his life and those things he said.

Loneliness was not a human emotion that ever burdened Kenny. Today, however, either the confrontation at the crash site or the effects of the substance in the bright sunshine of the spring afternoon, or both, suddenly left him feeling unfulfilled and lonely—feelings he neither recognized nor accepted easily.

Surprisingly, he sat motionless for the remainder of the long afternoon, entranced by the hypnotic glimmer of the slow-moving water in the distance. He forgot about calling Mary, and placed the phone on the ground next to the half-drunk vodka, the ice long since melted, while the feeling of solitude overwhelmed him. Suddenly, a line from a high school class came to memory.

"I go alone, like to a lonely dragon, that his fen makes fear'd and talked of more than seen." (Shakespeare's *Coriolanus*)

Loneliness was not the emotion felt by Mary at this time. The lawyer she'd been working with called her at work to inform her that a judge had issued the guardianship decree several minutes ago. Mary was now the kids' new mom in the eyes of the law. No happier woman lived this day. The moment she placed the receiver into its cradle, the whoop emitted from this petite, young woman seemed amplified in the ears of her co-workers throughout their small office. Mary had made no secret of her intentions once Virgil had told her that he realized he'd be in over his head with the kids. Her co-workers left their desks and came to her with supportive congratulations for the person they knew worked feverishly to make a better life for two great kids.

Mary floated through the remainder of the day. Her thoughts were of the kids and whether or not they completely understood the intensity of this accomplishment. She asked to leave early so that she would be there to pick them up when school let out. She just wanted to hug them now, knowing that everything would be fine with their little family. She thought of a hundred of their favorite foods she wanted to cook for them tonight. They needed to celebrate. She had them now and it was all legal.

On the ride home, nearing the summit of Cathance Hill, a feeling of foreboding took hold of her, an expected fear of having to tell Kenny, who'd been somewhat mild-mannered about the situation so far. She wondered how he would take the news of her guardianship. She feared him, but she knew there wasn't anything he could do to derail the forward movement of her plan for the kids. He'd have to live with it.

Then she laughed, more like a giggle, the very moment she cleared the summit.

"I'm their legal guardian. There is nothing he or anyone can do now. Virgil gave me his blessing. He gave his statement to the court, and the decree was handed down," she said to herself aloud, and with a feeling of self-control. She hadn't felt like this since she and Kenny had run away and gotten married. It seemed so long ago now.

She turned the radio up, and with the sound of rock 'n' roll blaring from the one good speaker left in the dash, she pushed the gas pedal down confidently, and headed downhill toward Chesterfield.

The heat of the spring afternoon was refreshing. Mary could see Kenny's truck parked in its usual spot in front of the barn, the glare of the sun's rays reflected off of the roof, but it wasn't until she turned into the driveway that she noticed the damage to the rear portion of the fender facing the house. Her heart

243

immediately thumped with an irregular beat, knowing how Kenny prided himself on maintaining a level of near-perfection of his belongings. The old truck was número-uno on his priority list.

"That damage wasn't there when I left for work this morning, so why didn't he call me at work to blow his lid about it?" she wondered. *"Something like this would normally be a good reason for his blood pressure to blow, with my ears being the sounding-board for his frustrations."* She wished she were back at work, if only for this moment when she would go in the house to find...

Upon entering the barn, she found it considerably warmer, obviously from the sun shining in through the small, southern exposed windows, yet the dank air of the closed-in area made her feel somewhat nauseated. The kitchen, however, was cool, and the fresh air coming in through the open windows revived her senses, yet the entire house lacked the normal vibes that always seemed to encapsulate it whenever Kenny or the kids were there. She wondered briefly if he'd gone off with someone and left the truck out front, as every room she entered was empty. It wasn't until she reached their bedroom that she saw Kenny, just outside the window. It appeared to her that he was sleeping, and from this distance, the redness of his face was a good indication of how long he'd been there. She went to the open window and called his name, softly so as not to jolt him from sleep. At the sound of her voice, one eye opened first; then, as if an alarm-clock had gone off, he sprang to an erect position, looking confused and starring in the direction of her voice.

"Well, mista' man of leisure. You've got quite a sun-burn thea'," she said.

She wanted to laugh, but doing so before knowing what type of mood he was in could be foolish. But the look on his face with the redness made it difficult not to laugh, so she bit her tongue and kept the humor of it inside.

He came to his feet slowly, picked up the glass with the remaining clear liquid and the phone before walking toward the house, scanning the area where he'd been sitting. He met Mary at the rear entrance.

"I don't know what in hell happened to the joint I had," he said. "It musta' fell into the tall grass."

She put her arms around his neck as he entered, and when her face touched his, she felt the heat of the burn.

"Wow, you are hot."

"That's what I keep tellin' ya', Mary, but it's like, in one ear and out the other." They laughed and shared that moment.

She wanted to blurt right out about the phone call at work and the good news from the lawyer, even though he'd been against her getting a woman lawyer in the first place, but she thought it best to see how everything had unfolded with the news of his day first, and she'd wing it from there. They stood by the rear door for several minutes. She watched as he grimaced after taking a sip from the air-temperature vodka and melted ice, then he asked, "What time is it, anyway?"

He seemed dazed when Mary told him it was 3:00 p.m. He wasn't sure how long he'd been out back, yet it felt much longer to him.

"Why are you home so early?" he asked.

She began smiling, a broad, happy smile, one like Kenny hadn't seen in quite a long time.

"I left early to pick the kids up from school," she said as she looked at her wristwatch, "...which is almost time now," she said, with a shortness of breath.

Kenny had a puzzled look on his face. He wasn't here usually at this time of the day, and his paranoid mind began to ask why, when, and how. He wasn't sure he believed her explanation.

"I'll go with you," he said and his suggestion surprised Mary, but excited her at the same time.

"Sure, I'll bet the kids would get a kick outta both of us picking them up."

Then, without thinking she blurted out, "Hey, what in hell happened to your pickup?"

"Yeah, that's another story, and there's another story I can add to that one. I'll tell you about it on our way," he replied.

They left quickly. Mary figured they would arrive at the school in the nick of time. The moment Mary started the engine of her car; Kenny began relaying the events of the late morning accident and the ensuing argument with Harry Circus. Mary's eyes were wide with anticipation at each new twist, yet it was unclear to her how much of it was being made up, because she knew Kenny was quite a storyteller, and how much of it had really happened.

"What about the girl, is she ok?" Mary asked. Kenny told her that she'd been taken in an ambulance, and Mary went on at that point with question after question, causing Kenny to experience a burst of anxiety. His patience began wearing thin with each additional inquiry asked at every tenth-of-a-mile increase on the odometer.

"Yo, yo, Mary, take a pill, will ya'? Who's tellin' this story, anyway?"

"Sorry, I just got worried for a minute. We don't have insurance on our cars, ya' know and…" He interrupted her at that point.

"She hit me, remember? That's the last thing on my mind now. Did you hear anything I said about the holy-roller cop and what I said to him? That creep is gonna cause trouble for me, and I'm not gonna take any shit from him or that little imp rent-a-cop, Ralph. One of them is gonna eat some lead," he said.

Mary couldn't believe his lack of concern for the young woman who'd been hurt and taken to the hospital. Everything was about Kenny.

His last comment sent a stream of hot bile from Mary's already nervous stomach to burn her esophagus. The happy feeling that had nearly overpowered her only a few short hours ago was gone, replaced by the fear and uncertainty of their life with Kenny Collins. Suddenly, she became excited with the sight of the school just ahead, and she hoped that he would refrain from going further with the story once the kids got in the car.

The school bell sounded as Mary entered the small parking area, and she pulled to the side next to the home-plate back-stop of the Little League diamond, so as not to block the way of any incoming school buses. A steady flow of excited children exited the building, which resembled an emergency evacuation drill at the nursing home; even the teachers standing by, who looked burned to a frazzle, made no attempt to maintain any type of order.

"Will you look at the faces on those teachers? I wouldn't want that friggin' job if they paid me double. I bet a few of them could use a good buzz after a day in there," Kenny said with a slight laugh to his voice.

Mary wanted to respond to that comment with something, knowing the true reason for the way the teachers looked, but saying what she thought of his comment now would only stir an already boiling pot. She wondered if the kids would notice her car. She hadn't told them, since she hadn't received the news until later in the morning, that she was coming to get them, and she didn't have to wait very long to know. Tabitha and Bobby walked out together holding hands, and Tabitha immediately saw the car. She smiled and pointed so that her brother could see the reason for her happiness. They ran together toward the car.

Their pent-up energy from spending a large part of the day inside the building was obvious. The speed at which they both spoke, at times together, then Tabi to Mary and Bobby to Kenny, forced the two adults to pay closer attention to accommodate the whirlwind. Kenny motioned with his hand his desire to get moving, and Mary told the kids to settle back in the rear seat as she started the car. All appeared normal until the bright color of the blue trooper car pulled alongside Mary's, and the look on Harry Circus' face did not resemble a happy parent there for a pickup. He said nothing, nor did he attempt to exit his car. He simply stared in their direction. Kenny and the trooper shared almost identical poker-face expressions.

Kenny's earlier curiosity about whether or not the trooper felt the same level of anger was confirmed. Then, the trooper nonchalantly looked away and pulled his car ahead slowly, taking every precaution for the thinning crowd of children, still wandering between the building and the buses. He parked his car besides the principal's and got out, never looking back toward Mary's car, and went inside the school.

"Oh...my...God. Was all that because of the accident this morning?" Mary asked. Two sets of ears in the back seat perked up.

"Never mind, just drive the hell outta here," Kenny said, watching the trooper.

Mary could no longer remain silent. Her nerves had gotten the best of her, and no level of fear could stop her from speaking.

"I'm thinking there was much more you were going to share with me about the little fender-bender this morning," she murmured, not wanting to use the word "accident," but then she realized it was probably too late for that.

"Well, you didn't let me finish..." And he was immediately interrupted by both kids, speaking in unison with questions.

"You were in an accident, Kenny?" they asked.

He inhaled a deep breath, remained still for several seconds, then responded along with the exhale. "Yes."

Bobby, seated directly behind him, placed a soft hand on his shoulder and asked, "How ya' doin', Kenny-boy?"—a small voice filled with concern.

"Well, I'm not mildewin', kid," Kenny answered, never looking back toward the boy.

Bobby appeared puzzled by Kenny's response, not fully understanding the play on words. Mary felt good to hear him so willing to share his concern; yet she was angry that Kenny had chosen to be so casually thoughtless in regard to Bobby's empathy.

With the trooper's last-minute appearance and Kenny's silence, there remained little time, Mary thought, before an eruption took place, with Kenny being the epicenter. It became very apparent to Mary the moment she pulled the car out from the school lot that Kenny had already begun building his psychological wall, which for all practical purposes, Mary knew from past experiences, could take several hours for him to come out from behind, if he came out at all this evening. He became quiet, withdrawn, and unmoving in his place in the passenger seat, and stared vacantly out the window.

The kids had become accustomed to Kenny's moods, and like Mary, understood what the behavior presaged. They immediately went still, not knowing what might happen next.

Mary adjusted the rear-view mirror, and was able to view both kids in the back seat and with the twist of the mirror. She spoke softly.

"So, how was your day, you two?" she asked.

They looked up from their books (which both had taken out when they saw Kenny slip into his mood), simultaneously looking, as if cued, directly into the reflection of Mary's eyes.

Tabitha went first. "Well, Mrs. Maher is piling it on for homework this week. She thinks it builds character in young people."

Mary remembered when she'd had Mrs. Maher for a teacher, and for some reason she thought she remembered that teacher telling her class the same thing. She shook her head with a smirk on her face, which she hid from the two kids behind her.

Bobby asked why they were being picked up instead of walking to Mary's friend down the road as they usually did until Mary got home, and the very second he asked, Mary pulled into her friend's driveway just to tell her she had the kids. Her friend and the kids saw each other simultaneously from their windows, and they all waved as Mary pulled out. Tabitha and Bobby waved, almost frantically, until they were out of sight from the house. Kenny never moved once. The late afternoon air was still warm, yet spring did not mean hot in the Down East area. It invigorated the senses and instilled a sense of freedom from the confinement of winter.

"*A new beginning,*" Mary thought, as she peered into the back seat and saw her children. She wanted to just blurt it out: "*I'm your new mom!*" Then she thought better of it.

Having Kenny in this mood was not how she'd imagined the scene playing out when she did finally tell the kids the good news. She would tell them later, when they were alone together. If she knew Kenny, and she did, he would probably sulk for most of the evening until he smoked and drank enough to let the feeling from his day pass, so that part, or all, of his wall would drop so he could open up to her.

His silence was intimidating. No one knew what to say or do. The kids talked to Mary only, and in low tones, so as not to distract him. Kenny went to his room shortly after they arrived home, and would not make an appearance until the kids went upstairs for the night. Several times, Mary toyed with the idea of asking him if he'd like something to eat or drink, and each time she neared the closed door, the thick smell of pot filled the area, and she withdrew without saying a word.

Both Tabi and Bobby had become accustomed to wishing Kenny and Mary a good night, with hugs for each. Tonight, however, Mary suggested they give her an extra one and she'd pass it on to Kenny later. It was as if he'd waited for the sound of their feet going upstairs, before leaving his self-imposed segregation for the evening. He fixed himself a drink, though it was probably the last thing he needed at this point, and sat on the couch thinking of the little divorcée as he waited for Mary to come down.

She hurried the kids along, but not in a way that they noticed, and all the while she was anticipating him being in the kitchen, wanting a late supper, or on the couch with another drink, ready to unload his grief on her.

Thinking ahead was a great way to prepare oneself for the unexpected when living with Kenny. Mary had found out early, and it appeared the kids were fast learners as well.

Once she got downstairs, she found Kenny on the couch. "Well, nice ta' see ya,'" she said

"Whatever."

"Can I fix you something? I haven't seen you eat anything since I came home this afternoon." She kept her focus on his expression as she talked.

"Yeah, you can fix me something. You got a recipe for lead-pie a certain trooper might enjoy?" He said just prior to taking a large gulp from the vodka. The ice tinkled against the glass as he rested it on his leg.

"Wow, what in hell happened out thea' today?" Mary asked. "You never finished tellin' me about it."

The day had been warm, but there was a noticeable drop in temperature now that it was early evening; Mary stoked the stove, and the burning hardwood snapped and crackled, keeping the house warm and cozy.

She wanted to know what it was that had set him off so dramatically, yet she wasn't prepared to prod him for information. She knew he would open up, when he was ready, no matter what. Knowing well that sitting quietly would allow him to come out of his shell, she bit her tongue and waited, and it didn't take long.

He began in a low voice, making it difficult for her to hear, but his tone rose in volume quickly as he descriptively unfolded the events of the day for her. He actually included his comment about Ralph having his finger crammed up his nose, and Mary cringed at that one. She couldn't stop herself from interjecting, however, when he spoke of the young woman's injuries and not knowing who she was, or where she was from. He simply shrugged her off and did not answer any questions about her. He rambled on for several more minutes, and then her curiosity got the best of her.

"What were you doin' a-way out thea in the first place?" she asked. She did not intend the question to be provocative. She had simply gotten a little too comfortable and let her guard down. And that was the little insignificant thing that touched him off.

"Curiosity killed the cat, Mary. Are you fuckin' kidding me! That dim-witted, two-legged fart-bag of a trooper asked me the same thing, now you?" With that said, he pitched the half-filled glass against the hot woodstove, sending shards of glass flying across the room and billowing clouds of steam rose up along the pipe. She pressed herself against the armrest, her only dead-end means of backing away, and the look he focused in her direction forced a rumble of fear to quake deep within her mid-section.

Before the microscopic splinters of glass settled, Kenny was moving toward the kitchen, while the sound of scurrying footsteps from upstairs forced Mary to a standing position, afraid to move in her stocking feet, for the glass was everywhere, but she did want to reach the staircase before the kids made it to the bottom.

Kenny had his leather jacket on over his shirtless torso, and seeing her approaching rapidly, thought she was coming at him for whatever reason his paranoid mind would have him believe. He turned quickly, a reactionary movement, and without Mary suspecting it, she walked headlong into his outstretched arm and closed fist, taking it on the right side of the jaw, knocking her backwards and flat on her back to the screams of the two kids, now standing in full view of what just happened. Without saying a word, or looking to see if Mary was injured, Kenny walked out into the cold night and was gone.

28

MARY WAS DAZED, BUT UNINJURED. The two kids were frantic as they hovered over her, trying to get her to her feet.

"Why?" Tabitha repeated the word over and over, seeing her sister lying before her disoriented and hurt. Bobby was the protective little bro now, staying calm and quiet, comforting Mary as best he could. The moment Mary sat up, with help from her brother, never thinking of herself or any possible injury; she reached for both children and brought them close to her, giving them the hug she'd intended to give several hours ago when she'd picked them up. Mary wiped the tears softly from her sister's face with her hand and tried to calm her, but the child shook with spasms of fear. Mary began crying, not for herself, but for the young woman she'd vowed to protect. Bobby was the pillar of strength. He held them both, never shedding a tear.

It was 9:00 p.m., somewhat early yet for Down East standards, though lights were out for most folks. Normally, the lights would be dimmed in the old farmhouse by the road. However, it was difficult to see the miniscule particles of fine glass, sprayed over the hardwood floor and surrounding scatter-rugs in Mary's living room.

The kids would not leave her side. Tabi had locked all of the doors and windows; fearing Kenny would barge in unannounced and right now, her anger was stronger than her fear.

Mary's jaw ached, but it didn't appear to be dislocated, or with any loose teeth, outside of her inability to bring her teeth together while her mouth was closed, indicating to her that swelling had begun. The thought of going to work looking like the boxer taken by the sucker punch did not appeal to her.

She wanted so badly to tell them about the guardianship, but Kenny had taken the love out of that one tonight. It somehow felt to her like an anti-climax. She would tell them as soon as she felt the time right. After all, nothing could change that decision now. Given the lateness of the hour, the thought came to her that she and the kids would take a sick day tomorrow, but they wouldn't be spending it here, in what felt to her as a very hateful place. The bad memories in this house were rapidly outweighing the good, and if she had any guts at all, she felt that she could burn the place to the ground and never be bothered with guilt.

All three of them jumped at the slightest sound from outside. Even the tinking sound of the cast-iron stove as it contracted from the rise in temperatures from the drafting chimney flue caused them to look in different directions. She tried to reassure them that all would be fine, without success. It was as plain to her as the painful jaw that she was as frightened as the kids of Kenny's obvious return. It wasn't if, it was the when he returned that kept them jumpy.

The early morning sun reflected off of the "Get Gas" sign out front of the Quick-Stop. Spring had sprung, and so had the attitude of Maine State Trooper, Harry Circus.

"I'll tell ya' what, Ralph, that *"little-man"* of ours is a pain where the sun don't shine."

The two men sat at their usual table, as Harry told his story about the accident scene and Kenny's behavior after Ralph left with the damaged car. The young woman who'd been rushed to the hospital would be fine. Harry had found out that she was here from Massachusetts visiting friends and was actually lost when the accident happened. A simple case of being in the wrong place…

"You should o' heard the way he talked to me, Ralph. That young man has no respect for authority, or himself for that matter. He is out of control. When I asked him simply, 'do you come out hea' much?' he got so smug with me."

Ralph had a bad feeling about all this. He would never tell Harry exactly how he felt—that was simply the politician in him. He respected Harry, but he took his own opinion just so far. That's how he was able to maintain his place with so many who'd gone before him.

The trooper went on at length about Kenny. He didn't come right out and say he wanted to pin something on him, but he kept referring to his father's words, "The law must sustain a monumental patience to apprehend the offender."

Ralph was beginning to think that Harry needed to go fishing. Take a little time away from the office, so-to-speak. He was about to suggest it, in a diplomatic way, when Harry began speaking again.

"Ya' know, Ralph, I think it's time we started digging a bit deeper where that photo is concerned." And Harry began verbally drafting out a plan and the part each one of them would play and in what direction they would go. Ralph sat patiently, dunking his stale donut, nodding his head in agreement and occasionally jotting something down; like the name of a place Harry suggested that he go, or something that he should do. It was obvious now that Harry had had enough of what Kenny Collins was shoveling, and the last thing he'd be ready to do was go fishing.

Filbert Cirone was not a violent man, but as the trooper and constable configured their plan on the other side of town, Filbert held his son, Amos, the oldest of his three children by the shirt collar and demanded to know where he'd gotten the marijuana cigarette.

"You aar' gonna tell me where you got this little stick o' crap," he said.

Filbert's eyes bulged from their sockets. The side of his face appeared to glow a dangerous shade of red, and the jugular on the side of his neck seemed prepared to burst as he shook the boy again, reaffirming his demand. They stood at the back entrance of the store, somewhat hidden from anyone who might pass by out front or on the side road to the bridge behind the store. Neither Amos nor anyone else had ever seen Filbert this angry. The boy was understandably frightened.

"I found it." Amos said simply.

"That is a bunch o' crap, and yaw' not gonna shovel any of it at me, young man," Filbert said.

Without warning, Filbert began to feel tightness in his left arm, the one stretched out with the hand that clutched at the boy's collar, and the hand began to go weak.

His pride would not allow him to show weakness in front of the boy, and he quickly released his hold and grabbed the boy with both hands by the shoulders. The feeling in his left arm, however, did not change, and he simply dismissed it for the heavy lifting he did alone, while emptying the newly arrived stock for the store. At that very moment, Heidi shrieked at the sight of them, obviously entangled in a physical quarrel.

Without a nanosecond passing since Heidi's scream, Filbert's mind exhumed the thought of the small group of teens who had originally uncovered the photo of Millie and the naked men behind the store. Now, he could not dismiss the possibility that his own son was part of that group, and his anger flared once again, shaking the boy in his effort to finally dislodge the truth. To the best of his knowledge, Heidi knew nothing of the photo, and if she did, kept the information to herself. Hearing the sound of her footsteps and her voice drawing nearer, he would not bring it up now, as much as he would like to.

In the real world, most sixteen-year-olds have already sampled the taste and smell of marijuana. The outside world had arrived Down East—not that it hadn't long ago—but in the minds of most everyone born here, and like any town in the world, denial can be as dangerous as the act being denied.

Bullet hadn't been seen in town, or anywhere else for that matter, for several days. It was a bit unusual, yet there were times he'd gone out to camp—he had a small place off the Stud Mill Road that not many knew of. He went out there when he needed to be alone, as he put it, *"When the fuckin' world's gone nuts and thea' droppin' thea' fuckin' shells all ova' the place."*

It seemed he took more hurt from finding out about the photo of Millie than he'd let on. True, it may not have been Millie he concerned himself with, it was the two boys. He didn't have a relationship with any of the three, and no one thought (at least by what he said) that he wanted to start anything up with the boys. It's just that everything that had happened to him as a youngster—losing his father the way that he did—had always left him with a heavy heart, and as an adult, it seemed nothing had changed for him when it came to family. He was nursing his feelings.

The fact that spring was in full bloom heightened his desire to be out there preparing for the late summer when his deer hunting season began. That was his sole reason for being at the camp—to scout out the deer activity in that area in preparation for the hunt that always came sooner than one could plan for. He had built the camp by himself several years before meeting Millie. He worked on it during the late autumn and early winter before getting snowed out, and then resumed construction, sometimes in the late spring when he needed to get away by himself as he did this trip. Looking out the window now and thinking back, he couldn't remember ever bringing Millie or the boys out here. It was a rustic cabin, a simple one-roomer with a cookstove, two sets of bunk-beds, and a sink with a hand pump and a black plastic PVC pipe directly to the lake.

Lake water was fine to drink as long as you boiled it first, and that wasn't a problem with a six-cover wood cookstove. The Lake was called Horse Shoe Lake, which was located on paper company land at the bottom of Hard Wood Ridge just north of the Stud

Mill Road, and the drive was several miles of fairly rough going. Back then, you could get a permit to build a place like this fairly easily, and that's what he'd done. Soon after it was built, the paper company had stopped allowing building permits in that area, and so his was and always would be the only camp on the lake. The fact that it was so difficult to reach made it all the more endearing to Bullet. He would return to his regular routine as soon as he got being out to camp out of his system, however long it took.

Unknown to anyone, Kenny was staying at a remote camp also. Not his, but Filbert's. Kenny had been given the key long ago, and now Filbert had forgotten, one Kenny never returned at the time of the eviction. From the moment he was given the key, Kenny used the camp as his own, much to his pleasure. As the crow flies, the camp was less than five miles north of Bullet's. It also was the only camp on a pond that had no name, so was even more remote. Neither man could know that the other was there. Filbert had built his camp long before Bullet knew how to drive a nail, and hadn't been out there himself for a good ten years. That was why he'd given the key to Kenny, knowing very well he'd use it.

The dew glistened in the early morning sun on the tips of saplings, sprawling ever closer to the shoreline. Kenny didn't go there to thin the brush for a better view of the water. He went there because of what had happened last night, to try and get his thoughts together with some uninterrupted substance use.

He was very much alone here, yet only once did he give a thought to whether or not he'd hurt Mary before storming out in only his leather jacket and sweats, which was all that he still wore now. He'd stocked the cabin long ago with coffee, salt, and pepper, canned goods of all types, and an assortment of freeze-dried foods to last for long periods without refrigeration. The camp was set up surprisingly similar to Bullet's; however, it had an addition on the rear which accommodated a full-sized, well-furnished bedroom, including a huge dresser with full-length mirror. It had an attached outhouse, which Filbert had added at Heidi's request.

"If I'm gonna stay out hea', I'm not walkin' out thea' in

the middle o' the night to piddle," she told Filbert, and he accommodated her wishes.

Kenny sat quietly, watching the sun reflecting brilliantly off the shimmering water. The sound of the chirping birds and the whistling, wind-blown pines once again gave him a feeling of loneliness. He swore aloud now, cursing the fact he'd brought no beer or vodka with him. All he had was a small bag of pot, a pipe to smoke it, and all the black coffee he could swallow. He hadn't planned on coming here last night until the scene with Mary.

It's strange how life comes around full circle at times. That is where Mary found herself, emotionally, the morning after Kenny's whack to the jaw. The children had seemed to be in a fog the remainder of the night. They both helped to clean up the broken glass, and were unable to snap out of it no matter how hard Mary tried to reassure them that it all was behind them now.

She was up before dawn, still jumpy at the slightest unfamiliar sound, looking through one window, then another. She hoped the kids would sleep in, allowing the healing effects of sleep to coax them toward a more peaceful demeanor, but before the thought could be fully absorbed into her conscious mind, she heard Bobby's quick footsteps scurrying toward the stairs and his trembling voice calling her name. There was no time for breakfast this morning, and without a second thought of what they would do, they loaded themselves into her car and drove directly to the old farmhouse down by the river, the old homestead, Virgil's place.

29

Preparing for summer sometimes starts during the height of a Nor-Easter, a white-out blizzard, and a long-lost Vesey Seed Catalogue. The pictures of enormous flowering plants and bulbous vegetables caressed the imagination on an excursion to the warmer days of the year. The old timer's rule of thumb was to not plant before the full moon of June, realizing that a frost could still be considered a threat until that late in the season; but before then, the small garden tillers could be heard across the countryside, and cow dung was now a lucrative commodity for every dairy farmer in the area.

As rapidly as time moves on, the long-anticipated gardens were planted, and if you were lucky, or had a green thumb you might serve up a decent-sized plate full of home-grown peas for the Fourth of July along with a freshly caught Atlantic salmon from the Paguagus River. Then it was all downhill from there. Before you knew it…summer was gone and you were tillin' that garden under and getting' ready for another winter.

The predictions were the same each year: the lack of snow cover during the coldest time of winter had probably burned the blueberry plants, and everyone should expect the price to be at the very bottom of the market; or with the desperate lack of rain in the spring the blueberry growers would cry poor-mouth early and predict the coming devastation to the crop. No doubt all would suffer (primarily the rakers) as the relentless ranting of the growers always seemed to drive the cost down to rake a half-bushel until it was time to harvest, and then everybody got paid and all was forgotten of devastation. All–in all, the crop, being wild from nature, always seemed to pull in a much larger harvest each year. People paid their past-due bills with blueberry money, got themselves ready for winter, and just tied up some of the loose ends that always seemed to be coming untied. When it came right to it, however, most everyone had enough to spend at the Bangor or Blue Hill State Fairs.

"Ayah," as the old timers would say, "the weather this spring had the makings of a great summer, and the buds on them trees and the blueberry bushes were plentiful." For the younger generation, those who'd been born here or transplanted, it didn't much matter if there were berries or not, as long as there was spending money for the friggin' fair.

Several days had passed since Mary had taken the kids to Virgil's. They returned home several times for forgotten items, still in fear that Kenny would be there, but it was obvious to them by the temperature inside that no one had been there since they'd left. They rummaged through a change of clothes for several more days, just the kinds of things you might take when going on vacation to make the stay more comfortable and then they always left quickly.

Mary was never as unsure of herself as she was at this time in her life. She told Virgil some trumped-up story about slipping and falling after a tugging match with Kenny over nothing and Kenny going out to camp afterwards, since that was the most obvious possibility.

Virgil appeared to be surprisingly unprejudiced over the entire matter, even overlooking the children's concerned expressions, yet they would stand behind whatever Mary said, knowing well that what she said would be in their best interest.

Overnight, the swelling of Mary's jaw subsided. She covered

the bruising that remained with make-up, and following their "sick day," all three returned to the daily routines they were accustomed to. Being with Virgil was a major restructuring of habit for all of them, yet in some minute way they all seemed to appreciate the time with their father, who remained attentive to their needs, and it all felt like a short period of time removed from reality.

Mary noticed that Virgil seemed to refrain from drinking while they visited, and he never questioned, in depth, why they were actually there. That alone was a welcomed lack of stress in their pressure-cooker life with Kenny. Several times, when Mary and Tabi found themselves alone, Tabi questioned her about when she thought they might return home, and the answer was the same: "We'll see how things are in the next couple of days." Apparently it was a good-enough answer for her, and she went about her business.

For the first time that Mary could remember, Virgil took to Bobby as a father to a son. They'd go to the barn workshop, spending hours after school there, and Mary had to call them for supper the first two evenings they were together. It was during one of those evening meals that Mary was able to tell the kids about the guardianship, and she thought it no better time than to have Virgil there so all could receive the news together. It was good, she thought, but knowing Virgil, it wouldn't last forever, and that was fine with her; but she worried how Bobby would handle the separation that was soon to come. She questioned everything about herself now and her place in her relationship with Kenny. All that she'd done to rescue these kids from a totally dysfunctional relationship had backfired, and now they burned in their own little hell, for which she could find no means to extinguish the flames.

The first thing Bullet made sure of upon returning from camp, rested and spewing of piss and vinegar, was to make sure he met the trooper and that little bag o' pus, Ralph Bailey, at the Quick-

Stop for their morning cup. The last person they wanted to see that particular morning was the man who had given them the picture they just happened to be re-examining again at that very moment.

As usual, Bullet sauntered in like he owned the place. "Well, well. It looks as though I'm right on schedule. You fellas getting off on that photo, aar' ya'? Or is it just stuck to yaw' fingers?" Bullet asked, with a sickening laugh.

"I suppose you think you're pretty funny. This here may be police business, and you, my friend, may just be interrupting." The trooper's voice held an official tone. Ralph did all he could to stifle a laugh.

"Oh, ya'… police business, how could I forget that, bein' in such company? I hope you don't forget who gave ya' the picture, Harry. Seems ta' me, if memory serves me right, I neva' said ya' could keep it faa' eva'," Bullet said.

Without moving their heads, the two lawmen looked toward each other with a slight movement of their eyes, and their expressions spoke volumes without the utterance of a word.

"Sit down, make yourself comfortable," Harry said.

"I thought you'd neva' ask," Bullet responded.

Ralph could feel the tension between the two men as Bullet sat close to Harry, as opposed to near the middle of the table, and immediately reached for the photo. But he wasn't quick enough. Harry flipped it face down toward his coffee mug.

The two men starred at one another for the longest moment, the silence at the table so thick you could cut it with a dull knife. Ralph studied them from his place with quick jerks of his eyes, and forgot to remove his stale donut from his coffee. When he finally lifted it, he realized that all of what he'd dunked was at the bottom of his cup.

"I guess my biggest question right now is why did ya' give this picture to me in the first place if ya' didn't want me to do something about it?" Harry asked. His stare was penetrating, causing Bullet to pause before answering, yet he never flinched from Harry's stare.

"Did I eva' come right out and tell ya' I wanted you to do somethin' about this? And I don't rememba' sayin' nothin' about you keepin' it," Bullet said, maintaining his penetrating stare. Harry remained quiet after Bullet's last statement, contemplating the truth in what he said. Harry had never given a second thought to Bullet asking for the return of the photo, but it was a definite deflation of his enthusiasm about digging deeper into it with the plan he and Ralph had discussed only days earlier.

"Look, I was simply considering the best interest of all who may be involved here—Millie for one—and I thought you were concerned for the boys." Harry realized he was stretching it a bit, and hoped Bullet didn't see through the ploy.

"You know better thun' that. If I wanted help from you or... your side-kick here," he said, staring at Ralph as he remembered the day Ralph had cuffed him, "I'd ask for it. Until then, I'd like the picture back."

30

WITH THE INTENSITY OF A STALKING CAT, after being brought up to speed about the reason for the confrontation between her two men, Heidi swung into action as only a mother can do when the time comes to protect her young, or to give them an education. She began her own investigation into her son's activities.

The first place she decided to start was at the school. She hated getting her feathers ruffled by anyone, and when she did, the last thing she worried about was ruffling a few feathers on the other bird, which could include a possible plucking. Where her only son was concerned, since he'd been found with pot in his pocket, plucking appeared to be the chore of choice. She made several calls, one to the principal, the other a short time later to Amos' teacher. In her mind, for whatever reason, getting to them separately, before they could discuss the matter of why she called for the late morning meeting, was paramount.

For the time being, Amos was grounded, and no longer allowed to ride the school bus with his friends, which for a sixteen-year old was an embarrassment of major proportions amongst his peers. The bus carried both grammar and high-school students, and his two younger sisters took that same bus. When it came to small town talk, children rivaled the adults as gossip-mongers. The plan was devised quickly. Filbert or Heidi would drive Amos to and from school until further notice. He would be at the store every day to help out, and he would be attending any meeting, including the one scheduled this morning.

In the meeting, Heidi held nothing back of her plans of discipline for Amos, which included random stop-ins at the school by her or Filbert whenever she felt the need, and she told them she was relying on school officials to monitor the situation. Several times, the principal interjected, simply to agree with her.

Most days following the meeting, if the weather permitted, Amos rode in the bed of the pickup, refusing to ride up front with either Filbert or Heidi, whoever was available to drive him, doing his best to maintain a low profile. He knew his parents— his mother especially—where discipline was concerned, and he knew his hell was only now just beginning.

It was while preparing for one such trip that Heidi informed the two younger children that she would be picking them up after Amos this afternoon. The same afternoon, Mary was picking Tabi and Bobby up from school. It was simply coincidence that the two women arrived at the same time, parking near the baseball back-stop fence. It was a complete and welcomed surprise for Heidi when she saw Mary, and she felt instant relief from the dysfunction, as she now thought of her life with Amos. She told Amos to remain where he was, got out of the truck, and walked directly to Mary's side of the vehicle.

"Mary, it's so good to see you dea'. We haven't been in touch as we said we would. I know, I know, busy, busy," she said with a smile. Mary returned the smile, pausing for a moment, thinking of what she might say, and that was all that Heidi needed.

"We went by yaw' place on aar' way to Ellsworth the otha' night. It looked as though the place was empty, dea'," she said.

Mary knew there was no use in lying, not about that anyway, but she'd be damned if she'd tell all at this point, at least not to Heidi.

"Yeah, we had a bunch o' stuff that belonged to the kids left-ta'-home at Virgil's, and thought we might just as well stay put while going through it. Dad was happy to have us thea'," she said, and realized she had just called Virgil "Dad."

"Well, is Kenny staying with ya'?" Heidi asked, and Mary shrugged her shoulders in an attempt to evade the question, looking toward the rear seat, and it was then that Heidi noticed the discoloration around the lower jaw of Mary's face, obviously an area that Mary had neglected to touch up with make-up before leaving Ellsworth.

Already shouldering the anger for her son's behavior, it didn't take much for Heidi's pulse rate to soar to new heights. She was now convinced that the little pig, Kenny, was hittin' them. Call it woman's intuition, or plain old life's experiences, no one was going to tell her different now. The little pig was outta the pen as far as Heidi Cirone was concerned. There was no longer any question in her mind now.

She wanted to come right out and ask Mary, but she knew that Mary would lie to her about what really happened. Heidi could be cold-hearted at times; it was simply the protective instinct in the law for her survival, but she felt only hurt for Mary and the two kids. She wanted to blame herself for not seeing it before now. All those months Mary had cared for Lulu while they rented the place by the river. She watched Mary's lips move, yet the sound faded in and out. Her thoughts of what might have happened behind closed doors were overpowering.

Then, her need to know coaxed her on.

"Mary, is everything all right on the home-front? I know that taking on the responsibility of havin' those two kids ta' home, well, sometimes it can put the old squeeze on a relationship. Ya' know what I mean, dea?" Heidi asked.

Suddenly, it felt to Mary as if her world was collapsing on her shoulders, and without even feeling the sadness overwhelm her, Mary broke down in tears.

After several days out at the camp, Kenny became restless. He burned many daylight hours walking around the isolated lake, contemplating his return home and his plan to ingratiate himself into Mary's and the kid's good graces. He was bored, and besides, there was no electricity out here and his cell phone was dead, and the service was periodic to none anyway, which meant no business contacts. Like most people, he did his best thinking while he was alone, and here, in the middle of the forest, the distractions were minimal. He felt that if he had to take another bite of canned beans with molasses brown-bread, he would go crazy. He decided he was leaving here today.

"Kiss my ass, trees!" he yelled. "I've got to get outta this place!" His voice echoed across the deserted lake, resounding off the distant tree-line, and he headed toward the cabin to prepare to leave.

31

WITH PHOTO IN HAND, Bullet headed directly to Filbert's store. Months had passed since the first conversation between Harry and Filbert which led them all on a fruitless endeavor in search for the mystery filmmaker. Each man felt anger from deep within himself; however, each was angry for a different reason.

Filbert continued to stew over finding the joint in Amos' pocket. It was simply a lucky find; the outline of the cigarette had simply shown through the material. Had the boy placed it anywhere else, Filbert might never have seen it. Filbert's first thought was to let the trooper in on it, letting him give the boy a good tongue-lashing, but Heidi would have none of it.

"Something like this will get around fast enough without bringin' in the law," she said.

Today, all Filbert hoped for was an uneventful day.

It was unlike Heidi to keep something, no matter how big or small, from Filbert. However, she had never told him of her encounter with Mary at the school. She'd left early this morning for Ellsworth and would, she thought, go over it with him at length when she returned.

When Bullet's pickup pulled up alongside the store, Filbert realized that it had been quite a spell since he'd seen his old friend, and imagining that he'd probably been out to camp. The door-chime rattled with Bullet's clamorous entrance.

"Well, mista'-man, did ya miss me?" Bullet asked, almost hollering.

"You, maybe…I'm naut' too sure about that voice," Filbert said with a laugh.

Bullet began looking around suspiciously to see if they were alone. Filbert recognized the gesture and nodded his head in the positive.

"Have a good look, big-boy. I got this from Harry, not ten minutes ago. If looks could kill, they'd be stretchin' me out on a slab right now," Bullet said.

Filbert looked down, took one look at the photo, and immediately flipped it over.

"What in God's name?" He wanted to turn the photo over again to have another look, but his hand would not move to allow him to do so.

"Ya' know, this is the first time I see this thing and it makes me feel so bad for Millie. Have ya' been able to locate her, or the boys?" he asked.

"No, but I haven't spent much time on it since I gave the picture to Harry. I've been out ta' camp for a couple o' days and got all fired-up about it again. That's when I decided to get this back from Harry and that little fart-sack, half-a-badge Ralph," Bullet said. "But the day I gave it to 'em, Ralph pointed out that he thought he saw a reflection in the background of this photo. He thought it might be the person taking the picture."

Without knowing it, both men were thinking the same thought, for when Filbert began speaking, so did Bullet.

"Go ahead, you started first," Bullet said.

"Well, I can't help but think that my old friend, Kenny has something to do with this. I have nothin' to go on but my gut feelin.'"

"Funny, I was just thinkin' the same thing."

Before turning the photo over for a closer look at the subject of Ralph's observations, the two men got themselves caught up on the going's-on while Bullet was out to the camp, and Filbert reluctantly told him about the fracas with Amos and the joint in his shirt pocket.

Both men displayed similar facial expressions, yet Bullet listened attentively—something he rarely did—without the utterance of a single word until Filbert finished. Then Bullet went back to the previous subject.

"Seems to me that our little friggin' friend Kenny's coaxin' for some lead-pie," Bullet said. There was something in the way he said it that gave Filbert a tremor of uncertainty from deep within him. Filbert motioned for Bullet to follow, going toward the rear of the store and more privacy in the event of a customer entering the front. He knew Heidi would be in Ellsworth for most of the morning, making the rear entrance secure.

"Take a good look at it, Filbert. I can't for the life o' me see nothin' in that flash; neva' mind somebody," Bullet said, while pointing toward the photo.

Filbert felt embarrassed gawking at what looked like a peep-show photo before him of the naked ex-wife of his friend, who was standing right next to him. He couldn't imagine how it would feel if the tables were turned and his ex-wife (if he had an ex) was in Millie's place and doin' what she was doin'.

The two men resembled school-boys, looking around so as not to get caught; however, there was anger in Filbert and resentment in Bullet, and the expressions would be wildly mistaken by anyone who saw them.

"Whaddaya make of it, Filbert? I see a major flash, but for the life o' me, that's all I see," he said.

"Outside o' the people in the shot, mostly it's all dark in the room. I can't say that I see more than the flash myself."

Someone came in the front door, and Filbert flipped the picture over and told Bullet to stay here with it, then went to see who had walked in.

While he was out front, Bullet brought the picture closer to the window to the side of the sandwich counter, turning his head frequently, making sure he was still alone. The added light simply glared on the glossy finish, and he realized that more light was not the answer. Studying the photo more intently than when he first received it from the kid's father, his mind guided his thoughts to his past with Millie. He had always thought of himself as a rebel, and when he'd first met her, their personalities seemed so alike, and that's what attracted them to each other. "*'Yeah, she liked her beer,*" he thought, "*but so do I. I can't believe she would stoop this low and let herself do something like this. And where were those two little rug-rats? What did she do with them?*"

"Did ya recognize anything?" Bullet jumped at the sound of Filbert's voice as he came around the corner from the beer cooler. He was carrying a frosty cold sixteen-ounce Bud, and handed it to Bullet.

"Whoa! You musta' been readin' my mind. I can use one o' thi'em' right now." Bullet's eyes reflected his joy at being handed his favorite drink. He popped the top immediately and guzzled about half of the contents before coming up for air.

The door-chime jingled once again, and it appeared that Filbert's wish for an uneventful day was just that, a wish. He was now preoccupied with thoughts of the photo, and made no attempt to hide his desire to move along from anyone whose intention it was to hold him in conversation about anything. So it was each time someone entered the store. He quickly returned to the sandwich counter, and on his second return, he brought two beers.

"Well, mista' man. A bit early in the day fa' ya' and that stuff, ain't it?" Bullet asked.

Filbert simply grunted and popped the top on his beer, took a respectful sip, and put the can down on the counter-top.

"What if anything have you seen different since I've been gone?

"Nothin'. I almost blinded myself from this glossy shit when I brought it to the window for a closer look."

Filbert took the photo in hand once again, and this time with his eyes rested from his jaunt to the front, focused his attention to the area around the flash and the faint silhouette of the person behind it. The sun was bright, and it reflected brightly on the counter-top. Filbert turned away from it, darkening the shot for a better look. He took another sip from the beer, and he noticed for the first time how labored Bullet's breathing was. He assumed it was a result of the amount of smoking Bullet did, and there was nothing he could do about it. Both men were silent in their study of the photo, as if cramming for an exam. Bullet looked up, then around, making sure they were alone and at that very moment Filbert let out a gasp.

"Well, tickle me easy!"

"What?" Bullet asked.

"Take a good look at this."

"Whatcha find?"

"I want you to take a close look at this picture, one more time. Take a close look."

Bullet nearly strained his eyes to the point of blurring his vision, yet he saw nothing that he hadn't seen before giving the photo to Filbert.

"Are ya lookin', or what?" Filbert asked. Then he began to swear mightily, which was completely out of the norm for him.

"I'm sorry Filbert," Bullet said helplessly. "I'm not seein' nothin' that wasn't here before."

"Let me tell you now, mista' man, you take a good look at that full-sized mirror thea'. You go ahead and tell me that's not the one in mine and Heidi's room out-ta' camp," he asked.

"Sonovabitch!" Bullet said.

32

IT IS INEVITABLE THAT ONCE THE HOURGLASS IS REVERSED, the sand will pass from one bulb to the next uninterrupted until it's finished, and so it is with life. Hour by hour, day by day, it just keeps sifting down. There are days when it appears that time stands still, yet as sure as rain falls on everyone eventually, so winter came and went and spring felt even shorter.

The spring rains came in damaging torrents at times, saturating the earth and maximizing the breeding potential of the mosquito and the infamous Maine blackfly populations. And right on schedule, those pesky blood-suckers appeared—and they were thirsty. It seemed strange, when spring finally arrived in full bloom, the weather Down East made you feel as though you'd passed over into Shangri-La, and the best time of the year to be outdoors was doomed by those flies, creating a hell on earth for man and beast alike. Nothing was spared from their vampire-like bite.

A level of solemnity came over Mary and the two kids while their stay at Virgil's was extended to well over a week. The threesome gave little to no thought of home, as they blended right in here at the old homestead, even though Mary still held a deep suspicion for her father that would most likely fester for the remainder of her life. As all good things must eventually end, so did their stay at Virgil's. Through it all, she couldn't help worrying (as hard as she tried not to) about where Kenny was, despite her anger toward him for creating this nightmare. To her own surprise, she hoped he was safe.

Mary prepared breakfast on their final morning, a larger, more leisurely experience than the usual quick glass of orange juice or a rapidly devoured cup of fruit yogurt at home. Here, almost religiously, Virgil required eggs, bacon, toast, and home-fries, all of which needed to be cooked in, or slathered in, real butter, and all had to be served with steaming hot brewed tea, juice of some sort, and always something sweet to top it all off. Mary never complained; she simply accepted it as the cost of running away from home again.

"The price of an education," she thought.

The kids had known the night before that today would be their day to go home. They each had a slew of questions for her, mostly about Kenny and what would happen when they got there. Virgil remained mentally removed from the reason they had come in the first place, but remaining removed didn't automatically make him ignorant of the fact that something stank on their home-front. He allowed the kids ample room in the mornings, realizing that their pent-up energy from the long night's rest had to be released, and so he sat back and enjoyed his last morning with the three of his kids together, and Mary's great breakfast, a change from the breakfasts that he would undoubtedly enjoy at the Quick-Stop's microwave in the mornings to come.

He watched, with a feeling he was never able to find for them while they all lived at home, yet it was as if they truly were born to someone else. He had been, all of his life, the epitome of a loner, and Mary had set him free when she took the kids. For that, he would be eternally grateful. As the kids finished up in the dining room and went off to get ready for school, Virgil had to say what he'd been thinking.

"I suppose you'll be headin' home after school and work tonight?"

"Yeah, we have all the stuff they'd left here and…"

She paused, searching for what she might say next, yet words failed her, and she looked out the window and the view where her mother had found such solace.

"If ya' want me to go with ya' when ya' go back home, I can. He may be a lot younger than me, but I ain't scared o' no man," he said.

For the first time since they'd arrived, Mary knew that her father had known all along why they were here. He'd simply said nothing to her or the kids. Her first thought was to let him meet them there. A show of force could only protect them from an unexpected outburst of anger from Kenny. It's what all three of them feared. Suddenly, she realized that Kenny had not tried to make contact since they'd gone their separate ways.

"Look, if you want to come over with us, that would be fine, but really, there's nothing to worry about. Everything is okay at home. Kenny's been out ta' camp, that's all." She wondered if that's where he'd really been. "He'll probably be thin and gaunt from lack of my cookin'," she said with a half-smile.

Virgil looked at her from the corner of one eye, as a slight grin developed on his face. "If ya' change yaw' mind, call me. I'll be here all day cleanin' up after you three." His smile was as broad as could be.

A sense of sorrow for having to leave began to tug at her emotions at that point. She knew she could never allow her feelings of mistrust for her father to change after all this time, not even if his denial for his loathsome actions of so long ago disappeared, and he came right out and said he was sorry and asked for forgiveness. For those that knew him, it appeared that Virgil, spending as much time as he was alone after the kids left, was on a different path to his own salvation. He would probably always be a drinking man, yet each time Mary brought the kids to visit, he was involved in some kind of home-improvement project, and he was sober.

For the time being however, everything had to stay the way that it was, if only for Mary's sake.

Before the sun rose and became visible over Eastport, Filbert and Bullet made their way through the still, dark morning out to Filbert's camp on the pond with no name. Heidi, much to her dismay, had opened the store, allowing the two to go off together. She never found the time to tell Filbert about the bruise she saw on the side of Mary's face, and he had purposely neglected to tell her where they were going and why they decided to take off.

With the photo tucked in his shirt pocket, Bullet rambled on about how he'd found things out at his camp last week, and how he thought the deer herd was healthy and the fish were jumpin'. Filbert nodded his head occasionally, but he had one thing on his mind, and that was the vision of the full-sized mirror in the camp bedroom. He couldn't imagine, in a place as close to nature and Godliness as his little camp was, that someone would use it for such ungodly smut as what had appeared in this photo. He swore to himself that if it were true, he would burn the place to the earth and watch it until the flames subsided and all that was left were ashes.

"*That place has many loving memories for me and Heidi,*" he thought. Then suddenly, as if he'd been hit with a bat, the realization of not having taken the key away from Kenny at the time of the eviction flashed into his consciousness.

"I haven't the fucking'est clue why I forgot to take that friggin' key from Kenny when I tossed them out in the first place."

Bullet, having absolutely no idea what he was talking about, looked toward Filbert with the dumbest look and asked, "What?"

"I gave Kenny a key to the camp a long time ago, when I was showin' him around and teachin' him things I regret teachin' him now. He's just a big-bag o' lazy, and if I'd 'a' known what I know now…"

With each mile driven, the road became narrower, and the natural isolation of the area should have calmed them as it normally did when they were out here, but it only added to the rising head of steam and anger. Bullet looked out his window and saw the sun as a huge, red ball of fire, illuminating the earth through the silhouette of the thick forest.

The pond came into view first, allowing both men simultaneously to expel a breath of relief at the sight, and at that moment the roof and the stone chimney became visible. The way into the camp area was off the narrow gravel road, continuing on two tire tracks through tall grass matted with pine-needles, several inches thick. Before entering the tracked way, Filbert noticed that a vehicle had been in and out, from the scuffed needles at the entry way. The tire scuffs were fresh.

"Well, I'll be damned. Someone's been in hea' all right, and it looks as though they left in one hell of a hurry," Filbert said.

Bullet looked around as if he might see something, yet all there was to see in the still, dim early morning light was the faint glimmering of the pond water. The two men fell silent in anticipation of what they might find in the clearing where the camp was, or in the camp itself. Upon arriving in the clearing, Filbert pulled to the far end and swung the pickup so as to face the cabin, and stopped. They exited simultaneously. Filbert reached for his shotgun hanging from a rear-window rack, and Bullet carried a .45 caliber pistol, tucked into his belt. Neither one feared what they might find, nor were they in fear of whatever it might be. It was simply a way of life to carry a firearm while in the woods.

The faint scent of a recently smothered fire came from the chimney, and Filbert hadn't been here in so long, he knew he didn't stack that fresh firewood by the door. No one from around here ever locked their doors at home or camp, but after someone had come in and stolen everything out of Filbert's camp many years before, he'd started locking up, thus the need for the key, which Kenny obviously still had. Filbert unlocked the door with his key, and they walked into a neat-as-a-pin cabin. The smell of fresh-perked coffee lingered in the air, and the cookstove was warm to the touch.

"Well mista' man, who's been sleepin' in my bed?" Bullet asked with a chuckle.

Bullet ambled about the kitchen area, looking for what, only he knew. Filbert, after leaning the shotgun against the door-frame, asked Bullet for the photo and without saying another word went directly to the bedroom addition. The room's furnishings had been moved from where he remembered them being, yet for some strange reason, nothing significant appeared out of place. He walked slowly through the room, while overtones of Bullet's noisy exploration of the other room reached his eardrums; then he stood in the reflection of the full-sized mirror, and slowly brought the picture to eye level for comparison.

"That good-fa'-nothin' hippie-bastard. If this ain't my mirror, I'll bite the head off a live Pa'tridge " Filbert said, at just above a whisper.

Bullet left the kitchen area at a quick pace and came to stand shoulder to shoulder with Filbert in front of the mirror.

"Well… Sonovabitch," he said.

33

U PON ENTERING THE HOUSE, which he'd been absent from for nearly a week, Kenny knew in a second that no one else had been here since he'd gone. Spring evenings can still be fairly cold, and had there been a fire in one of the stoves, the house would have retained the heat for at least part of the next morning. This house and these stoves were cold. Being Kenny, the first thing he did was to plug his cell-phone into the charger, and from the indicator, it would take some time to recharge.

He brewed a pot of coffee and rolled a couple of joints, and contemplated whether or not to call Mary at work, or just wait for her and the kids to come home, if they came back at all. He wondered where she'd taken them. His first thought was her close friend down by the school, but her place was too small for all of them. She could be staying with her friend in Ellsworth, the one that got her the job, whose name he couldn't remember.

"*Maybe she went home to fat-faced Virgil?*" he wondered.

While these thoughts played out in his imaginative mind, he suddenly realized that the .12-gauge shotgun, normally leaning against the kitchen door-frame, was not in residence.

"What the frig?" he said loudly.

He got up from the table where he sat and went to the door. He opened it, looking into the barn and around the door-frame there to see if for some reason Mary had put it there, but there was nothing. Besides, he would have seen it when he came in that way.

"*Guns were in the house for protection,*" he thought to himself. "*Why would she put it outside?*"

Panic immediately set in as he thought perhaps someone had come in while they were away. He began checking the house, feverishly, yet nothing but the shotgun was out of place.

Any thought of reconciliation went out the window with the smoke from his freshly lit joint. Coffee and something to eat became low priority. Frustrated now, he checked the phone charger for the second time as he passed it, smacking the side of the unit, thinking it wasn't working as the charged indicator showed no flags. He drew the smoke deeper into his lungs, and with each draw, his anxiety and paranoia increased. He walked to the phone on the shelf between the living and dining rooms, picked the receiver up and placed it to his ear. There was a dial-tone—"*probably originating from some black hole in space,*" he thought, and slammed the receiver hard back into its cradle. He stood quietly, looking down at it.

Kenny became more out of control with each passing second. His mind raced to Mary in Ellsworth and what she was doing there. He wondered if the rug-rats had told anyone about the punch incident before they all went their separate ways several days ago. He moved toward the phone once again, more determined to find out what Mary was up to.

It was strange sometimes how Mary's intuition could be right on the money. As she sat at her desk, unable to concentrate on the work in front of her, looking up at the clock on the wall now and thinking of Kenny, her desk phone rang. She could, if she chose, allow it to ring out a preset number of rings, and the central receptionist would automatically have the call routed to her desk in the event Mary was not at her desk. If her intuition was right, it was Kenny on the other end of the ringing. She counted the number of rings, and when the final one began, she picked up.

"Good morning, this is Mary."

"So, where've you been sleepin' these past couple o' days?" Kenny asked.

"Gee, I'm fine, how are you?" she responded coldly.

She kept her voice low and free of any outward sign of emotion, and no one in the small office appeared to notice or became distracted when she answered the call.

As usual, Kenny did most of the talking, Mary ah-hummed continuously, and for the first time for as long as she could remember, no pang of fear raised its ugly head in her mid-section. The sound of his voice in her ear was cold and demanding, yet she was not moved to feel the need to accommodate him.

"Where's the freaking shotgun, Mary?" he asked suddenly.

She'd forgotten all about it until this very second when he asked her. She'd removed it from its place by the door at Tabitha's request shortly after Kenny left the night he hit her.

"Oh yeah, I almost forgot, the shotgun. It's under our bed," she said.

"Why?" he demanded.

"We can talk about that later. Besides, I have a meeting to go to in a couple of minutes. I can't be late," she said, and was about to continue when he slammed the receiver down and broke the connection.

There could be no denying that he was pissed, yet she just couldn't be bothered with his needs right now. Suddenly, the thought of her father asking her if she wanted him to be there when they got home became a very delightful idea. For all practical purposes, though, she wasn't going to be the one to call him. It would seem peculiar that she gave the call no further thought, but

Kenny entered her mind several times during the remainder of that day. She went about her work, thinking of the kids often, and anxiously awaited the end of the day when she would face Kenny as she always did: just her and him.

The ride home was as monotonous as the ride in; however, when approaching the summit of Cathance Hill, the anticipated feeling of foreboding never entered her consciousness, nor did she give it a second thought. She arrived at the school hoping that Heidi would not be there today. She wanted the experience of the three of them going home to be private. School let out on time and without incident, and she could see the joy on the kids' faces as they ran across the school yard to meet her. They made haste of the small talk about the day—their goal was the same. They were going home together.

Their nervous energy was stifled at the sight of Kenny's pickup parked at its usual spot beside the barn. They just never knew what mood they would find him in.

Now, as all three exited Mary's car, it was impossible for them to hide their uncertainties about what would happen upon entering.

The late afternoon sun cast tall shadows from across the road, like monsters reaching out for them over the driveway. A slight breeze blew the net on the basketball hoop at will, yet the air was warmer than earlier in the day. Bobby looked around trying to find the ball, which he'd forgotten outside when they left the house, and they entered quietly so as not to disturb Kenny if he was enjoying a nap. But when they saw him seated in the chair facing the door, his look was actually far less threatening than they expected.

"Hey now, if it isn't my wandering group of gypsies! You got any bags, or stuff like that?" he asked.

It was difficult for Mary or the kids to respond, but Bobby

spoke up first, the little trooper that he was. "Uh huh, mista' man, we took caar' of it," he said.

Neither child would leave Mary's side. In fact, Tabi clung as though they'd been super-glued at the hip.

"So, it looks ta' me as though you've thinned down a bit. Not eatin' much lately?" Mary asked.

"One would want a nice body for summer, wouldn't one?" he answered.

"Guess so," she replied.

They continued to stare into each other's eyes, yet there was no sign of animosity in their facial expressions. Mary looked around the room casually, and noticed that the shotgun was returned to its position by the door.

She figured that he would be the one to bring up the crap that went down, causing them all to split, and no doubt he would bring it up at the least opportune time. But there were things to do, and unpacking and getting back to normal was one of them.

"C'mon, let's get your stuff up to your rooms. You both have homework, and I know it," Mary said.

Despite her confidence, she could not overlook Kenny's volatility, and said as little as possible to him, hoping her silence would not be seen as a means to provoke him. Her intention was to persuade him to make the first move toward discussing what happened. She didn't have to wait long. As her foot hit the first step, he began.

"You know, Mary, the other night was all just a big misunderstanding. I thought you were pissed and were coming at me with a good one. You know what I mean? That ain't my style, you know, slappin' women."

"Really! Well do you remember the bruise on my arm from our little conversation at the nursing home?" She asked. He laughed and shrugged her off with a slight shift in body language.

"Look—that was a mistake, too. I've…We've been under a

287

bunch o' stress lately. Slow time with money, the kids comin' here to live. You know, all the shit that makes up a life," he said.

It was her turn to shrug him off with a slight lift of her head. "Whatever." She turned and went up the stairs behind the two kids.

For his own selfish reasons, he wanted all of this behind them. Several days out to camp, and he'd lost a good deal of spending cash, which he was going to run out of in a very short time now. After his call to Mary in Ellsworth in the early afternoon, he'd begun making calls to people who'd been looking for him and his supplies. He was impatient, and generally he never used their home phone to do business, but with the cell phone still charging at that time, he was determined not to waste another minute.

He didn't know that one of the people he'd called was in trouble with the law, and had made arrangements with Harry Circus to let him in on some of the little things that Kenny Collins did. In so doing, the guy would loosen the noose from around his own neck. Harry had a little squeak. Ah! Honor amongst good-for-nothin's.

June, She'll change her tune.

July, she will fly.

And give no warning to her flight.

August, die she must.

September I'll remember,

A love once new has now grown old.

(Paul Simon, 1965)

34

THE SPRING AND SUMMER SEASON and the activities that embrace that time of the year seem to move more rapidly than all the rest. To Mary, it felt like yesterday that she and Kenny had stood at odds with each other, neither one willing to give an inch in their contest for control. She was still fearful of his temper tantrums, knowing well how quickly he could turn on anyone. Children tend to forgive and forget more readily than adults, yet Tabi and Bobby maintained a level of cautious respect.

Before anyone realized it, August came, and with it, right on time, the influx of transients with their dilapidated old cars, which for some, were purchased to tear up on the blueberry barrens in August. This added to the cash-flow for the local auto-parts store. Some came with back-packs, looking as ragged as homeless people, and some were sort of a homeless breed, living in tents, some with tarps tied to trees for a roof.

Those who signed on with the large companies were furnished with wood-framed, one-room camps with bunk beds, and fresh water was available at communal faucets for water jugs and the occasional reviving splash to the face. August could be incredibly hot Down East, especially on the hellish barrens.

Almost everyone worked overtime getting ready for August, and when it finally came, overtime was high on everyone's list: The blueberry company employees, local merchants, rakers, private landowners, state and local police—and one wouldn't want to forget that the local drug dealer was also working overtime.

It's strange thinking about how Kenny used to laugh when Lucretia would tell Mary that her intuition was working overtime, yet a little voice from deep inside his head told Kenny to stay away from Filbert's camp. Had he wished to use it now, he would have to break in. Filbert and Bullet had installed a huge hasp and padlock the day they'd gone out there. They even nailed plywood, stored in the shed out back (which Filbert cut when he built the camp) for winter protection over the windows and doors.

He really didn't need to go out there anymore, as the pictures he had in his so-called portfolio far surpassed his original intentions. He was simply waiting for the right time and place to use them. With the season in full swing, there was no time to head out to camp for any reason. He had his hands full with his trips over the barrens for the day-and-night needs of his clients. Kenny was a solo act now, unlike in years past when he and Mary were an item out here on the barrens, Mary was simply along for the ride. Since she was in Ellsworth every day, and had arranged with the nursing home to have the kids with her, now that school was out, Kenny had the freedom he needed to take care of business. Besides, the last thing Mary envisioned was Kenny in the summer child-care arena.

Unlike the past several summers though, every time Kenny turned around it seemed he saw a cop—not necessarily looking in his direction or directly at him, but close enough to make him nervous, and a nervous Kenny could be dangerous. One time it might be the trooper, the next time, the constable. Just the fact that they were there gave him the willies.

Unknown to him, those sightings were carefully planned by Harry Circus. The lawmen no longer met at the Quick-Stop for their morning caffeine needs. It was just too busy this time of the year, and neither one wanted to be witness to a shoplifting incident; with the countless numbers of strangers in town, they had their hands full of everything now.

They met each morning at the trooper's home, which was just up the hill from the Quick-Stop in Berryville. They could speak at will about their "little man," who now was an obsession with Harry. Ralph loved the coffee and fresh pastry Annie made. The trooper set surveillance in motion, utilizing his connections with friends and blueberry company employees to keep a vigilant eye open for the type of activity associated with the goings-on where Kenny Collins was concerned. There were other dealers who followed the transients and supplied them with their needs; they were under the same kind of watchful eye, but Harry was truly interested in only one. Those he chose to keep him up to speed, he trusted unequivocally. They were lifelong friends, or close associates.

The month of August started out rainier than normal, which for Kenny and his duffle bag of goodies, was a welfare breaker. Fighting off the boredom from confinement in the small living quarters the transients were subjected to, the drugs that our peddler provided helped to while away the hours and withstand the incessant tapping of rain on the roof waiting for the sun. In most cases, when it appeared that a client was interested in buying more than normal, Kenny hung in a bit longer than he might have and offered samples. If a young woman was involved…

The front seat of the pickup began to smell like cheap perfume, and when it was obvious that his clothing had come in contact with an essence somehow, he went swimming fully clothed, using a bar of soap he kept in the glove box. Sometimes it worked, sometimes it didn't; but he just didn't care anymore. His hair was long and tangled. He wore the same clothes for a week at times, and he now resembled the young man who, that first day in Chesterfield, had walked into Filbert's store raising the eyebrows of all who were there.

Kenny had come full circle, but the dreams he'd come with were now more of a nightmare, and the hopes that he and his young bride had envisioned for their future had been dashed to the gravel shoulder of the countless, forgotten back roads of Washington county. Hedonism became his reality.

Kenny was like a coyote. He blended into his surroundings, laying low when necessary so as not to bring attention to himself or those he supplied. If he wasn't in his truck, he disappeared into the vast, well-populated transient community. There was one instance when the constable was called to a minor disturbance at a tent-site where Kenny was, and because of his motley appearance, he went completely unnoticed by Ralph. As Kenny looked on in relatively close proximity to the scene, he found much humor in his disguise. Without much information being passed along to the trooper of Kenny's activities, Harry became obsessed with the young man's ability to remain unseen, and began spending more time on the barrens himself, which was his unrestricted jurisdiction as a Maine State Trooper, his authority ranging throughout the state.

35

Filbert and Heidi both refrained from unloading their thoughts on each other. Heidi continued to hold back about Mary's swollen, bruised jaw, though it had long since healed. Filbert suppressed the photo and mirror findings, knowing well that eventually it would get out through the grapevine, and then there would be hell to pay for not sharing what he knew. Heidi, knowing well how Filbert felt about her involving herself with Kenny and Mary's business, felt it was better to remain quiet for now. After several days, they were bursting at the seams, and as if an alarm-clock went off alerting both to the ensuing eruption, each finally thought it best to share their secret with the other.

The store was as busy as any August they remembered. Both of them were there to open the store together each morning, but with the persistent rain, the generally early influx was now bare-bones.

The butterflies in Filbert's stomach could have carried him off had the wind currents come from another direction that morning. Heidi avoided him at all costs, and both were afraid of the task at hand, but before the crowds appeared, she decided it was now or never. Filbert prepared to collect the trash from yesterday's accumulation, something Amos normally did the night before, but had not for some reason. These days his mind was always on something other than responsibility.

"Filbert?" Heidi called his name.

"Yes, dea'," he responded.

"I have a tiny ditty I need ta' shaar' with ya', dea'," she said.

Filbert's lower intestinal tract began to bubble with uncertainty from his guilt, forcing him to think she knew of his secret.

"*Well, if she knows of it, there's no need for me to throw myself on the tracks. When the train hits, that's all folks,*" he thought as he edged his way nearer to her.

She hesitated momentarily, allowing him a final gulp of courage, and then she spoke up.

"Filbert, I've been holdin' out on ya', dea'."

His eyebrows furled into a huge question mark as his surprise at hearing this nearly knocked him against the counter with relief, knowing however, his turn would come.

"I know how you feel when I…stick my nose where it don't belong, using your own words, dea'. And I really didn't stick it… really…it just kind o' got stuck in a situation all by itself, ya' might say."

At that point, he was more confused than worried and having absolutely no idea what in hell the woman was talking about, he asked…"What?"

She took a deep breath and proceeded to tell him how the chance meeting with Mary had come about and when. He shook his head slightly, indicating a minor form of disapproval, thinking that this might lighten the load he'd been carrying, but when she told him of the swollen, bruised jaw, there could be no holding back for him any longer.

"Why that, fleshy-headed, good-fa'-nothin' son-ova'-hoe-a'! And hea' I was ticked at you for stickin'…well, you know what I mean. You told me you thought he was hittin' her, and I should o' listened to ya' then." The jugular on the side of his neck grew to twice its normal size, and his face appeared to be glowing red.

"I didn't think I'd create such presha', Filbert. You'd better calm yaw' hormones, old man, before ya' pop that thing on the side o' yaw' neck," Heidi said with much concern.

"It wasn't just you and what ya' told me, dea'," he said.

She looked to him with questioning eyes, suddenly realizing there might be more added to the story.

"You stay put fa' a minute. I've got somethin' that's gonna curl yaw' haia'." He walked toward the back door and went out. The questions running through her thoughts at this moment would not allow her to concentrate on anything she'd set out to do in the store, and she couldn't imagine what had stirred Filbert so. She didn't have to wait long to find out. He returned in less than a minute, completely out of breath, near panting.

"What is goin' on?" she asked.

"You sit down hea' and have a good look at this, missy. I'll stand here and watch yaw' haia' curl."

In most cases, kids worked with, or for, their parents during blueberry season. It seemed that the residents of every second house throughout the area, in some way, were involved with the harvest at some level. The money earned by the kids, usually the teenagers, would generally be used to buy school clothes in the fall, and at least a couple of generous loads of books from the Mr. Paperback in Bangor, the older kids getting the latest new releases by Stephen King, and the rest, if they were normal, was blown at one of the State Fairs through August and September.

In one particular case, however, this wasn't true. Amos Cirone didn't get to work alongside his friends on the barrens. He spent his summer helping out around the store, especially on those days his mother didn't want to go in. Having Lulu at home was her excuse, and since a teenager could handle bundles and stock shelves, he had his job set out for him. Like most young men his age, there was a certain restlessness eating away at him, and he longed for the day he'd be free to roam the world without looking over his shoulder and seeing his parents hovering about with the infamous words, *"ya can't do this, or ya can't do that,"* just like every other kid growing up in Washington County and the world.

He was curious, like most his age, but he always found himself having to tell his parents the truth about everything, because his heart was pure. Most times, that's what got him into trouble. He just couldn't color the truth one shade off. His biggest problem was that he admired Kenny's bohemian attitude toward life, but until now, Filbert and Heidi had no idea how much he admired him. Working at the store did not make him a prisoner, nor did it keep him away from his closest friends, who were now raking berries on the barrens. And someone else was spending a lot of time on the barrens: his idol, Kenny.

36

I T WAS AS IF THE UNIVERSE HAD THROWN the mighty power switch when August came to an end. You could feel and smell the autumn season encroaching itself on everything. For anyone not prepared for the ensuing chill, the scramble was on to pull the susceptible crops from the garden before a surprise frost. Wood needed to be cut, split, and gotten under cover and made ready for winter. And for those who didn't have a full-time job to return to after the harvest, it was a manic time to research income statements for verification, with hopes of collecting unemployment.

The other choices were to follow the harvest north to the County to pick apples or dig potatoes. For those who lived in blueberry country, the latter was not a favorable or readily accepted option. True, for some, the season was extended for what remained of field clean-up raking, and for anyone who knew someone in the business, there may have been an opening at the blueberry factory. Other than that, the next seasonal endeavor was Christmas Wreath making, but that started in November. A person could get pretty hungry until then.

Having missed the Bangor State Fair, Bullet was determined not to miss the Blue Hill Fair, the last of the season's fairs within a reasonable drive from Isles Port. Generally, he gathered up a small tribe of adult delinquents he loved to play with, and spent the afternoon in the beer tent before promenading around the livestock pens and the horse-pulling events. He knew every other entry contestant in the barns in Bangor, but down in Blue Hill, his acquaintanceships were limited. Most everyone he knew went to Bangor, but this year, with funds being depleted quickly, he went alone. He figured he'd find some drunk down there to hang out with, and so he never gave another thought as to who he might run into.

He'd been in the beer-tent for about an hour, the servers now old friends; most everyone who entered the tent longed for an escape from the crowds on the mid-way and the heat. They loved their beer and enjoyed meeting people of the same interest. The sun was hot for an early September afternoon, and the cold beer went down as smooth as cream. Bullet contemplated not even venturing out and enjoying his annual fair experience, and staying right there at his table instead, when his heart entered his mouth and stopped beating. Millie walked in through the open flap at the far end from where he sat. She was alone, and at first glance, she appeared much thinner than when he'd last seen her a couple of years ago. She hadn't looked this thin in the photo. His heart then skipped a beat, then restarted, like a schoolboy at seeing his first love.

"Fuck me, Bullet-boy. Keep yaw' eyes in yaw' head and yaw' dickie in yaw' pants," he whispered to himself.

She didn't notice him until after ordering her beer, and when she finally laid eyes on him, his full focus was already on her. It wasn't as if she were stunned to see him, but she did display a surprised look, then grabbed her beer and purse and walked directly toward him with a smile.

"Well, big boy, long time no see," she said nonchalantly.

"Yah'…you could say that, little girl."

"What brings ya' down to this neck o' the woods? I thought you were a Bangor man."

He didn't reply to that, but motioned toward the seat opposite him, making an informal, County Fair-type of invitation. She walked around behind him, brushing his shoulder with her hip as she passed, causing the image of the photo of her to flash in his thought process. He remembered his anger, took a huge gulp from the beer, and immediately placed a cigarette between his lips, but before lighting it, offered her one.

"No thanks, I like filtas' on mine. I can't believe yaw' still smokin' them; they're so strong." She lit one of her own and blew the first drag of smoke in his face, then laughed, a naughty little laugh which made him quiver inside, then he laughed, too. It would seem to any one that knew them, somewhat queer that, having been separated for as long as they'd been, they were still toying with each other with a little puff of smoke.

That was Millie and Bullet though, as wild now as if no years had passed since dating. They looked into each other's eyes without saying a word, and it wasn't as if they were challenging each other to see who would talk first, they simply appeared to be taken with each other's presence. Several moments of silence passed before Bullet spoke first.

"Whea' aar' the boys?" he asked.

"They're at home, with a friend."

"I guess I'm not sure whea' home is for ya' anymore. Actually, I never knew whea' that was after ya' left," he said.

"Yah', well...ya' knew I took off with that carnie from Opie's Shows. He turned out to be a tiny shithead. We lived down in Monroe for a while, just for that winter, then he took off with the show, left me in a fucked-up little traila' with a leakin' roof. Come ta' find out he didn't own it, he just moved us in and told me it was his. The little leech bastard."

Bullet wanted to ask a thousand questions about her and the boys, yet all he could see was that goddamned photo and those bare-assed men. He wished now he'd never seen it.

She was wearing a black V-neck pull-over top that fit her contours perfectly, while exposing an invitational-sized peek at her enticingly deep cleavage. He tried not to stare, taking only an occasional glance downward, and from the expression on her face, it appeared to tickle her libido to think that she might be turning him on with her looks. He felt somewhat out of place, considering the way she was dressed, since he was in his blue-and-black-checked flannel shirt and black suspenders. He got up, and without asking, got them each another beer, while the heat from the mid-way wafted in through the open flaps on both ends of the tent. The beer continued to go down like cream.

"So, what's new around Isles Port?" she asked.

He stared at her for a moment, doing his best to hide his true emotions. He wanted to blurt out, *"You oughta know,"* but he didn't.

"Ya' know… same old, no-fuck-place, nowhea' to go, nothin' to do." He said it with such an overtone of sarcasm, she wondered if he was getting a little drunk, and usually, if her memory served her right, that was a good time to leave.

"Look, I don't want ta' hold ya' up, so…" She made an attempt to stand.

"Ah…no, no, Millie, I didn't mean it the way it sounded. Ya' know how it is down thea'…Sit down, dea', let's drink aar' bee'as," he said.

That sounded good to her, and so she sat back down from her half-standing position, giving him an unobstructed view down her top, almost to her navel, and he saw no evidence of a bra.

The moment she sat down, she lit another cigarette, and watching her deep-drag from it forced him, from habit, to light one of his own. They sat quietly for several minutes, Millie smiling at the distant sound of frolicking children. Then Bullet spoke up.

"Look, Millie, we neva' minced words ova' a bunch o' bull-shit. We always told it like it was. After all, when ya' thought it was time ta' leave, ya' didn't mess around, ya' left. But I have ta' tell ya', that pictua' spreadin' around town of ya' and them naked fucks set me back a bit. I ain't over it quite yet. I hope I don't know none o' them frigs', that's all."

Her eyes were as large as the base on her plastic cup of beer. Her jaw was agape, and suddenly all of the blood seemed to drain from her already pale face. Being uncovered in this way made her feel foolish—not that she was embarrassed, she just didn't expect it. Their eyes riveted on each other, yet neither one spoke. It looked to her as though Bullet's facial expression was more like one of hurt than anger.

"We…I…" Words failed her now, and she swallowed what remained in her plastic cup.

"I'm sorry I couldn't come up with a better way o' sayin' it. I saw the pictua' with you and…Christ, it's like everyone knows now. Why? That's all I want ta' know Millie, why?"

The thought flashed into his mind that he was very happy that he'd left the photo with Filbert, not knowing what he'd have done with it.

The silence between them was like a dull headache that just wouldn't go away. Neither drank, or lit a cigarette, and they appeared to share a type of cocoon while the world went round 'n' round. After several failed attempts, Millie began.

"Bullet, I don't mean to be a bitch, but your folks left you some money. I grew up in a foster home. I didn't even know my parents. After that carnie-punk took off on me, things got tough for me and the boys. I cleaned houses for a couple o' old lechers, who not only pinched pennies, but my ass, too. Then, the real owner of that leaking-toilet he left us in finally arrived, and figured that a little nookie could go a long way toward the rent. I think all you men aar' pigs. Then I met Kenny one night in Bangor, in that shit-dive bar under the bridge." Bullet drew in a noisy breath. "I can't even remember the name now. I remembered him from Chesterfield. He came to town just around the time I was leavin'. We had a few drinks, fooled around a bit in his truck, and he made me an offer I couldn't say no to." She looked down at the floor before meeting his eyes again. "I needed the money, Bullet. I was desperate!" Her voice broke and she fell silent. Bullet finally emptied his glass with one, huge swallow. He lit a cigarette, and drew deeply from it, looking out the flap at the far end of the tent.

"Did he force you to have sex with them pigs in that pictua'?"

Bullet asked. Then he began stumbling on his words, and nothing he said made any sense at that point, so he stopped talking. Their silence was far more tormenting than what they'd spoken about moments earlier. They sat without speaking for what seemed like an eternity, then Bullet asked, "Aar' ya hungry?"

"I could handle a bite," Millie said.

They strolled through the fair, sharing an Italian sausage with onions and green peppers, but they each demanded their own fried dough with powdered sugar, occasionally brushing against each other, then moving away quickly.

The afternoon moved along, and soon the evening crowds thickened. Millie wrapped herself up in the sweater she carried around her shoulders as the early autumn evening chill blew in on a sea-breeze from Blue Hill Harbor. No more was said of the photo. They spoke of the boys and how he would like to see them. She told him it could be arranged, and she smiled. The evening was getting late when he walked her to her car. The exiting cars, mostly filled with whooping teenagers on their way out, kicked up large clouds of dust in the fields used for parking, yet it didn't seem to bother them. Anyone seeing them and not knowing who they were could have easily mistaken them for lovers, because of their hushed conversations and obvious need to cling to the moment of togetherness. And then she was gone.

Bullet drove home alone, as usual. He didn't drink while he drove, but he did come away with a more empowered hate for Kenny Collins.

Though few saw Kenny during or after August, when anyone did, his mood was of such an empowering energy it was difficult not to be sucked into the vacuum of his ideals. His pockets were always filled with huge wads of cash, and the only thing he liked better than making it was spending it. With Kenny, spending money on those he loved was the number-one way to obtain forgiveness, for no matter what he'd done, or when. In actuality, forgiveness never entered his mind. It was just his way to forget the reason for needing to be forgiven. From Mary's point of view, she had long ago learned to accept him for what and who he was, and she knew that nothing and no one could change him.

The kids, on the other hand, enjoyed the lavish spending. For the most part, they were on the receiving end and there were no complaints from that peanut gallery. Mary kept a watchful eye from a safe distance. She would not allow herself to be drawn in again.

During the raking season, several of Amos' friends became accustomed to their daily consumption of pot, supplied by everyone's friend, Kenny. The pressure of going back to school added to their need to stay high, and the man with the duffle-bag of goodies was ever willing to please. The one time that Amos had been found with the joint in his pocket was not the only time he imbibed. He was the one who had found the picture of Millie in the snow-bank, yet being Amos, holding that little piece of the puzzle inside caused him to feel ill to the point of vomiting each time the event came into his memory. He was angry with himself at times for his honesty. It seemed so easy for his friends to lie to almost anyone while looking them straight in the eye and keeping a poker-face like a pro.

Filbert or Heidi would have long forgotten the joint-in-the-pocket incident had Heidi not overheard a conversation between Amos and a couple of his friends early on a Friday evening in September. She was not eavesdropping, though she'd been known to do so. She had heard voices from the small shed between the store and the house. Filbert stored long-forgotten things there, and it had been left unattended for so long that the boys used it as a meeting place to get in out of the cold wind to smoke cigarettes, but never pot. It was just too close for comfort, and up until now, no one knew.

Heidi approached slowly, on her way to the rear entrance to the store, not immediately recognizing the voices until she came to within several feet and heard Amos. Her eyes blinked rapidly in her attempt to hear better, and her heart rate tried to keep up.

The topic of conversation was drugs—marijuana to be exact—and the boys were talking about a huge shipment that was coming in any day now.

She barged in at the very moment one of the boys said, "Let the good times roll."

Her first thought was strangulation. Had she been five years younger, she might have attempted a good butt-kickin' for all, but instead, she found chastisement in bellowing tones of anger to be just as effective. She blocked the door, so no means of escape was possible. After threatening the other boys with calls to their parents and Harry Circus, she ordered them to leave her property. With her hand functioning like a grapple-hook, she seized her son by the shirt-collar, gouging his neck with her fingernails to the howling displeasure of the young man as she literally dragged him into the store to be confronted by both his parents.

After nearly an hour of parental interrogation in the basement of the store, the area best known for privacy, the young man, though he tried gallantly, gave in to his parents and began telling them of his experiences with pot. He was extremely proud of himself, however; he never gave Kenny's name, or the fact he was a supplier, though Filbert persisted in asking for the duration of the conversation.

With what they had now, using the context of Heidi's unintentional eavesdropping on the boys, it was clear that someone local was at the forefront of contributing to the juvenile delinquency of the local teens, and God only knew who else.

Since school had resumed, so did the restrictions on Amos. With September coming to an end and October just around the corner, he shivered at the thought of riding in the back of the pickup for another school year as he'd done during his last removal from the school bus.

Through all of it however, Amos prided himself on not giving Kenny's name up and finally being able to cut the cord of his need to be honest beyond reproach. He was naturally an honest boy (some things never change), and his love for his parents superseded any and all relationships outside of the home. Shit happens to everyone somewhere along the line, it just happens with different textures, is all.

One thing was sure. There was a new mound of it piling up for someone in this town, and for all practical purpose; his name just happened to be Collins.

37

WHETHER HE NEEDED TO OR NOT, Harry Circus made it a point now to drive by the Collins' place regularly, if not on a daily basis. Sometimes the mere presence of a trooper can be intimidating without a single word or direct action from the trooper. Kenny was well aware of the trooper's drive-bys, and did not like it very much, but the way he looked at it was that if the trooper didn't pull in, he didn't need to start taking aspirin yet.

Kenny made it a point to remain vigilant, and began to log in the dates and times he saw the trooper's car pass by his place, in either direction. No pattern seemed to be developing, yet as cold as the temperature was getting in the early mornings and evenings, Kenny spent as much time as possible outside so that he might be there when Harry Circus drove by. No one could ever remember Harry being this obsessed with anyone or anything before. He had stepped up his meetings with Ralph again at the Quick-Stop, his home, and even stopping alongside of the road, sometimes within sight of Kenny's, sitting in their cars for several minutes. Harry's father, the retired trooper, got wind of his son's activities, probably from Ralph, who kept an open line of communication with the elder Circus, and warned his son to be careful.

Chip-off-the-old-block that he was, Harry believed in the old man's own theory: "The law must sustain a monumental patience to apprehend the offender." With that said, the old man never brought up the subject again, knowing very well his son was in control.

Control and obsession are two very different things. Using reliable sources for information, digging long and hard for solid leads to an investigation, and good old-fashioned police work is what the old man was thinking. Harry wanted Kenny. He was a thorn in his side. No matter how hard he tried, he could never catch him red-handed, and this intensified the trooper's frustration. He was armed now with the information Heidi Cirone had offered from the boys in the shed, and he had visited each one at their homes with their parents present, yet the boys remained as tightly closed as freshly dug clams. He wasn't sure if the boys were not talking because they feared Kenny or the dealer that no one knew, but he was sure there had to be some fear, or else they were so far into their addiction that they needed to protect their only source. Whichever it was, no one, not even young Amos, talked.

Heidi had also happened to mention Mary's swollen, bruised jaw and the bruise on her arm on the awards night when the trooper had officiated. He seemed almost indignant toward her for having waited this long to let him in on it, but he knew how Filbert frowned on sticking their noses into other people's business, and he told her he understood.

"*Had Mary reported this to me, I could have had him right where I wanted him,*" he thought.

The trooper sat in his car with the engine idling while parked along a deserted section of gravel road near the river. He had chosen this spot to meet with Ralph, after he'd sent him on a fact-finding errand yesterday. Ralph was late. The brilliant explosion of color on the surrounding foliage warmed the trooper's nostalgic recollection of an easier time when, for him, all he had to pay attention to was schoolwork and fishing. As a boy, Harry hadn't needed to worry himself with the chores that most boys his age occupied their free time with. He never split and stacked firewood. His father burned oil. He didn't have to pull the remaining vegetables from the garden, because his mother was a stay-at-home mom. All he needed to do was excel in schoolwork and be better than most at sports, and his free time was for fishing. The sound of water cascading over the rocks just below him soothed his emotions somewhat, and suddenly his anxiety at having to wait unproductively for Ralph flowed gently downstream. Several more minutes passed before the sound of an approaching vehicle forced the trooper to look in that direction. It was Ralph.

The bright sun, low in the autumn sky, reflected off the windshield of Ralph's vehicle, making it impossible for the trooper to see past the glare. He squinted as the truck came nearer, and maintained his facial strain as Ralph pulled alongside.

"Sorry I'm late, Harry." Ralph reached out with a large, Quick-Stop coffee for him.

"Ah, just what I need. No problem on the lateness. I needed the time here. Do a little thinkin', ya' know?" Harry said.

"Ayah!" Ralph responded with a quick, inhaled breath.

Harry took a careful slurp from the hot coffee, listening to Ralph ramble on about how low the water was, the low water table, and how shallow-dug wells would probably go dry this winter, and how tough that would be for those who couldn't afford to have a well drilled. Harry could appreciate the hard-pressed financial situation most folks around the county had, but it certainly was not from experience. Since his father had been the resident trooper for so many years, the regular paycheck and benefits eliminated most financial worries.

The coffee was cooler now, and Harry began gulping, wanting the caffeine to begin its journey to his heart-rate.

"Whatcha' find out, Ralph?"

"Not what I wanted, but I think you'll be interested in what I did find," he said.

What he didn't find out, and what Harry had sent him out for in the first place, was whether he could find more kids being supplied by Kenny. The trooper frowned at Ralph's first news, and prepared himself for his second.

"Ok, go ahead. What else?"

"I just happened to run into Mista' Bullington Carter," Ralph said, though he would never have called Bullet that to his face. "Seems that he and Filbert come to find out where them pictures o' Millie and them nakeds were taken." The trooper remained unmoving in his stare and was all ears, yet he couldn't help but feel a surge of jealousy rise up inside of him not having been able to uncover the information himself.

"Them pictures were taken out ta' Filbert's old camp. Collins had himself a key for that place, and he was usin' it for quite a spell."

"How did they figure out it was his place?" Harry asked.

"Filbert recognized the big mirror with the flash," Ralph said.

"No actual proof that it was Kenny Collins behind the flash. It's simply conjecture on everyone's part, but it all seems to be leading in the same direction," Harry thought. But criminals were always innocent until proven guilty.

"We can't really prove that it was Kenny Collins who took the pictures now, can we Ralph?" Harry felt smug upon enlightening his counterpart with his police bravado.

"Don't be too sure o' yawself, Harry." It was Ralph's turn to enlighten. "Bullet told me he ran into Millie at the Blue Hill Fair about a week ago, and yaw' not gonna' believe what she told him!" Ralph paused while looking at the trooper with a how-do-ya–like-that kind of look. Harry waited.

Finally he asked, "Are ya' plannin' on tellin' me, Ralphie?"

"Oh…Yah'…Sorry, Harry. She told him that she was desperate for money. Kenny paid her to do those things with them…nakeds. She agreed to do that fa' money! Can you believe that, Harry?"

Another glitch in the trooper's plans was in the works.

The little squeak who said he would keep Harry informed of Kenny's activities had found himself being held at the York County Jail on an outstanding warrant after a minor traffic stop. What Harry had gleaned from him was all he'd get. There seemed to be no end to the trooper's frustration—everyday civilians were cleaning up on the information he and the constable should have obtained. There was a new thorn in the trooper's side now that felt more like a spike, and Bullet Carter, for one, was almost enjoying seeing the trooper in pain. He seemed to go out of his way at times, dropping in at the Quick-Stop when he knew the lawmen were having coffee. Harry again discontinued their meetings there.

Had Hannibal Lecter, the cannibal decided to take up residence in either Isles Port or Chesterfield, he would, most likely, have been given a warmer reception than the negative sentiment now building against Kenny Collins. It was becoming clear that many now had a stake in the illicit activities that in some way involved their children or adults that they knew.

Gossip, at times, plays as an important a role as actual facts. "I heard it from the horse's mouth," along with a few well-chosen phrases, can throw the truth a wicked curve, but it can and usually does lead to other things that would not have come to light otherwise.

Though Kenny maintained a decent arms-length from anyone he thought to be up-standing in the small communities, the depth of his ability to obtain information at times rivaled that of the trooper and the constable. Kenny had long ago aligned himself with the well-established counter-culture in the area, something that most upstanding, church-going citizens had always been and remained in denial of. Kenny had lost credibility with everyone who bet on, or against him, when he'd first arrived in the Isles Port, Chesterfield area. Even Forest Bagley, who had gone out of his way at times to open the door of opportunity for the young man from away, had now alienated himself from the drug-pushing womanizer who was married to his relative's daughter.

No one, however, could calculate how much some people hated Kenny.

38

BEFORE ANYONE REALIZED IT, the Christmas-wreathing season was in full swing. Kenny dismissed his original plan to give up the seasonal aspect of his entrepreneurial endeavors, realizing that other avenues of income would add a shade of allurement to cover up his main source of cash-flow. Besides, many of those who made his wreaths and decorations were also in need of his other supplies, which opened another door for Kenny. He had a small group working out of his barn making, stacking, and loading wreaths to be shipped to southern Maine and Massachusetts. The people making the wreaths scratched out a meager income, usually minimum wage. It was those like Kenny and the ones who trucked the wreaths that made the money.

For the first time in as long as she could remember, Mary had found a new lease on life. She thrust herself into her work, and when she wasn't there, she devoted herself to the kids, who were growing in body and mind thanks to Mary's guiding awareness.

Mary was letting the kids ride the school bus home in the afternoons; she continued to take them each morning, as there was something about that early morning connection she needed, and it was good for the kids also. Getting home long before Mary, they were subjected to the tail-end of the work-shift in the barn, yet both Tabi and Bobby enjoyed the characters that filled the otherwise dark, quiet barn with a strange continuous laughter, and the scent of fresh fir tips filled their senses with thoughts of the rapidly approaching holidays. They were still a bit wary around Kenny, and they stuck together all the time.

They were under strict orders from Mary. They were to get into the house and start their homework after a light lunch which Mary prepared before leaving in the morning. She trusted the kids, but she knew that kids will be kids, and she wanted them exposed as little as possible to the fools in the barn, as she called them. She hoped they would honor her wishes.

Kenny, on the other hand, encouraged them to hang out and try their hand at making wreaths, for which he said he would pay them. Each of them tried, but became quickly discouraged, as snapping the tips and twisting the coarse wire to hold them together was rough on young hands. Once they realized how little each wreath paid, they were off on other adventures, like their homework. They were both good students, and it was easy for them to remain focused on school stuff.

There remained a cool separation between Mary and Kenny, though; every time he came to her, day or night, the vision of that hit to the floor from his fist would not allow her to get close to him, or forget. She was still struggling with the issue of forgiving and forgetting.

Kenny no longer made a secret of any aspect of his lawlessness, and Mary was no fool. It was accepted, with much reserve, that Kenny would disappear for days sometimes, and return as though he'd spent the day fishing and simply wanted supper. Mary stopped asking where he'd been; she just didn't want to know.

Bullet and Filbert met at the store every day now, early enough to beat the rush. Hunting season was well underway, and the store vibrated with a life and breath that rivaled the harvest season in the summer. Strangely enough, most everyone Filbert extended credit to finally paid him off. Being free from the worry of unpaid bills gave Filbert more time to concentrate on the evils his son and his friends were exposed to by the "anti-Christ," Kenny Collins.

If it was the last thing he did, he would see that young man run out of town. Tarred and feathered wasn't the farthest thing that his mind conjured up, if only for effect. After being with Millie, Bullet had withdrawn into a state of depression, questioning whether he had caused the difficulties that had come upon her, but he finally decided it is what it is, and he let it go.

Generally, by this time—the third full week of deer season— the first dusting of snow had already fallen, increasing the chances of getting a deer. A fresh powder falling the night before a hunt left no doubt as to the direction a deer had traveled how many were in the herd and just how fresh the tracks were. Filbert's store was an official tagging and weigh-station, and it generally pumped with a life-blood of its own. With the lack of snow and an unusually mild November, all types of rumors were spreading about the type of winter that might be expected. Some folks cared, others could care less. Most left the weather forecasting to the Channel 2 weather man out of Bangor, and he got it right most of the time.

The massive, burning red ball of the early morning sun hung low in the late November sky.

"*Red sky in the mornin', sailor's warnin'.*" Filbert remembered his mother saying that as he looked out the store-front window.

"*Most of the time she was right on with that one,*" he thought. He wondered if it really was a good way to predict the weather. He hoped it was true now—maybe they would finally get the snow they needed.

Standing in the quiet store, waiting for his friend to arrive, his memory took him back to that morning not so long ago, feeling like a lifetime now, when Kenny and Mary had appeared, and Kenny spun her car feverishly around in circles in the center of the road on the freshly falling snow and sleet mix. He remembered the two of them sitting like love-birds afterwards in their nest out front by the single gas pump, ignoring Filbert, or so it appeared to him. And his mind brought up the picture of that swollen bruise around Kenny's eye. "*They were out o' control even then,"* he thought, while his mind raced back to how many times he'd dismissed the rumors about them as jealous ravings by those who had nothing better to do than stir up stories. He knew differently now. He also knew that Mary had estranged herself from Kenny, which for anyone who loved her and that was many, was a blessing. The more he thought of the past and Kenny, the more he became infuriated.

He needed to take his mind off the bad thoughts that overtook him, so he swung around looking toward the back corner of the counter where he kept the Christmas lights, and thought he might string them up during the course of the day. He hoped it might usher in some happiness for a change. Just then, he heard the rumble of Bullet's pickup pulling to the side of the pump, which was out of the norm. From where Filbert stood, it appeared that Bullet was either talking to himself, or scolding someone at the side of the building, although Filbert hadn't seen or heard anyone pass in quite some time. It didn't take long for Filbert to learn the source of Bullet's excitement.

With arms waving and his finger pointing to the back of the truck, Bullet motioned for Filbert to come out. As he did, a cold wind blew from around the corner of the building, forcing Filbert, in shirt-sleeves, to shiver uncomfortably. He wasn't two feet from the door when he came face-to-face with what looked to be a perfect, ten-point buck deer, glaring at him from the pickup's bed with dark, dead eyes.

"Well, mista' man, whaddaya' think o' this beauty?"

"Jeez, Bullet...He is a beauty."

They looked like school boys as they gazed at Bullet's trophy-deer. Suddenly, the thought of Kenny, or even the Christmas lights, were shoved to the back of Filbert's thoughts, and he dropped the tailgate to have a better look. As they inspected the deer, and Filbert acted as the official weigher of deer, the thickening black clouds began to cover the red sun, and an icy wind blew up from down along the river, yet neither man took notice. They appeared oblivious to their surroundings—the only thing that mattered at that moment was the deer.

From the time he'd been a boy, Filbert had killed so many deer he actually didn't care if he ever shot another one. He was happy for Bullet, knowing how much he relied on wild game of all kind. The sight of the pickup and its contents drew a small crowd, which for Filbert might result in business, and for Bullet, a chance to milk the thrill of victory. Tensions eased for both men finally.

While the men examined the deer, Kenny's pickup rumbled on its way up from the road by the river, and pulled to a stop next to the store. He looked at the crowd and with a stupid expression on his face, burned rubber across the length of the road and was gone.

39

"**G**ET THE FUCK OUTA' THE TOILET!!"
Kenny's voice bellowed throughout the entire house, shattering the nerve-impulses of everyone within earshot of the command. The sound echoed from the upstairs hallway, which at the far end accommodated a small toilet with a sink and mirror. The kids used it to get ready for school, as their bedrooms were only several feet from its door, so they weren't upsetting Mary's need to use her own bathroom on the first floor. Mary was in that one when she heard the sound of his angry voice, and couldn't understand why he'd be up there as opposed to simply knocking on the door here as he would normally do. She would have let him in. She put her robe on quickly and ran toward the sound of chaos.

Kenny was in the toilet when she arrived, and Tabi, eyes wide with fear, stood stiffly in the hallway against the wall opposite the door, as if ordered to be there by a frantic drill sergeant.

Mary spoke in whispers to her younger sister, resting a hand on one shoulder in an attempt at calming her, while the sound of what seemed to be projectile vomiting came from behind the closed door of the tiny room.

"What happened?" Mary asked.

Tabitha clenched a damp towel in her hand, the corner of which she had in her mouth, as a toddler might do with a security blanket.

"I was just getting ready for school when the pounding on the door came and he started screaming," she said. Mary turned her head toward Bobby's room and the still-closed door. Bobby was a solidly sound sleeper. Walking from his room now, fingering the sleep from his eyes, he became surprised at the sight of his two sisters in the hallway just outside his door.

"Waz goin' on?" he asked, not fully awake.

There had been few temper outbursts since Mary was knocked to the floor. It was as if Kenny was able to maintain his self-discipline while being around her and the kids, but Mary had kept the separation between them for an episode just like this. At the sight of Bobby and his inquisitive eyes, Mary herded them toward the stairs, hushing them as they went. The last thing she wanted was to be in plain sight when the door finally opened. She told Tabi to finish up in her bathroom, stressing the need to hurry, and almost force-feeding Bobby his orange juice and a couple pieces of burnt toast. He kept asking for an explanation as only a young boy can do, and Mary, pumping her open hands up and down (resembling a cop on the side of the road motioning to a speeding motorist to slow down), kept telling him to eat his breakfast and hurry up.

Thanksgiving wasn't much of a day as far as family went this year. Mary cooked a small turkey, and she and the kids brought it to Virgil's and made a quick meal of it. Kenny kept the wreath shop open for anyone who wanted to work. Nine of the eleven women and two men showed up, and that's how he spent his turkey-day. After the upstairs toilet ordeal, Mary could care less how he spent his time now.

After leaving Virgil's, the three of them stopped by Filbert and Heidi's. Mary and Heidi had resurrected their friendship, basically because of the children, but Filbert maintained a watchful eye, knowing very well where Kenny stood in the scheme of things. He also knew where he and his good friend Bullet stood. Heidi had invited them for dessert, several days before Thanksgiving.

Virgil had declined, yet unknown to all including the hosts, an unexpected visitor would soon arrive shortly after Mary and the kids. Bullet, knowing well that Filbert closed the store early on holidays like Thanksgiving, Christmas, and New Year's, drove directly to the house behind the store. Mary saw him before anyone else, causing a heart-palpitation and an instant upset stomach.

"Now who in a bucket o' gory is that?" Filbert asked, at the sound of the rumbling exhaust pipes. Both Tabi and Bobby, fearing it might be Kenny, got up from their seats immediately, going to the closest window. They simultaneously exhaled a sigh of relief at seeing Bullet. Being the character that he was, both Mary's and the Cirone kids really liked him. The fact that he was wearing some stupid-looking turkey-hat made his arrival all the more prankish and endearing to the kids. Filbert and Heidi burst out in laughter at the sight of him; Mary remained silent, somewhat unsure of how he might react at seeing her.

She was well aware now of the goings-on in town and the ill sentiment toward her husband, who would blow a gasket if he knew where all of them were and in who's company. Amos was absent. He'd left immediately after their dinner, which was served promptly (as Heidi loved to do things) at two-o'clock p.m., giving everyone a chance to unwind after the huge meal before their guests arrived for dessert in the late afternoon.

After some horsing around with the kids, Bullet settled down with a straight face and greeted his former kissing-cousin, and with that out of the way, the four adults relaxed at the dining room table to an assortment of pies and coffee while the kids played games in the crisp outdoors of the late afternoon. Suddenly, being with these adults on Thanksgiving Day caused Mary to miss her mother, and looking across the table to Heidi, who was overwhelming the two men with small-talk, it eased her pain somewhat. She pictured the family at her mother's table only last year, and began to feel melancholic over her passing.

After the men finished their sampling of pies and coffee, they excused themselves, walking toward the door. It was apparent that Bullet had used up all of his time without a cigarette, and Heidi allowed no smoking in the house. Heidi smiled at the sight of them leaving. She cherished the moment that she would be alone with Mary, craving the sole company of another woman. Besides the knitting circle on Wednesday nights, she spent almost all of her time in the company of her husband and customers. Outside of work, Mary also kept her free time for the kids and home, and though all of her work associations were with women, she rarely enjoyed a one-on-one girl-talk conversation.

She had, for all practical purposes, given up drugs and alcohol, and hadn't had much trouble leaving the latter of the two behind. She did, however, continue the filthy habit of smoking cigarettes, and after several minutes of Heidi's chatter, the desserts and coffee triggered the need for nicotine, so she excused herself and went toward the same door the men had exited from. Reaching the outdoors, she immediately appreciated the reviving coolness of the late afternoon air and took a long, considering look at her cigarette before lighting it, regretting her addiction.

The kids frolicked noisily on the other side of the house nearest the river, the two men were out of sight somewhere, and after lighting her smoke, she strolled slowly, with no particular direction planned. The sound of the children faded as she neared the rear of the store, yet she thought she heard the sound of Filbert's voice coming from the tool shed with an agitated tone. Moving closer now, she realized it was Bullet's voice she'd heard, and she began to make out more clearly what he was saying.

"That little fuck told 'em that if he wanted the picture back, he'd be glad to give it to 'em for five hundred bucks, or he'd send it to his old lady."

"You mean he's blackmailin' 'em for the picture with Millie?" Filbert asked.

"Ayah. That's what I mean."

"What's he gonna do, tell Harry?"

"Nope, he says he's gonna pay the shit-bag."

"That silly frig's gone too faa," Filbert said.

Knowing nothing about the subject they spoke of, Mary began to walk away, never having heard Heidi walk up behind her. They came face to face, in front of the shed.

Heidi had been there long enough to overhear the last several comments by each man, and now she cleared her throat as loudly as possible, causing Mary to nearly jump out of her boots and triggering an instant silence from the shed. Suddenly, the sound of rapidly moving footsteps was heard from inside, and the door swung open with great force. It opened out. Had either woman been standing in its path, it would have knocked one or both of them to the ground.

"Have you two been listening in on our conversation?" Filbert asked, in less than a Thanksgiving tone, while Bullet displayed a stupid grin and stuck a Camel cigarette between his lips and lit it.

"Well, we weren't here for that reason, but since you two've got such big mouths, maybe now would be a good time ta' fill us in on what you just said."

The two men looked at each other with fear, each hoping the other might start, but explaining this to these two women in particular was not the chore of choice for either man.

"Ah...Well...Ya' see..." Filbert began, and Bullet interrupted a second later.

"Ladies...Well..."

"Deep subject for a shallow mind, Bullet," Heidi interjected.

It was a very uncomfortable situation to say the least. All four stood, looking at one, then the other, and then to the original person, yet no one was able to speak.

Almost simultaneously, Heidi, Filbert, and Bullet became overwhelmed with apprehension for knowing what they all knew and having Mary standing this close to their knowledge. At the very second it appeared that Filbert prepared to tell all, the sound of approaching children forced an immediate silence to the conversation.

The kids were set up in front of the TV with folding tables and desserts, leaving the dining room for the adults. If it could have been avoided, Heidi would be the first to have protected Mary from it, yet it had all landed in their laps, and since they weren't psychologists, the only way to meet this devil was head on. The trio bearing the bad news did so with the utmost caution, and as much tenderness as could be afforded when sharing information of this type about someone close.

Bullet never spoke a word; Filbert spoke very little, while Heidi told her version of the events that had led them to this point, as graciously as any human being could in a situation like this.

Mary's face grew bewildered as Heidi spoke, and by the time the conversation was finished, a look of drawn horror had replaced the bewilderment.

The kids' noticed their sister's sudden emotional changes. Although they were still young, they were mature beyond their years due to their life's experiences. From the moment she abruptly gathered them up from the holiday festivities, they knew something was very wrong. Thinking that one of the adults had said something to anger her, they kept their distance, and made their goodbyes and thank-you's short and sweet. The two men never got up, almost ordered by Mary's facial expression and body language not to. Heidi walked them to the door with a consoling arm around Mary's waist, and she spoke in low tones, not allowing the kids (including hers) to hear.

Like an infection spreading wildly through the bloodstream, did the news of Kenny's sexually deviant activities cause Mary to immediately feel sick. She gathered the children to run away once again from the nightmare that was her life.

40

THE DRIVE HOME WAS SILENT and rerouted from the holiday happiness. It seemed almost laughable to Mary that the news given to her less than ten minutes ago by the same people she'd mentally divorced herself from and then resurrected the friendship, for the children's sake, had known everything they told her for some time now. She became heart-stricken with betrayal. The agony forced to her to think about taking the kids and leaving all this behind, disappearing where no one would find them, but that simply was not reality. Sooner or later, she knew, someone always found you and the gig was up. She immediately dismissed that as a way out. She drove in the opposite direction from home, and Bobby, sitting in the front passenger seat, was the first to notice.

"Where are we goin', Mary?"

"I thought we'd take a little ride along the coast for awhile. Is that ok with you?" she asked in a low voice.

"Fine with me," he responded. Tabi, looking out of the rear side window remained silent.

Along their ride, they noticed that people had begun displaying Christmas wreaths, hanging lights on shrubs and houses, and some were already lit. The Christmas season was on, and Mary had every intention, despite the woeful revelation about her husband, to decorate and celebrate the season for the sake of the kids. Kenny was an animal in her mind now. She was embarrassed to think that she had been so radically naïve, or as Kenny had once said about the people from Down East, "ignorant and arrogant."

She couldn't believe she was quoting him in her thoughts now, and suddenly, without a millisecond passing since that thought, a feeling of unadulterated hate began to well up from deep within her. She couldn't remember if she had ever felt this alone. In her most hidden thoughts, she wished Kenny was dead. She felt the heavy weight these thoughts burdened her with, when she became distracted by the sound of the kids' jubilant voices from their seats as they watched the Christmas lights go by. It snapped her out of the emotional dive and made her feel alive once again to hear them so enthusiastically upbeat.

"Can we put lights on the front of our house?" Bobby asked.

"Oh, look at that place. Are we going to have a big tree this year?" Tabi asked.

They had no idea what Mary was going through right now. Thanks to Filbert and Heidi's candid, yet heedful message, they had heard nothing, and knew nothing of what had taken place at the Cirones.

She didn't want the ride to end at this point, but reality bites. It was dark now. They had begun their day early, and even if the kids weren't tired, she was beat, and they turned around and headed for home when they got to Ellsworth. Mary drove slowly; about five miles per-hour below the posted speed limit. She was tired, yet she needed awhile longer to put her thoughts together for the moment when they arrived home.

They were about halfway down Black Bear Road when a light dusting of snow began to blanket the area. The thought suddenly occurred to her that a dusting here on the flat wooded section of road could turn into a slip-sliding crap-shoot at the top of Cathance Hill, and she pushed the gas pedal down a tad, now wanting the ride to be over as quickly as possible. The kids were happy to see the white stuff falling. It made them think of the approaching holidays. But until they were parked in the driveway and safe, Mary would be on the edge of the seat and white-knuckling the wheel for the rest of the ride.

It is nice how gainful employment allows the recipient who is devoted to their work to enjoy the simple necessities of life like a set of new studded snow-tires. Like most people Down East, Mary still drove the same old car, and probably would until the rust ate it from the inside out or the wheels fell off. Her steady income, however, helped to maintain it in sound, running condition, and the new exhaust system made her extremely proud now as the vehicle made its way up the steep, winding hill toward the summit without a single slip-away from traction.

She frowned suddenly when she glanced at the rear-view mirror and saw a set of high-beam headlights closing the distance between them quickly. She remembered Kenny telling her that the wider apart the headlights were, the newer the car might be. He'd developed this theory while he was keeping an eye out for a trooper, who would most likely be driving a late model car. She hated herself for continuously thinking of things he'd said in the past.

The vehicle continued its advance without slowing until it came to within a half-dozen car lengths from her. The driver dimmed the lights, and the car appeared to hover in its place behind her, never increasing nor decreasing the distance between them. Both cars reached the summit a few seconds apart. Mary didn't give a thought to where she was or that the snow was much heavier and deeper here than she expected. Her only fear now, knowing she would never pull over because she couldn't see the hidden shoulder, was to have the jerk behind her all the way down to the Chesterfield town line a few miles from the top.

"He's just gonna have to follow me down or pass me up, 'cause I'm not gonna speed up or pull over for whoever that is behind us," she said.

Both kids turned toward the rear window, which was partially steamed up from the difference between the inside and outside temperatures. This was the first they knew that a vehicle was behind them.

The two cars cleared the summit and began their downward trek, much slower now at the pace Mary set. The vehicle behind never altered its distance. The night was extremely dark, brightened only by the glistening white of the fresh powder blowing in front of the headlights. Mary realized that the driver behind the wheel of the following car was more confident in the snow, simply because of the rate of speed it had originally approached; yet whoever it was had not made any attempt to pass or intimidate her to increase her speed on the downhill side. That gave Mary a sense of calmness, and with that, a sense of control for the conditions. The little-bro that he was, Bobby continued his updates to Mary on the other car's position, and his concern warmed Mary's heart.

Mary exhaled a deep sigh of relief upon reaching the bottom of the hill, where the road leveled off. The road had been widened here a couple of years ago, and there were new guardrails and wide shoulders. Mary thought to herself that perhaps now the other driver would take the opportunity to pass, as a good distance of road ahead could be seen. The car remained in its place, well past the stretch where it could have passed safely. With less than two miles before reaching home, and for the first time since leaving the Cirones, Mary felt a pang of fear and uncertainty in her stomach, and her mind went blank of everything she'd gone over in her thoughts about how she would act, given the news nearly two hours ago.

The final bend before the homestead was directly in front of her, and she decided to alert the other driver early with her directional signal as she began slowing down. She looked in the rear-view mirror, and much to her dismay, upon entering the glow of the first street light on the road and for the first time since the two-vehicle encounter, the official blue paint of the trooper's car came into view, with his turn signal light on for the same direction.

She refused to tax her already-burdened emotional state of mind with the worry of why Harry Circus was pulling in behind her, knowing very well that Kenny would have an encyclopedia of questions for her being away this long without calling. She had prepared herself to face him, but not him and the trooper together. That was a match made in hell, and was not what she needed to end this already devastating day.

"That caar is followin' us," Bobby said.

"And… it's Trooper Circus," Tabi chimed in.

The car slid slightly on the greasy road surface as she applied the brakes, so she immediately eased off, and regained control. Harry's heavy, equipment-laden car pulled in behind her like a tank.

Kenny stood under the incandescent glow of the outside barn light while the tracks of wreath makers long since gone were hidden by the fresh powder snow. The flakes were large under the glare of the light, and clung to his jacket and the top of his head. The look on his face spoke volumes, yet his stare went past Mary's car and focused on the Maine State Police car behind her. The temperature had dropped since earlier in the day, but Kenny had no shirt on under the leather jacket he wore with his black jeans, and surprisingly, he was barefooted. The warm air from his breath rose and encapsulated the light directly above him. His lips moved, but what he said was inaudible to everyone but him, as no one had exited the vehicles as of yet.

Harry pulled his car to a location where he might easily exit to the road when ready, and in a position where he could speak to Mary when she passed and Kenny, simultaneously.

"No doubt yaw' gettin' good traction with that old buggy, Mary," Harry said.

"I'd betta', with what thea' chaagin' fa' studded snows now-a-days," she responded.

"I recognized yaw' caar as soon I came up on ya', near the top; snowin' a lot harda' up thea'," he said.

There wasn't an ounce of sarcasm in his tone of voice, and Mary softened her demeanor toward him. She was thankful he simply implied concern for the conditions. Like an alarm clock going off, she was suddenly reminded of what she'd been told earlier, and her defense mechanism forced her to tense again as she looked toward Kenny.

She wondered to herself just how many people knew of her husband's degenerate activity. Surely the trooper was wise to it. He was given information from everyone, whether it was true or made up, in order to score points with the law.

The kids ran past her, saying nothing to Harry. Bobby lifted his head and smiled as he passed; the trooper lifted his index finger in the form of a wave, yet said nothing.

"Is there a problem?" Kenny's elevated voice asked from his post at the barn door.

Both Mary and the trooper looked in his direction, but the trooper was the only one to respond.

"No problem. We just came over the hill with heavy snow, and I wanted to compliment her on her driving skills in the snow."

"She oughta be good, she's from the county, you know," Kenny said sarcastically, then turned and walked in the open barn door, slamming it behind him.

"Havin' a bad day, is he?"

"I wouldn't know. I've been out with the kids all day."

Immediately, the trooper's naturally suspicious mind began pumping out data as to why they wouldn't have spent Thanksgiving together as a family. However, the trooper knew that Kenny ran a wreath shop here in the barn, and discounted the thought as the reason.

Mary's need to speak with someone was suddenly overpowering. The trooper had never been a friend, and from childhood on, Mary had never allowed lawmen or women to get close. Her father and now her husband would want it that way. Though Virgil was a calmer man these days, Kenny was still out of control.

Perceptive as he was, Harry prided himself on his ability to read facial expressions, and Mary's revealed a wealth of unasked and unanswered questions. Several times since Kenny had re-entered the barn, it appeared that she was about to begin to say something, but then looked away from the trooper toward the house, obviously backing away from the thought.

"Did you want to ask me something, Mary? It looked as

though you…" She interrupted.

"No, just thank you fa' keepin' yaw' distance on the road. I would have been nervous had ya' got any closa," she said, and then looked toward the ground as if it wasn't exactly what she intended to say.

"No problem," Harry responded.

At that very moment, Kenny bolted from the barn and was now wearing boots, walking determinedly toward the front side of the car where Mary stood, appearing dumbfounded now at the sight of him. Harry's first thought was to get out of his car, yet Kenny walked open-handed, and no threat seemed apparent.

"Are you plannin' on spendin' the night?" he said to Harry. "I'm waitin' fa' my Thanksgiving dinner, and she ain't gonna get it started until you pull on outta here." Kenny appeared to be puffed up with anger as he stared at Harry.

"I'm not lookin' for trouble—we're just talkin' hea', Kenny."

"Get that blue piece of shit outta my driveway. It's bad for my reputation with some from around here."

Mary put out a hand in an attempt to calm him, and Kenny slapped it aside with a strong back-hand, the sound slicing through the cold, night air. At the sight, the trooper lunged from his car.

"You may try that stunt while in the privacy of yaw'r own home, but you'll be blessed if yaw' gonna' try that in front o' me," Harry said.

He reached for Kenny, and Mary flung herself between them, forcing the trooper to stop suddenly, while Kenny flinched in the opposite direction.

With Mary standing between them, the trooper's arms fell to his side and with the sudden refrain from violence from the two men, Mary looked toward the house. She saw no peeping eyes at any door or window. For that she was most grateful. As the vapor from their warm breath rose and then evaporated in the cold night air, all three breathe heavily from the stress of the moment. Harry held his ground facing Kenny, who had now side-stepped several feet from the other two.

Mary's mind was filled with what was happening before her

and the information she received a short while ago from the Cirones and Bullet, flashed through her mind's-eye.

Right now, had they been anywhere else besides the front of their home, she wished the trooper would slap the shit out of her man, yet the term, 'man', she pondered without respect.

After several minutes of the facial stand-off, the cold seem to dispel the anger that rose between the two men. Suddenly, Mary felt trapped in the middle once again.

Seeing her face and her obvious dismay, Kenny let loose with a forced, chaotic laughter, causing Harry to prepare himself in the event the 'little man' decided to make a fool of himself. He did not however, move from his place several feet away.

"You're out of control, Kenny. If I find out you've been hittin' on her", and he looked toward Mary now, "I'll be back and there won't be anyone to stand between us."

"Whatever", Kenny said defiantly.

At that very moment, Mary knew she would never confront him with the information she'd received at the Cirones. She felt it was simply a matter of time and Kenny would hang himself, given enough rope, but it was her deep fear from denial that would stop her again as before and her inability to confront her father. As the clock ticked the time away, Kenny turned and went toward the house, telling Mary that he was hungry and not to be long with the man in blue.

After they were alone, Harry offered his apology. "Mary, I'm sorry. Had I known my stopping here would have caused you this much grief, I would have kept right on going home. If you need me, for anything, please do not hesitate to call, anytime. He's digging a grave for himself and…right now, I don't think anyone can stop him."

There was so much Mary wanted to say, but she though it best to remain silent once again. "Thank you, Harry," she said. "I'm sorry you had to be a part of this."

With that said, Harry returned to his car, looked to Mary as he pulled out and wondered if there would be trouble here tonight.

41

GENERALLY, IT SOMETIMES TAKES AWHILE for it to snow, but usually after the first storm where the snow sticks to the ground, you can pretty much take it to the bank that it's going to keep right on snowing after that.

Thanksgiving that year was the first sticking snow. There weren't any huge storms between turkey-day and Christmas, but most every day saw a decent snow shower, guaranteeing a white Christmas. The weather tended to put most everyone in the holiday spirit, and even folks who didn't normally decorate did this year, and the glowing lights burning almost everywhere simply added to the archaic seasonal atmosphere.

Though Mary did not string lights around the outside of the house as the kids had suggested, she dug deep in the ornament box, and almost ceremoniously readied the house for the "happiest time of the year."

Like a prayer whispered in private, Christmas Day soothes many a soul with a peaceful state of affairs, until the children rise to have their tree and the treasures to be found in glistening packages with brightly colored ribbons and bows. Families gather in the privacy of their homes, frolicking amidst the pleasures of merriment, while the outdoors is generally absent of the daily routines of labor except for the clamoring blue jay noisily rousting the backyard bird feeders in search of a holiday feast.

Everyone celebrates the day with respect to their own traditions. Some begin the day with worship to their chosen deity, whatever that might be. Harry Circus and his entire family, including his and Annie's parents, began the day by occupying an entire pew that took up the center portion of the congregation, the section with isles on both sides and the first up front. For them, all other celebrating of the day was reserved for after church. The Savior had been born this day, and Harry, like his father before him, had raised his family in the sanctity of his belief. There was only one thing that rivaled that doctrine however; it was Harry's antipathy of others who did not share his views. He took his work seriously, and believed himself to be one of a chosen few. He felt there was no room in society for the evils of the devil to roam the earth in the guise of human form.

Although his attention to the words of his minister was nearly beyond distraction, for no apparent reason his thoughts strayed from the sermon to illuminate through his minds-eye the delinquent face of Kenny Collins, displaying a cruel and exaggerated frown, in chaotic laughter. The vision bewildered him. But despite the vision, which passed quickly, things went very well for the Circus family. The word of the Lord and their beliefs brought them a level of happiness that not many could know. The gifts under their tree were simple. They were frugal and careful in all that was their life.

"Waste not, want not" was the motto of his life. Everything had to be useful, like his new .12-gauge shotgun. His wife and father had collaborated on that gift for him. True, he was a man who needed to carry a firearm as part of his work to protect and defend the innocent and law-abiding citizens of the Great State of Maine. A shotgun, however, was a tool. Frugality knew many levels, and hunting was God's gift to man for his preservation.

"Law cannot persuade where it cannot punish."

(Thomas Fuller)

Bullet Carter woke up Christmas morning with the worst hangover he'd experienced since he began drinking in high school. His tongue felt swollen to at least twice its normal size, and was dry as a desert. As drunk as he'd been when he finally passed out and slept, he dreamed crazy dreams. Visions of things that were now sparse in his memory came back to him as he lay in the partial darkness of his room. Mary had been in one of the dreams, and so had Millie. It was Christmas in another, and his boys were there with a decorated tree, the tinsel glistening brightly. Mary appeared in that one also. But there were no decorated trees with brightly wrapped presents beneath them, not since Millie and the boys had gone away. Bullet was tired of being sexually desperate and waking up alone in bed. The way he saw it now was that Kenny Collins had taken both of the women he ever cared for away from him in some way. *"Sure, I ain't no saint,"* he thought. *"I got my own problems, and me and Millie fought like cats and dogs at times, but I neva' treated them like shit the way he treated them since he came into thea' lives"*.

With the back of his head still buried deep in the warm, soft pillow, he reached for a cigarette and lit it, the flame from the lighter illuminating the area around his head. The click of the closing cover was loud to his tender ears, and he drew the smoke deep into his lungs, feeling the instant relief from the nicotine. Christmas was simply another day for Bullet. He'd probably hang around until late afternoon, then after cleaning out the fridge of whatever beer was left from last night, he'd venture out in the snow and find his way to someone who would be willing to feed him more alcohol. After all, he'd do and had done the same for countless numbers.

What pissed him off most about today was that he woke up and that little bag o' crap, Kenny, had popped into his thoughts. *"That little frig' made a mess o' everything and everyone he came in contact with. Someone oughta put some lead in his oatmeal. Send 'im back to where he came from."* Then he spat into the bucket he kept beside the bed, and swore like a man possessed.

"We're all just tragic examples of how life can hold us captive."

FILBERT SAT IN THE LARGE ROCKER RECLINER in the corner of the living room. Christmas was one of those days he allowed himself a one-day emancipation from the store, and the smile on his face was natural as he watched the two younger kids shred the wrapping paper from the gifts while the steam from his cup of coffee with Bailey's Irish Cream rose up to fill his senses. The past several months had been emotionally draining for everyone who was connected with his and Heidi's life, yet all of it seemed to be swept under the carpet today, as the happiness on their children's faces was exactly what the doctor ordered to relieve the mental stress. The only family member not present was Amos. Heidi had called up to him several times, and his low-volume response was in the form of a grunt. With all of the presents nearly opened, he still hadn't made an appearance.

Last night's late-evening dusting of fresh, fine powder had left the entire earth's surface and anything left outside coated with the essence of diamonds. The sky cleared early to an endless, burning blue; the sun magnified the crystallization. Suddenly, the room brightened, dimming the luster of the tree lights. Filbert, thinking the time right to roust his teenage son, so that he would participate in the morning's tradition, got up from his chair and shuffled across the floor in his slippers. When he reached the bottom of the staircase, to spare himself the need to go up, he signaled with a series of hoots, allowing the boy to come down on his own. No sound came from the upstairs, and Filbert, with a moan of contempt for having to climb, began the steep ascent on the creaking, old steps. Unlike most old Maine houses with their narrow hallways, the top of these stairs opened to an expansive foyer, enclosed by a long extension of the balustrade, overlooking the stairs, with doors on the three remaining walls.

There was a doorway directly in front of the stairs that lead to an attic space over the kitchen below, and just to the right and diagonally across from the top of the stairs, a door that opened to Heidi and Filbert's room. On the same side after a large expanse of wall, that door led to the girl's room. The doorway directly adjacent to the railing, the interior of which spanned over the staircase, was Amos' room.

The very second his foot came to rest on the top of the landing; the pungent aroma of burning marijuana filled his nostrils. At first, Filbert mistook it for burning tea leaves, which he had smoked as a young boy; then, as if he'd been struck by a rogue lightning bolt, he recognized what he was actually breathing. The door crashed open against the wall, vibrating throughout the entire upstairs, revealing young Amos with the upper half of his torso hung out of the open bedroom window. He didn't hear Filbert enter. When Filbert entered the room, it was freezing inside. What he smelled now was what he'd smelled for the last several months, without actually recognizing it as pot. It seemed to permeate everything that was Amos. His room and his clothes reeked of it.

"What, in the good Christ are you doin', hangin' out that winda'? You've been smokin' that crap right along, haven't ya?"

Filbert reached the boy just as he pulled himself back through the window after flipping the remainder of his smoke out and down into the fresh snow below, where it disappeared quickly. Filbert made a grab for him, and the boy, being far spryer than he'd expected, dodged his father's attempt to restrain him, and ducked below Filbert's outstretched arm, heading for the door and the stairs. Amos was his father's height, yet lanky and lean. His long gait quickened as he bolted through his room's open door, stopping suddenly in the middle of the foyer at the sound of his mother's rapidly climbing footsteps. He had two choices at that point. He could continue on his course to the stairs, probably knocking his mother down, backwards over the stairwell, or he could face the wrath of his father's boiling anger.

Either way, the unwelcome ramification of whatever justice lay before him destroyed what remained of the buzz he got during his upper torso's journey out the window in the cold Christmas morning air.

It wasn't early by Down East standards, but it wasn't late in the morning either. The object of everyone's Christmas morning thoughts was still fast asleep, along with Tabi and Bobby. Mary sat quietly sipping her tea in the faint glow of the Christmas tree that had been left lit (a Christmas Eve tradition), cherishing the solitude of the peaceful living room. Looking down now, at the enormous collection of gifts under the tree, she realized that Kenny had placed the largest amount of them. She laughed to herself, knowing very well that he had paid the store where he bought them the additional charge for wrapping. Kenny had a difficult time wrapping a sandwich with foil. The gifts were beautifully wrapped with ribbons and bows, and the many colored lights reflected off the glittering paper. Through the drawn curtains, Mary saw the brightening from outdoors, and hoped this Christmas Day would turn out bright and sunny. She had invited Virgil for a mid-afternoon dinner, and the smell of the huge ham, which was already cooking, filled the house.

She hadn't tried to contact Heidi since her Thanksgiving awakening to her husband's lifestyle, nor had Heidi made any attempt to contact her. Both women feared another feud between them, but it was Mary's intention, as the day became distracted with kids, toys, and other things that she would make the effort to get a call out to Heidi, simply to wish her a Merry Christmas. It wasn't their fault. They had become the messengers that day. How could she hold a grudge toward them for that?

Suddenly, Mary's thoughts drifted, carrying her back to a day when she and Bullet... She tried to block it out—yet it's funny how, when you least expect it, you're reminded of things long asleep in your subconscious mind. It was as if she feared someone might overhear her thoughts, and her guilt caused her to jump up from her relaxed position on the couch in front of the tree, to go directly into the kitchen and busy herself with little things to keep her mind from drifting back there with Bullet.

After several minutes of poking the ham with a large serving fork and brewing more tea, she began hearing movement from upstairs. Whoever it was would most likely wake the others, and the surge for presents would be in full swing. Whether Kenny needed solitude or not, Mary, would be unable and unwilling to keep the kids quiet today.

When she heard both sets of footsteps, she eagerly went toward the stairs to meet them. From the looks on their faces, no directional assistance to the tree would be needed.

They exchanged starry-eyed wishes for a Merry Christmas, and she asked, simply out of concern, if they wanted something for breakfast before they blew by her like a Boston & Maine freight train bound for Portland.

Deep in her heart, she could have cared less now if Kenny slept his life away, but the kids had presents for him, and they at least wanted him to be there to exchange presents together. She thought it best to open their gifts from Virgil. He had dropped them off after they'd gone to bed last night, still considering them the little kids he had at home before they came here. But they were like miniature grownups now, and the Santa thing, well... There were gifts that had come with the mail-lady from relatives up in the County. They never forgot Mary and the "little ones," as they still called them. Tabi would shake her head while reading cards from them when they used that term.

Her second cup of tea was ready, and she joined them on the floor beside the tree. The house was filled with the aroma from the ham being baked, and the spirit of this day instilled itself into their minds. Each found and separated the presents with their names on the tags. Bobby pointed to a couple of big ones with tags for Mary. They were from Santa. From where she sat, she heard the sound of deep, throaty hacking coming from behind the still-closed bedroom door. It appeared that "Santa" was about to join the festivities. Had this been a year ago, she would have anticipated his awakening and had the coffee brewed for him. Now-a-days, he mostly fended for himself, and surprisingly, he didn't do much bitching about it. Even if he had, though she was extremely careful not to trigger an outburst of anger, she had become quite the politician when it came to evading a confrontation using calm double-talk, and he usually went away shaking his head. Mary heard the bedroom door open slowly, and Kenny, looking like death warmed over, dragged himself to within several feet of the tree before he noticed the three of them on the floor next to it.

"Merry Christmas," he said in a low, hoarse voice, glancing quickly at them as he made his way toward the downstairs bathroom. All three reciprocated as he disappeared into the room. It didn't appear that he was ill from whatever he'd done last night. Nothing seemed out of the norm, as far as Mary could tell. He'd stayed home most of the evening, but it wasn't uncommon for him to just up and leave, no matter what the time was, day or night. The kids looked to her for some sort of signal that might indicate any bad feelings, and Mary simply shrugged her shoulders as a sign that all appeared okay, and they resumed their paper ripping, as excited children and some adults do on Christmas morning.

All went surprisingly well at the Collins' place Christmas Day. Virgil came over around noon-time; he and Kenny hit it off with a descent dose of civility toward each other. It probably helped that Kenny had given Virgil a case of Narragansett sixteen-ounce'rs for a present, keeping them cold in the fridge. Mary did crawl into a corner as the day played out, and called Heidi. She was thrilled when Heidi answered. They made small talk for several minutes, and it felt good for the both of them to hear each other's voices. Mary extended an invitation for the two kids to drop by on New Year's Day for Bobby's birthday. Heidi, still shy from Thanksgiving, thought it was doable, and said she would drop them off.

She didn't share with Mary the type of hell they were in on this wonderful Christmas Day, with their only son and the eldest child high on drugs that Mary's husband had probably supplied him with. Only time would clear his head of the demon-seed planted by the demon of all the evil they knew now. Kenny Collins.

42

THE WEEK FOLLOWING CHRISTMAS often feels like the final step before entering oblivion. There is a lull that blankets all activity during that time; a peacefulness that encapsulates all life as though the planet needs time to recover and regroup itself for beginning a new year. Most people felt as if Thanksgiving had been yesterday; yet in a few days, the western world and everyone in it would be thrust into the beginning of that new year. The need for "recovery time" didn't appear to affect the children however; everywhere you went you could see them enjoying their presents for the out-of-doors. Sleds, cross-country skis, and things of that nature were cherished by those of lesser means. Those who lived in the palatial palaces along the river could be heard on the four-wheelers and snowmobiles from their Christmas.

The snow continued to accumulate with light dustings almost every night, and each day the snow showers lasted at least an hour. It appeared that winter this year would probably break many records for cold and snow.

Call it sentimental on Kenny's part, but he was dejected, remembering that it had been quite some time since he and Mary had been together romantically. Any closeness remaining between them had withered the moment she felt his hand upon her in a violent way, and with every tick of the clock, it seemed to her that something new was uncovered about her husband. Now, the marriage was one of simply convenience. New Year's Eve arrived to find Kenny with many needs. Since Mary was the closest possible object for attention, he began playing the little game of "chercher la femme."

Mary wanted no part of it. The kids were home and the temperature was minus-five outside—no one was going out to play, and as far as she was concerned, there would be no adult games going on inside, either. Kenny persisted, but when it became clear to him that his wife was as cold as the outdoors, he went for his duffle bag of tricks, and planned to warm himself with tidings of good cheer for the New Year.

With addictions, the more you do, the more you have to do, and when Kenny abused substance of any kind, he developed a real bad attitude, and that's when he became most volatile. Mary's intuition was usually right on, and she could see no good coming from the duffle-bag-shuffle, as she called it, but if she were careful with him, she thought she could avert any New Year's fireworks of the wrong kind. After all, she was preparing Bobby's eighth birthday party.

She'd always thought he had it pretty cool. One week he got Christmas presents, and then the very next week, he got a bunch more for his birthday. *"What a kick,"* she thought. Bobby liked it, too. He got that tiny bit more attention from family and friends which, until he'd moved in with Mary and Kenny, was one of the things lacking in his young life.

At times like this, during the holidays, both Tabi and Bobby spoke much of their mom and how she would have loved to see this or that. Mary could feel the extent to which they missed her. She missed her immensely, also, but she would have wanted them to be happy, especially today.

Mary looked out of the kitchen window just above the sink. The wind blew a slight gale of fresh powder snow into a whirlwind of glistening ice crystals up and around the open expanse of the turn-around driveway. The road out front was absent of the normal traffic, and probably would be for most of the day, adding solemnity to the atmosphere.

She made mental notes of things she needed to get done for tomorrow. She was baking the cake for Bobby... and suddenly, thinking of Lucretia again and seeing the icy effects out the window allowed a calming sensation to come over her, alleviating, for a short period of time, the stress that had built up within her, fearing what might come of her rejection of Kenny's advances.

He continued to spend much of his free time in the barn. He'd installed a small wood stove for when he ran the wreath shop, and used it throughout the winter and spring months, when the evening chills necessitated the burning of a little wood. He'd gone out there with whatever he needed to celebrate with, and was there now. On New Year's Eve in years before, the two of them would have been prowling the party circuits, staying out all night, sometimes having to stay over at one of the party stops. Back then, Mary would've been in the barn with him, enjoying whatever he had to offer.

She pondered that thought for quite some time, questioning herself as to whether it had truly been love that brought them together, or if it might have been her need to rebel against her parents by running away with a bad boy to spite them. Her mind was a million miles from where she stood when the slamming of the kitchen door forced her back to the reality of now.

There were two possible states of mind she could expect from Kenny when he returned from the barn. One, he could be the playful fool, or he could have become an ogre, depending on which end of the bag he'd pulled from. As it turned out, the playful fool entered, and since she knew him well, it was obvious to her that he'd been smoking pot. The thin slits in his eyelids and the redness of his eyeballs, along with the giddy laughter, was a true giveaway.

He went directly to the cupboard, taking out a large bottle of vodka and two glasses. She didn't want to physically turn her head toward him, so she simply moved her eyes to broaden her peripheral vision. He began speaking in what sounded like riddles, Mary having no idea what he was talking about, while his laughter sounded childlike, and this concerned her. He never asked her if she wanted a drink, he merely filled both glasses with ice cubes, filling one to the rim with the clear delight, and the other half full and topped with orange juice. Mary assumed the second glass was hers.

She was happy for right now that both kids were up in their rooms occupying themselves as they often did with reading and drawing. Kenny, being in a festive mood, began lighting candles around the house, then the tree—and what would New Year's Eve be without some Rolling Stones on the CD player?

The remainder of the day passed quickly and uneventfully. Mary was grateful for that. She indulged him that one drink; however, it took her until suppertime to finish it, adding ice and OJ along the way, and feeling little effect from the alcohol.

As usual, when the shadows of night began to envelop the earth in darkness, Kenny's phone began ringing with calls from the nocturnal creatures that depended as much on him as he did on them, and Mary knew it wouldn't be long before he left for however long it took to satisfy and be satisfied. With each ring answered, another spike of hateful agony was pounded into Mary's heart.

She fixed everyone's favorite for supper, "Poor Man's Dish." It's called by a variety of names, depending on where you live and what your background is, but theirs consisted of a layer of canned kernel corn, then a layer of ground beef topped with thick slices of sharp cheddar cheese, topped with garlic mashed potatoes. The garlic made it fancy for Down East, but Kenny wasn't from here. It was just the way he liked the dish.

Mary baked it, allowing a light crust to form on the potatoes, and served it piping hot. At the very moment she called the kids down to eat, with the table set and supper in the center, Kenny walked out the back door, never saying a word, or even saying goodbye. The kids arrived at the table the moment the door closed. Mary wanted to answer the obvious questions that appeared on their faces, but she thought it best to play it down, so at least the three of them could enjoy a quiet New Year's Eve together.

Mary and the kids were in bed long before the clock struck midnight. Generally she would hear Kenny come in, but either the stress or the preparation for Bobby's birthday had left her deeply fatigued, and she fell fast asleep the moment her head hit the pillow. She awoke to a thin beam of light filtering in through the edge of the curtains, and it became clear to her that the infernal racket of Kenny's deep, guttural snoring woke her. She lay quietly for several moments, puzzled at sleeping through whatever time it had been when he'd returned home and came to bed. She couldn't stay in bed any longer for the noise, and when she finally folded the covers off of herself, she felt the sudden chill in the air. It was obvious that the fire had gone out, and by the feel of the air, it had probably gone out before Kenny came home.

She slipped her bathrobe on and left the room as quietly as possible, closing the door behind her. Upon entering the living room, she immediately began gathering kindling wood from the wood box, and relit the stove in record time. It wasn't that uncommon for the stove to go out in the middle of the night, especially with the outside temperature so low, but she wished it had continued burning this morning. Within minutes, the fire crackled, and she fueled it with larger pieces of kindling, then topped it off with two large logs of hardwood, and went to brew her tea. The quiet of the early morning allowed her thoughts to drift, uninterrupted; she was happy that it was Bobby's birthday, yet she was still angry that Kenny had come home at all. She no longer wanted him in the house. Last night, she'd found herself wishing that he'd lose control of his pickup and freeze to death in some snow bank somewhere, alone... She felt guilty for that thought, but couldn't help herself.

Sometimes one feels the pressure of time running away from one when preparing for an event, yet when the day actually arrives, time flies like a rocket off a launch pad. For Mary, that's how the day went from the moment of her chilled awakening right through to the arrival of the first child guest for Bobby's party. She and Tabi decorated the house with balloons and streamers and there was a piñata hanging in the barn. The Christmas tree, surprisingly still well preserved, was lit from the time Mary had fired the stove, and would remain lit for the remainder of this day. After all, it was one of the traditions left unspoiled, unlike the changes to everything that meant the most in her life.

It was no surprise when Bobby strolled downstairs and greeted Mary with a sleepy good morning, followed immediately by, "where's my presents?" He stood, facing her in his blue pajamas, still not fully awake. Mary went to him, hugged him, and wished him a very happy birthday.

After calming his insistence on finding his presents, she fixed him a bowl of cereal, and they sat together at the table, her sipping tea, absorbing every second of their time together. She saw so much of Lucretia in his facial expressions and mannerisms now, and it made her feel alive to have been able to keep him with her like this. *"Sometimes life is just a bunch o' shit and all ya' have is family,"* she thought as she watched him mou-down on the Frosted Flakes she'd served him. *"Money talks and shit walks, but without family, all ya' got is shit,"* She thought.

They finished their breakfast almost sip for sip, and it didn't take long for the sugar from his to kick in, and he was off at lightning speed to search for any presents that might not be hidden well enough. Mary cautioned him to be quiet, knowing well that the king lay sleeping, and until she knew whether the monster or the playful fool would arise, discretion was the word.

New Year's Day was more frigid than the night before. Everyone would most likely prefer to remain indoors; yet by noontime, none of the invited guests had called to cancel. Mary had invited four of Bobby's closest friends, including Emily and Lulu Cirone, Filbert and Heidi's youngest. After inviting them, the worry of having made that choice was a constant draw on her mind as she wondered exactly how Kenny would react to seeing them. Every time she thought of it, she realized that he might not even be here for the party, so she hoped it didn't matter.

The party was set for 2:00 p.m. Kenny was just dragging himself out of bed as they finished their breakfast, looking worse than Mary could remember. What she was thankful for was that he did not appear to be in desperate need of disgorgement. In fact, he seemed rather together, except for what he looked like.

"Happy fuckin' New Year, everybody!"

Kenny's voice reverberated throughout the entire house, forcing a severe flutter of butterflies in the pit of Mary's stomach at the first sound of his crude greetings. She had perked a full pot of coffee, only for the sake of caution, and it was piping hot if he decided to have some. From the sound of his voice and the level of energy it projected, however, he was already well-perked on his own. Mary did not spend any time trying to figure out whether he was on something, because she knew he was; her concern was what he was on.

Bobby came running at the sound of Kenny's footsteps on the kitchen floor. "Whatcha' get me for my birthday, Kenny-boy?" he asked.

"Well, you're just gonna have to wait 'til the party, big boy," Kenny responded with excitement in his tone.

It was Mary's plan to lay out a buffet-style table in the kitchen for the partygoers. Tabi was as excited as if it were her birthday, whispering little secrets in Mary's ear, then playing head games with her brother to psych him up for the main event.

Kenny, for the most part, remained out of sight from the time he fell out of bed to several minutes before the first guests were due to arrive. He went out to the barn, and when he came back to roam through the house, he held tightly to his glass of vodka on the rocks.

The steaming tea and coffee pots and the activity throughout the entire house enlivened Mary's senses, and brought her back in memory to a time when the steam from her mother's tea pot added humidity to the dry, winter air, making the kitchen the warmest and most welcoming room in the house. The kitchen was where all guests were ushered in from the cold in winter and the heat of summer, where the ceiling fan cooled everything down.

Mary sat and sipped her tea. She couldn't remember when she'd felt happier, watching her brother romp from room to room with his young friends who'd arrived early trailing behind him, everyone smiling and enjoying the moment.

Finally, the long-anticipated knock sounded on the door. The only guests left to arrive were the Cirone kids. For a brief moment, Mary's heart leaped to her throat at the thought that perhaps Heidi had changed her mind and come with the kids. Then, as if her thoughts evoked action, and without warning—like he'd waited for this very moment—Kenny made a sudden dash toward the door, knowing well who the final guests were.

"Well, well! Look everyone; it's the young Cirone children. Come on in, kids. It's party time!" Kenny hollered out. Then, in a hushed voice he said to Lulu, "Where's your big brother? I thought he might come with you."

The child did not respond, she simply went directly to Bobby and never looked back at Kenny. Before he could leave the immediate area of the door, another knock came.

Kenny displayed one of his dumb looks, obviously thinking that perhaps Heidi had gone to park the car and let the kids come to the door first, so he would be the one to greet her. Mary, hearing the knock from where she stood in the kitchen, suddenly felt sick, thinking the same—that it might be her. They were both totally surprised, when Kenny pulled the door open hard, to see standing before him the outstanding blue uniform filled with a larger-than-life Harry Circus, directly in front of Virgil Bagley.

Had Kenny been swallowing at that moment, he would have undoubtedly choked at seeing these two particular men at his back door. Virgil, he could understand, but the freakin' state cop was something else. It was completely out of character to see Kenny speechless, but that is exactly how he was caught off-guard. Both men realized that Kenny was stupefied at seeing them, and began laughing together, which sent a bolt of anger up Kenny's spine, yet he remained motionless and incapable of speech. When Mary realized that no one had entered since the knock, she went to see what was happening. Standing now, by Kenny's side and seeing the trooper and Virgil at her door, she also appeared dumbfounded.

"Hey…little girl," Virgil said, still grinning.

At that point, Kenny obviously wanted to say something. Getting the last word in always seemed so important to him, so he finally spoke up.

"We usually send out invitations and I don't remember…"

Mary interrupted. "Yah', this, to say the least, is a huge surprise."

Kenny focused a dirty look in her direction, yet, she was, from the look on her face, unmoved by the apparent threat he intended to project.

"All my heat's headin' for the barn. If you're both plannin' to come in, now would be as good a time as any," Mary said with a playful tone and a school-girl grin.

This prompted all three men to believe she was teasing, which angered Kenny even more. The trooper threw an intimidating look in Kenny's direction as he passed. It wasn't until that moment that both Kenny and Mary noticed the trooper was carrying a small, wrapped present, which was a surprise to the both of them, not only that he'd brought a present, but that Harry Circus knew Bobby's birth date.

Mary remembered how he'd taken a liking to the boy on awards night, but never expected him to do something for his birthday, never mind show up in person. The smell of freshly perked coffee aroused the senses of both men, and upon entering the kitchen the trooper hoped that Mary might offer him a cup. Just as he was thinking it, Mary pointed toward the electric percolator, and both men nodded.

Harry, being Harry, didn't take long to scan the room in an

attempt to recognize all of the guests present, and immediately wondered why the Cirone kids were here without a parent.

"*It was last year to the day when I popped in at Filbert's store to chat about the 'little man' no more than an arm's length away from me now,*" Harry thought.

It was as if the junkyard dog in Kenny suddenly snapped his chain, and he stood right in front of the two men, mostly in front of Harry, as if lying in wait for an opportunity to maul something for a sample of bone. Harry did his best to ignore him, making small talk with Virgil, who seemed to be getting a big kick out of watching Kenny squirm. For the first time since Virgil had known him, he saw that the wind was knocked right out of his sails, as he remained quiet throughout the multiple conversations.

With every word that passed the trooper's lips, a flame of anger raged within Kenny, the likes of which he'd never felt before. He refilled his glass with vodka and drank deeply, yet it didn't satisfy his need. It was also impossible for him to conveniently slip out into the barn to take the edge off from the alcohol with a few good hits from his stash of pot while the trooper lounged in his kitchen, sipping coffee with his father-in-law.

Although Mary kept her distance from that area of the house, she occasionally glanced in that direction, and took much pleasure in seeing Kenny so uncomfortable in the company of someone he despised so vehemently. He had to put up with Virgil—after all, he was family, and during the past several months they had refrained from argument, especially in front of the kids. It became obvious to Mary that the tension in that room became dangerously thick when Kenny began making distracting noises with the cupboard doors and talking over the trooper, using his own form of intimidation.

The moment the trooper and Virgil displayed displeasure toward Kenny on their faces, Mary moved quickly to round everyone up and get the party onto high ground. Tabi brought the presents to the dining area after she helped Mary clean the table of the buffet, and she watched her brother's eyes bulge with each delivery. The cake, which Mary had decorated with a "Transformer's Robot" theme—a large "Optimus-Prime" standing guard in the center—would be left hidden until it was time for Bobby to blow out the candles. Mary was saving the cake for after he opened the gifts. She positioned Bobby as the star in the center of the table.

Harry's restlessness was obvious, and he moved toward Mary, brushing himself just slightly against Kenny as he passed, and asked her if he might simply add his gift to the others and leave, saying he didn't want to interfere any more than he already had. Had someone asked Kenny, the fact that the trooper showed up at all was damage enough. Mary thanked the trooper, and said that Bobby would be in touch. Everyone offered their goodbyes in unison, except for Kenny, who offered sarcasm.

"Here's your hat, what's your hurry? Hey, come back when you can't stay so long," he said, and laughed. Harry ignored him, while putting a hand on Bobby's shoulder and wishing him a happy birthday.

Bobby, always the little gentleman, said, "Thank you for coming, trooper."

Mary walked the trooper to the door under the watchful eye of her husband. When they had reached the apparent safety of the outside door, the trooper spoke to Mary for only the second time since he arrived.

"Mary, he's no good for you anymore and worse for the kids. Justice awaits him, like every evil that wanders the good Lord's earth. Free yourself from him Mary. Justice awaits him," he said again.

From the moment the trooper left, the tension subsided, and the time blew by faster than ever. Harry had given Bobby an honorary junior trooper's badge, which he immediately pinned to his shirt upon opening the gift. All Kenny had to say was, "Wow."

Soon, Mary was saying goodbye to the last three guests, including Virgil, and after the door shut behind them she drew a deep breath. The holidays were officially over.

The entire house was finally quiet, and very messy. She heard Bobby upstairs playing with the toys he'd received, and from the living room, though out of sight, she could hear Kenny speaking in low tones, obviously to Tabi. When she came around the wall that partially divided the two rooms, nothing could have prepared her for what her eyes fell upon. Tabitha was sitting on Kenny's lap and he was whispering something in her ear.

Mary stood frozen to the spot, while phantoms from her own hell as a child leaped into her thoughts with visions of those cold, winter nights when she couldn't wake her mother, while her tongue was tied in knots of fear. Her mind's eye replayed it for her, only this time it was her little sister appearing in the nightmare.

"Get the fuck away from her, you low-life bastard!" she screamed.

"I thought I heard you whisper softly to me in my sleep.

But with the safety clicking off your .12-gauge,

I bear witness to the sin.

(E. Matthew Barsalou, 2009)

43

IT TAKES A WHILE, but winter eventually slams its relentless, icy door on the earth. In the long, seemingly evil darkness of unparalleled cold, January slipped away rapidly, and surprisingly, a desperately welcomed January thaw arrived during the final week of the month and continued into the first week of February. The smell of thawing branches and the ground under melting snow in direct sun areas tempted the weather prophets to dwell on the possibilities of an early spring, which in reality was still a long way off. Nevertheless, the warmth of the sun defrosted even the most ice-like attitudes in some. Most people begin to feel the isolation somewhere between the middle to the end of January, some make it to February; but it generally affects everyone in some way, sooner or later.

Had it not been for Mary's job in Ellsworth, it's possible she may have ventured back to rely on her old substance-dependent ways when looking out of a window during a snowstorm. Most mornings now, she awoke and thanked her lucky stars for Tabi and Bobby. "They're my saving grace," she was heard to say in reference to them many times to others. Since New Year's Day however, her nightmare had persisted, yet she didn't have any knowledge of Kenny actually abusing Tabi. She took care to always keep a level head, mostly to protect her siblings from finding out about her past, and she relied on her intuition to guide her.

Each day was a struggle to leave for work and the drive over the hill was again a hateful endeavor to overcome in the snow. Even though Mary didn't speak a word about what had taken place on New Year's Day to her co-workers, it was obvious to them that she was again under an enormous amount of stress. Without prying or implying, they quietly supported her, as several of them knew exactly what she was going through.

At least when she was at work, she was able, with minimum distraction, to remain focused on the tasks at hand. It was during the drives in and home that her imagination ran wildly away with her. She began to feel pangs of uncertainty and fear when she got within several miles of home. She wished her husband would just pack his bags and go away.

Meanwhile, the kids, not knowing why Mary was in such a state of mind, tried every means afforded them to console her, but even with as much heart and soul as she could muster, she was unable to free her mind from the restraint of fear that the sight of Tabi sitting on Kenny's lap had instilled in her. She wanted to believe that Tabi would have told her had something happened. They were more than just sisters, they were confidants; but Mary knew first-hand that speaking of such things seems near-impossible even with someone you love.

Mary needed to talk to someone, but there wasn't anyone in her life that she could trust or feel comfortable with bringing up this subject of abuse. Sure, there was a counseling service available through work, and the nursing home would pay for her to go, but Mary, even as level-headed as she had become, was still from the old school of belief. Besides, the counselor probably had more problems than she did, and the last thing Mary wanted was to have all of her shit kicked around at some psychologists' happy hour sometime after she'd gone home.

She was simply unwilling to share any of this with anyone right now. She would sort through it like she did with the rest of her life, and she'd protect those kids to death's end. It was during one of her trips home after work, when the trooper's words sang out clearly in her thoughts, "Justice awaits him," that the situation hit her full in the face.

"Yeah…justice. All ya' need is a big bag o' money and ya' kin' buy all the justice ya' need," she thought.

She suddenly realized how difficult a situation it really was when she looked back to her own childhood abuse, and the way her mother had appeared blind to the whole thing.

"I'll be goddamned if I'll be blind to it," she said to herself at just above a whisper as she made her way down the slope on the Chesterfield side of Cathance Hill.

After the events on Bobby's birthday and Kenny's perception of the holidays as being shit in his face, his attitude was amplified by his constant anger toward everyone, making him all the more nasty. He remained away from home far more than he was there, and the separation between he, his wife, and the kids broadened. It appeared that the relationship between them was dead. When he did return home, it seemed that he'd slept in his clothes for days, and if someone got close enough, the telltale sign of body odor left no doubt. He spoke little to Mary or the kids, and he was always preparing to leave again. His cell phone seldom rang, and for the first time in a long time, no one stopped in at the house unless it was very late at night or around the time he was leaving again.

Mary maintained her composure, however. Supper was always at the same time, and there was always enough of whatever they were having in the event that someone stopped by unexpectedly, like Virgil. These days, though Virgil was a stranger to his three kids and Mary realized that the holidays and the beginning of the New Year always saw him drinking heavily and she made no attempt to deal with that part of him. She protected her space, yet hoped for the best. Long ago she had stopped caring about him in the way most would for a father.

Unlike before the holidays, when it was obvious to Mary that the trooper's and constable's cars were always somewhere close to their place, she rarely saw either one nearby now, or anywhere else for that matter. Being a chip off the old block, so-to-speak, there was no love lost for those who wore badges, but she was grateful for the level of respect Bobby displayed for all lawmen, or women, whenever he found himself in the company of one. She figured he had learned this respect in school, and deep down it made her feel good to think that another generation would not follow in the footsteps outlined by those who came before them.

The general consensus would be that a man with an enormous amount of money and free time would find much satisfaction with all that freedom. Kenny Collins was a breed apart. Had he used his level of intelligence to help his fellow man, there's no telling how far he could have taken it, but all that freedom for Kenny meant finding ways to piss people off, and he was very good at doing that. The warming trend during the beginning of February was forgotten quickly as the temperature dropped to below zero on Sunday night, the beginning of the second week. All bets were off for an early spring, and chimneys again vented the plumes of thick, heavy smoke from winter's last stronghold of dry firewood.

There was only one thing on Kenny's mind when pulling the covers over his head that night. School vacation began at the end of the coming week, and like a vulture circling for fresh, dead meat, he would cruise the roadways of the small towns looking for those little pieces of flesh wandering aimlessly in search of whatever would help them enjoy their school vacation. Surprisingly enough, Kenny now supplied as many adults as he did teenagers.

"Money talks and shit walks." He was known to say when collecting, with palms open and facing up, accompanied by his iconic, shit-eatin' grin. Deep down, though he said nothing to Mary, he resented the fact that she wasn't indulging any more. For him, having his partner partake in his own predispositions was part of his high. Now, supplying the needs of so many became his ego-trip, but like every endeavor and every practitioner in public demand, one accumulates friends and foe in numbers. For as many who deemed him their savior, so he was doomed to carry the load equally of the sentiment of those who would burn him at the stake.

It was as plain as the nose on his face, had he taken the time to look, just how many started out having so much faith in him and how many went out of their way to help and allow him into their inner circles, then he simply kicked the rich, wholesome dirt of Down East Maine right back in their faces. Kenny allowed very little time to dwell on the past, unless it helped to fuel his anger toward those who didn't see it his way. As Kenny might have said it, *"It's my way or the highway and anyone that doesn't like it should take the exit, now."*

Like cow-plop on a rock, he spent his time that week on the couch watching TV, drinking, smoking pot, and napping, waiting for Mary and the kids to get home. The remainder of the week passed uneventfully, outside of the endless sparring between Kenny and Mary for the right to control their own domain, although Kenny would have preferred to re-indoctrinate her to his. They went out of their way to evade the real reason for the fighting, skirting the issues that ate her up inside.

Through all of the bickering, it was Tabi and Bobby who suffered the most. As much as Mary catered to their emotional needs, the children ultimately had been subjected to their parent's style of raising them. Their parents had been drunks, and long before Mary straightened out and protected them as guardian, they had established their own means of coping in a dysfunctional relationship. Retreating to their rooms for art and reading was simply a way to extract themselves from the stress of the arguing. They weren't in their rooms for the artistic solitude; they were there with ears to the doors, shaking to the bones at the slightest sound that resembled a slap or a chair thrown against the wall in anger. They were young, but the farthest thing from naïve, and arguing adults were very familiar to them. They had grown to love both Kenny and Mary, but it was the fear of Kenny now that allowed them to tolerate him.

Finally, midwinter vacation arrived. It wasn't as though school kids really need that week off. After all, how much time off had they enjoyed since Thanksgiving? Nevertheless, teachers had to go to conventions, and all the kids got to play out in the cold or stay home and watch TV. Having been at the nursing home as long as she had, Mary had accrued a goodly number of vacation hours, and she'd saved this week to spend with the kids. No way was she leaving them home alone with Kenny, nor did she want them penned up in the nursing home all week, although it was an option offered to working moms.

They had their plans and Kenny had his, but since they were compassionate beings, the kids invited Kenny to everything they'd decided to do. He made excuses for everything, except telling them he'd be home for supper, and if they were good for Mary, he said he'd have a surprise for them when he got home. The only one intrigued by that was Bobby. Though Tabi and Mary hid their feelings well, they preferred it when he was away.

As he planned, Kenny set out to find the wandering, lost souls of the night.

Basically, he didn't make it home for many suppers during vacation week, and he didn't come up in many conversations between the three of them.

On Wednesday evening, while Mary tried to relax, (fat chance of that) on the couch with a Stephen King novel, the phone rang. The kids had long since retreated upstairs. At first, she hesitated to answer, thinking it might be Kenny, then giving that up as ridiculous, she reached for the receiver and picked it up.

"Hello," she said, in a low, relaxed voice, and the sound of the voice on the other end nearly knocked her for a loop.

"Hello yourself," Bullet responded. Then he paused. There was no caller ID on the old rotary phone, and since Mary knew very well that Bullet never had a phone at home, she couldn't help but wonder from where and why he was calling her. The momentary silence from each ear piece was smothering, yet for no apparent reason, she felt a sense of security, almost happiness, knowing that Bullet was on the other end. She wouldn't have been able to explain it had someone known what she felt and asked her why. All she was in tune with now were her senses. Mary spoke first.

"So, what's goin' on? The last time I saw or spoke to you was on Thanksgiving at Filbert and Heidi's."

"Ah, yah'…I'm just sittin' hea' thinkin' o' just that, that it was Thanksgivin' bein' the last time I saw ya' or talked to ya'." The phone went silent once again for a few seconds. Bullet began this time.

"I kinda just wanted to check up on ya'…" And he began to rambled on about things that made no sense to her, yet keeping what he said in her thought process, she couldn't avoid wondering and worrying what might have come from it had Kenny been here and answered the phone. She was wearing her bathrobe, and nervously tugged at the long, dangling ends of the waist belt. Without warning and like a flash of lightening, a vision from yesteryear exploded in her mind of her long ago, and until-now, unthinkable miscarriage of Bullet's baby. She tried desperately to neutralize the thought, but with the sound of his voice this close to her ear, it was an impossible task. She became more restless with each word that he spoke, though it was obvious that he meant her no harm, as his voice was a true reflection of his concern for her and the kids.

"Mary, you don't have to stay with him another minute. That shithead is diggin' his own grave, and you gotta know that by now." She knew that he really wasn't a violent man, but his words sank deep into her consciousness.

In a nervous twitching, she began scanning the house. First the book on her lap, then the TV which was off, and then, without knowing why, her eyes fell upon the shotgun by the door. The sight of it forced shivers up her spine, and she looked away quickly. She refused to answer his last question, remaining still, while a momentary thought brought her back to the lost baby. She felt a weight come over her at this point, and even though she'd never seen the baby, she couldn't imagine at her age then being a mother, and the loss of that tiny human being flooded her soul with sorrow, but it also implanted a seed of anger.

"Mary… Ya' still thea'?"

"Yeah, I'm still hea'. Don't you think it didn't make me feel like hell when you all told me about how my man became some kind o' shit head? I had my doubts, but you people added the color I forgot. And by the way," she said rather bitchily, "whaddaya think would o' happened if he answered when ya' called?" she asked.

"Well, he would have to be goin' like hell, 'cause I just saw 'im go through town in the other direction with Filbert's kid, Amos, in the front seat."

He went on about his feelings for a short time, and then as quickly as he'd come into her space, he was gone.

"Mary, I'm sorry I bothered ya', I only wanted ta' see if you were alright."

She began to say thank you and heard the receiver click, then there was silence.

She wasn't angry for his quick departure; she actually felt good now that he'd called, and as she reached to place the receiver into the cradle, she caught another glimpse of the shotgun resting against the kitchen door frame, and was unable to take her eyes from it this time.

The miserable quiet of the house overwhelmed her suddenly, and she fell back heavily against the couch cushions. She wondered how she could have allowed herself to be taken to such depths of unhappiness—to have started out, just the two of them, so crazy in love and free, and to end up here. How could she allow someone to rule her existence without fighting back for so long? *"When did it all start to go bad for us?"* she wondered.

She found strength in solitude at times, and each passing day lifted her to new heights of self-confidence. However, as difficult as it might be and as deeply as she might search her soul, she still loved Kenny and was unable to give him up despite the cruelty that he had shown. In reality, she knew the hate had to end. Nothing lasts forever.

During the day-to-day doldrums of being at work and at school, time often drags on to the point of hating what you are forced to do. The inability to just get up and leave makes it all the worse.

Being on vacation and doing all the things you want to do when you want to do them appears to make time fly much faster than normal. But we are all subject to the great equalizing twenty-four-hour day, and no one gets a minute more. And so it was with midwinter vacation. The time flew by.

Before anyone had realized how fast the time was going, they awoke to Friday morning and nothing but relaxation was enjoyed, except for Bullet's call to Mary on Wednesday night. Mary finished the novel she was reading, still held spellbound by the characters and events that took place within the multitudinous pages. Bobby finished a small book, and Tabi wrote several letters to a young friend who had moved away, so all in all it was a restful week.

Many thoughts continued to haunt Mary after she spoke to Bullet. She lay now beside a snoring Kenny, her head still entangled with the cobwebs of sleep, wondering if her life would ever be free from the tumultuous upheaval of the past and present. Her dream had been to take her siblings out of the hell they existed in at home, but she had opened the door to the hell that was her life with Kenny and brought them in, thinking that somehow Kenny would change once the kids were in the picture. But she knew now that she couldn't change Kenny. He was just as wild and arrogant (more so) than when she'd met him at Filbert's store a lifetime ago. Had he not been there in the bed next to her, she could have enjoyed solitude, wrapped in her warm covers, yet being this close to him and awake made her uncomfortable, and restlessness stirred her to begin her day.

The instant she rolled slightly and was about to extend one leg to the floor, she felt Kenny's hand grasping her gently by the shoulder. Since they hadn't been together sexually for at least a couple of months, his hand upon her not only sent a pang of fear through her, it also allowed a tingle of desire through to her groin.

He began speaking just above a whisper, making it difficult for her to hear, but it was obvious from the look on his face, faintly visible in the still partially darkened room that he was not interested in what might be available for breakfast. She knew how desperate she'd become for sex. As active as they had been together for so long, the yearning to have him inside of her was making her crazy, but she could not dismiss the reason for the forced abstinence, which took its toll on both of them, physically and emotionally.

Kenny was very persuasive. With a few well-placed kisses to her neck and shoulders, the ice that coated Mary's good intentions began to melt; the occasional right word at the right time overtook her, and finally she turned and gave herself to him completely.

Both of them appeared to be floating on air all day Friday. The kids, always willing to forgive and forget, were delighted to see them once again in high spirits and exhibiting a tender regard for each other, but they couldn't know the true reason why. It was as if the world had declared another truce so that Kenny and Mary could be in the same room at the same time, talking in low tones and not screaming at each other. Love is truly blind.

Even though the weight of sexual frustration had been lifted from their lusts for the flesh, Mary still maintained an emotional distance between them that she was afraid Kenny might pick up on, but if he did, he never gave any indication. Several times when his attitude surfaced, she regretted what she'd done, but the feeling passed, and they went on to have a very good day all together. The kids acted like this was the way they loved life to be.

Saturday flew by. Snow showers came often; they sometimes do toward the end of February. For the first time that winter, the four of them went cross-country skiing together on the trails Kenny had cut along the river a long time ago. It was peaceful away from the road and the neighbors. It gave Mary some time for solitude, so that her thoughts became more vivid to her.

Suddenly, the vision of Tabi sitting on her husband's lap exploded again in her memory, and for a split second broke her concentration on the approach to a slight downhill section. She crossed the tips of her skis and went down like a fifty-pound sack of potatoes in the center of the trail, entangling Bobby, who was following closely. The commotion caused the two up front to stop and break out in laughter as the pile-up looked like something right out of the Three Stooges, minus one stooge. Bobby was on top of Mary, their poles and skis crossed in every direction, both struggling to right themselves, to the continuous laughter of the other two.

The trail home was long and tiring, and nothing further was said about the pile-up. It agitated Mary.

Evening came quickly. Mary fixed hot dogs and beans, and for the first time in a long time and after a couple of drinks, Kenny sat down with them to supper. He teased Bobby like he used to, and they sat there like the happy little family Mary had hoped they would always be. But each time she looked at her sister, she saw her sitting on Kenny's lap, and she knew she would have to confront him, and that it needed to be sooner than later.

With Mary however, the fear of confrontation and her inability to deal with the truth of abuse, rumbled through her mid-section.

It wouldn't be tonight, however. By the time Tabi and Mary cleaned up the kitchen, the frigid outside activities of the day had taken their toll on everyone, and with the heat from the freshly stoked stove, one by one they retired their bodies and minds to the comfort of their beds. Mary was at ease and fell fast asleep, while the kids seemed very calm and relaxed after the togetherness of the day. Kenny remained awake and took solace from substance.

Sunday morning arrived, the last day of vacation. During the long winter months, Mary and the kids had remained active indoors and out, but the ski excursion along the river yesterday let them all see just how out of shape they really were. They all slept in, well past their normal waking times. It was Tabi who stirred everyone awake with the aroma of fresh-perked coffee and the steaming kettle of water for Mary's tea. Even Bobby hadn't ventured down until then. About 8:00 a.m., Mary wrapped herself tightly in her robe, and sauntered through the living room, peeking out as she passed the still-closed curtains to a cold, bright winter day and making a mock shivering motion. She relished the warmth of their home. In her mind, her plan for the day was to reorganize the entire house after the week-long absence from housekeeping. She hoped it wouldn't be difficult to get the two kids back on course with the normal routine.

She hadn't heard Kenny come to bed the previous night, nor did she hear him if he'd left. Whether it was intuition, or the stack of empty beer cans on the counter, it seemed he must have stayed home. She hugged Tabi good morning, and thanked her for making coffee. They stood close, speaking softly about how good yesterday had been. Tabi spoke of things she planned for the week, and Mary thought about how much alike they were as she watched Tabi's face as she spoke, still looking for any telltale sign that she might be hiding something.

Just then, Bobby ran up from behind her and bear-hugged her around the legs, allowing her final thoughts of Tabi to dissipate into the ionosphere. She was so grateful for this moment, being alone with the two of them, warm and safe together.

"It's funny, and maybe funny's the wrong word, but when ya' think it's all peaches and cream, your memory digs up some crap and it all starts over again," she thought.

For Mary, it felt like an invisible puppeteer tugged on her emotional strings, even more forcefully since Friday morning. Her mind jerked her thoughts from the kids at the table having breakfast now and some long-ago forgotten vision from her and Kenny's past. She sipped slowly from the hot brew in her cup, watching Bobby dredge his spoon through his cold cereal, making sounds like a back-hoe, while Tabi flipped through the pages of a recently started novel. Then her thoughts flew back to some day on the barrens when Kenny delivered his goods, and she was simply happy to be along with him for the ride. Suddenly, Kenny's black pistol grip became visible in her memory—the day it stuck out from his leather jacket. Those early days with him were exciting for her, yet now those thoughts were menacing interruptions in her life.

Without a sound, Kenny came up from behind her, wrapping his arms around her upper body, forcing her to twitch with surprise.

"Wicked! Ain't we just jumpy this mornin'? How we all doin'?" he asked, in a gruff, yet friendly, low tone.

The kids spoke quickly with their "okays." After all, their thoughts were still on yesterday. Mary simply smiled as he came around her and placed a light peck with his lips on her cheek, and amazingly, it sent a shiver up her spine. She almost hated herself because she felt it. Kenny tapped Bobby lightly on the head as he passed and went for the coffee pot, filling his cup with only black coffee. Then he sat in his usual chair at the table.

"Well, I'm not sure 'bout the rest of you, but I feel as stiff as a piece of cardboard tacked to the side of the barn in an ice-storm after that ski trip yesterday," he said.

The kids burst out laughing. They loved his silly quotes. Mary, not being angry at him for anything at the moment, and feeling mentally bloated from her mind's race through the past, simply looked at him and smiled.

"Look! I'm digging a grave," Bobby said, as he lifted his dripping spoon from the bowl, and without another word, he dropped the spoon with a splash and was gone with only the telltale sound of his footsteps, pattering up the stairs. Mary wondered if he'd been thinking about his mother's funeral.

Tabi left soon after Bobby, and it now felt to Mary and Kenny that they'd sat down only minutes ago, but it was 10:00 a.m. when she looked up for the first time.

"Where in hell is this day going?" she asked.

"You got any plans for the day?" Kenny asked.

Before answering, she looked around to see where Tabi had gone, and saw her sitting on the couch, absorbed in the book and oblivious to her surroundings.

She began telling him of her plan for getting the house in order and preparing the kids to get back on a normal schedule for the next week.

There was still tension between them, obvious to both of them, so each trod lightly with the other, and Mary maintained her vigilance for any sign of an eruption from him.

"Yeah, well, I've got a few things to do myself early, and I thought we might throw somethin' on the grill for a midday dinner," Kenny offered.

"That could work. I'll make macaroni salad and take some deer steaks out to defrost," she said without a moment's consideration, and then immediately regretted saying it so quickly.

"Look…Mary …" Kenny was staring at her, expressionlessly. "We really need to talk, don't you think?"

For the life of her, she couldn't figure out what had come over him during the last several days. Her mind would not allow her to believe that just because they had sex, everything could change.

"Ya', sure, we can talk."

With that said, and Mary never giving it a second thought, they went about their business. Kenny left about a half hour later, and Mary heard him come back within a short time, but he left the truck running, and never came in the house. Shortly after his return, Mary heard the rumble of the pickup, and figured that he'd left again. She remained on course with the original plan, though she was interrupted several times with phone calls from a good friend and co-worker from Ellsworth and Heidi Cirone. They hadn't communicated since Bobby's birthday. Mary was still embarrassed about the way Kenny had acted toward Harry that day. There could be no question that Heidi's kids had gone home and told all.

While they spoke, Mary looked through the partially frosted window at the outside thermometer. It read a chilling 16° Fahrenheit, and she was grateful to be inside. Nothing in Heidi's tone of voice indicated that she might be prying for anything. She seemed sincere, and it made Mary feel good to hear her voice. They agreed to meet soon for lunch, hopefully in Ellsworth when Heidi came there to run errands. They said their goodbyes, and Mary looked up to the clock as she placed the receiver into the cradle.

It was 1:00 p.m.

—

Later that afternoon, she exhaled a deep breath, feeling a slight pulse of anxiety, and wished she could start the day over fresh. The house was picked up and back in order. The meat was nearly defrosted and the macaroni noodles were cooling on the counter when the rumble of Kenny's exhaust pipes came to within several feet of the house. This time Kenny turned the engine off.

He didn't come in the house, and Mary assumed he was in the barn doing whatever it was he'd set out to do. About the same time she was searching for the ingredients for the salad, Tabi came in and asked if she could help. Mary loved it when they were in the kitchen together—it was something she'd never done with Lucretia. Though she might be a mother figure to the kids, she had never exaggerated her place in their lives. She was the older sister, and wouldn't trade that place for all the money in Bangor.

A sudden gust of wind rattled the window on the south side of the house, and when it did, they caught the pungent whiff of charcoal-lighter fluid from the smoke of the grill, which Kenny had obviously fired up on his arrival. She wondered why he was so family-oriented all of a sudden. She liked it this way, but there was a lot of water over the dam at this point in their lives, and she would remain firm in her caution.

Bobby recognized the smell of charcoal, and bounded downstairs toward the barn, with Mary's warning about getting too close to the fire trailing behind him. It was mostly the men-folk who made outdoor fires. Mary and both kids arrived at the door at the same time, and immediately noticed the drop in temperature in the barn, yet it was toasty in there even with the garage door wide open.

Kenny had a roaring fire in the grill, and the open flame from the fluid on the charcoal was over his head when they arrived. It was like old times; grilling in the middle of winter.

There is something about the smell of deer steaks cooking over an open grill that forces hunger pangs in the midsection of almost anyone who comes within close proximity to the cooking, and so it was with everyone but Tabi. She was a vegetarian, even before the lifestyle was made popular by some of the hippies that came from away during the eighties. After all was said and done, they sat down to a wonderful, mid-afternoon dinner around 3:00 p.m. Tabi, who had earlier followed her mother's recipe for popovers, served them hot. They were lighter than air, to everyone's delight, and as the frosty wind dominated the outdoors, the warmth of family ruled indoors.

The kids did most of the talking during the meal, and it seemed that the thought of going back to school in the morning made them nervous. Kenny and Mary glanced at each other occasionally, but remained quiet for the most part. His earlier words to her, *"we really need to talk, don't you think?"* rang loudly in her thoughts, causing momentary pangs of uncertainty that kept her somewhat uncomfortable.

The afternoon soon became evening, and the time passed as swiftly as the entire week had. The crackling fire soothed any ill feelings that might have festered in either of them, and the four sat in the living room watching TV. Bobby was sprawled on the floor with a toy; Tabi lounged in the blue chair in the corner reading. Kenny and Mary, leaning against an armrest at opposite ends of the couch, shared an occasional laugh at the performance on the screen. Without warning, the question came from out of the blue.

"So, you give any thought to what I said this morning?" Kenny asked.

She wanted to blurt out a definitive, "YES!", as it was all that she'd thought about since the words left his mouth, but she was uncertain about being too ready to walk his ground.

"I agree that we should touch base on a few things that seem to be eatin' us up from the core. There is one, in particular, that's been buggin' the hell outta me," she said.

"Go ahead, Mary, let's deal the cards. See how they fall."

Their serious voices trailed off, causing the kids to look toward the couch with concern, and at that point, Mary suggested they both get ready for bed early, and then they could watch TV until it was time for bed. Without saying a word, perceptive of the conversation that had begun, they went off without dissent.

With the kids upstairs, they began in low tones hashing over some of the little things that obviously meant a lot to the both of them. Mary trudged along, keeping the most concerning issue, like the plague, in the back of her mind, and realized that subconsciously she actually hoped that she wouldn't have to bring it up with him. He sat quietly looking at her.

"Do you realize how much physical and emotional hurt you've put on us lately? You can't possibly tell me you've forgotten Bobby's throw to the couch and his bloody lip. And, what about my fist ta' the face act you pulled on me." Mary was warming up. She began to feel a strength come over her that had been hidden for quite some time.

"Ok…my turn," he said. "What about you taking that job and not letting me in on it until it was too late?" He had very little on Mary and he knew it. He reached for the ashtray when right in the middle of one of Kenny's unarguable pet peeves, his phone rang. Although he tried to dismiss the ringing, the caller remained persistent, and though he became visibly perturbed, he eventually surrendered to answer it.

His face grew more serious by the second as he talked on the phone, yet he kept his voice so low that it was impossible, even as close as Mary was, for her to understand a single word.

At least five minutes had passed when Kenny ended the call, without saying goodbye, and as if no call had taken place, he resumed their talk where he'd left off. Mary interrupted and asked who the caller was, and he simply blew her off with a nonchalant swat of his hand.

He immediately lit a joint, and began speaking in gibberish for several minutes, confusing her, but the flame inside her suddenly lit up with what he said next.

"You know, what really pissed me off, Mary, was that you never told me why you called your old man a 'crusty ass,'" he said, looking her straight in the eyes.

The heat of her anger began to rise from deep within her, and she felt her ears getting hot. Her thoughts of that evening when they'd found Lucretia came alive in her mind's eye, and the reason for using the words "crusty-ass" to describe her father brought the terrifying reality of her past to the forefront of her existence. *"Why...Why would he bring that up now?"* she wondered. *"Everything that's gone between us and a stupid phrase that came out of nowhere from my frustration is what pisses him off."*

They stared intensely at each other. Neither spoke, or blinked for the longest moment, and then, Mary began with a low, determined tone. Suddenly, she realized nothing in the world mattered anymore.

"Ya' know what really pissed me off were those nights when ya' came home with the smell of cheap perfume on yaw' fuckin' pants and the thought of you with our little-pig land-lady. My old-man is a 'crusty ass', and yaw' a 'crusty ass' too!" she said boldly. Her eyes bulged in their sockets.

Kenny sat stunned and speechless with her sudden outburst, angry that she'd steered his question away from her and thrust him into the spotlight.

And now, out of nowhere, she asked him, "Ya' wanta' tell me what Tabi was doin' on yaw' lap after everyone left on Bobby's birthday? You sure had a funny look on yaw' freakin' face when I came in the room." She looked at him accusingly.

"Are you outta' your fuckin' mind?" he bellowed.

From that point on, the volume of the intended "little talk" grew to the ear-splitting torrents of a full-blown fight. Tempers flared for better than an hour. Oddly, Mary never felt an ounce of fear, but fear kept the kids in their rooms, with their ears to the doors, neither one moving.

It was 9:00 p.m. when a deafening silence finally blanketed the house. It was obvious that they were drained physically and emotionally. Kenny stood at the kitchen counter; Mary sat with her head back against the couch cushion, as if in a trance. The silence was disturbed by the sound of a vehicle entering the driveway, and simultaneously, they both looked toward the kitchen window, but neither one spoke. The sound of Kenny's footsteps going toward the door caused her to turn her head in that direction and their eyes met as he reached the coat hook and took down his black leather jacket.

"Who's that?" Mary asked.

He shrugged his shoulders, indicating no concern, while flinging his jacket over his shoulders, and lifting his arms, it slid onto him. As he opened the door to leave, he stopped suddenly and looked toward her. They stared, speechless and then he spoke softly as if his voice had no volume left.

"Look…Mary—let's talk about this when I get back," he said. She maintained her stare, yet said nothing, and simply motioned toward him with an upward jog of her head.

He turned slowly, and the reflection from the dimmed garage light glared softly on the arm of his leather jacket as he closed the door gently behind him and left. It was 9:30 p.m.

On the evening of February 27, 1983, Kenny Collins left his home on Black Bear Road in Chesterfield with a person or persons unknown. He appeared to know the people he'd left with and went willingly, according to his wife, the former Mary Bagley of Chesterfield and Aroostook County. He never returned home. His body, covered lightly with a fresh dusting of powdered snow, was discovered the next morning by a passing motorist at the summit of Cathance Hill, in the neighboring township, just a few miles from his home. He had been shot.

"Well, he wasn't always a down ta' earth kinda guy, but he's in tha' earth now. What can ya' do?"—Forest Bagley, while chompin' on a ham and cheese sandwich in Filbert's store, two days after the murder.

"WELL, IF YA' REMEMBA' WHEN I STARTED tellin' ya' this story, I told ya' my closest buddy and th' first person I eva' met when coming here to Isles Port was Bullet Carter. For a time thea'—ya' prob'ly notice I've picked up th' Down East accent—we were like Siamese twins, but it was about th' time that Bullet and I came across young Kenny Collins poachin' them fish and they got into that verbal squabble. I thought it might come ta' blows, me bein' in the middle of it, and that was the last place I wanted ta' be. I could see no good could come from it. I knew from th' start, th' very day Kenny walked in Filbert's store, that no good would come between them two. It was that day at th' fishin'-hole I made my decision then and thea' ta' cool it with Bullet. Sure, we stayed close, but not like before. So everything I've told ya' since that day I guess ya' might believe it was hearsay, but them that told me these things, I took it as true.

They neva' found out, ta' this day anyway, who killed Kenny. Oh ya, there were some that knew and those who thought they knew and a lot o' speculation, and some weird things happened after th' murda', but no one ever figured it out. He was blasted with a shotgun and ya' caan't do no bullet-tracin' from that.

Not that long after th' murda', old Filbert fell ova' dead from a heart attack right in front o' Heidi.

Filbert's heart attack and sudden death left a huge void, not only for Heidi and the kids, but also for the many that knew and confidentially shared so much of their personal lives through everyday palavering with him at the store.

The weeks following Filbert's death were a blur for Heidi; she never attempted to open the store. Many had offered to help, but for her, the mere thought of even walking through the front door and coming face to face with the very counter that had been so much a part of Filbert's life for so long was unbearable. She sent the two oldest children, Amos, who was nineteen at the time, and Emy (short for Emily), who was fifteen, into the store to clean out the perishables from the coolers and the stock room, bringing the contents to the local soup kitchen. Lulu, the youngest at seven years old, found it difficult to understand fully the loss of her fatha', but was able to comfort her mother with simply her presence. Starting over is never easy, especially following such a trial of hopelessness. Somehow, even shortly following his death, they knew that they would make it. The four of them were on their own, and nothing could stand in their way.

The old store's shut down; empty now. Heidi wanted nothin' to do with it after that.

She never did want nothin' to do with it anyway. The two girls are still at home with Heidi. Young Amos is out in Bangor now. He don't come 'round hea' much.

To this day though, I still get all choked up about my friend, Bullet. Sure enough, mista' man, he drank himself into a fit one night. Harry Circus and Ralph Bailey had their hands full.

It's true how things come 'round full circle. By th' time they had 'im' handcuffed, and it was Ralph who cuffed 'im like that night long ago, part o' Harry's shirt and badge was on the floor in one corner o' the room, and his Stetson was smushed in the othah'. It took both o' them to get 'im in the troopa' caar. Crazier still, they brought him up ta' Bangor Mental Health for observation. Poor bastard's still there today. I caan't figure that out.

There was anotha' murda' shortly before Kenny's. Local

bankah' from town got whacked 'cause he was foolin' around and got caught by his wife, who was foolin' around with someone else. I don't rememba' it all, but Harry got even more religious than he already was, and after Kenny got shot, well…that mighta' been the boink that tripped his trigga'. He retired after this one. He got real frustrated at not bein' able to solve the murda'. He went fishin', I think. They say you could hear 'im, on th' river-bank, just a' preachin' away and no one around ta' hear 'im.

But the strangest thing may not be so strange when ya' think about it. Mary had Kenny's body sent home to his family. I think she was th' only one eva' found out who his family was and where they were; in New York, somewhea'. He never talked about 'em.

I don't think Mary and th' kids even went to th' funeral. Well… right afta' they shipped the body out, she packed th' three o' them up and left town. Don't have a clue whea' they went.

About a year ago now, they found Virgil, stiff as a cedah' post in the same bed whea' Kenny and Mary found Lucretia. Damned, if he wasn't lookin' out that same friggin' window that Mary said her mama was lookin' out. No one could find Mary, so she was never contacted about her fathah's death. The local undatayka took charge of it all. The house and land were left ta' her in Virgil's will, but ta' this day, none o' th' three eva' came back, and that big ol' house in that field down by th' rivah is just rottin' into th' ground.

Well, like I told ya' before, I could see no good would come from any of it. I do miss hangin' around with my buddy, Bullet. I guess I miss all that deer meat and bee'a we used to do together. I still consider 'im my closest friend, though I can't bring myself to go up and visit 'im.

Funny how some things neva' change, though. Ralph Bailey just got voted in as town constable again. This time he'll be workin' with the rookie state troopa' that took Harry's place.

Ayah, my name's Adva Bagley. No relation to them Bagleys upriva'.

CREDITS

Edward O. Barsalou

AKA E.D. Ward

1950-2016

E.D. Ward's works are being published by his wife,
Louise Y. Barsalou

Keep an eye out for the last installment in the Harry Circus Series

Before the Leaves Change Color

By E. D. Ward

www.ingramcontent.com/pod-product-compliance
Lightning Source LLC
Chambersburg PA
CBHW051520250626
47156CB00001B/170